# THE
# SHADOW
## OF
# CAELUNARRA

### THE PROPHECY UNLEASHED

# SCOTT A. HATFIELD JR.

The Shadow of Cáelunárra – The Prophecy Unleashed

For information contact: scotthatfieldtheauthor@gmail.com

Development Editing By: Jessica Streibel (JSH Proofreading and Editing Services (jshproofandedit.com))

Line Editing By: Jessica Streibel (JSH Proofreading and Editing Services (jshproofandedit.com))

Copy Edited By: Steven Moore (Condor Publishing)

Secondary Copy Edit By: Jessica Streibel (JSH Proofreading and Editing Services (jshproofandedit.com))

Proofread By: Steven Moore (Condor Publishing)

Secondary Proofreading By: Jessica Streibel (JSH Proofreading and Editing Services (jshproofandedit.com))

Book and Cover Design By: Daniel Schmelling (Schmelling Designs | scmellingdesign.com)

First Edition: August 27, 2025

10 9 8 7 6 5 4 3 2 1

To my daughter Lillian, thank you for inspiring me to write again. Also, to my wife Jessica, for always supporting me in all of my endeavors.

# CONTENTS

# DEPARTURES

IT WAS A COOL spring morning, and the grass glistened with frozen dew as far as the eye could see. A biting chill lingered in the air after a storm had swept through the high country, leaving Mount Nebo as white as a cloud in the sky.

The morning unfolded in stillness at the local high school. Remnants of the previous night's state championship baseball game; black and red confetti, tangled streamers, and weathered banners all lay scattered across the grounds. The maintenance crew had made little effort to clear the mess, aware that today marked the last day of the school year, with the graduation ceremony set to follow.

The small class of one hundred twenty-seven would soon throw their caps in the air, marking the beginning of their adult lives. This proved pivotal for many. Some returned to family farms; others pursued higher education or careers, while still others began new lives through marriage and family. Though their journeys would take them in different directions, this moment was one they all shared; a celebration of the years that had shaped them.

Families would gather in the parking lot and fill the gymnasium as they lined up to find their seats for the commencement ceremony. The air would fill with jubilation; smiles, laughter, and the eagerness of students who had reached a momentous milestone in their lives.

As the day carried on, the gymnasium buzzed with excitement. The ceremony proceeded with speeches into the latter hours of the afternoon from teachers, the principal, and the valedictorian. As the final orator concluded, the students stood up, clad in their black and red gowns. The speaker's words echoed through the space: "Class of two thousand twenty-six, you may now toss your caps!"

With a unified cheer, caps soared into the air, the flurry of black fabric catching the afternoon light. The gymnasium rang with laughter and applause. The sound mingled with the complex feelings of four years of shared experiences; friendships formed, lessons learned, and life-changing moments not yet fully understood.

Among the sea of elated students, Ethan Johnson stood out. His semi-muscular build and thick brown hair, effortlessly tousled, gave him an air of confidence, while his hazel eyes reflected the energy of the moment. Charismatic and well-liked, Ethan had earned the respect of both classmates and teachers alike. Yet, like everyone else standing beneath the fluttering caps and stage lights, he was just one of many stepping into an uncertain future, their stories still unwritten.

Ethan caught his cap, grinned, and turned to his friends nearby: Jake Miller, Ryan Davis, Emily Carter, and Hannah White.

Jake was a simple young man from humble beginnings, having grown up on a farm with one hundred fifty head of cattle and four times that number of sheep. He spent most summers in the High Uintas with the sheep herd his father would push. Towering over his friends, he had a scruffy beard, piercing blue eyes, dirty-blond hair, and a husky frame.

Ryan's deep brown skin and wiry build gave him his own presence among the group. Having just secured their school's third state championship by beating Carbon—their rivals—for just the second time, the catcher was still elated.

The shortest of the group, Emily had short brown hair that grazed her shoulders, freckles, and square black-rimmed glasses that outlined her intelligent green eyes.

Hannah was a classic Utah girl, with fair white skin, blonde hair, blue eyes, and a can-do attitude. Well-liked by almost anyone who met her, she balanced out Emily's sarcastic quips with smiles and kind words, bringing lightness and ease to their group.

As the crowd dispersed, Ethan motioned his friends closer. "Guys, I've got something amazing to tell you," he said, his eyes sparkling. "My dad has a surprise for us. Your parents even agreed to it. You need to pack for a two-week adventure! Here's a hint: plan for tropical."

His friends' eyes widened, and they all started bombarding him with questions, causing quite a scene.

Hannah exclaimed, "Are you serious, Ethan?"

"And where exactly is 'tropical'?" Emily added.

Jake chimed in, "Are you sure my dad is good with this?"

"Dude, is this for real? How did you pull this off?" asked Ryan, barely containing his excitement.

Rolling his eyes, Ethan threw his arms around Hannah and Emily. "Guys, guys, chill... It'll be fun. This will be a nice break before Hannah goes to Switzerland, Emily starts med school, Jake works for his dad, and Ryan goes to college and plays baseball in Minnesota. My dad and I will be by each of your houses before six tonight to pick you up."

"This is unbelievable. I can't believe we're doing this!" said Hannah incredulously.

Emily nodded. "Yeah, Ethan. You've outdone yourself this time."

"This is going to be epic!" Jake said, grinning from ear to ear.

Ryan clapped Ethan on the back. "Man, I knew you had something up your sleeve, but this... this is next level!"

Ethan laughed. "Just wait until you see the plane. Now c'mon guys, let's get out of here."

The five said their goodbyes and headed to their cars in a hurry. They left the jammed school parking lot.

\*\*\*

A few hours passed, allowing each of the friends to take photos, say goodbye to their families, and share a few warm embraces. At the appointed time, Ethan and his father, Lucian, went to the graduates' homes to collect them and their bags. They then transported everyone to a secluded municipal airstrip near Nephi, nestled amid farmlands. A small parking lot and three white hangars, along with a small air traffic control tower, were located near the field. Lucian, using his immense authority and privilege, drove to the airfield security checkpoint, presented his identification card, and proceeded directly to his private plane's hangar. The oversized and bulky vehicle came to a screeching halt, the engine shutting down, and everyone hopping out.

Jake took a deep breath, looking around the tarmac. Letting out a low whistle, he said disbelievingly, "I never thought I'd be flying on a private plane."

Emily smiled, almost skipping as her excitement bubbled over. "It's like something out of a movie. I can't believe we're actually doing this."

Exchanging unsure glances with one another, they approached the aircraft, doing their best not to show their enthusiasm too much. The white plane, emblazoned with Lucian's Blackwood Real Estate emblem; a black palatial manor with cursive font, waited audaciously on the concrete between the hangars and the runway.

Behind the teenagers, Lucian stepped out of his imposing black F-650. The massive vehicle towered over everyone, much like the man who emerged from its depths. Planting his feet on the ground, he swung the truck's heavy door closed behind him with a thud. The vehicle's polished surface reflected the world around it, but nothing could outshine the figure that now stood beside it.

Tall and commanding, Lucian instantly dominated the space. Long golden hair cascaded down his back, shimmering faintly in the fading light like molten gold, a stark contrast to the deep, inky blackness of his attire. His enthralling blue eyes, sharp and cold, scanned his surroundings with a calculated gaze, like a hawk surveying for prey. They were eyes that held secrets and a depth of intelligence and cunning that left no room for doubt. This was a man who saw everything and missed nothing.

A thin scar ran just above his upper lip, a faint, almost imperceptible line that added a rugged edge to his otherwise flawless features. It was a mark of past conflicts, perhaps a warning to those who might think to challenge him, though few would dare. His clothing: tailored black trousers, a sleek coat, and mirror-polished boots perfectly complemented his aura. With each step he took forward, it resonated with authority.

The blackness of his outfit seemed to draw in the surrounding light, creating an aura of shadow that made his golden hair and piercing eyes even more striking. Lucian commanded attention effortlessly. Darkly elegant and undeniably powerful, he smiled in satisfaction at his son's friend's reactions, even in his relaxed state.

"Come on, kids, gather up in front of the plane. We should take a group photo. It will be a great way to commemorate this day." Lucian's voice was smooth, almost hiding his slightly odd accent; though barely noticeable, it was enough to know he had other roots than American. Brandishing his sleek smartphone from his coat pocket, he opened the camera and prepared to frame this moment within the lens and screen of the device.

The five friends gathered near the stairs up to the plane to pose for the photo. He tapped his phone screen, capturing the photo. This preserved the day, not just in their memories, but as long as the photo existed.

"Are you all ready to hear where you're going?" Lucian said with a playful wink.

They all exuberantly replied, "Yes!"

"Given your academic achievements and inevitable secession from one another, I thought a two-week Fijian vacation would be the perfect send-off." Lucian declared, a wide smile stretching across his face.

Cheering, Hannah and Emily jumped up and down while Jake and Ryan high-fived, ecstatic to have an all-expenses-paid visit to another country. Lucian hugged them all and then introduced who would take them to their destination.

Mark, the pilot, was a rather tall man with glasses, a military haircut that was slightly graying, and a sharp pilot's uniform.

Following Mark, the friends climbed the stairs into the main cabin of the plane, and its breathtaking opulence overwhelmed them. Plush, cream-colored reclining leather seats outfitted the cabin; each had its own small, high-resolution flat-screen television affixed to the chair in front of it. Elegant wooden paneling and ambient lighting added to the sophisticated atmosphere.

A state-of-the-art entertainment system, with gaming consoles and surround-sound speakers embedded into the cabin walls, sparked animated chatter among the boys. The cabin also featured a cozy lounge area with a large comfortable sofa and a sleek glass coffee table. A private sleeping area at the rear offered luxurious bedding for those who wanted to sleep. The flight attendant, dressed in an immaculate uniform, greeted them with a warm smile, ready to cater to their every need for the duration of the flight.

Following them onto the aircraft, Lucian hugged each of them again before heading off to the captain's cockpit. Passing through the compact yet fully equipped kitchenette, he stopped briefly to greet the personal chef, already preparing some gourmet snacks before continuing through to the front of the aircraft.

Lucian shook the pilot's hand firmly. "We'll see you in a few weeks. And, Mark, take care of my kids, will you?"

"Will do, Mr. Johnson. Will do," Mark replied. Nodding briskly, Lucian turned and exited the aircraft.

Back in the cabin, the five friends had all settled into their luxurious seats, relaxing and soaking in the experience. The flight attendant, attentive and professional, brought them an assortment of snacks and drinks while they waited for flight clearance. Ethan opted for sparkling water with a hint of lime, while Jake and Ryan indulged in freshly squeezed orange juice. Emily and Hannah shared a plate of artisanal cheeses and crackers, marveling at the quality of the spread.

As the plane's engines hummed to life, the friends couldn't help but feel a sense of anticipation. The pilot and the few crew members at the small airfield conducted their last checks, ensuring everything was in perfect order for their journey.

A voice crackled over the intercom.

"Good afternoon, folks, this is your pilot. We are about to begin our journey. Ensure your seat belts are fastened. In a moment, our flight attendant Jane will begin the pre-flight safety demonstration."

The flight attendant rehearsed her quirky and swift version of the demonstration. The presentation was over quickly, and Jane efficiently gathered the few loose items scattered about before stowing the leftover refreshments. Then, she carefully ensured everyone's seatbelts were fastened.

Making her way up the cabin to the cockpit, she leaned in and informed the pilot, "We're all set for takeoff," before dimming the lights and strapping herself into her chair.

With a slight jolt, the plane taxied down the runway, stopping briefly at the north end before gaining speed rapidly as it raced along the tarmac.

"Here we go!" Ethan exclaimed, his eyes filled with anticipation.

The friends traded eager glances, their excitement overflowing as the landscape outside blurred.

"This is it, guys," Jake said, gripping his armrests with a mix of nerves and thrill.

As she glanced through the tiny window near her seat, Hannah murmured softly, "Goodbye, Nephi," a tinge of sadness coloring her tone.

The plane lifted smoothly into the air, with a gentle pressure pushing them back into their seats. Gaining altitude, the landscape diminished. Below, their high school, homes, and other beloved Nephi landmarks faded.

As they climbed higher, the sun cast a golden glow over the Wasatch Front. Mount Nebo, majestic and snow-capped, stood tall in the distance, its peaks bathed in the soft evening light as the aircraft veered southwest.

Offering an unparalleled view of the rugged terrain, the plane soared around the mountains. The friends could see the highway winding through the valley and the patchwork of fields and towns below. The sight was mesmerizing, and they couldn't help but feel a sense of wonder at the beauty of their home state.

They leveled off, heading toward the vast expanse of the Pacific Ocean. The flight attendant brought them another round of beverages and snacks, and they settled in comfortably, chatting about the adventures that awaited them in Fiji. With the fading evening blue sky stretching endlessly before them, they felt a sense of freedom and possibility, and were eager to embrace whatever this journey had in store.

Static crackled through the intercom, followed by Mark's voice. "Alright, kids, sit back and relax. Tonight, you'll enjoy some fine dining from our chef, Michaud. We've got about seven hours to Honolulu, with an expected arrival around nine o'clock Hawaii-Aleutian Standard Time, where we'll land and spend the night."

The intercom clicked as he hung up.

Menus were handed out by the flight attendant shortly after takeoff, and on her next rounds, they eagerly ordered food, gleefully anticipating the gourmet meals. Chef Michaud's culinary creations filled the cabin with rich aromas. The friends indulged in dishes of coq au vin, truffle risotto, and chocolate soufflé. They watched movies, played games, and laughed together, reveling in the surrounding luxuries. They were living the good life, if only for a few weeks, and for tonight, they wanted this experience to last a lifetime.

Many hours passed, the energy levels waning until all of them eventually fell asleep. It wasn't until the aircraft began its descent into Honolulu that they stirred. The lights of the city sparkled below in vibrant contrast against the dark ocean. The plane landed smoothly at Daniel K. Inouye International Airport, and the friends gathered their belongings, their enthusiasm filling the air despite the long day.

A black luxury sport utility vehicle awaited them on the tarmac; though not a standard practice at such a large airport, Lucian had spared no expense. They all entered the immaculate vehicle with ease, sliding in and securing themselves in their seats. The driver turned the engine on and departed the airport, escorted by another vehicle across the tarmac.

They drove through the streets of Honolulu, soon arriving at the elegant Halekulani Hotel, with its serene courtyards and impeccable service.

Upon checking in, the staff showed them to their spacious, beautifully appointed rooms, each with a stunning view of the Pacific Ocean. The beds were plush and inviting, with crisp white linens that promised a restful night. They were all jittery and ecstatic, knowing that tomorrow they would be in Fiji, enjoying the sun and the beach.

Their untamed excitement, combined with their naps on the plane, made it hard for them to find sleep. The events of the day caused their stomachs to swirl with elation, keeping them awake, talking and laughing until the early hours in Ethan's room.

Eventually, exhaustion caught up and overtook them. They all said goodnight before departing for their own rooms in the same hallway. After completing their nightly routines, they succumbed to their tiredness and laid down in their luxurious king-sized beds. One by one, they drifted off to sleep, the sound of the ocean waves pouring through their open windows providing a soothing backdrop to their dreams.

# THE UNEXPECTED EVENT

THE NEXT MORNING, VARIOUS alarms awoke them at eight o'clock. After going through their usual routines; showering, brushing their teeth, dressing, and packing their bags. They each prepared for the second leg of their trip. Today, they would land in Fiji, ready to enjoy the pristine beaches, crystal-clear waters, and lush South Pacific landscapes. Chatting excitedly over breakfast, they anticipated snorkeling and diving. They envisioned the warm sun on vibrant coral reefs and immersing themselves in the local culture.

After breakfast, Mark and Jane met them in the lobby. They entered what they assumed was the same black sport utility vehicle that had brought them to the hotel and headed back to the airport.

They navigated through the bustling security checkpoints, filled with the sounds of announcements, the chatter from the many conversations, and the occasional clatter of luggage.

Eventually, they reached their terminal and boarded the familiar plane from Utah. Each of them cozied up and settled in while the flight attendant cared for them during the flight to Nadi International Airport.

As the plane took off, they watched the vibrant cityscape of Honolulu recede below them. Gently humming, the engines soon had them soaring above the Pacific once more. The friends talked animatedly, their late night and early rise doing little to diminish their energy. The clinking of glasses and the rustling of snack wrappers added to the surrounding atmosphere. They could see the vast expanse of blue ocean beneath them, occasionally dotted with tiny islands.

Hours passed, and the five were enjoying their lunch and a movie when, suddenly, the plane jolted abruptly. Glasses toppled and dishes jostled, sloshing drinks and scattering food across the furniture.

Jane rose from her post and rushed up to the cabin, assertively instructing the friends to return to their seats. A second, more emphatic jolt caused not only her but also the five friends to struggle to remain standing.

Mark's voice chimed over the intercom.

"Kids, it looks like we're heading right into a storm, and unfortunately there is no way around it without turning back to Hawaii. We'll be hitting some rough patches. So, sit back in your chairs and buckle up. Remember what Jane taught you to do in case of an emergency. But don't worry. I flew under much worse conditions when I was a pilot in the military. We will reach and land safely in Fiji."

The intercom clicked off with a loud screeching noise, causing the passengers to cover their ears.

Ethan, Jake, Ryan, Emily, and Hannah all frantically rushed to get secured in their seats. The girls were tense, their eyes wide with anxiety as the plane rumbled louder.

"Not like we're going to crash or anything," Ryan said with a laugh, high-fiving Ethan as they both chuckled, although they followed the pilot's directions without argument.

Meanwhile, Jake was hyperventilating at each toss and jolt of the aircraft, having never flown before this trip.

Occasional flashes of lightning illuminated the darkened sky outside, casting eerie shadows within the plane. The turbulence grew more intense, causing the plane to rock and sway. Metal creaked as the wings flexed, engines groaned, and the contents of the overhead compartments rattled. All the while, the friends held onto their armrests, trying to steady their nerves as the plane continued its turbulent journey.

The girls became more worried as the storm continued, letting out whines and shrieks with each jolt, fervently holding onto the pilot's promise that they would land safely. Ethan and Jake exchanged worried glances while Ryan vomited in his lap because of the nauseating experience as adrenaline pumped through his body, instigating Jake's reflexes to do the same.

Jane moved swiftly and calmly down the aisle, helping everyone don their flotation devices from under their seats while offering comforting words. Despite her reassuring demeanor, the tension in the cabin was visible. Despite their efforts to stay calm, concern showed on everyone's faces.

There was a deafening crack, followed by a series of wrenching, metallic groans. The goods in the overhead compartments overflowed, sending bags and personal items flying. Distressing cries filled the cabin. The plane lurched violently to one side, throwing all loose items against the walls. During the commotion, a small luggage bag came hurtling through the air and slammed into Jane's head with brutal force. The blow ripped open the flesh just behind her neatly pulled-back hair and her right ear, splitting it wide enough that blood poured out in thick streams, running down her neck and staining her clothes. The wound was so deep that the whiteness of her skull gleamed through the torn skin, a stark and horrifying contrast to the crimson flow. Her body crumpled where she stood, collapsing onto the floor, where she now lay utterly still, her chest unmoving. Lifeless.

Suddenly, a strange sound rose through the cabin. It did not belong to the groaning metal or the trembling windows. It came from somewhere deeper, somewhere that did not belong to the world they knew. It pushed through the roar of the engines and the shuddering frame of the plane until every other noise felt small beside it.

The teenagers lifted their heads at the same moment. Each felt the air shift. The lights flickered. A pressure built along their skin, a faint hum beneath their ribs, as if something unseen had stepped into the narrow aisle and breathed in.

Then the echoes began.

They did not sound like memories or recordings. They sounded alive. Men shouting. Steel striking steel. The low rolling thunder of horns calling an army to formation. The heavy, hungry roar of battle rising and falling like a tide. The sounds carried weight and grit, as if the air itself strained beneath the force of it.

Jake twisted in his seat, searching for a speaker or a failing engine. Emily pressed her hand against her chest, feeling her heartbeat stumble. Ryan leaned forward, brow tense, listening as if the noise might suddenly form words. Hannah gripped her armrests, unable to decide whether to pray or scream. Ethan stared straight ahead, frozen, the sound reaching him in a way that felt almost familiar, though he could not understand why.

The war grew louder. Closer. The cabin lights dimmed again, this time as if a veil had brushed across them. Shadows thickened along the ceiling. The aisle seemed to stretch, widening for a moment before snapping back to its narrow shape.

The friends looked at one another. Each face reflected the same realization. The sounds were not in their minds. They were not part of the storm. They were not of this world at all.

Something was bleeding through.

Something ancient. Something violent. Something that did not care whether the plane survived the next minute.

A final clash of steel rang out, so close it seemed to spark across the cabin itself. The teenagers flinched as one, bracing for a blow that never came.

Silence followed.

A silence that felt like the breath before a door opens.

Through the cockpit windows, Mark saw what lay ahead—a massive, rugged cliff face, towering with the raw power of nature. Dark basalt columns rose sharply, weathered by relentless wind and sea. Granite outcrops jutted out proudly, adding to the cliff's imposing presence. The entire facade shimmered with veins of quartzite, reflecting the lightning's luminous cracks in a dazzling, yet ominous, display. This awe-inspiring sight, though beautiful, was an unforgiving and immovable obstacle in their immediate path, and Mark desperately performed evasive maneuvers to keep them alive. Mark did everything he could to navigate the plane, narrowly missing the cliffs.

Without warning, an intense flash of light flooded the cabin, blinding everyone momentarily.

Screams erupted throughout the cabin, a chorus of terror that matched the cacophony of the storm outside. The plane plummeted, the wind catching the wings as it turned. All the while, the force of the descent pushed everyone back into their seats. The engines whined and groaned loudly as they struggled against the wind. Cracks started spider webbing across the windows under the pressure.

Inside the tiny galley, Michaud fought against a world that had turned upside down. Pots, pans, bowls, and sealed containers tore free from their cabinets; latches failing, as if some unseen hand had ripped them open. Knives clattered across the counter, rolling and sliding with each violent shudder. Michaud reached for them on instinct, grabbing at anything sharp before it could fly toward the passengers in the turbulence. A metal bowl struck his shoulder. A cutting board slammed into his ribs. His breath hitched, but he pushed forward and snatched a long chef's knife from the edge of the counter. He tried to force it into a drawer, holding it down with one hand while he fought the trembling latch with the other.

The plane lurched. His feet slipped. The world tilted.

The galley exploded around him as every unsecured item launched into the air. A jar burst against the ceiling. Silverware scattered like falling hail. Michaud pitched forward as the counter vanished beneath him. The knife in his hand drove inward from the impact, the full weight of his fall pressing it through his chest. His eyes widened once, a soft and startled breath leaving him as the chaos swallowed him completely.

The aircraft continued to buck and twist as if caught in a giant's grip; the wings flexed unnaturally. Another violent shudder and one wing tore away with a gut-wrenching scream of metal, sending the plane into a spiral.

Everyone on the plane could hear the frantic beeping of alarms from the cockpit mingling with their cries. Ethan clutched his jeans, his eyes darting around to his friends. Jake was hyperventilating, tears streaming down his face, while Emily and Hannah clung to each other, their faces pale with fear. Ryan, usually calm and collected, wore a look of sheer panic.

The ocean looked closer than it should through the fractured windows, a vast, dark expanse churning with restless waves. It was a heaving mass, illuminated sporadically by lightning bursts that split the stormy sky, casting eerie, flickering light across the tumultuous water below.

Mark's voice crackled urgently over the intercom.

"Brace! Brace! Brace for impact!"

The last moments before impact seemed to stretch into an eternity, filled with the sounds of wrenching metal. With a bone-jarring crash, the plane hit the water, skimming violently across the surface before breaking apart.

With the fuselage torn open, icy seawater flooded in, engulfing the passengers. The force of the impact tore the plane's occupants from their seats, plunging them into the freezing darkness. What were once mighty engine roars were now gone, supplanted by the cacophony of churning water, contorting metal, and survivors' muted cries.

In the pitch-black night, the remains of the plane bobbed on the furious waves as the sea tried pulling it under with its terrifying grip. The sky above was a relentless storm, with bursts of lightning illuminating the wreckage for moments at a time.

Heads bobbed at the surface. The survivors gasped for breath; the saltwater stinging their eyes and throats. With the debris of the plane and its contents scattered around them, the once luxurious aircraft was now a twisted, sinking ruin.

The friends clung to their flotation devices. They shivered in the cold water, disoriented by the impenetrable darkness around them. They did not know where they were, only that they had survived the crash. In the distance, the outline of a mysterious land stood, barely visible against the stormy horizon.

They struggled to make headway toward one another. They were guided only by the distant veins of lightning in the sky, the brief reflections from their life vests, and an occasional scream of:

"Ethan!"

"Jake!"

"Over here!"

"Hannah!"

"Emily!"

"Almost there!"

"Ryan!"

Eventually, they were able to lock arms to help keep each other afloat.

The storm raged on, and after what seemed like hours of being thrashed about in the frigid ocean, Ryan shrieked, "Guys, my foot touched something!"

All but Ryan popped their heads up and saw a large orange flotation raft. They started cheering hoarsely, exhilarated as they beheld this life-saving miracle. It was a glimmer of a chance at survival. Ethan helped them get in one by one. Ryan and Jake then pulled him in.

While it seemed unwarranted because of the entire ordeal they all had just endured, they all fractured with laughter despite the deafening sound of waves slamming into the raft, incredulous that they had somehow survived this catastrophe.

The night pressed in as they floated. With all of them safe and secure inside, the reality of their situation sank in. It was cold and unforgiving as they awaited dawn, bobbing like a loose buoy in the sea. They were stranded far from any civilization that could save them.

Huddled together for warmth on the small raft, their teeth chattered uncontrollably. The only light came from a blinking orange beacon and their life vests. The rain pitter-pattered, and thunder rumbled low. Waves crashed and water sloshed against the raft, a hypnotic combination of sounds.

In the early hours of the morning, the storm finally abated, the water calming until it gently lapped at the edges of the raft. Exhausted, the teens succumbed to their heavying eyelids.

# SHADOWS ON THE SHORE

HANNAH WOKE WITH A gasp. She jolted forward. Vivid flashes of the crash played through her mind. The ocean's icy grasp had seeped deep into her bones, her clothes offering no warmth as they clung to her, still saturated by the salty water.

Hannah tried to rouse her friends, but none of them stirred. Each of them was still too enervated from their ordeal. With panic rising when they didn't wake, she checked their pulses. Though weak, she was relieved to feel the dull, steady rhythm of life beneath her fingertips. Like her, they had torn clothes, and scratches marred their faces and limbs, but nothing seemed life-threatening. Closing her eyes, she whispered a thankful prayer to God for their survival. Slowly, she crawled to the opening of the raft, where the vinyl door flapped gently in the ocean breeze.

Peering out, she saw a vast, seemingly endless body of water stretching before her on the horizon. Two never-ending landmasses encapsulated them on the right and left. In the distance, she heard the muffled cries of seagulls. Below them, hundreds of fish teeming in the bright blue depths surprised her as she gazed down into the water. Idly, she noticed the raft was snagged by a tether to a coral reef far below, anchoring them like a marker in the now gentle, forgiving waves near the coast.

Pained groans from behind caught her attention and made her investigate who they were coming from.

Through the vinyl door, the vibrant pink and orange colors painted the sky as the rising sun replaced the black and blue.

Hannah sat still, her breathing shallow as she watched Ethan, unnoticed.

He rolled over, his movements slow and stiff from the night

spent on the raft. When his gaze fell on the landscape, his eyes widened with a mix of awe and confusion.

The majestic green cliffs formed a vast shoreline; an alien sight compared to the tropical scenery he'd expected in Fiji. Farther down the beach, a plume of smoke curled into the morning sky, its blackened tendrils standing out against the golden sunlight that danced across the glistening white sands.

"Guys! Hey, guys!" Ethan called out to his friends.

Hannah crawled over to him, placing her hand on his back.

He looked back when her hand touched him and smiled weakly, saying in a hoarse tone, "Glad you're okay."

She smiled back.

He took a deep breath, coughed, and continued, "We need to get there." He made a vague gesture toward the distant beach. "I think that is what's left of the plane. Maybe we can use the communication devices in it to reach someone. Call a mayday out? What do you think?"

Hannah nodded in agreement.

"Yes," she said. "Let's do it."

A quiet, tense moment passed between Hannah and Ethan, but before anyone of them could act on their feelings that ran between them, the others awoke like a flock of startled birds in the night.

Many frantic questions fraught with confusion and coupled with groans of displeasure and coughing fits ensued. Ethan and Hannah tried to keep their friends calm, but they were in a state of panic. In their altered states, they almost capsized the raft with their frantic movements, allowing seawater to splash in through the doors.

"STOP!" yelled Ethan, his voice cutting through the tumult and bringing some sense back into everyone. "We need to remain calm. We can't afford to sink this raft; besides, we can't all swim that far. Somehow, we'll need to paddle to reach the shore. Once we get there, we can reevaluate our situation and come up with a game plan."

The logic and authority in Ethan's voice quelled the rising panic. The friends exchanged anxious glances, but slowly nodded in agreement.

Hannah interjected, "Ethan, we're stuck on the reef by some sort of rope. We'll need to free the raft before we get anywhere."

Ethan moved to the edge of the raft, dipping his arm down as far as he could, carefully pulling and twisting the tether to free it from the reef. The others watched in tense silence, their breaths held as he worked quickly, but deliberately. Despite his efforts, the tether remained stubbornly entangled, and frustration built. Determined, Ethan reached further down with both hands, yanking with renewed ferocity. His shoulders strained and cracked under the immense force he exerted until, at last, the cord came loose.

With the tether finally free, Ethan gave a nod.

"Alright," he said, scanning the raft and assessing who was best suited for the next task. After a moment, he added decisively, "I'll get out and kick first."

Ethan slipped out of the raft into the cool, clear water and began kicking toward the distant shoreline. The task of propelling the raft through the water was long and arduous, and Ethan's legs quickly grew tired, as he had underestimated the distance. However, even though his legs cramped from the exertion, lack of sustenance, and the wreck, he didn't want to burden his friends with the task. So, he kept on kicking, using the sight of the beach and the promise of solid ground to keep himself motivated. The sun continued to rise as Ethan labored, casting a warm light over the green cliff face and sparkling white sands.

As they got closer to shore, more details came into focus. They saw the vast, inviting beach, but the partially submerged, listing remains of their plane on the distant shoreline caught their attention. With growing alarm, they saw that the flames now engulfed a section of the downed aircraft.

The crash of waves on the sand grew louder, blending with the distant shrill cries of the seagulls circling overhead. The shallows made progress difficult with the shifting rip current, pulling them back with each arduous kick. As the raft hit the wet sand, Ethan heaved it ashore and stood up on the nearby sandbar. The others jumped out and joined him, wading through the foamy surf until they reached the shore. As soon as they felt solid ground beneath them, they collapsed, their breaths ragged, muscles aching, and minds struggling to process the reality that they had finally made it.

They lay there for what felt like hours, the gentle waves lapping at their heels, staring into the light blue sky; their exhaustion was too overwhelming to allow any movement. Lulled by the rhythmic sound of waves crashing against the rock coves on either side of the beach, their eyes slowly grew heavy, and they drifted off.

Amidst the steady clash of waves, the sound of approaching footsteps reached their ears, but they were too weary to react or check who it might be. Their enervation kept them still and clouded their better judgment, leaving them unaware of whomever might be near.

Emily's eyes fluttered open as a shadow fell upon her. She recoiled at the sight towering over her. A cloaked humanoid creature, imposing in its stature, planted itself near her head. The figure wore black, tattered robes from head to toe, its face encased in pitted steel armor, revealing only its eyes. Its eyes were chillingly white, with a single pinpoint red pupil that seemed to cut through her very soul. A foul stench accompanied the creature's presence, a rancid odor, as if its flesh was rotting beneath the armor.

Emily let out a blood-curdling scream as it leaned down and grabbed her by the shirt and began dragging her away. Ethan, Ryan, and Jake shot up quickly, only to face five more of the devilish creatures. Hannah stood up too, her face devoid of any color as she stumbled back into the sea. The sixth creature continued to drag Emily toward horses in the distance, its movements swift and deliberate. The creatures mumbled in an unfamiliar language. At least, they thought it was a language—to their ears it was just a guttural, demonic-like croaking. The sounds were menacing and sent chills down their spines.

"Thrụụg grọkrạn ọr ạtzlọ!," one muttered while drawing his sword and pointing it at Hannah.

In an unknowing and surprising defiance of the creature's authority, Ethan exploded toward Emily, knowing he must do something to save her, but one of the assailant's fists clattered into his chest and halted him. He flew backward, landing hard, skidding across the sand on his back in the surf. He gasped for air with every attempt at breathing painful.

Ryan and Jake took off after Emily. But it was for nothing. An invisible force of energy struck Ryan and Jake, sending them sprawling back into the ocean. The force of the impact left them dazed. Struggling to regain their footing.

Hannah screamed at the top of her lungs, her voice piercing through the discord. With the others incapacitated, one of the five creatures turned their attention to her, their eyes glowing with a sinister light from beneath their hooded helms.

The scene was one of utter pandemonium. The other three creatures entered the water in pursuit of the dazed boys, while they were too stunned to fight back. They easily took Ethan, Ryan, and Jake by the hair, while the last advanced toward Hannah as she backed further into the water. The creatures began chanting something under their breath together; it was incoherent for the friends as they struggled in vain against the grasp of these demonic beings.

Ethan, out of the corner of his eye, caught that Hannah was being pursued through the advancing waves across the beach. Seeing that increased his desperate struggle to free himself from the firm grasp on his hair. Ethan threw all his weight into it as he let his body go limp and fall to the ground. With an outstretched leg, he swept his captor's feet out from underneath it, tripping the creature. The other two, seeing this unfold, loosened their grips on Ryan and Jake, slamming the boys' bodies into the ground and leaving them gasping for breath again. Leaving Ryan and Jake stunned on the sand, the masked and cloaked personages drew their swords and advanced.

Ethan's assailant stood up, brushing off his blackened robes from the sand now coating it. Unfalteringly, they pressed on, chanting their song.

Terrified by the three creatures' advance, Ethan frantically searched for a weapon. He needed a rock, a stick, anything to fight the monsters.

He heard another scream and turned his attention back to Hannah as she narrowly avoided capture. His distraction allowed the creatures to close in, and he scrambled back, stumbling over the strands of loose kelp.

Suddenly, two of the creatures jolted forward, landing hard on the ground. Ryan and Jake raced around the fallen attackers, having pushed them down to aid Ethan. The boys huddled together, slightly reassured by each other's presence, but their slight success was short-lived as the two creatures quickly recovered and returned. They charged the boys, forcing them to scatter to avoid the creatures' swiping blades.

Faced with such ruthlessness, the boys were helpless and forced to resort simply to avoiding injury or capture.

Despite the pain he felt pulsing throughout his body, Ethan forced himself to his feet after he had stumbled while trying to parry a strike. From where he stood, he could see Emily was perilously close to their attackers' mounts. The girl was fighting back, kicking and hitting the creature, and the sight renewed his determination.

"We can't give up! We have to fight them!" he yelled, trying to rally his friends.

But the creatures were relentless, their strength too much for the weary survivors, preventing Ethan, Ryan, and Jake from gaining any ground in the desperate struggle.

The three boys grouped together again, their agility allowing them to move more swiftly than their armored opponents. Helplessly, they watched Emily flail as the creature tried to tie her to one horse, while Hannah was only barely avoiding capture. Looking at each other, they nodded, knowing what needed to be done, however futile their efforts were. They split, racing in different directions as they tried to get past the three monsters that had forced them away from the girls. But it was for nothing. The monsters blocked and forced them back again and again. It was another ineffective attempt. Swift, brutal punches to their faces knocked them to the ground. Downed, their assailants began kicking them remorselessly, their armored boots landing devastating blows.

The one who pursued Hannah grabbed her by the hair, and she thrashed wildly, her arms and legs flailing to break free. With brutal force, the creature slammed her head into the sandy beach, and she went limp, unconscious, blood beginning to trickle from her ears, nose, and mouth. The creature then hoisted Hannah onto its shoulder and sprinted toward its comrade, who was still struggling against Emily's fierce resistance.

The merciless assault left the three boys desperately fending off attacks, helpless in their attempts to rescue their friends.

Unexpectedly, loud cracks and whipping sounds echoed across the sandy beach. Miniature lightning bolts of pure energy bombarded the creatures.

The boys hesitantly raised their heads as their attackers turned their attention to who or what was attacking them from the forest beyond the shore.

A funny-looking man with a long beard reaching mid-body, cloaked in red robes and a pointed red hat, came into view, following this strange phenomenon.

He was screaming, "Begone, evil agents of the Dark Lord," as more of the streams of light began making contact with the evil creatures.

The black-robed figures began extirpating into black mist even as they shot red and black darts of vaporous energy at the man amid their groans.

The strange man yelled, "Behind me, children!" An orb of light enveloped him.

They just looked at the person who yelled at them, caught between the creatures and him, unsure what to do.

"Don't just stand there! Come," he yelled again. "Hurry! Hurry now!"

Ethan, Ryan, and Jake snapped back into reality and fled from the ground toward him as he fought the dark monsters.

Emily quickly stripped the bindings from her feet after the substance hit her captor as she freed herself. Emily ran to Hannah, who had fallen but lay still on the ground. Grabbing her friend by the dress, Emily dragged her to the safety of their friends and the mysterious person who had come to their aid.

With this new foe, the remaining creatures retreated toward the cliffs. They deteriorated into clouds of black mist as they did. The strange man pursued the retreating brume, determined to ensure the departure was absolute.

Emily tended to Hannah as she briefly regained consciousness, mumbling incoherently, almost as if she were speaking in a foreign language. Emily gently patted her head with cold seawater, causing Hannah to wince in her stupor from the salt stinging her open wound.

Meanwhile, Ethan, Ryan, and Jake stood nearby, disheveled, mesmerized, and confused, completely at a loss for words after the chaotic events that had just unfolded.

The odd-looking man turned and began making his way back to them, repeatedly saying "friend" while lowering his hands, palms down, in a gesture of peace.

He towered over them. Up close, he didn't seem so odd, more like a crazy old grandfather with shimmering blue eyes, a quaint demeanor, and wacky clothing.

He then said in a funny accent, "Glad I was around to save you from them nasty Shadewalkers, eh." He paused and looked to the side, pointing at some newly erected headstones. "Your friends, I'm guessing? They didn't have the same fate as you. A bit lucky you are."

"Who... who are you?" asked Ethan, dumbfounded.

Smiling, the old man replied, "Ándróniüs."

# ANDRONIUS

THE FOUR SNAPPED OUT of their shocked state as Ándrôniüs gave his introduction after the quick but intense skirmish. They all started firing off questions simultaneously.

"What were those things?" Ethan muttered.

"Andrinius?" a puzzled Ryan asked, stumbling over the name.

"Where are we?" chimed in Emily.

"Hold on… What just happened? Is this a dream?" Jake stammered.

"Children… children. Please, one at a time," Ándrôniüs chuckled. "I think introductions are in order. Then I will answer all your questions to the fullest extent I am able."

Each one responded:

"Emily."

"Ryan."

"Jake."

"Ethan, and that is Hannah," he said, pointing to her limp form on the sand.

"Oh, you poor girl. That looks deep," Ándrôniüs murmured, kneeling down beside the unconscious Hannah, gently parting her hair to examine the laceration on the back of her head.

"We should get you back to my tower. I'll have the finest Naïads from the ponds near my home tend to you," he added, carefully wiping away the blood, hair, and sand from the side of Hannah's face.

"Naïads?" Ethan questioned, raising an eyebrow.

"A type of healer of sorts, a creature in this world that can be trusted with such things," Ándrôniüs replied, looking up at Ethan with a reassuring nod.

As they spoke, the weather shifted quickly, almost supernaturally. Towering thunderheads raced in from the ocean, spitting misty droplets and unleashing increasingly fierce gusts. "We must hurry if we do not want to end up like wet dogs out here," said Ándrôniüs as he grunted, picking up Hannah. "This way, follow me. It's not but a thirty-minute jaunt through these here woods. You have my word; you will be safe."

"Ethan, what about the plane? What about our stuff?" asked Ryan.

"What about sending a mayday?" added Jake, grabbing Ethan's shoulder as they walked with Ándrôniüs.

"What are you children on about?" questioned Ándrôniüs, looking over his shoulder as he headed toward the forest.

"Stop!" Ethan urged as he ran in front of Ándrôniüs. "We need to go back to the plane."

He looked back and pointed at a pristine beach as if it were unscathed from the wreckage and recent skirmish. There were no remnants of the debris visible. "Wait! It was just there... where did it go? How? What just happened?"

"There's nothing left for you in the old world; this is your home now. The time has come, and you have appeared. I know it'll be hard, but I'll do everything in my power to ensure a smooth transition," Ándrôniüs stated seriously, before changing the subject. "You know, for as dainty as this lass is, she's heft' like a horse," he said.

"What do you mean?" shouted Ethan angrily, feeling as if something sinister was amiss.

"The prophecy, children. The prophecy is what I am talking about. Now, I insist we trot along before that storm catches us... Or worse, them Shadewalkers return, but with more than a half dozen," jabbered Ándrôniüs, stepping around Ethan.

The four friends huddled together momentarily before silently agreeing to follow the odd figure. They ran to catch up to Ándrôniüs who had carried on, unbothered that they had fallen behind. Hoping they would be safer with him, they staggered after him into the confines of the forest.

Ethan hesitated at first, but took a few steps forward. But

something gnawed at his insides about everything that was unfolding. He paused for only a moment more at the edge of the trees, looking back at the beach and at this strange land, wondering where the wreckage had gone as lightning filled the now-blackened sky with thunderheads approaching the coast. Unease filled him as he turned and entered the forest after his companions.

The forest was full of large green ferns and towering pines that swayed in the wind. It was quiet within the columns of trunks, almost too quiet, with only the occasional scurry of a mouse or the peep of a bird to break the silence and give life to the environment. It was as if the creatures that called this place home knew another violent torrent was making landfall.

The rain picked up, creating a dissonant drumming on the ferns. Rumbles from above became more prevalent. Ándrôniüs picked up his speed as he felt Hannah's shivering quicken even in her unconscious state. The path they followed became more of a stream than a walkable route through the trees.

Thoroughly soaked, the small group came to an abrupt stop before a small moat, which blocked their path to a modest keep and manor house enclosed by a stone wall. A drawbridge spanned the water, providing access to Ándrôniüs's home. Two guards stood at the entrance, their figures illuminated by an array of cressets and torches surrounding the gate. Two men, clad in white armor from head to toe and wearing red capes, stood directly in the middle of the path. In one hand each held a white-and-red rectangular shield, and in the other, a formidable halberd.

As Ándrôniüs approached the guards, he called out, his voice carrying through the air with authority. "Áelfwînë! Come help at once!"

Áelfwînë moved with haste, his face etched with concern. As he approached, his eyes scanned the surroundings for any signs of danger that might have followed.

"What is it, Sire?" Áelfwînë asked, his tone serious.

Ándrôniüs, his arms trembling, replied, "The girl... take the girl to the tower. My arms are spent. I will be right behind."

The urgency in Andrôniüs's voice as he gave Hannah to the

guard suggested a serious problem. He took her gently but firmly, ensuring her safety as he swiftly ran off toward a quaint yet imposing tower in the distance.

Ethan, upset, yelled, "Take her to what tower? I will not allow us to be separated from one other."

Ándrôniüs responded firmly, "Ethan, that is enough. There is no reason for you all to be so worried."

"Worried?" Emily mused sarcastically.

"I'm not worried," Ryan said with a shrug to his shoulders.

"Yeah, stop it, Ethan. We're fine! Let's just get out of this rain," Jake added.

Ethan crossed his arms in defiance as his friends seemed to be quick to trust someone they did not know.

"How are you guys okay with—" Ethan said sharply, but was ultimately cut off by Ándrôniüs's.

"Shh. Shh. Ethan, you five are quite alright. Now! Enough jibber-jabber. Come now. Come, children, this way. We are only a few paces from my hall, where we can feast and warm our bodies by the fire within." He then pointed off to the right as they followed Áelfwînë through the archway of the gate. "I will see you settled. Then I must visit my tower and ready it for the Naïads to tend to your friend."

"No!" roared Ethan as he advanced on Ándrôniüs angrily.

The remaining guard rushed over, knocking Ethan into the waterlogged soil. "Mind your manners, boy, or your next words will be your last."

"No, no, Áethelwûlf. I appreciate your diligence in protecting me. At another time, such actions might be necessary, but tonight is not the night. I assure you, Ethan is all bark without fangs. He is no more threatening than a drifting feather. So, please go summon Câllirrhöe. We desperately need her. Our efforts will be wasted if we fail to save the girl, forcing us to wait another age," Ándrôniüs declared, preventing the guards' advance.

The four friends exchanged worried and confused looks amongst each other.

Áethelwûlf nodded stiffly, clanking with every step as he moved purposefully through the rain, which continued to fall unrelentingly. The sound of his armor and the pitter-patter of the rain created a symphony of urgency as he hurried to the ponds, determined to bring Câllirrhöe, who lived on the other side of the defenses of the manor walls, back to help Hannah.

"Shall we?" Ándrôniüs smirked as he brought his hands together, intertwining his fingers. "This way," he added, beginning to amble toward the manor house entrance, not bothering to check if they obeyed.

Though hesitant, they followed Ándrôniüs, their eagerness to be dry and fed overriding any suspicions. Ethan brought up the rear, his mind warring between doubt and exhaustion.

Intricate wooden doors, lined with iron, opened with a bellowing creak to reveal the interior of the building. The crackle of fire came from the fireplaces at either end of the great room. The interior walls were whiter than snow and almost as bright as the outside on a midsummer day. On one side of the space was a large table with ten wooden chairs, a runner on the surface, and a triad of candles providing warm light. On the other side were plush embroidered chairs that looked like they belonged to a king. Directly opposite the door was a staircase leading to unknown rooms above.

One by one, they stepped into their protector's home. As they crossed the wooden threshold, something strange befell them—something magical. Their clothes, which moments ago had been soaked, tattered, and clinging to their skin, were now completely dry. Not a single thread dripped, nor was a single thread missing. The grime and dampness were gone, as if they had never existed.

They stared at one another in disbelief at what had just happened.

"Huh?" Emily said, her face frozen in wide-eyed wonder.

"What the—" was all Jake and Ryan managed, the words slipping out in unison as they turned to each other, equally dumbfounded.

Scratching the back of his head, Ethan said, "It's like there's magic or something. First those weird bolts of lightning, then that invisible shield, those things traveling by smoke or something,

and... and... now this? What's going on?"
Ethan turned to Ándrôniüs, who was now stepping through the door. Water poured from his robes as if wrung from a sodden beast—yet within seconds, the soaked mess gave way to the appearance of a regal personage once more.

"Oh, it's just a charm, my friends," Ándrôniüs said with a half-hearted smirk. "You'll get used to it. In the Republic, such things are... well, ordinary."

He had always enjoyed these little moments—watching newcomers gape at the mundane spells, charms, and other magical abilities he and his kin no longer thought twice about. What amazed them was routine to him. And yet, their awe stirred something familiar—a quiet reminder that even the simplest magic still held wonder.

Smacking his lips, Ándrôniüs muttered, "Home sweet home." He turned and cocked his head slightly. "Have a seat. I'll call Ísolde, my love, and she will feed us whatever delectable concoction she has made this evening. Once fed, I will try to answer your questions. But until then, warm up and sit tight."

Ándrôniüs walked over to the base of the stairs, clapped twice, and called loudly, "Ísolde, dear! We have company!"

Sounds of thuds and creaks came from above, followed by a cheerful voice. "Ooo, visitors!"

Running down the stairs in utter excitement, one hand in the air and the other holding up her skirt, a slender woman with black hair and green eyes, dressed in a tight white blouse and pleated long brown skirt, made her way into the room. She ran up to each of the four, giving them a hug and a kiss on each cheek.

"Praise be to the Allfather that you are here and safe!" Ísolde exclaimed as she made her way to a few cupboards affixed to the walls and retrieved bowls and utensils, and placed them on the table. She then pulled out six chairs but hesitated at the seventh, her eyes running across the visitors in her home. "Oh my, I thought there were five of you. Where is the fifth?" Ísolde asked, worried.

"Hannah is with Câllirrhöe, my dearest. Hopefully, after a few days' rest, she will be on the mend," answered Ándrôniüs.

"Oh, children, she's in the best care in all of Eldôria, don't you worry!" Ísolde said with a warm smile. "We must feed you now. This evening, I whipped up the finest stewed fish and cabbage south of the Âldâmûr ports."

"Stewed fish?" said Emily with a tinge of distaste.

"Âldâmûr?" Ethan questioned.

"Listen, Em, at this point, we haven't eaten in... wait. I have no clue how long. It could be roadkill for all I care," scolded Jake. "Have some manners!"

"Roadkill?" Ándrôniüs asked, a puzzled expression on his face.

"Oh yeah, it's when a vehicle hits an animal and it's left on the road until something eats it or it's removed," replied Jake.

"How barbaric, just leaving an animal to spoil after a hunt. But what is this vehicle you speak of?" Ándrôniüs pulled his seat closer to the table, eager to learn more.

"You don't hunt with a vehicle, Ándrôniüs. A vehicle is a motorized mode of travel to get people from one place to another," replied Jake with a chuckle. He then paused for a moment and continued, "Do you not have vehicles here?"

"I'm still not quite sure what this vehicle you speak of is, or what *motorized* means. Quite simply, we walk from here to there, or from there to here. Occasionally, if we are lucky, we ride a horse or ox-drawn buggies," responded Ándrôniüs, still quite stumped by the unfamiliar words he was learning from his visitors.

Ísolde then brought over the cauldron of stewed fish and cabbage, filled each of their bowls, and passed out small rolls. She left the basket on the table with at least half a dozen rolls left inside, in case anyone ate more.

It then hit Ethan, and he voiced his thoughts out loud.

"Guys... I think we went back in time."

"Actually, sideways, upwards, downwards, or something or other," Ándrôniüs stated while swirling his spoon in unison with his statement. "It's a bit odd actually how these things happen from other worlds. One minute you're there, the next you're here, and sometimes you'll pass on to another. I've dedicated over a semi-quincentennial studying the phenomena since the last came and failed. Before that, it was an age before that when we last had visitors who also... failed at fulfilling the prophecy."

"Enough. Enough! Ándrôniüs, at least let them get a good night's rest and an update on their friend before we bog them down with hearsay," touted Ísolde.

"Dear! It is not hearsay," Ándrôniüs slammed his fist on the table in dismay, putting quite the scare in Ethan, Ryan, Jake, and Emily.

"Alright dear. On that note, I will retire to my quarters for the night, seeing as I overstepped my boundaries. Children, it's been lovely. I'll have apple porridge ready for you when you awake," said Ísolde as she made her way up the stairs.

Ándrôniüs sighed heavily as she left. "My deepest apologies. See, I'm a believer in the prophecy, seeing as I was a young man, having just graduated from the academy at the time of the last visitors. And Ísolde, she is a nonbeliever of the prophecy. But I assure you that the prophecy is real; it's living and breathing, just like you and me. All the High Mages of Eldôria have been looking forward to your arrival. Unfortunately, I am not at liberty to expound upon my knowledge of the prophecy as I am bound by higher powers, and only at the right time, when you have passed the tests, to prove you are our chosen five, then the prophecy's words will be bestowed upon you by the Grand Mage," Ándrôniüs monologued in a diatribe-like manner.

"So, what you are saying is, we don't get answers after all, even though you promised us when we left the beach?" Ethan said in a disgruntled tone.

His friends echoed his words, nodding along and urging the old man for an explanation.

"Precisely," Ándrôniüs stated, pausing for effect as they all sighed. "But imprecisely."

Ethan palmed his face, Jake mumbled under his breath, Ryan rolled his eyes, and Emily smashed her face into the table in frustration.

"But children, perhaps maybe you four are just not asking the right questions, the answers of which I am at full liberty to divulge to you. But we must hurry with our conversation; I still have to set your beds up..." Ándrôniüs stated before being interrupted by a voice from up the stairs.

"No, dear, they are ready," yelled Ísolde, taking full pleasure in derailing his conversation and attempted escape.

"Fine... fine... your beds are ready." His shoulders slumped slightly before a thought occurred to him, and he brightened. "Oh! I must tend to Hannah in the tower, send a messenger sparrow to notify the Grand Mage about your arrival, and prepare myself for the tasks ahead," Ándróniüs stated, rolling his eyes. "Now, ask away! Hurry! Hurry now!"

"Well, I know I sure as hell would like to know what those things were," stated Jake earnestly.

"Those were Shadewalkers. They are agents of the Dark Lord of Khạrzọnọv," Ándróniüs replied with a troubled look on his face. "Though they have many names in the various tongues of the races of this world. Some call them Az'ụgụl, others Izzârrë, and yet others call them Khóâzzë. Simply stated, in the common tongue, which is used across all the realms of this world, they are Shadewalkers."

Ethan chimed in abruptly as Ándróniüs finished, giving no one a chance to ask further questions about the creatures that nearly killed them earlier, this Dark Lord, or where and what Khạrzọnọv was. "Who are you, and why should we trust you?"

Jake, Ryan, and Emily exchanged looks, annoyance hewn upon their faces, before Jake smacked Ethan on the back of the head.

"Come on, he literally saved our lives from those shade demons—"

"Walkers. Shadewalkers, Jake," Ándróniüs corrected, promptly cutting him off.

"Shadewalkers," Jake said slowly, correcting himself.

"He's letting us stay with him and taking care of Hannah," snarled Emily, adding her two cents to the conversation at hand.

Ryan was too busy stuffing his face with stewed fish and sneaking a few extra rolls from the basket left on the table to contribute verbally to the conversation at hand.

After a moment's pause and silence, Emily shyly asked, "Wait... we get to stay with you tonight, right, Ándróniüs?"

"Why yes, that was never not an option, darling," chuckled

Ándrôniüs. "However, Ethan, you will learn to trust me in time. I know you're a bit quick-tempered.

"That's not true!" shouted Ethan as he stood up, his chair clattering to the floor, disliking such criticism from someone he hardly knew.

"Settle down, Ethan. You are simply proving my point by lashing out. This is not a time for harsh tones. We are friends," Ándrôniüs said calmly. "Now, to answer your question, I am Ándrôniüs, as I've already told you, one of the High Mages of Eldôria. To settle questions that may arise as to what a mage is, it is a practitioner of magic—we can manipulate the elements, cast spells, and harness the supernatural through our deep knowledge, rituals, and the use of arcane symbols. "My home is Pinemarsh Hollow, and this is my manor," he exclaimed proudly.

After Ándrôniüs's declaration, the room fell into a momentary silence; the friends grappled with the information they had just received. Emily again was the first to break the silence, her voice a mix of disbelief and confusion.

"Pinemarsh Hollow? Where is that?"

Ándrôniüs nodded, a patient smile on his face. "My dear girl, you are in Pinemarsh Hollow. It's within the Republic of Eldôria, as I previously stated."

His confusion deepening, Ryan clutched at his side as if trying to ground himself in reality. "Eldôria? I've never heard of such a place."

"Of course, you haven't," Ándrôniüs replied, his tone calm, yet slightly amused. "Eldôria is on Arcánüs Májörá, a system within yours but many, many light-years away."

Ethan's eyes widened in shock. "Wait, what? We're not on Earth anymore?"

Ándrôniüs tilted his head slightly, as if considering how best to explain. "You are on an Earth of sorts. Not entirely false, you see; just not your Earth."

"Not on Earth... Eldôria... Arcánüs Májörá... Pinemarsh Hollow?" Jake said with a stammer, still trying to process what left the mouth of the man that saved them.

Ethan, frustrated, cut in sharply. "I think what Jake is trying to say is we need a more direct answer, Ándrôniüs."

Ándrôniüs, a glint of humor in his eyes, replied, "Yes, everyone, to clarify: we are on our Earth, which is called Arcánüs Májörá. The manor where we now sit is Pinemarsh Manor, located within the High Mage Republic of Eldôria, on our continent of Cáelunárra, which comprises our republic and the five other kingdoms."

"Ethan, did you hear that? We're not on Earth," Jake said, still bewildered at the events transpiring.

"Yes, Jake," Ethan replied, trying to keep his irritation in check. "We all heard. Just... let's try to piece this together."

"Ándrôniüs, how did we end up here?" Ryan asked, his face wrought with confusion.

Ándrôniüs's expression became more guarded. "That, I'm afraid, is information that the Grand Mage will share with you in due time."

"Screw the fricken Grand Mage! You're here now! Just tell us!" Ethan demanded, his frustration boiling over, sharp and unfiltered.

Ándrôniüs chuckled softly, a sound that only added to Ethan's irritation. "Patience, Ethan. I have reasons I cannot tell you now, but eventually, I will reveal everything.

"Great, more mystery," Emily said with a mix of sarcasm and sincerity.

Ryan, still grappling with the concept, asked, "But... what exactly is a mage?" He had forgotten that Ándrôniüs had already explained this, his attention then more consumed by the meal before him than the words being spoken.

Ándrôniüs turned his attention back to Ryan. "A mage, as I mentioned earlier, is a practitioner of magic."

"You've already told us that, Ándrôniüs," Ethan said, feeling unsatisfied and sidelined.

"So, are you like a wizard, then?" Emily asked.

Ándrôniüs smiled, a twinkle of amusement in his eyes. "Not quite a wizard, Emily. Here, we are mages, or, in our ancestral tongue, the Áírrmá; however, in many of the worlds I've studied, those terms might be used interchangeably. It just all depends, circumstantially speaking, of course."

"I feel like we're getting nowhere and everywhere at the same time," Jake said, exhaling in exasperation.

"Indeed, Jake. Indeed," Ándrôniüs said, letting out a hearty laugh.

Three loud knocks echoed throughout the manor, interrupting the semi-informative conversation at hand. Áelfwînë popped in through the door, bowing. He was now in much more casual attire. Black boots, loosened for comfort, completed his outfit of a matching brown wool tunic and hose.

"Ándrôniüs, sir, Áethelwûlf is back on guard. We've been waiting for you. Hannah has regained some of her cognizance with Câllirrhöe's help, though she says the girl may need more than a few days to recover because of the extent of her injuries. May I retire to my quarters, sire?" Áelfwînë groggily reported, clearly worn from the day.

"Indeed, my friend," Ándrôniüs responded in an appreciative and welcoming manner. He stood and walked to the door, escorting Áelfwînë out before peeking back in. "Now, children, please head up the stairs, where you will find your quarters. Men on the left and women on the right. No mixing, you four; there are strict rules in place here, not to mention a fun little surprise I have in place to ensure no funny business goes down. But not to worry, as long as you don't pass over each other's thresholds, nothing will happen. Now, I really must tend to Hannah this evening and send Câllirrhöe on her way."

"But we have more questions that ne—" Ethan said quickly.

Though it was too late, Ándrôniüs closed the door before the question could be asked. Ethan, Ryan, Jake, and Emily sat there in the comfort of the manor and this new world. They listened in silence to the crackling and popping of the fire, the ticking of a rudimentary clock that had no rhyme or reason to it, and inhaled the sweet smell of incense that was burning.

A long quiet settled over them, the kind that arrives only when every thought has been spoken and nothing more needs to chase the air. It stretched across the room like a soft blanket, filling the spaces between the flickering firelight and the shifting shadows along the walls. No one moved. No one felt the need to. They simply let the stillness rest with them, heavy yet gentle, as if the house itself were taking a final breath before the world pulled them back to their feet.

"Well then," Ryan said, then stood up, stretched, and yawned. "Shall we?"

With differing expressions of agreement, they all stood up, pushed their chairs in, and made their way up the creaking stairs. On the left were three different doors; in the middle, there was one; and on the right, there were three as well. Each door was elegant in design, handcrafted to perfection, and lined with blackened iron.

"Well, I guess this is goodnight," Ethan said, his demeanor deflated and lacking his earlier passion.

Before retreating into their accommodations, they exchanged hugs. While not an uncommon occurrence among the friends, this time they embraced each other a bit more fiercely, considering the events they had endured. They knew they were safe for tonight, but none knew what lay ahead of them in this strange new place.

Ísolde popped out of the door in the middle, now in a white gown for bed. "Children, this is my room. If you need anything during the night, please do not hesitate to knock. I will try my best to meet your needs. I've put linens, a hot bath, and some clothes—hopefully in sizes that fit you all—in each room. Oh, and have a very good night's rest."

She then shut the door firmly, and the four retired to their rooms, where they found small beds on wooden and iron frames, small square windows, and opulent claw-footed bathtubs filled with warm, steaming water.

In their separate rooms, they all availed themselves of the soothing heated water. Once finished, they dressed in the provided nightclothes before crawling into bed and resting their heavy heads and battered bodies.

One by one, they experienced dreams of their past and felt the warm embraces of loved ones, yet the possibility of never seeing them again lingered. But for now, the hope of returning home sustained them, enough to comfortably lull them to sleep, lulled by the pitter-patter of rain on the roof and the croaking of frogs in the distance through their propped-open windows.

# PINEMARSH MANOR

MANY DAYS HAD PASSED since Ándrôniüs had brought them to Pinemarsh Manor. During that time, the four friends had not seen Hannah, who remained in the tower under the care of Cấllirrhöe and their host. Their concern for her well-being grew daily, compounded by their inability to visit her and the lack of any updates about her condition. The increasing isolation of Ándrôniüs, who had become substantially reclusive, only added to their unease.

Ísolde, Áelfwînë, Áethelwûlf, and the occasional trader bringing supplies by handcart, were the only faces they encountered regularly. The four friends spent most of their time under the large oak tree in the courtyard adjacent to the tower, sitting on a log that had been converted into a makeshift bench. They yearned for any sight or sound from the many windows that lined the walls of the tower. The manor and its defenses, more akin to an outpost than a village, offered little in the way of distractions or activities for them to ease their angst.

The children and wives of the guards, Áelfwînë and Áethelwûlf seemed wary and rarely left their thatched-roof, wooden-framed houses. Occasionally, they would peer from windows that overlooked the partially dirt courtyard with its uneven red brick paths, making sure the newcomers were not too close.

Ethan and Jake had fashioned a makeshift checkerboard on the ground using sticks and rocks. Though they didn't fully understand the rules of the game, it was a way to pass the time. Ísolde had been bringing Emily a few books each day from her personal library, satisfying the girl's addiction to literature. She would sit in the bifurcation of the oak tree, propping her back on one side and her feet on the other, lost in the words of the texts she received.

Ryan, on the other hand, was still visibly suffering from the crash and the Shadewalker attack. His movements were stiff and pained, each shallow breath sending sharp pangs through his bruised ribs. Ísolde had examined him the morning after they had arrived. She assessed him and found his ribs unbroken; with significant rest, he would recover in a few more days. Despite this, every day was a struggle for him. He did his best to remain still, lying on his back to avoid aggravating his injuries further.

The sun dipped low on the horizon, signaling the end of another day in this new world. A gentle breeze stirred, carrying the evening chorus of crickets and frogs. The rich aroma of something being cooked wafted through the air, tantalizing and impossible to ignore.

Impatience gnawed at Ethan, despite his best efforts to suppress it. He had never been one to wait for things; his father always made sure that whatever Ethan wanted happened swiftly. Now, as thoughts of his father crept into his mind, an intense feeling of longing for the comforts of his home and his father pierced through him.

Unbeknownst to him, thoughts of their homes and families similarly occupied his friends' minds, although they all maintained their silence. There had been a pseudo-unspoken agreement among the friends to avoid discussing their lives before the crash, though from time to time someone would slip up. The uncertainty of their current situation consumed their thoughts just as much, and the slim, but near impossible, hope of returning to their old lives and families made the past feel like a fragile dream; one that could easily shatter if examined too closely.

Ísolde emerged through the front door of the manor. "Children, dinner is ready! Please come join me."

Ethan and Jake stood up from the ground where they had been sitting cross-legged while Emily jumped down from the tree. Ryan signaled for someone to help him get up, and the three turned to assist him. As they helped Ryan to his feet, he made slight groans and grimaces of pain from the movements.

"I feel like we're prisoners here; this is complete crap," huffed Ethan, supporting Ryan with his right arm.

"At least you're not in as much pain as I am," Ryan replied, wincing with every step.

"Yeah, I get that, Ryan! But we have heard nothing about Hannah. We're stuck in this place, and no one is giving us the time of day," Ethan argued.

"You literally say that three times a day, Ethan; we know. But seriously, you're not a prisoner. You're just dramatic, and not to mention downright voracious. And you most definitely lack restraint," Emily countered with a sarcastic laugh.

"They're right, man. While, yes, we don't know what's going on with Hannah or what we're gonna do, we could be substantially worse off," Jake said, supporting Ryan with his left arm over his shoulder.

"Exactly! We're being fed, clothed, kept safe from danger, and we're alive. Those are things to be grateful for," Emily encouraged, walking backward so she could face them.

Emily reached the door first, turning around to hold it open for the others. Juggling Jake between them, Ethan and Jake maneuvered inside, making their way to the table and helping Ryan to a seat. Just as Emily was about to step inside and close the door, a familiar voice called out her name.

"Emily! Emily! Hey, Emily!"

Emily turned around immediately on the third call. Hannah, dressed in a semi-loose-fitting brown ankle-length dress with her hair pulled back and a bandage around her head, was being escorted into Pinemarsh Manor by Ándrôniüs. Emily dropped her books on the doorstep and sprinted toward Hannah, the door slamming shut behind her.

"Oh, Hannah!" Emily screamed as she quickly sprinted, reaching her friend and hugging her. Ándrôniüs smiled and then continued walking, allowing them to have this moment between them.

Noticing that Emily had not come through the door, Jake peeked out and saw the two girls in each other's arms. "Ethan! Ryan!

Hannah is out in the courtyard!" he yelled over his shoulder and then pushed the heavy door open, sprinting toward her.

Ethan followed suit, leaving Ryan behind.

Suddenly alone but happy, Ryan muttered, "Well, I guess I'll just wait here."

Out in the courtyard, Ethan, Jake, Emily, and Hannah were all smiling and happily hugging each other. Ryan had made it to his feet but had not gone outside. He was standing in the window, waving at them, the movement catching Hannah's eye. She turned, a warm, beaming smile crossing her face as she waved back enthusiastically.

"We are so happy to see you," Jake said ecstatically.

"I have been... I mean WE... we were so worried about you," Ethan said, staring at Hannah. "Tell us everything!"

Hannah smiled. "Let's eat dinner, and then I'll tell you what I am able to do so."

She locked arms with Emily, and the two of them made their way back to the doors of the manor, Jake trailing after them.

Ethan remained standing in the courtyard, replaying Hannah's words in his mind. "Wait. What exactly do you mean by you'll tell us what you're 'able'?" he asked, a hint of anger creeping into his voice.

Hannah, knowing Ethan's perception of things, turned and looked at him, her smile fading slightly. "Ethan, it's not what you think."

"Not what I think?" Ethan questioned angrily, running up to the door, blocking the way, and throwing his hands in the air in rebuttal. "Did they tell you not to talk to us or something?"

"Calm down, Ethan. All I remember is us being back in Honolulu and boarding the plane," Hannah said calmly, trying to diffuse the situation. "I'm still fairly fatigued, and I have a bad case of amnesia. I'll tell you what I remember once we sit down."

Emily, Jake, and Hannah pushed past Ethan as he stood there, angrily confused. Ethan fought his thoughts, debating whether to go with his friends or run into the woods. He contemplated an array of other things in that moment, many being indiscriminate. In the back of his mind, a nagging voice became prevalent in his psyche, though the words were distant, muddled, and indiscernible.

He gave his head a good shake to clear the ruckus he was hearing. Once he could no longer hear it, he saw he was alone in the courtyard, near the door.

"You coming, Ethan?" asked Hannah, peeking through the door to where he stood, lost in thought.

Ethan hesitated, his voice uncertain as he responded slowly, "Uhhh, yeah, sorry, I'll be right there," the pauses between his words betraying his overwrought mind.

He turned, took a few paces to the door, and caught it with his hand just before it slowly shut, stepping across the threshold into the room beyond. His gaze immediately landed on Hannah, who was embracing Ryan tightly, her expression a mix of relief and joy. Nearby, Emily and Jake had already settled into their seats, their plates holding modest portions of potatoes, greens, and a small, whole fish—an unassuming but hearty dinner.

At the bottom of the stairs stood Ísolde, her posture poised but her eyes soft as she observed Ethan where he lingered in the doorway, his expression blank, his thoughts distant and heavy. Ísolde watched him for a moment, reading the unspoken confusion and concern etched into his face. Without a word, she approached, wrapping her arm around him in a quiet gesture of reassurance. She pressed a gentle kiss to his cheek and whispered, "Everything will be okay."

Stepping in front of him, she took his hand in hers, the warmth of her touch grounding him. With a delicate nudge to his chin, she coaxed his eyes to meet hers; her smile was steady and unwavering. Tugging him toward the table, she pulled out a chair and gestured for him to sit, her touch tender but firm. Ethan followed her lead, allowing himself a brief moment of calm amidst the ramblings in his psyche.

She sat down next to him, grabbed Ethan's hand again, and stated with beaming emotion, "You must all feel over the moon that you survived and that our dear Hannah is back with us and well on her way to recovering. Ándróniüs told me he didn't think anyone could have survived by what he saw. Yet here you are, all in the flesh, alive and well."

"Partially well," chimed in Ryan as he grimaced, pulling out a chair next to Ethan after he had made his way back from standing near the window.

A small bout of laughter echoed around the table, though Ryan didn't think it was something to laugh about. However, he decided not to let it bother him too much. During the laughter, Ándróniüs had descended the stairs and joined the table, sitting next to Ísolde. She took her hand away from Ethan and leaned into her husband, resting her head on his shoulder.

Everyone dug in except for Ethan, who shot glares at Ándróniüs, still not fully accepting of or trusting the old mage. Despite his sullen mood, the group enjoyed each other's company throughout the meal. Night fell over Pinemarsh Manor as they ate, the cool breeze coming through the open windows carrying the singing of the crickets outside. Their song reverberated through the manor, mingling with the crackling of the fire to create a soothing ballad.

Once they were all full and feeling lethargic from the meal now sitting heavy in their bellies, Ísolde stood up and began collecting the empty dishes. Emily quickly rose to help her. Ándróniüs was deep in thought, and was scribbling something on a piece of parchment with a quill.

Ethan noticed the pauses growing longer and the silence tightening around the table. He held his thoughts as long as he could, then finally let them slip free.

"Hannah, what happened? We haven't seen you in forever!" he blurted out.

Hannah sighed, looking at Ethan with her blue eyes. "Ethan, can you ever give anything a rest?"

"No," he simply replied.

Placing the small stack of ceramic plates she held back down on the table, Emily walked over to Hannah and placed her hands on her shoulders. Meeting Ethan's gaze across the table, she said, "This is not the time, Ethan." She grabbed Hannah's hand. "Hannah, let's get you ready for bed. I'm sure you're tired."

Hannah nodded, stood up, and hugged Ryan, Jake, Ándróniüs,

and Ísolde. As she walked by Ethan, she placed her hand on his shoulder and muttered, "Please, for once, let me do things on my terms."

Everyone heard this; though it was a quiet mutter, it echoed throughout the room like a bomb being set off in everyone's ears. Surreptitiously, they all eyed the pair, wondering what she could be referring to and what more their relationship had once possibly entailed.

Jake pushed off the table, glared at Ethan, and followed Emily and Hannah. Ryan found the strength to stand up, completely ignoring Ethan's "Ryan, please don't go," and also made his way slowly but surely up the stairs.

Realizing it was just Ethan, Ísolde, and him, Ándróniüs stood up, grabbing his parchment. "On that note, I will excuse myself," he said, departing out the front door and back to his tower.

Ísolde finished cleaning up the table while Ethan sat there stoically. She wanted to give him a few moments to cool down. Once done, Ísolde dried her hands with her skirt and then approached the lonesome Ethan, who still sat perched on his dining chair. She took a deep breath and rested her hands on his shoulders, as if to help ease the restlessness in his soul.

Ethan looked up at her, their eyes connecting. At that moment, he felt safe. The care of a woman was something he had not experienced for some time. He thought about the times he had with his mother, who had passed when he was a child. Somehow, Ísolde felt like her and she even slightly resembled her, too.

His reminiscing ended when she sat beside him.

"Ethan, can we speak for a moment?" she said after a few moments of staring at him.

Unwilling to face more criticism about his tone, his words, and everything left unspoken, Ethan suddenly stood up in a burst of frustration. His abrupt movement startled Ísolde. Words erupted from within him, laden with anger and desperation.

"What's there to talk about, Ísolde? They all think I'm a jerk for simply asking questions. I just want answers!"

Ísolde calmly responded, "Sit back down, Ethan. I'm not here to judge you." She paused as Ethan took a deep breath and sat back down in his chair, then continued, "I understand you're frustrated. But sometimes, demanding answers can hurt those we care about. You just have to find restraint. Patience is key in all situations."

Ethan glared at Ísolde and responded, "Patience? I've been patient! We've been here for days, and no one tells us anything! Back home, I had control; I could make things happen. Here, I'm powerless!"

Grabbing his hands and firmly turning him to meet her eyes, Ísolde said, "I see now. You feel lost, as if someone stripped you of everything familiar and the power you once possessed. It's difficult to navigate this new reality, isn't it?"

Ethan's voice cracked and almost broke as he replied, "You don't understand. I was someone back home. I could protect my friends; I could make decisions. Here, I'm just... nothing."

"You are not nothing, Ethan. Power and control can be comforting, but they aren't everything. True strength lies in understanding, patience, and empathy. "Even if they don't show it, your friends are scared too, and they look to you to be the leader they know," Ísolde said with a smile.

The sudden rage that had momentarily consumed Ethan faded as he slumped back into his chair, drained. "I just... All I want to know is whether Hannah is alright. I want to understand what's happening to us... I want to go home," he said, his voice tinged with frustration, a tear falling down his face.

Ísolde smiled again. "I promise we will do everything to help you understand. But right now, Hannah needs gentle care and time to heal. And your friends need to know that you care about them. There are other ways to be strong besides getting worked up over all these little things."

Ethan looked down, conflicted, as tears welled up in his eyes. "I don't know if I can do that. It's not who I am."

Smiling warmly, Ísolde said, "It is who you are, Ethan. You just haven't had to rely on those strengths before. Trust in yourself and the people around you. Show them you care by being there, by listening, and by being present."

"I'll try. I don't want to lose them. I just... I need to know they're safe," Ethan stated, his words faltering in his uncertainty.

Ísolde stood up and hugged him from behind as he stayed sitting at the table. "They are safe, Ethan. You just have to see it and accept it."

Ethan leaned into the hug and replied, "How do I make it right, Muh... I mean, Ísolde?" He stood up quickly, trying to cover up what he almost said, avoiding her gaze and the feelings welling up inside him.

Reaching out, she grasped his hands and waited for his eyes to meet hers.

"Time is the best healer of all, but in this instance, you must be patient with yourself, patient with them, and trust that things will work out the way the Allfather intends them to," Ísolde said, looking up at him. "Now head up to bed, because tomorrow we all head for Vâloríâ."

"Who is this Allfather? And what is Vâloríâ?" questioned Ethan.

"The Allfather is the master creator. His hands crafted everything you see in this world. We owe our lives and this beautiful land we call home to him," Ísolde said solemnly.

"And Vâloríâ?" Ethan added.

"It is the capital of our republic," she responded.

"And what will we be doing there?"

Ísolde gave him a tolerant but firm look and responded, "Ethan, this is exactly what I—"

Ethan cut her off. "Patience, yes, patience." He paused, looked at the stairs, and took a few steps toward them. He looked back at Ísolde and said, "Thanks, Ísolde... for everything."

Ethan made his way up the stairs, and Ísolde heard the door close. Someone else heard this as well, and the front door opened. In walked Ándrôniüs. He cocked his head to the side and smiled at Ísolde.

"You do have a way with children, my dear," he said.

"Well, considering we... well, that's not important," Ísolde replied, and sighed. "He is very much like Ancülí. There are many things like his words, how he talks and walks, his insufferable impatience, and, not to mention, he is nearly the spitting image of him."

"Indeed, he is," Ándrôniüs responded thoughtfully.

"I felt as if I had seen him before. So, I refreshed my memory the day they got here. I found the painting of the last chosen. And he has an uncanny resemblance to Ancüli. Everything you've said and obsessed about; all your worries and conversations with me, is completely accurate," she said as she approached her husband.

"Ísolde, are you telling me that after all these years, you are becoming a believer?" Ándrôniüs replied with excitement.

"I think so. It's uncanny how everything is falling in line, just as the original Ythâríôn said it would. Things that would happen to the visitors. Things that are happening to you... and to me... and our world leading up to their arrival. We are being pulled into something. What? I don't know. That is not by chance, Ándrôniüs," Ísolde said, her speech starting out tentative but increasing in pace and confidence until she was rapidly firing off her words.

"Not at all, my dearest," he replied, embracing her in the middle of the room.

"I have one last question, love," Ísolde said, her face full of concernment.

"What is that look for?" Ándrôniüs said, his face now wrought with the same expression. "Could the boy... could the boy really be?" she asked, choking on her words.

"Let us not worry about that tonight, my love."

"No, dear," she said, her temper rising subtly, "Tell me!"

"Ísolde, my dear, very well, he could be. That's all I can say. As I've told you many times during my tinkering, there is no guarantee that he is."

Ísolde dropped her head, loosening her intent gaze upon her husband, and let out a defeated sigh.

"Let us get some rest now," he said, offering her the slightest peck on her cheek.

Together, they made their way to the stairs and proceeded to their quarters, silence descending on the manor in their wake.

# THINGS LEFT UNSAID

ETHAN SAT JUST INSIDE his door, his back pressed against the wood as he listened to the world beyond. The thin walls allowed Jake's thunderous snores to carry, for the rhythmic trickle of water to be heard from another room, and for the soft murmurs of Ísolde and Ándrôniüs conversation to drift through. Further down the hall, muffled giggles from Emily and Hannah broke through the soft noises that filled the mages' home, their joy infectious even in its muted form.

Ethan's thoughts drifted. They pulled him back to simpler days. To a time in his favorite place above all others, the Uinta Mountains. He could almost feel the cool alpine air and hear the crunch of gravel under his Jeep's tires as they escaped the stifling summer heat in the valleys below. He remembered leading his friends to secluded lakes, fishing under the sun, diving into icy water, and lying beneath a sky painted with stars as brilliant as those here. They'd laugh, tell stories, and live immersed in the moment. When the magic of the secluded wilderness wrapped them in its timeless embrace. Even back to when the world was less frightening.

The memories stirred something within him, and he felt compelled to speak with Hannah. He rose to his feet. Ethan eased his door open, careful to muffle the creak of its hinges. Slipping out into the hallway, he tiptoed toward the room where Emily and Hannah's soft voices emanated.

Inside, the two girls sat immersed in quiet companionship. Dressed in a flowing white nightgown that brushed her ankles, Hannah was perched in a chair by the bed, her posture relaxed. Dressed similarly, Emily knelt behind her on the mattress, a brush in hand as she gently worked through Hannah's hair, mindful of the healing wound on her scalp.

The scene was one of comfort and nostalgia, their whispers and shared smiles rekindling a bond forged long before the trials of this strange new world. They savored the moment, unaware of the figure standing just beyond the door, hesitating on the other side.

Ethan pressed an ear to the door to hear the words. Upon placing it firmly against the wooden surface, the words were more discernible.

"I don't understand how you deal with him after all these years," Emily said, her voice tinged with exasperation.

Hannah smiled softly. "He's not that bad."

"Not that bad?" Emily echoed, raising an eyebrow. "He's kind of pretentious, and a... Well, you know, a jerk."

Hannah chuckled. "Well, it's easy when I know a bit more about him than you guys. Not to mention there is a small history between us."

"Oh?" Emily's curiosity piqued.

"Yes," Hannah admitted, reaching behind her back to smack Emily's knee.

"Tell me everything," Emily urged.

"There's not much to tell," Hannah said with a shrug. "We kissed one night after he was brave enough to take me on a single date to Burraston Ponds for a picnic and some fishing. But then it never happened again, and we promised never to talk about it."

"Do you wish it had been more?" Emily asked.

"Every so often," Hannah replied, a reminiscent tone in her voice. "I think I'll always feel something for him, maybe just not in the same way. Maybe there's still something... maybe not. Emily, I don't know. I'm confused by everything, and it doesn't help that there's so much unknown right now."

"Oh, really?" Emily teased playfully, poking at Hannah.

"Yes," Hannah said with a small smile playing at her lips.

"Do you love him?" Emily asked.

There was no answer from Hannah. She just sat there mulling things over in her mind, when a sigh betrayed her and was released.

"You do... don't you?" Emily said the question caught halfway between hope and fear, as if either answer would wound her.

"Enough, Em," Hannah said, putting an end to the topic.

Another silence settled over them for a moment as Emily tucked a strand of hair behind her ear, contemplating her next words with apparent care; though not as much as she should have. She wanted to hold back, to bite her tongue, but as was often the case, her mouth moved faster than her thoughts, outpacing both reason and restraint.

"Well, I have to admit something... I've always felt a little overshadowed by you. I'm jealous of how much he watches you. I've always, well... had a crush on him, if I'm being completely honest. Despite his infuriating nature, I can't help but be infatuated with him."

Hannah, hearing this proclamation of her friend's feelings toward Ethan, felt a sting of jealousy. "Emily, why do you have to say such things? You've known since junior high that I've wanted him."

Feeling the awkward discomfort rise between them, Emily wished she had said nothing. She had thought she could trust her lifelong friend with her declaration, seeing as they had always been truthful with one another. Apparently not, Emily thought. Trying to divert the conversation, she asked, "Where are we going tomorrow again?"

"Vâloríâ," Hannah simply replied.

At that moment, there was a knock on the door. Emily slid off the bed and walked toward the door. Opening it, her expression turned sour when she saw Ethan.

"Go away," she demanded.

"No," Ethan began, but then, realizing the girls were indisposed, he covered his eyes in embarrassment. "Sorry."

Hannah walked over, sliding her hand onto the door, and gently nudging Emily out of the way. "Ethan," she whispered.

Emily sighed and rolled her eyes, retreating into the room. Hannah smiled and took Ethan's hand.

"Can we talk?" Ethan asked.

She paused for a moment, glancing back and spotting a robe

draped over a chair. "One second," she murmured, quickly grabbing the garment and ignoring the loud huff from the direction of the bed.

The pair made their way downstairs, carefully avoiding the creaks in the wooden floorboards and the whine of the manor's old door. Every sound seemed magnified in the night's stillness, heightening their senses as they tried to remain unnoticed.

Once in the courtyard, they paused, listening for any signs of someone who could discover them. Áethelwûlf, standing guard, noticed them out of the corner of his eye. They momentarily froze with apprehension, but to their relief he smiled, nodded, and returned to staring out the gate of the manor's defenses, allowing them their privacy. They continued walking over to the oak tree and settled on the bench beneath its wide, protective branches.

Hannah, feeling the chill of the night air wisp through her robe and light clothing, moved closer to Ethan, seeking warmth and comfort. Unspoken words and lingering unresolved emotions, a blend of past memories and present uncertainties, filled the air between them. They hadn't been this physically close in years, and the closeness brought a longing that neither of them fully understood.

As she leaned her head on Ethan's shoulder, Hannah felt the familiar, comforting presence she had missed. It was a moment of quiet reflection, both of them grappling with the remnants of their shared history and the new dynamics of their circumstances.

"Remember the kiss we shared in tenth grade?" Hannah began, her voice barely above a whisper. "How did you feel about me back then?"

Ethan sighed, looking into the distance. "I felt so stupid for never taking you out again. I've always liked you."

She looked up and smiled, remembering the words exchanged between Emily and her earlier, and gave out a small laugh. "Were you spying on us, Ethan Johnson?"

"Not particularly. I just overheard that part," Ethan chuckled.

"Just that part?" Hannah teased, resting her head back on his shoulder.

"Yeah," he replied softly. "I miss this."

"Me too," Hannah said wistfully. "But I miss it with all of us. That part of our life is more than likely over. We need to figure out how to be here now and how we are going to fit into this world."

Disheartened, Ethan sighed, "Okay."

"But," she continued, "we never know what might happen. Things could be different here. You could be different here. I know there was a lot going on with your dad and things at home back then, but maybe you could leave that all behind here. If you really try to change, maybe we can find a way to work things out."

Ethan got down on his knees. "I will change," he said, trying to kiss her.

Hannah deflected the kiss, instead opting to kiss his head. She looked down into his eyes and said, "I love you, Ethan. It's there. You just have to earn it again. I've always loved you. But you push me. I'm not just a possession. Especially not one that you can acquire by looking at me a certain way or saying the right flattering things. You continually try to get your way, and not just here, but back home; I am my own woman. I make my own decisions. You need to respect that."

Ethan sighed and put his head in her lap.

She caressed his hair. "Everything will be fine," Hannah mumbled.

"There's no going home," he said, his voice heavy with despair. "We're just stuck."

"I wouldn't be so sure," she replied. "But it will take dedication from all of us as a team; so says Ándróniüs. And if we get home, then maybe, just maybe, you can ask me out on that second date."

Hannah gently lifted Ethan's head from her lap and crawled to the ground. Ethan followed her lead. She rested her head on his chest, and together they lay there in each other's arms.

"What do you know, Hannah? What won't you tell me?" Ethan asked, breaking the silence.

Hannah sighed. "Ándróniüs shared some things with me, but I'm still in the dark just as much as you."

Ethan huffed in frustration.

"Don't you do that! I'm not keeping anything from you," she said, pushing off his chest and smacking him lightly. "This is what

I'm talking about, Ethan."

"I'm sorry," he said quickly, reaching for her. "Please come back."

Hannah hesitated at first, but then obliged, settling back into his chest. "Look... all I know is that Ándrôniüs and Câllirrhöe believe I'm healthy enough to handle the journey to Vâloríâ and then take part in these tests, whatever they may be. Ándrôniüs also told me if we pass and are successful at our tasks thereafter, we might be able to go home. He just didn't mention how long that would take, if at all."

Ethan tensed at this new information and had to restrain another outburst demanding answers. Battling down more frustration, he sighed and said, "I understand."

"Just trust me and have faith that I'm okay, that we will make it through this. Believe me, I'm telling you all I know. Because of that crash and what those Shadewalkers did to me... it truly and really hurt me," she said, her voice gentle but firm.

"I'll try," Ethan whispered, the weight of the situation pressing down on him.

Hannah nestled closer to him, the warmth of their shared body heat providing some comfort. "We're in this together," she murmured. "We have always been."

Ethan wrapped his arm around her, holding her close. They watched the stars twinkling in and out of sight with the drifting clouds above. The sounds of the gentle rustling of leaves in the breeze created a soothing symphony. As the night grew deeper, the cool air settled around them, and the exhaustion from the day's events finally took over.

Hannah's breathing slowed, and she drifted off to sleep first, her head rising and falling with Ethan's steady breaths. Ethan followed soon after, his mind filled with thoughts of their journey and the promise of home. The serenity of the night embraced them, and they slept soundly under the canopy of stars. The night faded away, making way for the break of day as the sun peeked over the horizon, breathing life into the forest.

# THE JOURNEY BEGINS

THE BIRDS BEGAN THEIR early morning chatter, and the inhabitants of Pinemarsh Manor stirred. Despite the bustling activity, Ethan and Hannah remained asleep. Even as they brought an ox into the courtyard, hitched to a wagon loaded with tents, clothing, bedding, food, and other essentials for the journey to Vâloríâ, their slumber remained undisturbed.

While the others enjoyed a delectable breakfast prepared by Ísolde, Ethan and Hannah slept soundly, unaware of the preparations being made. Emily, Ryan, and Jake sat at the table, their faces etched with concern as they exchanged glances, puzzled by the pair's absence.

Emily, her brow furrowed, glanced around the table before suggesting, "Maybe I should go look in their rooms to see if they're still asleep?"

The others nodded in agreement, and Emily rose from her seat. After a few minutes, she returned downstairs.

"They're not up there," she announced, her voice puzzled.

Ryan, showing modest improvement, stood up and scanned the room as if expecting the two to appear. "I wonder where they could be," he mused, his thoughts racing as he tried to piece together their absence.

Ísolde, after gathering the breakfast plates, meandered to the window. She looked outside into the courtyard. She spotted the two figures lying beneath the old oak tree. Looking back over her shoulder at the others, her eyes sparkled with a touch of amusement. "Found them," she said, a smile crossing her face. "But you might want to wake them before Ándrôniüs finds out. He's quite the traditionalist and wouldn't like that sight."

Filled with curiosity, the three hurried outside. As they approached, the sight before them took them aback. Beneath a large hide blanket; one that had mysteriously appeared in the middle of the night. Lying a few paces forward below the tree were Hannah and Ethan, who were still fast asleep, oblivious to the world around them.

They quietly approached, moving with gentle steps. Ryan walked to the left, his thoughts racing with amusement at the scene, while Jake mirrored him on the right, a grin already forming. Emily, standing at the feet of their sleeping friends, felt a sting of jealousy as she gazed down on the two cuddled together under the oak tree. She took a steadying breath and brushed it off. She then looked at Ryan and Jake. She forced a smile and held up three fingers. Smiling knowingly, the boys gave her nods.

Emily quietly counted down, her voice barely a whisper. "Three... Two... One..." Then, on cue, all three shouted, "Wake up!"

The sudden outburst jolted Hannah and Ethan awake, their screams of surprise filling the air as they scrambled under the blanket. Their friends burst into laughter, their joy ringing out in the early morning light. Hannah, embarrassed at being surprised, instinctively clutched the blanket tightly around herself for protection. Ethan, still half in shock, sprang to his feet, ready to defend them both against whatever threat had arisen.

Jake, unable to hide his grin, teased, "Oh, so are you two a thing now?"

"No, it's not like that!" Hannah exclaimed, her cheeks flushing as she glared at them.

"Yeah! We just came out here to... talk about... my attitude... and how I need to be more... patient... and understanding," Ethan explained, standing in his long brown nightclothes. His voice broke at each point, the nerves clear in his words. "We laid down to stargaze like we used to in the Uintas... and we must have... fallen asleep!"

"Yes, yes, we just fell asleep, is all," Hannah added, now standing and wrapped in the blanket. "I really must go get ready." With that, she hurried off, her steps quick and her head held low.

Emily, Jake, and Ryan exchanged a skeptical glance, their doubt clear, though they tried to hide their amusement.

"Guys, it's totally not what you think," Ethan insisted, his exasperation clear. He sighed, his shoulders sagged as he followed Hannah's lead to get ready.

The three friends watched as the pair scurried back into the manor. Two couldn't help but laugh amongst themselves at the situation, while the third sulked unbeknownst to the others.

Jake chuckled, shaking his head. "It's about time, don't you think?"

Emily, with her arms crossed as she watched them disappear inside, heaved a sigh. "It's kind of sickening, if you ask me." She paused, her expression softening as a thought crossed her mind, then added, "I really think Hannah deserves way better." Her tone carried a hint of concern for her friend.

Ryan nudged her playfully. "C'mon, Emily, you know Ethan's always had a thing for her. They are our friends, and we should support whatever they have."

"If anything," Emily said sarcastically, suppressing her feelings deep within her chest.

Instead of going back inside, they sat on the bench and watched the life that had erupted at the manor. There were more people around than they had ever seen before at Pinemarsh Manor. Men and women of all ages, children running about, horses tied to a hitching post, and a loud, distinct chatter filled the air. Many people were staring at the three on the bench and pointing from time to time. This made them feel somewhat vulnerable but also excited, and the boys in particular didn't understand why there was so much commotion.

"What is happening around here?" Ryan asked, puzzled, scratching his head.

"Not sure, but it looks like someone is about to head out on a trip," Jake added.

"It's for us," Emily said.

The two looked at her, their confusion evident, and in unison said, "Wait, we're going somewhere?"

Jake, his brows furrowing as he processed the information,

continued, "Why didn't you tell us?"

Ryan immediately followed up with, "Yeah!"

Emily took a deep breath before responding. She admitted, "Honestly, I hadn't considered it until now," her voice betraying the frustration of being accused of withholding potentially unwelcome information.

Jake, looking more irritated than before, shook his head in disbelief. "Man, everyone is keeping secrets from everyone around here." He paused, the thought lingering in his mind, before turning to Ryan with a raised eyebrow. "Wait... are you hiding something, too?"

Ryan, almost offended by the suggestion, straightened his posture. "Not at all. You should know better. You know everything about me, considering I can't keep my mouth shut," he replied, his voice sharp with a hint of defensiveness.

Emily, watching the back-and-forth between them, her expression a mix of exasperation with a touch of humor. "Exactly why I said nothing," she added, the words carrying an edge of finality.

Back in the manor, Hannah decided to bathe, taking her time to wash the grime from her hair and skin. The warm water enveloped her, and she soaked in the tub, savoring the moment of cleanliness. The simplicity of the act was a small but much-needed comfort amidst the flurry of preparations.

Ethan, on the other hand, felt no need to wash again, having done so the previous night. He moved through the manor with an easy pace, his thoughts more on joining his friends than on the process of cleaning himself. As quickly as he had gone upstairs, he returned to the courtyard, biting into a sweet roll he had swiped from the table inside as he rejoined his friends.

"Hannah still in there?" he asked, pointing back to the manor, a casual tone in his voice as he leaned against the tree.

"Do you see her here?" Emily snapped, her irritation flaring as she rolled her eyes.

Feeling the spark of frustration in her tone, Ethan shot back, "Emily, calm down. Can you give the attitude a rest? I was just asking." His voice carried a defensive edge, mirroring her irritated tone.

As the friends conversed, Ándrôniüs left his tower and made his way to the group seated by the oak tree. As he approached, he waved at the four of them, his movements deliberate but not hurried, as if he had all the time in the world. His eyes, sharp and calculated, scanned the group, noting the way they sat as they waited for Hannah's return.

He wore his usual robes, though today they were brown rather than the flamboyant colors he often favored. His hat, typically pointed with an air of grandeur, sagged slightly at the tip. He carried a staff in his right hand. Intricate carvings etched the staff. And at his side, bouncing off his hip with each step, was a black leather satchel that hung from his left shoulder.

"Beautiful day, isn't it?" Ándrôniüs stated. The four shrugged their shoulders and nodded in agreement. The mage continued, "It is a fine day for a journey. There's a sweetness to the air; not too hot, not too cold, just right. The woods are alive and ready for us to embark on our journey to Vâloríâ."

"Vâloríâ?" Jake asked with a puzzled look.

"What's Vâloríâ?" Ryan followed up.

Ándrôniüs completely ignored their questions about the journey. His gaze drifted briefly, as if lost in thought, before he abruptly asked, "Where is Hannah?"

"Here!" yelled Hannah, who was quickly walking with Ísolde along the brick path toward them.

Hannah looked refreshed and far less rattled than she had earlier that morning. As she approached the group, Ándrôniüs gave her a brief nod before turning to address them all.

"Where are your things?" he asked, his eyes scanning their empty hands. "We can't very well set off without proper supplies."

Jake opened his mouth, confused. "Wait... we were supposed to bring stuff?"

"I wasn't told we were leaving right now," Emily said, glancing around.

Ísolde chuckled from nearby. "Relax, children. While you were out here, I packed your things. Clothes, food, water, and a few other essentials are ready to be loaded in the cart. I wasn't about to let you run off unprepared."

The five teens exchanged a few surprised glances with one another as she handed them their satchels with supplies.

"Wait... you packed everything?" Emil said with astonishment. "That quickly?"

"Even added a few apples," Ísolde said with a wink.

Jake looked impressed. "You're kind of amazing."

"I know," Ísolde replied with a sly smile.

"Well," Hannah said, brushing her hair back, "I guess we really are ready."

"As ready as we'll ever be," Ethan murmured, stepping closer to the cart and eyeing the packed supplies, adding his satchel to the cart.

Ándróniüs gave them all a satisfied look. "Then no more delays. It's time."

With the ox cart loaded, the two guards, Áelfwînë and Áethelwûlf, positioned themselves before and behind the small caravan. Ethan, Hannah, Jake, Ryan, and Emily stood nearby, waiting for direction.

Ándróniüs looked at the group and said, "We're about to embark on a significant journey. Our destination is Vâloríâ, a place where you will begin to understand your purpose here. It is crucial that you remain vigilant and stay close. The path to Vâloríâ is not without its dangers. Though it's unlikely, we will run into anything of significance."

With a curious look, Emily inquired, "So, what precisely is required of us in Vâloríâ?"

With a reassuring smile, Ísolde replied, "In Vâloríâ, you will undergo tests to prove your worthiness. These tests are designed to prepare you for your destiny. Each of you has a role to play in fulfilling the prophecy."

"What kind of tests are we talking about? Are they dangerous? And what if we don't want to do them?" Jake asked, with a slight frown playing at one side of his face while he glanced at Ándróniüs. The others, sensing his discomfort, exchanged glances but said nothing.

"Most are perilous, some not, but nonetheless they are

necessary," Ándrôniüs replied, his voice steady as he gave a solemn nod, his eyes reflecting the gravity of the situation.

Ryan, still sore from his injury, shifted his stance. "Well, great. And what about what Jake asked? What happens after the tests, if we even do them? Will we get answers about how to get home?" Impatience and hope tinged his voice, as if he needed something more concrete to hold on to.

A mischievous grin spread across the mage's face. "The rest of that information is not important... but... if you don't go, we will just have my guards here shackle you and drag you straight to Vâloríâ," Ándrôniüs said, his voice carrying an edge of amusement, though his eyes remained unreadable.

A stillness settled over the friends, the very air becoming thick, each one uncertain whether he was speaking in jest or if they would indeed be bound, shackled, and marched to their destination. Their eyes lingered on one another, hesitant, as if searching for a way to make sense of the mage's cryptic threat.

Ísolde leveled Ándrôniüs with an unimpressed glare as she smacked his chest lightly, a playful but firm gesture, before speaking. "He's only kidding, children. But there is no way around this. If you do not partake in these tests, there are consequences not only for you, but for our entire world. However, if you follow through and succeed, you will learn more about the prophecy and your role in it." Her voice softened slightly, though the fullness of her words lingered. "As for getting home, we're not sure, but the world has a funny way of working those things out."

Ethan rolled his eyes and swallowed the comments he wanted to blurt out, the effort clear on his face as he took the first steps toward exercising his will to be more tolerant and open-minded. His internal struggle simmered beneath the surface, but he remained quiet, knowing he needed to adjust.

"What if we fail?" Hannah said timidly, having quietly drifted toward Ethan during the conversation. She gently took his hand, seeking reassurance, her own doubts mirrored in the uncertainty in her voice.

"The Dark Lord already knows you're here. His agents were no doubt sent to find you on the day of your arrival. Their failure means that our failure at this point in time... is not an option," Ándrôniüs said, his eyes softening as he looked over the group. He paused, noticing the doubt on their faces. "Believe in yourselves. Believe in each other. You are capable of great things. I know this. I have seen it. In each of you."

Ethan, trying to mask his true thoughts, couldn't shake the lingering memory of last night's conversation. He also thought back to his earlier conversation with Hannah, her grip on his hand tight, a silent plea for reassurance. In the intense quiet, he mustered the strength to shift his tone, to change his way of thinking at that very moment. It was a conscious effort, one he knew he had to make for the sake of the group.

"C'mon, guys, we can do this. Surely we'll be able to face whatever comes next as a team," he said, his voice firm, though his inner doubts remained hidden beneath the surface.

Ísolde nodded, her eyes full of warmth as she smiled at Ethan and the others. "That's the spirit. Now, Ándrôniüs, lets climb aboard. It's time to depart."

Ísolde and Ándrôniüs climbed up into the cart, preparing to steer it for their journey ahead. The cart groaned under the weight of its newly added passengers and load, a stentorian creak splitting the air as the ox joined in with snorts and huffs. As Ándrôniüs settled into his seat, there was a small, subtle movement from his black satchel that went unnoticed. From within, Câllirrhöe the Naïad, peeked out, her delicate wings fluttering just enough to be noticed by the sharpest of eyes but hidden from everyone else.

Ándrôniüs took a deep breath, his eyes scanning the road ahead, before raising his hand to signal the start of their departure. "Onward to Váloríâ!" His voice was steady, filled with purpose, though the weight of their path lay heavy on him, known only to himself.

The ox lumbered forward, and the small caravan set off down the path, leaving Pinemarsh Manor behind. As they crossed the bridge, the manor's familiar sight faded, its silhouette shrinking. The gate creaked as it closed behind them, sealing off the manor and the reassuring sense of security it had brought to the five misplaced teenagers.

# SALAMANDER SNAIL STEW

THE CART CREAKED AND swayed as it traveled along the dirt path through the forest. The dense canopy overhead offered shade from the blistering heat. A crisp, sappy scent carried a tang that teased their senses. It was inviting at first, like split resin on warm bark, but gradually became unpleasantly sour by the faint seep of rot buried under leaves and old needles. In contrast, the pleasant sound of birdsong brushed their ears, softening the smell in the air.

As they ventured along the path deeper into the woods, the canopy thickened, casting dappled patterns on the forest floor as sunlight filtered through. Birds chirped from the branches above, while small mammals rustled in the underbrush. In the distance, larger creatures bellowed, their calls echoing through the trees. A cool breeze passed through the forest, bringing brief moments of relief before fading back into the warmth.

"It's beautiful out here. Reminds me of the hikes in the foothills we used to take back home," Ethan said, walking near the front of the cart, his eyes fixed on the ever changing scenery. His words carried easily into the quiet, and for a moment the forest almost felt familiar.

Hannah glanced toward him, then let her gaze drift across the trees.

"This place is certainly magical. Though... I never thought I'd miss the comforts of home so much, ya' know? But this world is growing on me little by little," she said, her voice soft. Her comment settled over the group with a warmth that matched the filtered sunlight.

Ryan shifted beside her, rubbing his ribs as the cart bumped along. "Do you think we'll run into any more of those Shadewalkers?" he asked, using the question as much to ground himself as to break the quiet that followed Hannah's words.

Ándrôniüs, guiding the cart, glanced back at them with a measured look. "It's possible, considering they found you on the edge of the sea, but it's unlikely this far into Eldôria. The flying contraption you all arrived on could be seen streaking across the sky for miles. Quite the scene for anyone from our world, considering we have no such things. That was more of a one-off chance. You see, here the canopy of this forest acts like a shield, concealing us from prying eyes or those with ancient seeing stones. We mages enchanted it to ensure safe passage for all who travel under its protection." He adjusted his hold on the reins and returned his attention forward. "However, we must always remain vigilant. Danger can come from many places at any time."

Step by step, the day wore on; the heat growing more oppressive, and the earlier morning breeze all but disappearing. Sweat trickled down their faces, and salt crusted on their brows and lips. The air grew heavy, pressing on their chests and stinging their lungs. Though the forest now provided ample shade, the sun's rays that cut through the leaves above amplified the sweltering discomfort.

By midday, they stopped to rest near a small clearing where a brook babbled cheerfully over the smooth, tiny stones in its bed. The cool, clear water was a welcome sight, and they took turns splashing their faces and filling their canteens, grateful for the refreshing break.

Their quiescence quickly ended, and they resumed their journey. The afternoon sun began its descent, casting a warm golden glow over the forest. The path grew more rugged, with fallen trees and thick underbrush to navigate. Despite the nagging challenges—clothing snagging on thorns, skin stung by nettles, toes stubbed on loose rocks, and frequent stumbles over hidden branches—the group's spirits were high. They told jokes and bantered, buoyed by their shared perseverance through the adversity of their trek.

As evening approached, Ándrôniüs called for a halt.

Áelfwînë and Áethelwûlf briskly got to work, unloading the cart and setting up their camp. Under Ísolde's direction, Jake and Ryan gathered firewood, while Emily and Ethan laid out bedrolls and arranged supplies. Hannah, her head swimming and aching, moved to help, but was emphatically told to sit and rest by the older woman.

As sunset approached and the night sky began its vibrant display, painting itself in an array of colors, the first day of their journey to Vâloríâ was coming to a close. They gathered around a small campfire, its flames dancing and crackling, casting flickering shadows on their faces. Ándrôniüs passed around a pot of stew, the warm, savory aroma filling the air. Using a ladle, they dished out portions into the bowls they had received from Ísolde, eager to enjoy their meal.

"This is actually pretty good," Jake said while spooning his dinner into his mouth. "Better than I expected."

"It's nice to have a hot meal after a long day," Emily added with a firm nod in agreement.

Áethelwûlf said, with a smirk on his face, "Not sure you'd be saying that if you knew what it was made of."

A ladle whipped through the air and struck Ryan squarely on the shoulder mid-gulp, causing him to cough and nearly spill his stew. He let out a sputtering groan as the utensil clattered to the ground.

Ísolde didn't say a word. She simply crossed her arms and gave Áethelwûlf a pointed smirk—half warning, half amusement—her message loud and clear: let the children eat.

But the damage was done. The seed of curiosity had been planted. The five friends had stopped eating, each of them now staring wide-eyed at the guard.

"Why do you say that?" Emily asked, taking a big slurp of her stew.

"Just trust me. Your kind is always squeamish when they find out about our delicacies," Áelfwînë added, mirroring his counterpart's smirk.

"Oh, c'mon," said Ryan, shrugging his shoulders. "Just tell us... It can't be that bad, not if it tastes this good."

The two guards looked at each other, chuckling.

"Oi, let me tell them, brother," said Áethelwûlf, winking at Áelfwînë and slapping his knee.

"Be my guest. Just let me grab my things before you tell them," Áelfwînë said, letting out a long sigh as he stood up.

Resigned, Ándrôniüs, and Ísolde also stood up, following his lead and stepping back from the fire ring, leaving Áethelwûlf and the five friends still sitting.

"So... are you gonna tell us?" Ethan said, stirring the stew instead of eating it.

He prodded at the surface with the edge of his spoon, watching the broth shift as if it might reveal something hidden beneath. The steam rose around his face, and he narrowed his eyes at the mixture, turning it slightly as though intense scrutiny alone could expose whatever he suspected they were keeping from them.

With a grin on his face, Áethelwûlf said, "That'd be Ísolde's famous giant salamander and snail stew."

The five teenagers all looked at each other and immediately turned green. Their faces then flushed. They began heaving or spitting out the spoonfuls they had just eaten onto the ground. Ándrôniüs and Ísolde, the two guards, roared with laughter at their companions' revulsion towards the meal's contents. The friends poured the rest of their stew onto the fire, causing it to hiss and spark. The adults took their places back around the fire on the stumps or rocks they had been using as seats.

Meanwhile, the teenagers reacted to the trick played on them by huffing, sighing, or rolling their eyes. Gradually, they all settled down, their irritation fading into quiet murmurs before even those slipped away. The fire's orange glow softened across their faces, and the stillness of the night took hold, broken only by the crackling of the flames and the distant hum of the forest.

As the quiet deepened, their attention drifted upward. Through breaks in the canopy, the first stars emerged, faint at first, then sharpening into clearer points of light as thin clouds moved lazily across the sky. Ryan watched them for a long moment, his earlier frustration melting into something more restless and uncertain.

Gazing up at the stars that began to peek through the canopy of trees and the thick clouds drifting high above, Ryan asked, "Will we get any answers in Vâloríâ, Ándrôniüs?"

"You may... you may not. In Vâloríâ, great wisdom and power reside, and the very fabric of our lands is recorded there. If you seek something, ask, and it will be revealed to you; but likely in a book you must read completely. Like any answer you seek, you must put in the work, Ryan. The High Mages will set you on the path to fulfil your role regarding the prophecy. Vâloríâ is the place where you will conduct your test, and you must prepare yourself for whatever they place before you... And well, of course, all of you," Ándrôniüs said with a thoughtful look at each of them.

Ethan, ever the inquisitor, demanded more. "You still haven't told us what kind of tests they are."

"It's hard to say. Each test is tailored to the individual," Ándrôniüs said, with a shake of his head, a wry smile etched upon his face as if he were holding back.

With a loud huff, Ethan followed up with, "You never give us anything to go off of, Ándrôniüs. It is downright infuriating... It's... It's just so damn annoying."

With a roll of his eyes, Ándrôniüs answered snidely as he leaned back. "Almost as annoying as your persistence."

"What was that, old man?" Ethan said with a snarl.

Ethan stood up and towered over Ándrôniüs, almost as if he was squaring up to fight the older man.

"Watch your tongue," Áethelwûlf interjected, taking hold of the hilt of the sword near his foot.

"What are you going to do? Murder me?" Ethan said, turning his attention to the guard instead of the mage. "I'm just demanding answers we deserve to get."

Áethelwûlf spit on the ground near Ethan's feet, stood up and said, "If only I were younger and less wise, I'd cut that selfish head from your neck for your insolence to my master, boy."

The two were now mere inches from each other's faces. Ethan's friends were trying to calm him down, and Áelfwînë was pulling his counterpart back from the boy.

"Now, now, boys... settle down. Maybe it would do all of you some good to take in the effects of a small cutty of drangoon weed.

I have some extra if you'd like," Ándrôniüs said, trying to diffuse the tension, pulling out a few small papers that were rolled around an herb of sorts.

"Thank you, master, but you know I don't like that dwarvish garbage," Áethelwûlf said before sitting down and brushing off the scuffle with Ethan.

Ethan rolled his eyes at both of them, pushing off his friends. "No, I don't partake in things like that."

Those still standing took their places back around the fire.

"Well, if they won't, my lord... I surely could use a few puffs. Here, toss one to me," Áelfwînë said, with an outstretched hand.

Ándrôniüs threw a small package of fags over to him. Áelfwînë catching them, opened it swiftly. The mage retrieved one of the smokes after a long time examining the rolled herbs for the perfect one. He lit the end of it in the fire, leaned back, and started puffing on the cutty while staring up at the stars.

The conversation gradually faded, fatigue from their laborious day beginning to take over. One by one, the companions retreated to their bedrolls, the comforting sounds of the forest lulling them to sleep. The gentle rustling of leaves, the distant hoot of an owl, and the soft murmur of the nearby stream created a soothing orchestra.

Ethan, feeling restless, lay awake for a while, staring at the canopy of leaves above. His mind raced with thoughts of the journey ahead, the prophecy, and the strange new world they had stumbled into. Despite his doubts and fears, he held onto the flicker of hope within him. He hoped they would stay together, so they could face whatever confrontations lay ahead, united.

# No Way But Forward

THE FOLLOWING MORNING OF their journey dawned with a hazy sky and a breeze that tugged gently at their faces, carrying with it the scent of damp earth. The early morning light filtered through the forest canopy, casting a soft green glow over the camp.

Ethan was the first to awaken, groaning as he shook off the grogginess of a restless night. His body felt stiff from the previous day's hike, his muscles protesting with each stretch. He took a deep breath, savoring the quiet serenity of the morning before the day would commence.

One by one, the others stirred. Emily shifted first, still more asleep than awake, and rolled straight into Ethan before she realized where she was. She rubbed at her eyes, mumbling about the absence of coffee and how no sane person should be conscious at such an hour. Ethan let out a low laugh. She had always pushed against the stricter parts of their shared faith back home, especially the rules she was never supposed to break. Her complaints were familiar enough that they softened the edge of morning.

She forced herself upright, blinking at the pale light filtering through the trees. Her hair was a tangled mess, and she made a halfhearted attempt to smooth it before giving up entirely. Jake and Ryan were not far behind her, both moving with the slow resignation of men who would have much preferred another hour of sleep. They began packing their gear with the heavy motions of people still negotiating with the day, each breath fogging softly in the cool air as they tried to gather themselves.

Hannah, in contrast, was calm and methodical as she folded her blanket with precise movements, her face a mask of quiet focus. Her meticulousness provided a spot of order amidst the morning's lethargy, though the others took little notice. She seemed almost detached, lost in thought as she prepared.

The surrounding forest was already alive, with birds chirping a lively morning chorus, their songs filling the air with a brightness that contrasted the somber mood settling over the group.

After a meager breakfast, they finished loading the cart and departed the camp, gradually putting miles between them and it. It didn't take long before sweat dripped down their faces and their muscles ached from the effort of moving through such unforgiving terrain. The once serene forest now felt like a hostile environment, its beauty overshadowed by the sheer difficulty of the path. Even the canopy above seemed more oppressive, with the dense foliage blocking out much of the sunlight, casting the path ahead in shadow. The forest's song, once filled with lively birds and rustling leaves, now seemed quieter, as if the wildlife had retreated in the face of this rugged landscape.

Every step forward was hard-earned, every small victory over the terrain a testament to their resilience. Yet, with each passing hour, the forest became ever more uninviting, its thick underbrush and uneven ground turning the path into a grueling trial of will.

Ethan led the way, his eyes scanning the path ahead for any signs of danger. He moved with purpose, keeping a distance between him and the others.

Hannah noticed Ethan walking alone and ran up to join him. She grabbed his hand, offering a bright smile. "Why are you up here by yourself?"

Her voice broke Ethan's focus on the path. He hesitated before replying, "Everyone except Ísolde treats me like I'm some sort of disease. Even you four, whom I've known most of my life. All I want is answers. To know... to... Never mind, I can see the look on your face. I should just stop."

Ethan quickened his pace with Hannah in tow, causing her to chase him as he sped off down the trail.

"Ethan, stop!" Hannah said, stomping her foot on the ground and pointing to him.

He halted, turning to look at her.

"You're being childish. Stop this. Whatever this is. This isn't the Ethan I know," Hannah continued with a stern look plastered all over her face.

"Why are you saying these things? You're just proving my point... anyway, what do you want? Do you just want to go with the flow here? Should we just keep dealing with all of this blindly?" Ethan said, unable to comprehend her easy acceptance of being in this new world, a place he struggled to acknowledge and so desperately wanted to leave.

"What other choice do we really have, Ethan?" Hannah said, approaching him beseechingly.

Ethan took a small step back, his face set in hard, angry lines. "Tons!"

Hannah softly took his hands in hers. "Then what is it we should do then?"

His shoulders slumped at the question. "I don't know," he replied, stumped, unsure of the correct course, only that he believed this wasn't it.

"Exactly my point, Ethan," Hannah said, taking him into her arms and wrapping him tightly in her embrace, running her fingers through his hair. "I know Ándrôniüs and the others are basically strangers, considering we only met them a week ago, but I believe they have the best intentions. The rest of us are trusting them. After all, they have fed us, clothed us, put us under their roof, and even helped me heal. That has to count for something, right? Now tell me, what is really bothering you?"

"I feel that this is all my fault. I told my dad I wanted a big graduation trip with you all... not this, of course. But if we hadn't planned it, we wouldn't have been on the plane, in that storm, and ended up wherever this is," Ethan mumbled, still holding onto Hannah, his head pressed firmly against her shoulder. The admission took away any more desire to fight, and he slumped against her.

Hannah reflected on his words for several moments. "There's no way you could have known this would happen." She squeezed him tighter, silently offering reassurance that everything would be okay despite his worries.

Someone in the back of the group released a heavy sigh, breaking the pair out of their conversation.

Emily, lagging behind the others, began complaining. "Well, isn't that image just disgusting... You two are just... Never mind. I'm so over this place. This walk. I just want to be wherever we are going, just sooner. Not to mention... I just want a nice fluffy couch, a good book, and some ice cream right about now," she groused.

Jake and Ryan looked at each other, a sudden longing overcoming them at Emily's words.

"Ice cream," they both said in unison.

"What is this couch and ice cream you speak of?" Ándróniüs asked, lurching back, his curiosity piqued at yet another unusual set of words.

Emily squealed. She swatted and huffed in frustration at the bugs that dove like kamikazes, and had particularly chosen to swarm around her. After a few more unsuccessful swats through the air, she let out another shrill scream before answering.

"A couch is much like the furniture you had near the fireplace in your manor. And ice cream is a creamy mixture of milk and other ingredients that are sweet, cool, and refreshing."

Her frustration grew as she described it, her voice tinged with longing.

Ándróniüs brightened at her explanation. "Oh! A double chair. I see, I see." He paused for a moment, his expression thoughtful, clearly still puzzled by the concept of ice cream. "Well, when we get to Vâloríâ, if we have the time, I will fetch the best milk in all the land, so I too can know the taste and desire you have for this ice cream."

Emily kept swinging at the cloud of bugs pestering her as she shoved past the shrubs snagging at her clothes. She snapped angrily, "Ándróniüs, I'm not even certain we can make it here." Letting out another sharp scream of frustration, she added, "I HATE these pestilent little bugs and these fricken thorny plants!" With a stomp of her foot, she pushed past Jake, the cart, and the guards, seeking a clearer path ahead.

"Is she alright?" Ándróniüs inquired, sitting in the cart and watching her storm off as the cart passed by Ethan and Hannah, who had stopped to allow the rest of the travelers to catch up with them. He looked down at Jake, waiting for a response.

Once the cart had passed them, Hannah and Ethan pressed on, opting to stay behind the cart a way so as not to eat the dust it was stirring with the churning of its wooden wheels over the dusty soil along the path.

"She was never a fan of the outdoors," Jake said, chuckling softly before yelling after the young woman. "Think of it as an adventure, Emily. We're seeing places and things we'd never have dreamed of back home."

Emily turned around quickly and spewed, "But we're not back at home, Jake, are we?"

Everyone remained silent for much of the day after Emily's eruption. Chatter resumed when the group paused for a brief rest under a large tree, its branches providing a welcome respite from the sun. They drank water from their flasks and shared a few bites of dried fruit, the simple fare doing little to lift their spirits but enough to sustain them.

Once revitalized, they resumed their trek; the path grew even steeper, and the rocky terrain gave way to a series of narrow switchbacks that wound up the side of a hill. The air grew cooler as they gained elevation, and the dense forest thinned, offering glimpses of the surrounding landscape. The view from the top was breathtaking, with rolling, forested hills stretching out as far as the eye could see, a patchwork of green and brown painting the horizon.

After a long day of traversing hills, climbing up and down endless switchbacks that seemed to tug at their weary minds, the group finally set up camp in a small clearing near a bubbling spring. The water pooled among the rocks before trickling down the hillside, its gentle sound providing a soothing backdrop as they prepared their simple dinner.

Ándrôniüs sat by the fire, his staff resting across his knees, deep in thought as he puffed on a small cutty. The others gathered around. Silence dominated the space, their fatigue quelling any thoughts of conversation. The crackling fire and the murmur of the nearby spring were the only sounds that filled the air as they ate their less exotic meal.

They finished their meal in the night's stillness, each lost in their own thoughts. Some rubbed their aching feet, trying to ease the spasms that had plagued them throughout the day, while others popped the blisters that had formed from the relentless trekking. A few stretched their stiff limbs, seeking to regain some flexibility. The fire continued to crackle and pop, sending occasional sparks into the night sky where they disappeared, becoming one with the stars above. One by one, the companions retreated to their bedrolls, letting their minds drift away from consciousness.

Ethan, much like the night before, lay awake for a while, staring up at the sky. His expression tightened as if lost in thought, his body tense against the whispers of the night. Though the surrounding forest remained still, a faint unease lingered in his demeanor, a shadow of something unseen gnawing at his focus.

He shook his head and pressed his fingers against his ears, the motion subtle enough to avoid drawing attention from the few still awake or stirring. The steady breathing of his friends and the occasional snores from Áelfwînë and Áethelwûlf offered a reassuring rhythm, a reminder of their safety. Slowly, he closed his eyes, his chest rising and falling with deliberate breaths as he willed himself to sleep, seeking the rest that eluded him.

# WILLOWDALE

WHEN MORNING CAME, THEY quickly fell into their routines, efficiently packing up camp.

Ethan, who was the last to wake this morning, arose to the chatterings of each doing their assigned tasks. He stretched and looked around, taking in the sight of his friends getting ready. Emily was brushing her hair, Jake was tending to the ox, and Ryan was checking their supplies. Hannah quietly hummed to herself as she prepared breakfast, a small smile on her lips.

"Breakfast is ready!" Hannah called out.

Approaching the mess area set up in the camp, Áelfwînë groaned, "Porridge again?"

"Yup!" Hannah replied cheerfully.

Áelfwînë shook his head and muttered, "I think I'll pass. I'd rather have that bread from the other morning that tasted like gritty dirt." A mischievous grin spread across his face as Ísolde shot him a sharp glare, clearly offended by his remark, as she had made the bread the morning before.

Hannah carefully dished out the sloppy porridge into the bowls they had collected from Ísolde at the oxcart.

As they ate, Áelfwînë and Áethelwûlf, who usually kept to themselves in private conversation, finally broke their silence.

"You all seem to be adjusting well to this journey," Áelfwînë said, his deep, steady voice carrying across the camp. "It's difficult traveling through these woods; you've shown surprising resilience."

"Indeed," Áethelwûlf added with a nod. The slightly shorter and stockier guard continued, "We've been through these parts many times, and it's rare to see first-time travelers handle it as well as you all have."

Ísolde, who had been quietly observing, smiled warmly. She seized an opportunity to speak, something she rarely managed with this group, and blurted out, "The five of you are doing well, as they both mentioned. I know I would not have made it this far without the oxcart. I am just so proud of you all!"

"It sure doesn't feel that way," Ethan groaned, pushing his half-eaten bowl of bland porridge away.

With a playful smile, Ísolde waved her hand dismissively. "Oh, come on, Ethan. You're doing just fine, and you know it."

Shaking his head, Ethan replied, "I wouldn't call this 'fine.' I mean, do we really have a choice? I'd say we're just surviving at this point. Not to mention we're being forced to do this journey when all we want to do is go home."

Letting out a soft chuckle, Emily leaned forward. "Oh, stop being dramatic, Ethan. I think we all agree that we're rolling with the punches. But honestly, back home, I don't think I could've even imagined doing any of this. I know I've been complaining a bunch, but this place has been growing on me."

Ísolde beamed, clapping her hands together. "See? I told you, Ethan. Each of you is stronger than you give yourselves credit for."

Ethan shrugged, though a small grin tugged at the corners of his mouth as the group cleaned up. They washed their utensils and bowls in the spring. The gentle trickle soothed the remnants of their weariness from the previous day. Each splash against the rocks seemed to cleanse not just their bowls, but their spirits, too.

As they placed the cleaned dishes back into the chest on the oxcart, Jake let out a contented sigh. "Well, no point in sticking around. We've got more ground to cover."

"Indeed!" Ándrôniüs shouted at the top of his lungs as he hoisted up his robe and started marching down the trail.

With a last glance at the clearing, they got underway, Ándrôniüs already far ahead in the distance.

As they descended the treacherous hills they had camped atop, the forest gave way to a bog, its waist-to-neck-high water brimming with insects. The bugs swarmed like miniature clouds of black smoke, biting relentlessly and leaving painful, itchy welts on the travelers' dry, dirty skin.

Emily, who was continuing her Sisyphean assault on the bugs that pursued her, lost her footing and sunk up to her neck in the muck. Áelfwînë quickly sloshed over, pulling her out and back onto the path.

"Watch your step!" Ándrôniüs called out, his voice echoing through the dense, humid air. "This bog is more treacherous than it looks. One wrong step and you'll sink, never to be seen again! Emily, you were mighty lucky! Stay between the logs outlining the path. They mark the safest route, placed there long ago by the locals."

Disgruntled at the late notice, Emily climbed into the back of the cart to avoid further struggles in the bog. Unfortunately, the added weight caused the cart, already burdened by its load, to sink. The others had to push and pull to free it from the mire, their patience wearing thin with the infuriating task.

Emily wasn't the only one struggling. Ethan floundered against the thick mud as he swatted futilely at the swarming insects, gritting his teeth as he pushed the cart. "These bugs are unbearable!" he exclaimed, swiping at the air. "It feels like they're trying to eat us alive."

Hannah, her dress soaked with the contents of the mire and sticking to her legs like a second skin, nodded in agreement. "We need to keep pushing," she urged. "Come on, guys!"

"I've never seen so many bugs in my life," Emily grimaced, flailing frantically at the swarms around the ox cart.

Ándrôniüs smiled facetiously. "Indubitably; the Créquhiêvins are quite galling today." He paused, watching as everyone rolled their eyes. "I daresay we've all had just about enough of these pests."

"I don't care what they are, Ándrôniüs." Emily snapped. "I just want them gone. Isn't there anything you can do about this?"

His face unchanged, Ándrôniüs replied, "Of course there is! C'mon boys! Push harder! Give it your all!"

"Pay no mind to him," Áelfwînë said with a huff as he strained against the cart. "The craykies are always a pain. There's not much we can do but just push our way out of the quagmire."

Jake and Ethan worked together with the guards at the back of the cart, struggling against the weight to push it forward through the wet ground.

"Keep pushing!" Jake encouraged, his face streaked with sweat and mud. "We're almost through this."

The group pressed on, their fortitude unwavering despite the oppressive conditions. Each step through the endless bog was a battle against the sucking mud that threatened to drag them down.

With a loud splash, Jake strayed outside the logs marking the path and fell into the muck. He let out a yelp as his head briefly disappeared beneath the surface. Áelfwînë and Ryan lunged forward, grabbing his flailing arms and hauling him free.

Áelfwînë, his armor clinking with each movement, took the lead to ensure they made it out unscathed. "Stay close and keep your eyes on the path," he grumbled. "We've already had two of you take a plunge; we need no more."

"What path?" Emily fired back sarcastically, her annoyance evident.

"Ahhh, shush, Emily. We've faced worse," Áethelwûlf replied, covered in sludge but undeterred. "Just a bit more, and we'll be on solid ground again."

With one final push, the cart reached the edge of the bog, the ground gradually becoming firmer beneath its wheels. Jake and Ethan heaved at the back, and together, the group emerged from the mire with a collective sigh of relief.

"Thank heavens," Emily muttered, brushing the mud from her clothes after climbing down from the cart. "I thought we'd never make it."

Hannah smiled, her face streaked with dirt from swatting away the swarms of insects. "Let's just keep going. The further we are from it, the fewer bugs we'll have to deal with."

As Hannah scurried off, the others exchanged amused glances and pressed on, leaving the bog behind.

By mid-morning, the dense forest thinned, gradually giving way to open fields of golden wheat. And by late afternoon, a small village came into view, nestled peacefully in a valley between imposing hills. Smoke curled lazily from chimneys, and the faint sounds of human life drifted through the air—a welcome contrast to the solitude of the forest.

Ándrôniüs guided the cart toward the gates that interrupted the palisade surrounding the village.

"Welcome to Willowdale," he announced as they arrived. "We'll rest here tonight before making the last leg of our journey to Vâloríâ."

The villagers greeted them warmly, their curious eyes lingering on the newcomers. Willowdale was a quaint settlement with modest homes and a small market square. The group was led to an inn. The inn's haphazard construction suggested numerous additions throughout its lifetime. Two posts jutted out from the top of the door with lanterns adorning them, swaying in the light breeze. The door had seen better days than even the inn; the wood was worn and split. However, the well-maintained architrave above the door bore a cartouche of a majestic lion. The name of the inn, "The Lion's Labyrinth," was written in fancy cursive script beneath the lion's carved bust.

Once inside, the innkeeper showed them to their rooms. The accommodations were humble, but after three days of rough travel, even the simplest bed felt luxurious. Before settling in, they happily washed away the grime of their journey and changed into clean clothes from their satchels.

That evening, they gathered for dinner at the local alehouse across from the inn. Taking the opportunity, Ethan asked Ándrôniüs about their destination, attempting to catch the older mage off guard, hoping he would slip up.

"What can you tell us about Vâloríâ? What should we expect?"

Ándrôniüs sighed, a hint of irritation creeping into his voice as he rolled his eyes. "Ethan, for the love of all things sacred left in this world, haven't I answered this already? Vâloríâ, yes, it's beautiful, full of wonder, blah, blah, blah. The tests? Yes, of course there will be tests. You know this. And the prophecy? If you are the chosen ones—and I am fairly certain you are—it will be revealed in due time. But, Ethan, you don't need to keep badgering me like a child asking, 'Are we there yet?' All is well, so stop worrying. You're going to give yourself wrinkles."

Ethan's swift-kindled frustration boiled over. "Enough, Ándrôniüs! You're always repeating the same vague nonsense! It's getting old. 'The tests, the prophecy, the chosen ones.' Do you even hear yourself? We've been dragged into this, and you keep dodging our questions. Just give us something tangible! What you're telling us isn't enough. We deserve more than what seems like riddles!" His voice was sharp, filled with contempt.

Emily tried to intervene. "Stop it, Ethan—"

"Ethan, what did we talk about?" Hannah interrupted, eyeing him with a firm look and pointing a finger at him.

Emily rolled her eyes and let out an audacious huff at Hannah for cutting her off.

"I'm sure we discussed this as well," Ísolde added, seizing the opportunity as confusion flickered across Ethan's face.

Ísolde winked reassuringly and smiled conspiratorially at the puzzled Hannah.

"It's not just that. We should be entitled to some understanding of our lives being upheaved as they have been," Ethan said, his voice softening slightly but remaining resolute.

"I've told you in due time, you will understand everything," Ándrôniüs replied, striving for calm, though his patience was clearly worn thin. "You need to have patience, Ethan, and all will be revealed."

"Didn't I say that, Ethan?" Ísolde added, offering Ándrôniüs a reassuring glance as she touched his back lightly.

Ethan sighed, muttering, "Fine, whatever. I'm just trying to be proactive, while all of you seem okay with what's happening."

"No, Ethan. We've just come to terms with the fact that we're not going home. We need to start our lives here if we want to survive," Jake retorted.

"Yeah, man, we all miss home: our parents, the comforts, what we were supposed to be enjoying in Fiji. But we don't even know if going home is an option," Ryan added.

Emily turned to Ándrôniüs and asked hesitantly, "Is it possible to go back, Ándrôniüs?"

"Maybe... maybe not," Ándrôniüs replied thoughtfully. "There have been strangers from other lands beyond this planet, like you. All arriving... never any leaving. But there's always the possibility of something, anything, or nothing, regardless of the situation."

Sighs of frustration escaped from the five friends, weary of Ándrôniüs's endlessly cryptic responses. While they had tolerated his vague answers before, this time felt different. Their fatigue and the unanswered questions left them mentally drained and on edge.

After dinner, they made their way into the inn's common room and claimed a spot near the hearth. The fire did its work slowly, warming their faces and loosening the stiffness in their shoulders and feet. No one rushed to speak, but when they finally did, the words came easier than they had at the table. A few small jokes, a few tired smiles, nothing loud or forced, just enough to remind them they were still together after a long and difficult day. The roof overhead and the steady crackle of the flames eased the tension that had gathered since morning and especially after the mess at dinner.

That is when a funny memory popped into one of the minds of the boys.

Ryan leaned back in his chair and let out a chuckle. Grinning, he turned to Ethan. "Remember that time you tried to impress, oh, what's her name?" He snapped his fingers trying to jog his memory. "Oh, yeah, Anna. That's it. You tried impressing her by climbing that old tree on campus to grab her assignments that had blown up into the branches, only to get stuck halfway when your belt got tangled. You were just hanging there!"

The memory seemed to cut through each of their tiring minds and bodies, as Emily burst into laughter, her joy lightening the mood in the room. Even Ethan, despite his earlier frustration, couldn't help but crack a smile.

"Oh, don't remind me," he groaned, rubbing his temples. "But I was not stuck!"

Jake laughed, shaking his head. "Man, you were stuck up there. Quit messing around. You looked ridiculous. All the while, Anna just walked away with the rest of the cheer squad."

Ethan blushed, shaking his head. "Yeah, yeah, laugh it up. At least I didn't get chased by a goose, Jake."

The laughter over Ethan's tree incident was interrupted as Jake, still grinning, said, "Seriously though, that goose was out for blood! It left a scar, see?"

He pulled down the hem of his pants, exposing his lower back, where a small brown scar was visible.

Raising an eyebrow, a hint of amusement playing on his lips, Ándrôniüs said, "A scar from a goose, Jake? You must have truly angered the creature."

Áelfwînë, with a teasing glint in his eye, added, "You let a goose best you? I'm not sure if I should be impressed with the bird, or concerned."

Shaking his head, Áethelwûlf smirked. "I've fought off many things, but a fowl? That's a new one. Maybe we should knight the bird for bravery."

Giggling from her corner, Ísolde joined in, her voice light and teasing. "Oh, Jake, you'll have to tell everyone in Vâloríâ how you earned that battle scar. They'll think you're quite the warrior!"

Jake rolled his eyes, laughing along with them. "Alright, alright, enough about the goose. Just wait until one of you gets chased by an angry... an angry... chicken or something."

Ethan, grinning from ear to ear, said, "I'll take my chances with the chickens. You can keep the geese, Jake."

Laughter erupted again, filling the common room. For a few moments, their shared mirth lifted the burden of their travels. The warmth of the fire, the camaraderie, and the shared experiences softened the memory of the harsh words spoken over dinner.

The merriment faded, a comfortable silence settling over the group. And as the night deepened, Ándrôniüs stood, stretching his back and smiling at the group. "Get some rest. Tomorrow is another day, and the great white city of Vâloríâ awaits us. But first, the Kítspäk Mountains."

# THE BALLAD

MORNING CAME HARD AND fast as Willowdale burst awake around them. Voices called out across the village before the sun had fully cleared the roofs. Pots clattered in nearby kitchens. Someone shouted instructions from down the lane. The blacksmith's hammer struck metal in sharp, ringing blows that cut through the cool air. Dogs barked, chickens scattered, and horses stamped and snorted in the stables as the day took hold. The noise rolled through the streets in waves, shaking off whatever sleep they had left.

The group woke to the commotion, dragging themselves upright as the village's morning pushed against the surrounding walls. They pulled on their boots, gathered their things, and moved with the heavy steps of people not given a gentle start to the day. Once ready, they headed down the rickety stairs of the inn, each creaking step announcing their descent, before stepping out into the cool air outside.

The guards were already waiting, the ox, and cart readied for departure. As the group stowed their belongings, Ísolde noticed Emily wrestling with her satchel, the sides bulging with the supplies she had picked up the night before on their way back from getting their meal passing through the market. Emily tried to force the flap closed with her knee, muttering under her breath as another item slipped loose.

With a gentle smile, she walked over. "Let me help you with that," she said, her voice soft and reassuring.

Emily smiled gratefully. "Thanks, Ísolde. I appreciate it."

With her help, Emily was able to reconfigure her satchel to fit all of her things. Ísolde then threw the bag, along with her own, up to Áethelwûlf, who was in the cart securing the goods in place for the next stretch of their journey.

Once the cart was loaded to the brim, Ándrôniüs flicked the reins, urging the ox forward, and leading the way out of the village. The villagers waved them off. The path ahead appeared clear, as if the forest was welcoming them with open arms.

As the hours passed, the terrain shifted from dense forest to rugged hills, the distant outline of mountains gradually becoming more prominent on the skyline. Cool, crisp air filled the surroundings, dotted with a vibrant array of wildflowers. The narrow path forced them to walk single file, with the oxcart trailing behind, rattling as it collided with stones jutting out of the footpath. Áelfwînë and Áethelwûlf took the lead, their eyes scanning the landscape for any sign of danger.

Ethan, who was walking behind Ándrôniüs, couldn't ignore the burning desire to ask the questions that he felt he and his friends were entitled to know the answers to. He tried focusing on the trail, pushing the queries to the back of his mind, but they were irrepressible, whispering through his thoughts until they were front and center again. Before he could stop himself, his mouth opened, and he spoke.

"Ándrôniüs?"

The mage stopped in his tracks, sweat dripping down his reddened face, and turned to face Ethan. "What is it?" he asked. "If this is what I am thinking it is about, I caution you to hold your tongue."

"Well..." Ethan started sheepishly.

"No, not well, Ethan..." Ándrôniüs said, his face tightening. "Well... get on with it, if you must."

Sensing the old mage's growing irritation, Ethan tread carefully with his next words. "It's just... we're almost there, right? I mean, you're a mage. You seem important. I've seen how people treat you. Shouldn't you be able to tell us more about these tests? Like what we'll be facing? At least it'd give us something to talk about while we're suffering out here."

Ethan's friends let out a collective sigh.

Ándrôniüs pinched the top of his nose, trying to maintain what little composure he had left. "Ethan… I know I've told you this already. Over and over. But since you must know and are so worried about these tests, all our previous chosen have passed. Not one of our chosen has failed their test. The Grand Mage will tell you when the time is right. But if you cross me and keep up with this pestering, I will push you right down this hill. And I will sleep just fine tonight without *any* regrets. There have always been more of you that come every age, meaning there will be more of you if I end you."

Letting out an exasperated sigh, trying to maintain his own composure, Ethan responded, "Yes, Ándrôniüs, I know. You've said that every day since we started this journey."

Taking a step forward, now nose to nose with the boy, Ándrôniüs said, his voice cold and biting, "And yet you ask the same question every day, as if I'll magically change my answer. What part of 'the High Mage Council will decide' and 'the Grand Mage will inform you' is so difficult for your simple mind to grasp?" His eyes flared with irritation. "Do you think this is some game where I'll pat you on the head and tell you exactly what's coming if you ask enough times? Grow up, Ethan. The world doesn't cater to your endless demands."

Ethan stood, stunned. He was used to his father's shouting and drunken threats, but the old mage's sudden shift in tone, laced with what seemed and felt like genuine menace, caught him off guard. What unsettled him even more was the harshness of Ándrôniüs's words, which were usually wrapped in kindness or delivered with pompous indifference. There was something different in the mage's eyes; something teetering on the edge of deflagration. Ethan felt his own anger rise, bubbling just beneath the surface, but the words he wanted to say never came.

Instead, the voice he tried so desperately to suppress—the one he never dared to speak of—whispered again. It urged him to draw the dagger given to him by the guards back at Pinemarsh Manor for this journey and plunge it into Ándrôniüs's heart. Horrified, Ethan shook his head violently and clenched his fists. Without saying a word, thrusting down his own feelings of contention tempering them, he shoved past the others and stormed off, putting distance between himself and the group. His pride stung, and his thoughts were in turmoil.

A heavy stillness followed him as he stalked away, the air left behind feeling tight and unsettled. No one reached for him or called after him. They all felt the edge in his departure, a rawness none of them were prepared to test. Even the surrounding forest seemed to hold its breath, waiting to see what would break first.

But there was no rest. The old mage waved an arm forward, and the oxcart moved down the trail, following slowly behind Ethan's wake. As they pressed on, the group replayed Ándróniüs's words in their minds, exchanging uneasy glances. These weren't the cryptic musings they had grown accustomed to; this was different. Ándróniüs's sharp tone had caught them off guard, revealing a side of him they hadn't seen before. His usually calm demeanor had fractured, anger bubbling to the surface. Though none of them wanted to admit it aloud, seeing Ethan—normally the most tenacious of them—silenced so quickly made them think twice about engaging Ándróniüs with any of their own queries.

The group moved on in subdued silence, traveling well into the late afternoon without stopping for lunch. The hills rose sharply beneath their feet, and the path turned rough, littered with boulders, charred trunks, and broken limbs of trees long dead. The land felt stripped of breath, as though nothing living had touched it in years. No one dared speak.

Their route eventually brought them to a rise where the ground leveled out into a broad meadow tucked high in the mountains. They had noticed its open shape earlier in the day on the other side of a large alpine lake, a pale stretch of green glimpsed between distant slopes, though they could not reach it until now. A wide stream cut across the meadow, its cold, clear water rushing hard over polished stones. Deep pockets carved by the current churned dark and quick, making any attempt to guide the oxcart across far too dangerous.

Jake took the lead, carefully scouting for a decent crossing point. As he stepped onto the rocks, he suddenly slipped and tumbled into one of the deeper pools, completely soaking himself. His companions burst into laughter at the sight, their attempts to muffle the sound barely concealing their amusement. Jake's ears turned red, but he stood up, brushed himself off, and with a wry smile, said, "Watch your step. The rocks are slippery."

"Really, I couldn't tell," Áelfwînë said sarcastically, a smirk on his face, his comment amplifying the surrounding laughter.

One by one, they carefully made their way across. Further downstream, Áelfwînë found a place where the path forward was just wide enough to allow the cart to pass. With his guidance, Ándrôniüs was able to steer the ox cart across the stream.

Once the two mages rejoined the company, the group pressed on, feeling lighter as the sun dipped in the sky. The strain from the earlier scuffle having subsided, stories and jokes started flowing between the companions, livening the atmosphere for the latter half of the day. The unrelenting heat intensified with altitude, yet it could not dampen the cheerful mood of the group following the path.

As evening's sunset approached, painting the sky in hues of orange and pink, they found a suitable campsite near a small grove of trees. The ground was soft and level, and a gentle breeze rustled the leaves above. They moved efficiently, setting up camp with practiced ease: establishing a fire ring, pitching Ándrôniüs's tent, finding flat ground for their bedrolls, gathering firewood, and ensuring everything was ready for dinner. Ísolde began preparing a warm meal, her efforts promising a comforting end to the long day's slog.

Ándrôniüs took a seat beside the fire, his expression thoughtful. "I'm happy to inform you all that tomorrow, we will reach Vâloríâ," he said, his voice carrying a note of relief. "You should all really get some rest. It won't take long for the High Mage Council to determine what each of you will be facing."

Ignoring the morning's warnings, Ethan piped up with a snarky tone. "If only there were someone... anyone who could tell us what this High Mage Council might decide."

A jeering look in Ándrôniüs's direction followed his words.

Ándrôniüs abruptly stood and hurled his half-eaten meal into the fire. The flames hissed, and a plume of smoke rose as he huffed in frustration. "Ethan... I've had enough of your petulant remarks," he snapped, his voice rising in anger. "Tests, prophecies, riddles, and the gods for sake chosen! Ahhhh! Why... Allfather, why did you curse me with such a task?" he screamed, storming off into his tent, the flap slapping shut behind him.

Everyone else sat in stunned silence, eyes wide, unsure of what to say.

Ísolde broke the awkward silence. "It's okay," she said gently, trying to ease their concern. "He's just had a long day. Too much sun. He'll be fine after some rest in Vâloríâ." She stood and offered a reassuring smile. "Good night, everyone," she said before following her husband.

After her departure, the group finished their meal and cleaned up. Ryan grabbed a bucket of water to douse the fire for the night, but Áelfwînë quickly stopped him.

Áelfwînë and Áethelwûlf stood together. "Before we rest, we'd like to share a song," Áelfwînë announced, his deep voice resonating through the quiet night. "It's an old tune that has brought comfort to many weary travelers in times of uncertainty."

Áethelwûlf nodded and stood, walking over to the cart without a word. From beneath the bundled tarp, he retrieved a peculiar instrument. It was an oaken-bodied contraption with a crank on one end and a curved fingerboard made of bone on the other. Faded script covered its surface, and a leather strap held a single brass key near the top. As he returned to the firelight, he settled the instrument against his knee, turned the crank slowly, and pressed the keys with practiced grace.

A low, droning hum emerged first; somber and ancient, like the voice of the earth itself. Then came a series of resonant notes, almost mournful, but rich and full of depth. The tones stretched through the evening air, beckoning something deeper from the soul.

After a few bars, Áethelwûlf hummed a gentle melody. His voice, warm and soothing, blended harmoniously with Áelfwînë's. Though the lyrics were unfamiliar, the song carried a sense of hope and fellowship, filling the night air. The group listened, comforted by the harmony, finding peace in the moment's simplicity.

*Over Möchí Möchí's rolling crest,*
*Through Fünchâ's windswept breast,*
*We march as one, through storm and sun,*
*For light will stand the test!*

*So stride on, press on, bold hearts true,*
*The road is long, the night is cruel,*
*But dawn shall rise, o'r field and fen,*
*And free our land again!*

*Through Olëstrë's drowning mire,*
*Where willows whisper dire,*
*Through shadow's claw, through biting flaw,*
*Yet still we climb up higher!*

*So stride on, press on, bold hearts true,*
*The road is long, the night is cruel,*
*But dawn shall rise, o'er field and fen,*
*And free our land again!*

*O'er Kítspäk's ice-bound throne,*
*Through Valoríâ's gates of stone,*
*We lift our song, though days be long,*
*For Cáelunárra's own!*

*So stride on, press on, bold hearts true,*
*The road is long, the night is cruel,*
*But hope still burns, through war and woe,*
*The dawn shall come; this we know!*

As the company took to their bedrolls that night, the song replayed in their minds, its echoes calming their thoughts. One by one, they curled up, pulling the fabric tightly around their tired bodies.

# VALORIA

THE LAST DAY OF their passage on the way to the city of Vâloríâ began with a sudden crash of thunder, followed by a relentless downpour. Ethan jolted awake.

"Wake up, everyone! We need to move now!" he shouted over the storm. Half-soaked and disoriented, the group scrambled to break camp.

"Yes! Yes! Children, Áelfwînë and Áethelwûlf, we must get a move on!" shouted Ándrôniüs as he held his gown up from the muddy ground, heading from his tent to the oxcart to secure the animal, ensuring it would not run away.

The group hurried to gather their things, frantically loading the cart. Hannah and Ísolde struggled with Ándrôniüs's tent, their hands slipping on the wet fabric and mud.

"Need help over here!" Hannah called.

Jake hurried to her side, grabbing one end of the tent. "Got it. Let's fold this up and get moving."

Ryan, drenched to the bone, packed supplies into the cart with the help of the guards as the others brought them things. Just as they finished, the rain abruptly stopped altogether, as quickly as it had come.

"Of course, it stops just as we finish," Ryan grumbled, shrugging his arms to shake off the water.

Emily, wringing out her wet hair, muttered, "Great timing, as usual."

Ethan took a moment to catch his breath, glancing around at the gloomy sky. "Let's just get going."

"Indeed!" Ándrôniüs piggybacked off Ethan with fire in his voice.

They wrung out their hair, clothes, and any other items that were completely soaked. Quickly, they prepared themselves with whatever clothing they could wear from the dry wares. They opted to eat just jerky and dried fruit instead of a prepared breakfast. They hung their damp clothes and bedrolls on a drying line along the wagon, fashioned from a rope that was now being repurposed. Once done, they checked their camp for anything they might have forgotten and took their first steps of the day toward Vâloríâ. After leaving the thicket, their trail descended from the mountain plateau, and the fullness of the tree line came back into view. As they inched closer, the hair on the back of their necks lifted, giving them an unsettled feeling.

Upon stepping foot back into the forest, there were no sounds of wildlife. No birds chirped. No animals scurried. Not even the usual hum of insects could be heard. This foreboding quiet enveloped them, making every footstep seem unnaturally loud as a heavy fog lazily crept in, cloaking the forest in a thick, oppressive mist. A loud crack shook them, and the five friends screamed at the top of their lungs. Ándrôniüs jumped in his seat at the sound, and even Ísolde let out a squeal with them. The guards simply rolled their eyes.

"It was just a branch snapping as the cart rolled over it, ya' pansies," Áethelwûlf barked, kicking the now snapped branch off the path.

"Get on with it," Ándrôniüs said impatiently, as he readjusted himself on the cart's seat, having nearly toppled out of it.

Slightly embarrassed that it had only been a broken branch, the friends looked at one another with darting eyes. Still, something didn't sit right. A strange feeling lingered. Quiet returned, save for the worn groan of the cart's wheels and the heavy snorts of the ox pulling it forward.

Emily shivered. She was the first to break the group's inability to talk amongst themselves as she pulled her cloak tighter around her. "It's so quiet. I don't like it."

Nodding in agreement, Hannah scanned the shadowy trees, her eyes catching something. "Did you see that? There in the woods," she said, pointing toward a large fallen log. She blinked, and whatever she thought she saw was already gone.

Everyone followed the gesture, noting nothing more than columns of trees and moss as far as the eye could see. That is until the fog came creeping back in with a gust of wind.

"What are you on about, girl?" Áethelwûlf questioned, his tone laced with vexation.

"It looked like a person. I saw a person in the dark, wearing ragged clothing. It cloaked them and those eyes, they were creepy," Hannah said, her voice cracking with wary distress.

"Ándrôniüs, could it be a Shadewalker?" Ethan asked as he ran up to the cart, chomping at the bit.

"Oh, hush, you two. There are no Shadewalkers this close to Vâloríâ. Let alone anyone as foolhardy as us to be traversing these paths at this time," Áelfwînë said, mimicking the same tone and patience of his counterpart in helping to guide and guard them.

Ándrôniüs lashed the reins softly to have the ox pick up speed. The cart pulled forward with everyone in tow. Still uneasy, the five continuously scanned the trees on either side of the path as they carried on.

"Hannah, do you think you saw a Shadewalker?" Ethan questioned, worried about what could happen to her, let alone all of them if they encountered those creatures again.

"I don't know. I don't even remember that day on the beach or what they look like. All I know... I saw something or someone in black," she responded as Emily took her arm and they kept walking, opting to catch up to the cart and stay as close as possible to it.

"Hannah, quit dodging the question," Ethan said, anger evident in his tone. He continued to press. "Did you or did you not see a Shadewalker?"

"Stop it! All of you! Just keep walking. I promise all will be fine!" Ándrôniüs snapped, clearly done with the talk of Shadewalkers and that something sinister afoot.

"What he means, children, is stay close. We're truly not far from Vâloríâ. I know the fog can be dizzying. But if my love and the guards are not worried, then neither should we be," Ísolde said, turning to them with a reassuring smile from her position in the cart. "So, hold on as some of you are. All will be fine."

The two guards looked at each other with knowing glances. They did not change their expressions, but something unspoken passed between them—brief, faint, and easy to miss. One of them gave the smallest twitch of a smirk before it vanished just as quickly.

"Many weary travelers have perished in these woods and remain lost. Keep your wits about you. This silence isn't natural," Áelfwînë said, his tone laced with derision as he walked alongside Emily, his words only heightening the group's unease.

Áethelwûlf nodded, and in the same tone as his counterpart, he added. "I've seen these woods play tricks on the minds of those who aren't vigilant."

"Didn't I tell you two to stop it? If you don't, I'll just have to make you," Ándrôniüs said, reaching for his staff. "You kids! And that includes you two," he added, lifting his staff and pointing it at the guards, "should just find something to occupy the time with. It's just your consciousness playing tricks on you!"

"Don't think about the bad things, everyone. Focus on something good, like... oh, yes! Just think of the warm beds and hot meals waiting for us in Vâloríâ," Ísolde said, trying to lighten the mood.

"I don't care about any of that; let's just get out of here as fast as possible," Ethan said with a sense of urgency.

The dense fog continued to swallow them, coming in disorienting waves, often reducing their visibility to only a few feet as they pressed on.

Ándrôniüs's voice cut through the mist: "For once in quite sometime, I am with Ethan on this, children. Keep your hands firmly on the cart and don't stray."

As the minutes dragged on, the fog seemed to stretch time itself. Silence shrouded the world, muffling their footsteps. The cold seeped into their bones, making each step heavier. Occasionally, a gust of wind would part the fog, but it quickly closed in again, as if alive and intent on swallowing them whole.

Gradually, the sun's rays broke through the clouds, and the fog lifted. Relief swept over them as the forest thinned, revealing a vast amalgamation of farmland. Beyond it, Vâloríâ stood in all its splendor.

The city was breathtaking, with its white castles, towers, and buildings glistening in the sunlight. A fortified wall encircled the city, dotted with platforms bearing war machines.

A cheer erupted from the group.

"We made it!" Emily exclaimed, her face lighting up.

Áelfwînë and Áethelwûlf exchanged wary glances. Áelfwînë turned toward the old mage, stepped close, and murmured something into Ándrôniüs's ear. Whatever he said tightened his expression at once.

"Shhh... this is not the time to cheer. Everyone, be on your guard," Ándrôniüs said, his voice low and urgent.

A short, uneasy pause followed. The shift in him was sharp enough that even the forest seemed to fall still. Ísolde lifted a hand and quietly motioned for the children to gather around her. They came without a word, their steps small and cautious as they moved in close.

The two guards stepped forward at once, fanning out and taking positions near the front of the group, each watching the treeline with a tense, practiced focus.

Áelfwînë turned back to Ándrôniüs and gave him a single, sober nod.

"What is it, dear? What is wrong?" Ísolde asked, her brow furrowed at his sudden change in attitude.

Only then did Ándrôniüs speak, his voice directed to the others behind them.

"Emily, Hannah, hide in the cart with Ísolde, and cover yourselves with the supplies," Ándrôniüs instructed, his voice edged with urgency. "Ísolde shield them. Áelfwînë senses them."

The group exchanged confused glances, unsure of what was unfolding, but the girls quickly obeyed, clambering into the wagon and pulling the items over themselves as instructed.

"Sensing what?" Ethan questioned.

"Yeah," both Ryan and Jake echoed.

"Not now! You two," the old mage snarled.

Ísolde jumped into the cart and immediately began rummaging

through the cart and gathered hidden weapons from beneath the baseboards of the wagon.

"Come over here, boys!" Ísolde

Ethan, Ryan, and Jake each received a hefty broadsword and a small wooden shield. The boys took up arms with a mix of determination and uncertainty, unsure if they were even properly handling the weapons.

A final gust of wind cleared the remaining fog, and a chilling sight gradually emerged: twenty Shadewalkers, their shadowy forms flickering ominously, materialized between the group and the distant city of Vâloríâ. The malevolent creatures, with their glowing red eyes and ever-shifting silhouettes, seemed to absorb the light of day, casting an unnatural gloom that seeped into the very air around them.

Then a familiar set of sounds rang out toward them. "Thrụụg grọkrạn ọr ạtzlọ!," the center Shadewalker growled.

"Never!" Ándrôniüs screamed back at the group of Shadewalkers standing in their way.

The Shadewalkers looked at each other and moved toward them in a line.

Ryan gripped his sword tightly. He winced as the weight of the blade sent sharp pangs through his bruised ribs. Ethan and Jake, though unsure of their footing, tightened their grips on their swords, their eyes locked on the advancing threat.

Meanwhile, Hannah and Emily, hidden away in the ox cart under a pile of gear, could feel the change in the air. The muffled sounds of the Shadewalkers' approach seeped into all their ears, making their hearts race with fear.

The Shadewalkers moved slowly, their advance deliberate, as if savoring the fear they were invoking. Each step they took felt like a drumbeat, growing louder in the ears of the travelers, who could feel the palpable threat creeping closer with every passing second.

Ethan's gaze darted between the advancing figures and his friends. They were now face-to-face with the embodiment of their darkest fears, once more their bodies tensing as they braced for the imminent confrontation.

Ándróniüs, his expression stern, said, "Stay strong, and fight with all you have. We are outnumbered, but not outmatched."

The three mages then stepped forward and let out a defiant battle cry as the Shadewalkers began running at them. Before they knew it, the creatures were upon them. The clangor of metal on metal and the zing and zap of bolts of magic filled the air.

Ethan swung his sword at an approaching Shadewalker, the clash of metal ringing in his ears. Before he could react, a shadowy hand gripped his face and threw him to the ground. Ryan and Jake quickly moved to help, taking swings at the creature looming over Ethan.

Despite their efforts, the Shadewalkers countered each move with precision, deflecting attacks and forcing the group back toward the forest. Encircled and outnumbered, they braced themselves as the shadowy figures closed in.

"Stay together!" Ándróniüs shouted.

In unison, the Shadewalkers pointed their blades at the group.

The largest of the Shadewalkers, his stature unmatched by his counterparts, took a step forward, and said, "Grǫz vrųn ęnzǫk vąrzmąg. Vąrz grǫznǫm drąv grǫkrąn, ǫr ątzlǫ."

"And..." Ándróniüs said, looking at all of them from the corner of his eyes, his drawn sword pointed back at them in defiance. "I say no, you foul beasts!"

The Shadewalkers advanced, their cloaked personas closing in. Suddenly, a deep, resonant horn bellowed in the distance, echoing across the fields and breaking the intrusive thoughts of utter defeat that consumed some, but not all, within their small group. Before the horn call faded away, a foreign noise rang out as the gate of Vâloríâ slammed open, the sound rolling across the land as hundreds of mages poured out, racing to their aid. The Shadewalkers hesitated, their advance halted.

With fire and light, the mages set ablaze some Shadewalkers. The acrid smell of burning flesh filled the air, mingling with the agonized shrieks of the Shadewalkers as they perished. A maelstrom of light, darkness, magic, and steel consumed the field.

In the midst of the fray, a Shadewalker lunged for the unassuming Jake, who was countering another attack. Áethelwûlf appeared, sweeping the boy's legs out from under him, and thrusting his sword into the assailant. Jake turned quickly onto his stomach, pressing himself up to stand, only to see the guard being grabbed by the neck. A Shadewalker lifted him up as his feet dangled and kicked, gasping for any semblance of air. However, the grip was too strong, and a sickening crunch followed, his trachea crushed in that unyielding grasp. Áethelwûlf gasped for breath, his eyes wide with terror. The Shadewalker threw him to the ground and jabbed its jagged sword into his sternum. The guard's mouth opened in a silent scream of pain, but only a hoarse gurgle emerged from his crushed throat.

"Áethelwûlf!" screamed Jake, his cry filled with disbelief and horror as the life drained from the guard's eyes. The shout drew the attention of those in the immediate vicinity, and many turned to see the guard let out his final breath, his mouth beginning to pool and drip crimson fluid.

"Áethelwûlf!" Áelfwînë cried, rushing to his side. A blast of dark magic struck him as he kneeled at his friend's body, the impact knocking the wind out of him and sending him sprawling across the ground.

The small force from Vâloríâ pressed forward and fought with relentless fury, pushing back the remaining Shadewalkers. Surrounding the group, the mages, once upon the travelers, created a protective barrier with their combined efforts. The last of the Shadewalkers present were nearly all vanquished, their bodies turning to embers, leaving trails of dark black smoke in their wake as others fled through the sky away from the battlefield.

The companions stood amidst the waning havoc, panting, their weapons still at the ready. The soldiers and mages around them screamed victoriously, celebrating their success. Yet, among the triumphant cheers, there were those who cried, mourning the loss of Áethelwûlf and several others who had perished in the fight with the Shadewalkers.

Ándrôniüs knelt beside Áethelwûlf's lifeless body, his expression one of sorrow and respect. "He fought bravely," he murmured.

With tears streaming down his face, Áelfwînë nodded. "He did.

He was a true warrior and a brother I'll never have again."

Áelfwînë leaned over and closed his comrade's eyes. He pressed his lips to his forehead before collapsing across the still body, wails of grief slipping out as he failed to maintain his fragile composure.

Three loud, rapid blasts of a horn were let out, startling the group. The leader of the company from Vâloríâ stepped forward. He was a tall, imposing figure with sharp features and a commanding presence, and he carried himself with the authority of a seasoned mage and warrior.

His armor, like that of his fellow mages and soldiers, was white as snow, though now covered in dirt, mud, and a black humor that resembled sludge-like blood. The metal's intricate etched designs still shone through and flowing horsehair plumes decorated his helmet.

"I am Thâlôr," he announced, his voice steady and reassuring. "Welcome, chosen ones. You have arrived at Vâloríâ. We will ensure your safety and honor the sacrifice of your fallen comrade. The Grand Mage Órynë awaits your arrival. We mustn't delay. There are likely more enemies on the way. Safety can only be guaranteed within the great walls of the city."

"Grand General Thâlôr!" Ándrôniüs said, a smile stretched from ear to ear when he saw him appear. "My friend, my colleague, I have the utmost gratitude this day for your aid in the fight here. We surely would have perished without your help."

Ándrôniüs approached the Grand General with open arms and firmly embraced him. They pushed off one another and looked deep into their eyes, clearly relishing their time together.

"Come to thrust us into another campaign against the Dark Lord, are we?" the Grand General said, looking back and forth between the five and his old friend.

"You know me all too well," the old mage said with a laugh as he smacked the shoulder of Thâlôr and turned to Ethan, Ryan, Emily, Hannah, and Jake. "Children, this is Thâlôr one of the many you can trust within these walls. Now shall we? I am tired of walking and would sure like to get off my feet."

Thâlôr nodded and waved them forward. With their escort, the group approached the city. The thick wooden gates reinforced with iron bands were nearly as majestic as what they saw when they first laid eyes on Vâloríâ. The opening gates revealed a wide avenue lined with marble statues and lush gardens. Vâloríâ's streets bustled with activity, people of all races and backgrounds going about their daily routines.

Thâlôr turned to the group, his expression softening. "Welcome, chosen... to Vâloríâ. We will find our way to the Hall of Mages, where you can rest and prepare for what lies ahead."

The buildings within the walls were grand, each one a testament to the city's wealth and power. Spires reached toward the sky, and stained-glass windows caused hues of color to dance upon the marble streets.

Thâlôr led them through the bustling streets. The residents paused in their tasks, taking in the sight of the newcomers. As the unfamiliar group passed with Ándrôniüs, whispers filled the air. Curiosity, hope, and recognition sparkled in the eyes of the onlookers, for they hoped these newcomers were the chosen ones, though their expressions were mixed with uncertainty.

As they continued deeper into the city, they passed exquisite churches, lush gardens, vibrant squares, and a grand open-air theater alive with morning color. The streets narrowed slightly as they neared the heart of Vâloríâ, and then an imposing structure rose ahead of them, dominating everything around it.

Ísolde had spoken of a magnificent place where they would stay, hinting at it during many of their dinners on the road. Yet none of them were prepared for the sight before them.

There was only one building it could be: the Hall of Mages, the seat of the city's dignitaries, the center of knowledge, and the place where magic itself was developed, studied, and governed.

# THE HALL OF MAGES

THE HALL OF MAGES was a transcendent marvel of architecture and design. White marble formed the building's exterior, its smooth surface reflecting sunlight and giving the hall an ethereal glow. Tall columns lined the front, each intricately carved and placed upon a pedestal.

"Inside, you will find all the provisions you need. The High Mages will meet in due course to discuss the tests and your roles in the prophecy. Until then, make yourselves comfortable. You are among friends here," Thâlôr said as he gestured for them to enter.

As they stepped inside, a vast, open space that emanated an aura of ancient power and profound knowledge greeted the group. The ceiling was a vaulted masterpiece; the frescoes depicting scenes of magical feats and legendary battles, the colors vibrant and lifelike. Some even seemed to play out before their eyes through some sort of enchantment. Crystal chandeliers hung from the sublimated ceiling, casting a soft, golden light that bathed the hall in warmth.

Towering bookshelves, each filled with ancient tomes, scrolls, and manuscripts, lined the walls. The smell of aged paper and leather filled the air, mingling with the faint scent of incense that burned in ornate braziers located strategically around the room. Alcoves interspersed the shelves, holding statues of past High Mages that stood in silent vigil, their eyes seemingly following the newcomers with curiosity.

The arrangement of chairs and plush couches in small clusters around the hall created intimate spaces for conversation. Rich, deep blue and gold fabrics upholstered each piece of furniture, and comfortable cushions complemented them.

A grand staircase on one side of the hall took visitors up to a mezzanine level, where they could see more bookshelves and study areas.

At the far end of the room, a large, arched doorway led to private chambers where the High Mages held their meetings and conducted their most important work. Heavy velvet curtains embroidered with silver thread framed the doorway, adding to the mystery.

In the center of the hall, a long table made of dark, polished wood stretched out. Platters of fruits, breads, cheeses, and meats were laid out for a feast. Goblets filled with fresh water and fine wines were placed alongside each plate.

Every detail of the Hall of Mages amazed the five friends. It was a place where the past and present converged, a sanctuary for learning and a fortress of wisdom. The group could feel the lingering footprints of centuries of magical study, the power embedded in the walls igniting a sense of awe and respect for the place that would be their refuge in the days to come.

Ísolde, looked around in admiration, then whispered, "This place never ceases to amaze me."

Ethan nodded, his eyes wide with wonder. "I've seen nothing like it."

His friends echoed the sentiment in hushed tones.

"This place is surely like nothing else in this world. At least in my opinion," Thâlôr said with a smile tugging at his lips. "But rest now, bathe, and in time, the real trial will begin."

With that, the Grand General turned and left them to their repose.

After Thâlôr exited the hall, the companions walked to the table, drawn to the enticing spread, careful not to soil the beautiful furniture with their travel-worn clothes.

Ándrôniüs, splitting off from the group to approach the stairs, addressed them. "I must see Órynë at once. Stay here, children, with Áelfwînë and Ísolde. I will only be gone a moment—"

The sudden sound of a booming voice resounded through the hall, exuding authority.

"Ándrôniüs! Welcome! Welcome to Vâloríâ."

Órynë, the Grand Mage of Eldôria, appeared at the top of the grand staircase, descending with an air of regal elegance. He was an imposing figure, tall and slender, with long, flowing argent hair that cascaded down his back like a waterfall of moonlight. His eyes were a piercing shade of blue, radiating wisdom and a gentle yet formidable power. He wore robes of deep blue and gold, adorned with intricate patterns of sterling thread that seemed to shimmer and move with a life of their own. Around his neck hung a large amulet, a brilliant sapphire set in a frame of gold and glowing with mystical light.

Reaching the bottom of the staircase, Óryně and Ándrôniüs interlocked in a heartfelt embrace, the bond of old friends evident in their greeting.

"It seems like ages since we last saw each other when the last chosen graced our lands. You hide away in that marsh you call home, when you could live like a king among us here."

"Yes, my friend," Ándrôniüs replied, his voice filled with emotion. "It has been too long."

Óryně, seeing the soiled state of the five as they hovered around the table about to take their seats, immediately took charge. "STOP!" he commanded, his voice firm. "You must soil nothing. Please, through those doors and down the hall are your quarters. Warm baths will be available to you, and fresh linens for you to change into. Please return once finished."

The friends tugged self-consciously at their clothes, soiled from travel and their recent skirmish. Meanwhile, Óryně's eyes darted around the room.

"Elârâ!" he boomed.

At his call, a graceful woman entered the hall. Kindness and hospitality were evident in her petite figure and warm, inviting demeanor. Her youthful face, bright green eyes sparkling with intelligence, was striking. She tied her auburn hair back in a loose braid, embellishing it with small violet flowers. She wore a simple yet elegant dress of forest green, embroidered with delicate patterns of vines and leaves.

Óryně introduced her with a motion of his arm. "This is Elârâ, and she will escort you there."

Elârâ nodded, and curtsied, her smile radiating warmth. "Follow me, please."

"Come! Come, Ándrôniüs, we have much to talk about while they ready themselves for dinner," Órynë muttered quickly as he ushered his friend up the stairs and through the doors he had clattered open.

Elârâ turned toward the doors that the Grand Mage had earlier indicated. The companions minus one followed her. Jake was frozen in place, his face flushed like salmon during the spawn. The pleasant young woman's entrance struck the young man dumb.

Looking back, Elârâ noticed his lack of movement. Her eyes caught his, a small smile tugging at her lips. "Are you coming?"

"I... uhhh... yeah... yeah..." Jake stammered as he tripped not only over his words, but his feet trying to catch up with the group.

Elârâ let out a giggle and turned to lead them toward their accommodations. She would never say it aloud, but she appreciated the obvious admiration of someone she found quite handsome and endearing in his blatant attraction to her. While she struggled to maintain her composure, she led them down a corridor lined with tall windows that allowed sunlight to stream in, casting a golden glow on the stone floor. They passed through a set of ornate double doors and entered a spacious area lined with open doors that led to individual rooms.

Every room was a haven of tranquility. Tapestries depicting serene landscapes were hung on the walls. A large, comfortable bed with plush pillows and soft blankets dominated each space, and a claw-footed bathtub filled with steaming water stood off to the side, surrounded by shelves stocked with fragrant soaps, oils, and linens. A small fireplace crackled in the corner, providing warmth and a comforting glow. Richly woven rugs covered the stone floors, and a wooden wardrobe stood ready with fresh clothing.

The friends, grateful for the hospitality, quickly separated and got undressed in the privacy of their rooms, dropping their sullied clothing at their feet and entering the baths, the warm water soothing their aching bodies. The scents of lavender and eucalyptus filled the air, relaxing their minds as well.

Eventually, they all emerged from their rooms dressed in the clothing provided by the Ward Steward of the Hall of Mages.

Ethan, Ryan, and Jake each wore robes of deep emerald, a color that highlighted their strong features and gave them an air of noble stature. The soft, luxurious fabric elegantly draped over their shoulders and fell in graceful folds to their ankles, forming the garments. Intricate silver thread embroidered the hems and cuffs. A simple yet sturdy leather strap belted each robe at the waist, accentuating their athletic builds.

Meanwhile, Hannah and Emily wore flowing gowns of soft lavender. The delicate, shimmering material of the gowns caught the light with every movement. Tiny, delicate beadwork, sparkling like stars, decorated the bodices, while the skirts flowed gracefully to the floor, trailing slightly behind them as they walked.

The transformation was remarkable; they were no longer just weary travelers caked in grime, but rather the chosen ones, destined for greatness.

Once at the table, chatter broke out among the five and Ísolde, who had joined them for the meal. Áelfwînë was also present, but contributed little to the discussion, mourning the passing of Áethelwûlf with a tankard of mead.

"Ísolde, when do you think we will hear about the tests?" Emily asked.

"I don't know," Ísolde replied, trying to sound reassuring. "I suppose it will take time to gather the council for deliberations. Eldôria is rather large and vast. Then, as I aforementioned; the deliberations... each of your tasks for the tests will not be a small discussion at that. They are politicians, after all. They love the sound of their voices."

"More time... more waiting... it's not like this is our lives or anything," Ethan grumbled, a sudden flurry of anger flaring inside him.

All but Jake looked at him, growing irritated by his persistent angst on the matter.

Seeing their disapproving expressions, Ethan receded into his chair. Though the conversation continued on without him, his mind heard something, a whisper, almost. He looked around for the source before realizing it was that nagging voice again. It was at the back of his mind. He tried to understand it, but it was nothing more than inaudible grumblings. Something else was at the forefront, and feelings of resentment toward all those around him began welling up. For a moment, he had a sudden urge to strangle someone. Then a voice rang out, clearing his mind of the dark thoughts that had briefly consumed him.

"And what about Áethelwûlf? What will happen to him?" Jake asked, glancing at Áelfwînë.

Jake's own thoughts absorbed him, the sight of the mournful warrior bringing back the fateful events outside of Vâloríâ earlier that day. His interjection into the conversation was sudden and jarring, reminding the group of the tragic loss they had all witnessed. He also unknowingly saved Ethan from the real possibility of doing something he might have regretted later.

Áelfwînë, his eyes filled with sorrow, murmured. "The gods will take him to the halls of the Allfather and praise his sacrifice against the Dark Lord of Khạrzọnọv. Tonight, we will light a pyre in his honor and burn his body, sending him to the heavens above. If the lights in the sky dance with the Elyrëndhôr, it means the god of war, Vâlgârd, has taken him to be with those above."

Ísolde gently placed a hand on Áelfwînë's shoulder. "For now, let's honor Áethelwûlf. The rest will come in time. You five just relax. You've been through much since you arrived. Take this time to explore Vâloríâ; there are many exciting things to do and see!"

As she spoke, Órynë and Ándrôniüs appeared through the doors, laughing as they descended the stairs and took their seats at either end of the table.

"Ísolde is indeed correct; we will honor Áethelwûlf tonight," Óryně announced. "After dinner, we will attend the ceremony at the Cathedral of Life. Tomorrow, you may explore this grand city, but for now, let us fill our bellies!"

# THE CATHEDRAL OF LIFE

ONCE THE ILLUSTRIOUS DINNER concluded, Órynë and Ándrôniüs gestured for the group to gather outside, and the two mages led them through the streets.

The Cathedral of Life was another magnificent structure within the city. Its spires rose like some sort of celestial being's fingers, reaching ever upward to the sky, yearning for a touch from the divine. Gleaming silver crowned each pinnacle, casting moonlight over the entire edifice. Grand arches and flying buttresses added to the architectural splendor, giving the building a sense of both strength and delicate beauty.

Towering wooden doors, inlaid with precious metals and gemstones sparkling in the torchlight, greeted them as they approached the main entrance. Fragrant incense filled the air, and a distant choir carried through the halls, their voices rising in a hauntingly beautiful hymn that seemed to come from the very heart of the cathedral itself.

Upon entering, the vastness of the space struck the teenagers within. The ceiling soared high above, supported by towering columns, each one wrapped with golden vines and sculpted with such precision that they appeared almost lifelike. Stained-glass windows, each one a masterpiece, lined the walls, depicting scenes of divine intervention and heavenly battles, their colors vivid and radiant as they caught the candlelight.

From the main hall, they passed into a long corridor lined with urns, busts, and sarcophagi, each marking the resting place of those who had served within these sacred walls or had given the ultimate sacrifice protecting the people of Cáelunárra. The corridor was dim and quiet, enshrouded with the legacies of the people laid to rest there.

Through a golden-washed door, the corridor opened into a breathtaking courtyard. Here, the open-air design of the cathedral was revealed in all its glory. The sky stretched above them, visible through a central oculus. It was surrounded by a delicate lattice of silver and gold that cast exquisite patterns of light and shadow on the ground below. The courtyard was a space where the sacred and the earthly met, an awe-inspiring bridge between the mortal and heavenly realms.

In the center stood a sacrificial altar, a grand structure made of pure white stone and carved with a golden script that glowed softly around its base. On the ground surrounding the altar burned hundreds of candles.

Taking in the grandeur of the Cathedral of Life, the sheer majesty of the place filled the teenagers with a profound sense of solemnity.

Óryně and Ándrôniüs directed the group to an open space near the altar, the two mages occasionally stopping to shake hands and share a quick word with one of the other mourners. Once situated, the teenagers looked around, amazed at the sheer number of people present. Hundreds of people had gathered to pay homage to the fallen warrior. People had reverent conversations as they awaited the archbishop.

A door opened, and the congregation found pews to sit upon while two lines of guards entered. Between them, they held aloft the sacred shield upon which rested Áethelwûlf's body. Ceremonial garments glistening under the soft lighting clothed the guards. Their robes were pristine white, trimmed with elaborate silver embroidery. Golden sashes crossed their chests, symbolizing their duty and honor in this sacred task. Each guard moved with grace; their faces were set in many expressions of sorrow.

The archbishop, a towering figure of dignity and authority, entered behind them regally. He took his place behind the elevated altar, his presence commanding the attention of all gathered. His ornate robes, woven from rich velvet in deep hues of crimson and gold, shimmered in the candlelight. A heavy golden chain hung around his neck, bearing the sigil of the cathedral; a radiant sun with a heart at its center, symbolizing the life-giving force of the divine. He raised his hands, and the room hushed. His stern yet compassionate face, framed by a mane of silver hair, radiated both wisdom and strength as he addressed the congregation.

"Tonight, we honor Lieutenant Áethelwûlf of the Vâloríân High Guard of the Vaerônthíloch, a faithful warrior and servant of the Republic, who gave his life in the battle against the darkness," the Archbishop intoned, his voice resonating throughout the grand space.

The Archbishop declared, "We will remember his sacrifice, and the sacrifices of the other men and women, in the coming days."

The archbishop then peered into the heavens, raising his hands and calling to a higher power above. "Vâlgârd, god of war, we offer this stalwart soul to you. May his spirit find peace in the hall of the Allfather."

As he spoke, guards appeared from a darkened hallway toward the altar and placed Áethelwûlf's body upon the sacrificial table. They moved with practiced precision, their movements choreographed and deliberate, honoring the solemnity of the occasion.

The Archbishop continued, his voice steady and filled with reverence. "Vâlgârd, mighty god of war, hear our plea. Accept this noble warrior, whose courage and valor shone brightly in the face of darkness this day. Let him join the ranks of the honored dead in the Allfather's eternal hall."

The guards then retrieved and set about pouring oil over Áethelwûlf's lifeless body, anointing him with a fragrant mixture that filled the air with a rich, earthy scent. Once done with the unction, they turned their attention toward the unlit torches on a rack that had been brought forward by two young priests. Each member of the ceremonial guard retrieved one of the torches and took up a position nearby. The Archbishop, seeing they were ready, took a few steps forward and approached a brazier. He reached inside his pocket and retrieved a vial of liquid. He opened it and poured the contents onto the charcoal-filled brazier. From the other pocket, he pulled out a flint and steel. He struck it once, and the brazier ignited in a magnificent roar of flames.

"Come now, brethren of the High Guard, and light your torches. Send our brother home," the Archbishop said, bowing his head. The High Guard moved forward in unison. They fell into single file and lit their torches from the flame-filled metal container, passing without turning their heads as they dipped the torches into the fire. As each torch roared to life, the guard would raise it back up and move past in one fluid motion.

The ceremonial guards then took their places around the altar where Áethelwûlf's body lay. One at his head, one at either side of his body, and one for each arm and leg. Once in position, the guards lifted the torches high into the sky, pausing only for a moment before they lowered the torches ever so slowly in concord. Fire met oil, and the altar was consumed in a blaze of purifying fire.

The guards then about-faced from their positions and fell into formation as they left the ceremonial chambers of the Cathedral of Life.

As the flames raged and the body disintegrated into shimmering white flakes, the Archbishop and congregation remained behind, watching the ash float upward like delicate snow. The sight was both beautiful and heart-wrenching. The sky above the open roof changed, the darkness giving way to vibrant hues of pink, green, and yellow: the Elyrëndhôr. Across the heavens the colors danced, divinely confirming Vâlgârd's acceptance of Áethelwûlf into the sacred hall of the gods.

The assembly watched in silence, their hearts uplifted by the transcendent beauty of the ritual. It was a moment of profound spiritual connection, a reminder of the eternal bond between the mortal and the divine.

As the flames lost their fuel, leaving behind nothing but the ashes of Áethelwûlf's body, the ceremony came to its conclusion.

The group felt a pang of sadness as they left the Cathedral of Life. This brave warrior had died for them. It would be a sacrifice they would not soon forget.

In the streets of Vâlloríâ, an all-consuming reverent quiet

settled over the city. The usual bustle had faded, softened to a hush as citizens offered their own respects to the fallen warrior, releasing hundreds of thousands of tiny paper lanterns that drifted upward toward the heavens above.

Órynë led the way back to the Hall of Mages, his steps purposeful and steady. The group's footsteps echoed softly on the cobblestone streets, each one heavy with the day's emotions. As they walked, the grand spires of the cathedral slowly disappeared behind them, replaced by the towering presence of the Hall of Mages in front of them.

Once inside, Óryně turned to face them, his expression gentle but firm. "Tonight, we honored Áethelwûlf's sacrifice," he began, his voice resonating with authority. "In the coming days, you will face tests that will determine if you are indeed the chosen ones of the prophecy."

Ándróniüs, standing beside him, nodded in agreement. "Áelfwînë and Ísolde will ensure you have everything you need for the rest of the night. Take this time to gather your thoughts and rest. The journey ahead will not be an easy one."

Not wanting to burden their two companions, the friends dispersed to their rooms, each person lost in their own thoughts. The ceremony at the Cathedral of Life and the unknown surrounding the tests hung over them, casting a shadow of anxiety on their steps.

Ísolde and Áelfwînë watched them depart, Ísolde's expression becoming concerned as she noticed their weariness. She called out to them, "Do not burden yourself with what has passed. The Allfather is watching over you... all of us. This was simply destined to happen."

Though still grieving for Áethelwûlf, Áelfwînë added to her statement. "And trust in the gods. They have brought you here for a reason."

Despite the reassurances, a sense of isolation overcame the friends as they entered their individual rooms. The rooms had been sanctuaries of comfort earlier in the day, but tonight, they felt like places of introspection and solitude.

Ryan lay on his bed, staring at the ceiling, his mind racing with what-ifs. He replayed the day's events over and over, questioning his actions and doubting his readiness for what lay ahead.

Jake tried to distract himself by pacing the room, but his thoughts kept drifting back to Áethelwûlf's sacrifice. The image of the brave warrior's body becoming one with the flames was etched into his memory. Frequently, his mind also returned to the girl, Elârâ, and how her immense beauty had captivated him and seemed to have taken possession of his thoughts. He wished he could glance upon her once more and maybe spark up a conversation.

Emily sat by the window, looking out at the night sky. She thought about her family back home and the promise she had made to herself to protect her friends at all costs. The magnitude of that promise felt heavier tonight than when she first came to this land.

Hannah found herself thinking about Ethan and their past. The uncertainty of the future made her long for the simplicity of their old lives, but she knew deep down they could never go back home.

Ethan sat on the edge of his bed, staring into the flame of a singular candle at his bedside, his mind a whirlwind. The candlelight pulled him in. He became hyper focused on its whimsical dance, being drawn deeper into its enticing glow. Within the flame, he thought he saw a personage take shape. A man draped in black clothing, nothing visible but a silver face with blond hair draping down his shoulders. The man's mouth moved, but he could hear no voice. A ringing in his ears consumed his thoughts, becoming all that he could hear.

A loud metallic chime rang out, breaking through the Hall of Mages from the bell-tower high above, marking the end of the day. The abrupt sound caused Ethan to lurch from his seat as the room darkened, the candle now smoking from being extinguished. He relit it, frantically searching his mind. Had he imagined it, or dreamt it? Not once did it cross his mind that this strange occurrence could have been real, as real as everything he had endured thus far. In his mind, he hoped it was nothing more than a strange dream in a cruel nightmare.

With one last glance at the candle, Ethan climbed into bed,

accepting that this night was for rest and he could search for answers in the morning. As his head hit the pillow, exhaustion hit him full force, his mind overwrought from the exertions and the turmoil from the day. Within moments, he was drifting into a dreamless sleep.

In the surrounding bedchambers, Ethan's friends also found their peace for the night. Outside their accommodations, the Hall of Mages was silent. Beyond the halls of this sanctuary, the city of Vâloríâ rested, awaiting dawn.

Morning would come soon enough, bringing with it uncertainties. But for now, in the night's quiet, they found a brief respite from their worries.

# DRANGOON WEED

IN A ROOM IN one of the highest towers that overstood the skyline and the Hall of Mages, Ándrôniüs and Órynë reclined in their dusty yet plush chairs. The room was simple, unlike the rest of Vâloríâ. This was Ándrôniüs's chamber, a place he had not visited in many decades. Its stark stone walls and minimal furnishings contrasted sharply with the opulence of the hall below. The smell of dust and musk clung to the air, permeating the nostrils of the two friends despite their evening activity. A single, large arched window offered a breathtaking view of Vâloríâ's glittering spires under the moonlight, while a modest hearth offered warmth against the chill of the early summer night.

The two old friends shared the finest drangoon weed from the halls of Brâldôr, a specialty pipe weed grown and smoked by the dwarves. The rich, earthy aroma filled the room as they inhaled deeply, the effects of the medicinal herb bringing a sense of relaxation and heightened clarity to their busy minds.

Órynë leaned back in his chair, exhaling a cloud of fragrant smoke. "This visit from a new set of chosen ones is certainly unprecedented," he said thoughtfully. "The High Mage Council wasn't supposed to convene with us for at least another seven hundred years or so. Who do you think could be responsible for this early arrival? You? Certainly not me! The Dark Lord? Or perhaps the nature of time is so different in their world compared to ours here on Arcánüs Májörá and an age has passed in their world already? Or could it be that the Allfather is quickening his work to bring about the Zültzëmmë?"

"The Zültzëmmë? No... I think not, my friend. Most definitely it is not that. All of us seers know how it comes. I can assure you that this is not that." Ándrôniüs furrowed his brow in contemplation. "It is a mystery indeed. We knew that the chosen of the prophecy were due to be delivered, but not so soon. I have pondered this much since they arrived. Could it be a shift in the cosmic balance, or has some dark force accelerated their coming, as you said?"

Taking another long draw from his pipe, Órynë sent the smoke curling around his head like a mystical halo. "Time is a fickle thing," he mused. "What seems like an eternity to us could be but a blink of an eye in their realm. Nonetheless, it is still troubling. The Dark Lord's influence may be stronger than we anticipated, reaching across worlds to bring about these events sooner. I have an undeniable feeling welling up inside me that Ancülí is *back* with him. And if he is back, you know what he is capable of, my friend. You also know that the people of this land see him as a seer-like being from the other world, even as a god. He could have brought these five as a ruse."

Ándrôniüs sighed, leaning forward with his elbows on his knees. "While I admit we must be cautious, Órynë, and the council will need to be prepared for any eventuality, that is not possible. He was exiled without the option of returning."

"Are you not hearing me, my old friend?" Óryně asked, urgency laced upon his furrowed brows and contorted face.

"I heard you. The same worry that seems to consume you this night is to in my heart, but I'm choosing to ignore it. I can assure you that Ancülí *is* and will *forever* be banished from this world. I promise I hear you. I even understand your words and perturbations. I am not playing one of my many mind games; you know I am capable of. But it does not change what I said prior. The council will need to be prepared for any eventuality, but there is nothing proving that the Dark Lord is involved or even has another working in Ancülí's stead. But that is talk for when the council is called. For now, in this moment, let us revel in good company and let the effects of this wondrous herb allay our minds," Ándrôniüs said firmly as he sat back in his chair.

Yielding to his friend's wisdom, Óryně nodded. "Indeed. We will discuss this further during the council meeting in the morning.

For now, let us finish our pipe and let the drangoon weed work its magic on our overwrought minds."

Ándrôniüs looked up, concern etched on his face. "What do you *mean*, tomorrow? What about the rest of the council? Are they even here? There are others who are not just from Vâloríâ and its outskirts. It could take some on the Vaerônthíloch many weeks to get here, if at all."

Órynë rose to leave, placing a hand on Ándrôniüs's shoulder. "We will get to the bottom of this, my friend. But for now, rest. Meet me promptly in the morning, and we will discuss this further with the council."

"Órynë, answer me. Are they here?"

Pausing at the door, Órynë gave him a reassuring smile. "Your messenger sparrow reached me just in time. We notified them. And in that time, when the fair girl was doing her healing and your travel thereafter from Pinemarsh Hollow; they answered the call, arriving last night. They seemed quite eager to come. Now, good night, my friend. We may have a long day ahead of us."

Órynë then left the room, the door closing softly behind him. Ándrôniüs sat for a moment longer, staring into the dying embers of the hearth. He took a last draw from his pipe, encapsulated in his previous draw; smoke swirled around him like a protective shroud before he extinguished the flame, exhaling one last time. He walked through a door on the other side of his quarters and entered the bedchamber. Preparing for bed, he turned as he heard the door behind him open. Ísolde entered and moved to change into her nightgown behind their modesty screen.

Her voice drifted over the partition as he sat heavily on the mattress. "How was catching up with your old friend?"

Rubbing his eyes, Ándrôniüs responded with a grumble. "He seems changed."

"How?" she inquired as she emerged.

"I'm not sure, but something is off. I can't put my finger on it," Ándrôniüs said, turning to watch as she moved around the room. "Perhaps it has been too long since I was last here. I am quite removed out there in the marsh. I'm not one to meddle in politics. It was never my thing. I fear I've buried myself in my books too much, given that these five arrived here abruptly. But there is something he said that truly puzzles me."

"What is it that puzzles you so deeply, dear?" she said as she pulled her covers back and fluffed the pillows.

Ándrôniüs scratched his head as he stood and followed his wife's lead in preparing his side of the bed. He let out a faint scoff under his breath, then said, "Oh... It's nothing, dear. I shouldn't bother you with such things."

She cocked her head and smiled. "My love, you wouldn't have brought it up if it weren't important. Now tell me."

"He mentioned Ancülí."

Ísolde's eyes shot open, the exhaustion wiped from her face as she swallowed deep enough to break any silence. "An... but... but you... you banished him? Did you lie to me?"

"No. You know how immensely difficult it is for me to lie to you, my dear. Indeed, he is banished. But Órynë believes he is back. Or is back somehow among the fold of the Dark Lord, possibly even communicating with him from another world. Maybe I have been too lax in my duties as the Seer, opting to stay cooped up in our tower tinkering with my experiments, my books, and my studies," Ándrôniüs said, desperation etched clearly on his face as he tried to unravel the thoughts in his mind.

Ísolde kept her eyes fixed upon Ándrôniüs and tried to muster up a forced smile. "Nonsense!" she said, nodding her head and crawling into their bed. "Your experiments keep the darkness at bay."

"Oh, Ísolde, my mind is wrought with the what-ifs, the could-haves, the should-haves, and so much more. If only I had been more present. Oh, never mind all of that. I think I need sleep. I know without a doubt that it will surely escape me this night."

"My love, just let the medicinal effects of the drangoon weed ease your mind," she said, looking to her husband.

"No herb, no drink, no spell can ease these thoughts," he said, taking a seat on the bed.

"Well... then what can I do to ease your mind?" she said, sitting up in bed and rubbing his shoulders.

Ándrôniüs turned to face her. He gave her a quick peck and

brushed a strand of loose hair from her face. "I think you've done all you can, circumstantially speaking. You should not let my problems hinder your sleep tonight. I'll just try closing my eyes and hope that I am carried off to the lands of my dreams."

"Well, I guess for now, just do your best to get some sleep, my dear. As you say, 'Things will sort themselves out according to the gods will,'" Ísolde said reassuringly.

She nuzzled up to him as he put an arm around her body, pulling her tightly against him. "You are truly right, my love."

# THE MARKET

HANNAH STIRRED AS DAWN broke, her eyes fluttering open to the soft glow of morning light streaming through the open window. The cool air drifted across her face, and she stretched languidly in bed, her hair a tangled mess from the restless night. Rising, she wrapped herself in a robe and settled by the window, brushing her hair in slow, deliberate strokes. The sunlight caught the strands as they smoothed out, making them shimmer like gold. Outside, the rustling of leaves and distant birdsong created a peaceful melody, though the calm did little to ease the knot of anxiety twisting in her chest.

Her mind swirled with thoughts of the day ahead, questions left unanswered, and emotions she couldn't quite decipher. Determined not to let her unease take hold, she decided she needed to talk to someone. None of the others would likely be awake at this hour except, perhaps, Ethan. With that in mind, she stood, opened her door quietly, and padded softly down the hallway to his room. Outside his door, she hesitated briefly before knocking gently.

The muffled sound stirred Ethan from his repose, though he barely registered it until a second, louder knock followed.

"Yeah, who is it?" he said. His voice was groggy.

"It's Hannah. Can I come in?" Her tone was soft.

Ethan jolted upright, panicked, as he realized he was only in a light linen nightshirt. Scrambling to pull on his clothes, he stumbled in his haste, landing on the floor with a loud thud. He froze, half-dressed and hoping she hadn't heard the commotion.

When he finally opened the door, his hair was rumpled, and he had slightly askew clothes, but his smile was warm; if a little sheepish. "Morning, Hannah. Come in," he said, his voice still heavy but carrying an unmistakable fondness.

"I hope I didn't wake you too early," Hannah said, stepping inside.

Running a hand through his tousled hair, Ethan shook his head and leaned against the frame of the door. "No, it's fine. I was just about to get up, anyway. What's up?"

Hannah hesitated, looking around his room. "I just wanted to talk... about us, I mean." Hannah paused, collecting her thoughts.

Ethan's expression softened, and he gestured for her to sit down. "Sure. What's on your mind?"

She sat on the edge of his bed, her fingers nervously fidgeting with the edge of her robe. "We've been through so much together over the years. Elementary, junior high, high school, our date, that kiss we shared... it keeps replaying in my mind. Not to mention the crash, all this, this... "tumultuosity," she stumbled, giving a small, self-conscious laugh. "I know that's not even a word." She paused, her voice trembling with uncertainty. "Sometimes I wonder if there's more between us. More than just friendship. I want there to be, but... I can't. I want to, I really do, but you just don't know how to. Gosh! The words are so hard to find. Things just aren't making sense, Ethan."

He took a few steps over to her and took a seat next to her.

"Hannah, it makes sense," he said gently, putting his arm around her shoulders. "While I want that with everything in my heart. I know you need time. That much is apparent. I get it now. Sorry, I didn't earlier. I also know that time may never come. Though... I will promise you this: I'll always be waiting; there will never be another from this day forward."

She leaned into him, resting her head on his shoulder as she continued.

"Which is why we shouldn't," she whispered, her voice barely audible. "It's not fair to you. I just don't think it'll happen. I mean, at least not right now. There's too much at stake, but you're the only one I find comfort in. When I look at you, I see everything we could have been, but here... I don't know what to say, feel, or think. All this talk of us being 'chosen ones', these tests, this odd prophecy... I know why you've been impatient and hounding Ándrôniüs all the time. But I also don't think it's helping. You've got to work on that, okay?"

He gently lifted her chin, guiding her gaze to meet his. "Let's take a walk. I know how much you love them."

Hannah sat up, her eyes locked with Ethan's, surprised at the unexpected suggestion. "A walk," she repeated softly.

Ethan smiled and winked. "A walk," he repeated, adding a playful tone to lighten the mood.

She sighed, a hint of a smile tugging at her lips. "I'm sorry I brought all this up. This wasn't the right time to do that. We have too much on our plates as it is."

He reached out, gently touching her arm. "Listen, Hannah, we can talk about it whenever you're ready. As I said, I'm not going anywhere. *Ever*."

She smiled, grateful for his understanding. "Thanks, Ethan. Let's take that walk."

Ethan led Hannah out of the room, but before they left, she embraced him, nuzzling her head into his chest. He wrapped his arms around her, savoring the moment of closeness.

When they got to the hallway, a mischievous grin spread across his face. "You might want to get dressed if you don't want to parade yourself around the town in a robe and morning gown."

She looked down at herself and began chuckling. "Alright, I'll be no more than ten minutes. Meet me in the hall."

He smiled and walked down the corridor.

Hannah watched him as he strode away, smiling to herself. She slipped back into her room, still confused, but somehow, in this moment, calmer. With a sigh, she undressed and donned the red and white dress given to her for the day. She braided her hair quickly, threw on her shoes, and walked out.

As she closed her door quietly, ensuring it didn't slam shut, Hannah failed to notice Emily peering out from her own slightly ajar door. Emily cleared her throat to draw her friend's attention as Hannah started down the hallway.

Hannah turned around, surprised. "Oh! I didn't know you were awake, Emily."

Stepping out into the hallway, Emily mumbled, "Of course not." Pausing, she added, "You're doing it again, Hannah."

Confusion colored Hannah's voice as she questioned, "Doing what?"

"You're falling for him again, and you know where that will lead. I remember when he did it the first time, though I didn't know it was him, but now it all makes sense," Emily said, her tone riddled with condescension.

"Oh, come on, Emily. No, there is too much going on for that," Hannah replied defensively.

"Sure," Emily said, her eyes narrowing slightly. "Don't come crawling back to me when he snaps your heart in two again because he can't figure out what he really wants."

"Stop, Emily. What is wrong with you this morning?" Hannah shot back, trying to deflect, but ultimately her temper boiled over, and she couldn't resist letting one last line slip with a roll of her eyes. "Don't be mad that he chose me. Not just once, but twice."

"Ugh... of course, you would bring that up, wouldn't you?" Emily rolled her eyes, letting out a bombastic scoff. "Also, there's nothing wrong with me. I just know what feelings you used to have for him. It will end the same. He'll get bored and find another person to be with," she retorted, her voice rising.

"Stop," Hannah said, turning to leave. "Just stop."

"Fine. Be that way. Don't expect sympathy from me," Emily snarled, slamming her door shut.

"I won't!" Hannah yelled. She stormed her way down the corridor toward the hall, her steps quick and determined.

Ethan, who had been lounging on a couch, looked up as she passed him. "What was that all about?"

"Nothing," Hannah snapped, stomping across the floor toward the door. "You coming?" She added tersely, inadvertently letting out some steam at him.

Ethan got up quickly and scurried to the door as it almost shut on him, confused by her sudden mood change. He had to sprint to catch up as she was already halfway down the street, leading him to an as yet unknown destination. Though this was supposed to be a leisurely walk, it turned into more of a game of chase as

Ethan struggled to keep up with her.

Still seething, Hannah marched down the street with Ethan trailing behind her, sometimes catching up and sometimes falling behind, like an unintended yo-yo. They ended up at a bustling market square. Everything around her seemed distant and muffled as her mind swirled with anger and frustration. She barely registered the sights and sounds of vendors hocking their wares, the lively chatter of townsfolk, or the aroma of freshly baked bread and exotic spices, things she would normally adore and immerse herself in if she weren't drowning her thoughts.

Ethan grabbed her arm, finally stopping her as they reached a stall behind which stood a plump, cheerful woman, who greeted them with a warm smile. She had rosy cheeks, sparkling green eyes, and a friendly demeanor that almost instantly helped ease the moment. Her hair was a riot of curls, tied back with a brightly colored scarf, and she wore a simple but clean apron over a floral dress. The stall itself was a charming display of her baked goods, with neatly arranged trays of pastries, buns, and cakes that filled the air with their sweet scents.

"Good morning! Would you like to try my famous honey cakes?" She asked, her voice inviting as she gestured to the tray. The sight of the golden honey cakes drizzled with glistening syrup was enough to make anyone's mouth water.

Hannah, lost in her thoughts, nodded absentmindedly. The woman continued talking, but her words were drowned out by the echo of Emily's accusations and the tumultuous emotions within her.

"One second," Ethan said to the woman at the stall. He nudged Hannah gently, bringing her back to the present. "Hannah, did you hear what she said?"

She blinked rapidly and shook her head. Hannah turned to the vendor, her cheeks flushing slightly with embarrassment.

"I'm sorry. Could you say that again, please?" she said.

The kind lady chuckled, her eyes twinkling. "Of course, dear. I said, would you like to try my famous honey cakes? There is strawberry, blueberry, or blackberry. These are the best on the market! I'd go for the strawberry if I were you."

Hannah nodded in agreement. "We'll take some of these for breakfast," she said, pointing to the suggested strawberry honey cakes.

Using the coins that Ándróniüs had given them back in Willowdale, Hannah bought a dozen of the pastries. The merchant carefully packed them into a charming wrap made from a sturdy, light brown waxed papyrus. A delicate twine secured the package with a small bow on top. The aroma of the honey cakes wafted through tiny air holes, allowing the hot pastries to breathe, and making the wrap itself a tempting treat to carry.

Ethan and Hannah continued to explore the market, immersing themselves in the vibrant atmosphere that offered a brief reprieve from their worries. The market continued to be lively; vendors called out to potential customers, showcasing an array of colorful goods. The stalls were a clash of colors, displaying everything from ripe, juicy fruits to intricate handcrafted jewelry. Musicians played jaunty tunes on lutes and flutes, adding a cheerful soundtrack to the bustling scene.

A fruit stall was where they stopped next. The vendor—a wiry old man with a toothy grin—offered them samples of his freshest produce available. They savored the sweetness of ripe blackberries and the tangy zest of fresh apples. Hannah couldn't resist buying a small basket of assorted fruits, each piece carefully selected for its plump ripeness.

Next, the pair visited a spice merchant, where the air was thick with the heady aroma of exotic spices. The merchant, a tall woman with dark, flowing hair and extravagant clothing, spoke passionately about her wares, describing the origin and use of each spice. Ethan picked up a small pouch of cinnamon, enchanted by its warm, sweet scent.

They also found time to stop by a stall selling fresh bread, the warm, yeasty smell drawing them in. The baker, a burly man with flour-dusted hands and a kind smile, handed them a steaming loaf straight from the oven. The crust was golden and crisp; the bread inside was soft and fluffy. Hannah purchased the loaf, unable to resist the enticing scent.

In their wandering, they stumbled across a young girl selling flowers. She had a basket full of vibrant blooms, their colors bright against the drab backdrop of the street. Hannah bought a small bouquet of wildflowers; its fresh fragrance was a reminder of simpler, more peaceful times.

With their purchases in hand, they began the walk back to the Hall of Mages. The morning air was still cool, and the breeze carried the sounds and scents of the bustling market. Though the confrontation with Emily earlier still hung heavily on Hannah's mind, the energetic atmosphere of the market had offered a brief reprieve, lifting her spirit, if only for a moment.

They bobbed and weaved through the streets and people, trying to glimpse the grand structure that was their destination. Out of the corner of her eye, Hannah finally saw the bell tower.

"Look!" she exclaimed, pointing.

"Well, there it is. It seems like we can take this alley to get there faster," Ethan said, peering down the narrow side road.

"But Ándrôniüs said to stay on the main streets," Hannah said, uncomfortable with the dirty and shady side street.

Ethan scoffed, waving his hand dismissively. "Screw what the old kook has to say. It's not that far. Plus Vâloríâ seems to be safer than any city we could find back home."

Still reluctant, Hannah hesitantly agreed. "I guess you're right."

"You guess?"

"Yeah," she said.

"Do you not trust me?" Ethan mused.

"Nevermind... you're right. You're absolutely right. There is nothing to worry about." Hannah said, more to herself than to anyone else.

"C'mon, just follow close to me. We'll be fine!" Ethan said confidently.

They walked together into the alley's shadows. The first several feet were clear enough, but the farther they went, the more they second-guessed their decision. Enclosed by buildings on either side, a darkening passageway emerged, riddled with broken glass, rotting food, and the overwhelming stench of body excrement. Hannah grabbed Ethan's hand, squeezing it so hard her knuckles turned white. Following the alley as it curved, they encountered two men playing dice, blocking the way through.

The men had possibly seen better days, but now they were filthy, with missing patches of hair and clothing that was browned and stained with holes and tears. As the two rounded the corner, they looked at them, eyes glinting greedily. Toothy grins emerged from their cracked and bloody lips.

Instinctively, Ethan pulled Hannah slightly behind him. "We don't want any trouble; we just want to pass," Ethan said, his voice cracking.

The smaller man on the right answered. "Horses and sheep, and sheep and horses," he said, then let out a sinister cackle, which devolved into coughing. Spitting bloody phlegm at his feet, his eyes shot back and forth, struggling to focus on Hannah and Ethan. He had obviously lost his mind.

While the two focused on the first man, the other man stood up and slunk closer. Lunging forward, he grabbed Hannah by the wrist, wrenching her from Ethan's clasp. Hannah let out a bloodcurdling scream as she struggled to pull free.

"Hey!" Ethan yelled, grabbing her free hand and trying to tug her back. "Get your hands off her!"

"Oi, she's a pretty fine one. Your bride will be mine, and there ain't nothing you can do about it, youngin'!" the man said, jerking the girl back toward him with surprising strength, the motion causing the basket of wares to fall to the ground.

The crazed one jumped up and wrapped his arms around Hannah, helping his companion wrestle her out of Ethan's reach, even as she kicked and twisted. He cackled some more. He even pulled at her dress, fighting back the layers of it until eventually finding her bottom, giving it a quick squeeze and slap.

"Oh, she's young and ripe! Come to play, have ya, missy?" he said with malevolent pleasure.

Hannah screamed once more and pleaded. "Stop it! Please... let me go! Ethan, don't just stand there. Do something!"

Ethan looked around frantically, trying to find a tool or weapon of some sort to even the odds. Finding nothing, he steeled himself.

"I said, get your hands off her!" Ethan yelled, drawing himself up and raising his fists.

The taller man released his hold on Hannah before reaching into his pocket and drawing out a dagger. It had obviously seen better days, evident by the rusted hilt and blade. His companion shoved Hannah against the wall while he focused on Ethan. Approaching the boy, he stretched the dagger out threateningly.

"If you want her, you'll have to get through me, boyo!"

"Stick the little man," the other said, struggling to hold Hannah against the wall.

Ethan pressed forward, keeping his eyes on the blade. Feinting left, he threw a punch with his right hand, but missed, hitting the hard brick wall instead. He let out a yelp of pain as he shook it.

"This is who you choose to be your protector, lass?" the man with the dagger jeered.

Grabbing Ethan by the hair, he thrust him face first into a pile of questionable decomposing refuse. He let out a hearty laugh as the boy flailed in the muck, turning to his companion, who copied his mirth. He approached Ethan, who was attempting to stand, slipping in the substance.

Once upon him, he raised his leg and with a swift and brutal kick of his foot wrapped in a tattered leather boot. It collided with Ethan's face. The poor boy's face erupted with crimson fluid spewing from his mouth and nose. Ethan reached up and felt his nose, now crooked, his lip split in multiple places, and his jaw forming a goose egg. He couldn't see it, but from the force of the boot and his nose nearly shattering under the pressure, his eyes blackened and were bloodshot; he was nearly unrecognizable.

Ethan flailed, trying not to gag on the horrid stench. The hold on his head lessened, the man distracted as his focus shifted to his companion. Kicking out, Ethan managed to hit him behind the knee, sending the man to the ground. The dagger clattered as it fell, sliding across the cobblestone alleyway.

The man slipped, struggling to maintain his footing on the less than sanitary cobblestones. Reaching for and grabbing his dagger, he pointed it at Ethan, his face contorted in rage. He stepped forward menacingly, ready to thrust his weapon deep into the boy's body.

His toothy grin reappeared as he muttered, "Cheeky bast—"

"Lower your weapon, sir," a voice called out from the shadows, cutting him off.

Everyone froze.

Hannah recovered first and used the surprise to push her attacker away and scurry back to Ethan. Ethan was still cleaning the muck from his face, shirt, and pants while simultaneously trying to stop the bleeding. The feculent concoction of waste still clung to everything; his efforts only smeared it around, worsening his state.

The two miscreants turned to the shadows.

"And who might you be?" said the man with the dagger, waving the small weapon in the air.

"Ancüli."

The two aggressors froze again before turning to each other, mirroring looks of incredulity on both their faces.

"No... It can't be. You were banished!" the knife-wielding man said, even as his counterpart took off running down the alley.

"Yet I am here in the flesh, standing before you. I suggest you leave. Or, I'll gladly spill your entrails upon the street," Ancüli said, drawing his sword from its sheath.

The man dropped his pitifully small knife, and it clattered to the ground, sending a metallic sound ringing in the air as he ran after his friend.

"Thank you, sir," Ethan said, still wiping the thick viscous sludge from his face.

The man turned as Ethan blinked, only able to make out a man in a black cloak and a silver mask. "Tell Ándrôniüs, Ancüli is back."

The dark figure turned on his heel, swirling his cloak around him, and disappeared into a thick cloud of smoke right before their eyes.

"Where'd he go?" Ethan asked, giving up on his fruitless efforts to tidy himself up.

"I'm not sure, but I don't think we should linger here any longer, Ethan," Hannah said as she retrieved her waterskin, helping him to rinse his face. "He disappeared like one of those Shadewalkers."

"They wouldn't be here in Vâloríâ. Everyone has told us we are safe here. And if he was one of those Shadewalkers... why would he save us? They've been trying to take us or, worse, kill us since we arrived."

"Oh, I suppose you are right, Ethan," she said. "Sorry, I'm just a little frazzled, is all."

"So, who do you think the guy was, anyway?" Ethan asked as Hannah retrieved the wares that had knocked out of the basket during the attack, securing them to the top of the basket holding their wares.

Hannah grabbed Ethan's hand and gave him a tight embrace. "I think he said Ancülí, or something like that."

"Weird. That name sounds familiar. And his voice..." Ethan paused, reaching for something buried deep within the confines of his mind.

"Ethan?" Hannah said, gently touching his shoulder and bringing him back to the present.

Snapping back to reality, Ethan looked into her eyes. He didn't speak, still puzzling out what his subconscious was trying to tell him.

"He sounded... what? Familiar? Why did the man's voice stand out, Ethan?"

"It's... its... never mind. It's not important," he said. "But you're right; we should get going. Ándrôniüs should know what happened. I heard him and Ísolde mention that name in the manor one night. He has to be someone important, right? That must be why he wants us to tell him he's here. Maybe he is an old friend?"

"What is important is that you bathe. You smell rotten," she said, pushing off of him and letting out a little chuckle.

Catching a whiff of his new cologne, he cringed. "I guess you're right. But seriously, are you okay, Hannah?"

Wrapping her arms around herself, Hannah tried to forget the feeling of those grubby hands on her. "Yeah, I'll be fine. Luckily, they didn't get what they wanted."

Ethan scrutinized her face for several moments, unsure if he believed her. "If you say so."

Hannah smiled and raised her arms to hug him, but then realized she didn't want to soil her dress any further. "Well, let's get back. But on the long path."

Ethan smiled. "Alright, after you."

They turned around and headed back the way they came, relieved when they were back on the bustling streets of the city again. In making their way, the hall eventually rose in front of them. They entered through the doors, their arms laden with their purchases, ready to share their morning bounty with the others.

Ándrôniüs was waiting for them. His expression was serious, but he smiled warmly as they approached. "Good morning. I see you found some treats at the market. I hope the excursion was enjoyable, but Ethan, what in the Allfather's name happened to you? You're definitely smelling ripe this morning. And your face? Lost a fight to Hannah again, did you? Or, is this a new look?"

"How does he know that?" Ethan said, momentarily forgetting he still needed to tell the old mage what had happened in the market.

Hannah laughed. "I do not know, but I remember that day now. Fifth grade. Kickball during phys ed. You charged me like a bull and still lost."

"How do you know that, Ándrôniüs?" Ethan asked, turning back to him.

The old mage shrugged with a small smile.

"No, tell me," Ethan insisted. "How do you know everything?"

"I have my ways," Ándrôniüs said with a wink and a playful nudge to Hannah's side. She only laughed, happy to revisit the old memory.

"Now," Ándrôniüs said, shifting his attention back to them. "Did you enjoy the market?"

Setting the basket of goods on the table, Ethan nodded. "It was enjoyable. But something happened on the way back that we need to tell you."

Ándrôniüs looked them over. "I can see the worry in your eyes," he said, his voice steady but firm. "First, Elârâ fetch a healer!"

Elârâ who was on the other side of the room, stopped. She had been dusting the shelves. Placing the feather duster down on one of the many bookcases, she headed off within the Hall of Mages to find a healer at the Medical Ward.

"Second, let's not dwell on this right now. I'm sure it can wait, whatever it is. I'd rather not start my morning with endless questions about the tests or things that seem important, but likely are not. Instead, let's gather the others and Ísolde and enjoy breakfast together."

Undeterred by the mage's dismissive attitude, Ethan said, "A man by the name of Ancüli saved us from some men that attacked us in an alley. He wanted you to know that he was back. I heard you and Ísolde talking about him back at Pinemarsh Manor. Who is he?" Ándróniüs continued after she had left.

Choking and gasping exploded from the old man, wracking his frame. He pounded his chest, trying to catch his breath. Hannah fetched him a cup of water hurriedly from the table near where Elârâ had been working. On her return, she grabbed his empty glass from the table beside where he sat and filled it, handing it over to him. Ándróniüs sipped as trying to quell the tickle in his throat, that fashionably arrived at the mention of Ancüli's name.

"Ancüli? Where? When? What happened? Tell me everything right this inst—" Ándróniüs started, before a powerful voice cut him off.

"Ándróniüs! There is no time to waste! The council must convene immediately!"

Órynë appeared at the top of the stairs, halting with a grand, almost theatrical flourish, his robes billowing behind him. "We have urgent matters to discuss."

Ándróniüs sighed, giving Ethan and Hannah a regretful look. "Do not speak of this to anyone. Duty calls. Prepare yourselves and remember what I said. I will return as soon as I can. And Ethan, for everyone's sake, take a bath. Then see the healer!"

Hurrying up the stairs, Ándróniüs left Ethan and Hannah alone in the vast hall. They shared a look, reeling from yet another unanticipated experience.

"Why is he always telling us not to talk about stuff?" Ethan said, turning to Hannah with a confused expression.

"Who knowns. But Ándróniüs is right. We should wake the others and find Ísolde," Hannah repeated, dismissing his question. "And seriously, that smell is getting worse. You should really get cleaned up. And your poor nose. Just don't... just I wouldn't worry about the rest for now."

Ethan nodded reluctantly, slightly annoyed at her lack of curiosity. "Yeah, let's get everyone together."

"Can you get the others after cleaning up?" She beseeched him with a guileless smile on her face. "I'll set everything up."

"I can do that," he said, turning to the corridor where their rooms were. He banged on his friend's door and retreated into his own room before he had to answer questions about his messy appearance.

Hannah, meanwhile, decorated the table with the wildflowers they had bought and set out the various sweet and savory goods from the market.

***

Slowly, everyone gathered.

"Wow, what an incredible smell," Ryan remarked, breathing in the scent of fresh pastries.

Jake grinned as he took a seat. "The food at this place is top-notch."

"It's from the market," Hannah said with a wink.

"Then the food from the market is top-notch!" Jake said, correcting himself

But before anything else could be said, someone they knew appeared. Ísolde turned up at the top of the stairs that Órynë and Ándrôniüs had recently disappeared up. Her beauty was more striking than ever, with her long, flowing hair cascading down her back, and dressed in a gown of deep green that accentuated her radiant presence. For a moment, her elegance captivated everyone.

Hannah asked, "Why are you so dressed up?"

Ísolde, brimming with excitement, responded. "This is a special moment! Today is a day to dress up and celebrate. Soon, you will learn what your tests entail. Apparently, nearly all the High Mages that sit on the council have already gathered in the city and are meeting at this very moment."

Ísolde walked over to the table, taking a seat near Hannah and gracing her with a warm smile.

Hearing the tests mentioned as he reentered the hall in fresh clothing, Ethan perked up, his attention focusing on what else she might say. But nothing more was forthcoming on the topic.

Instead, they all found their places around the table. As they exchanged light conversation and enjoyed the cozy atmosphere, they shared the delicious food. The mood was cheerful, and laughter filled the hall as they savored each bite of the delightful breakfast, even Ethan setting aside his previous disappointment.

With a loud thud against the floor, Emily finally showed up, looking stern and composed. She didn't exchange words or even look at anyone, just plopped herself into a chair and began eating.

Ethan tried to talk to her. "Emily, are you okay?"

She snapped, "I'm fine. Just leave me be."

Everyone responded in unison with a surprised, "Whoa," taken aback by her attitude.

Hoping to deescalate any issues, Ísolde gently took Emily's arm and guided her to an outdoor courtyard near the hall, allowing the girl some space. As the one in charge of the teenagers' care, Ísolde had been informed by some servants that there had been some words exchanged between Hannah and Emily earlier that morning.

After Emily and Ísolde left, Áelfwînë made his presence known as well. He entered the room, greeting everyone with a warm smile.

"Good morning, everyone. Seeing you with joy upon your faces this morning is truly uplifting," he said, his voice brimming with genuine affection.

The companions at the table welcomed him warmly, Ryan even nudging the chair beside him out so the guard could join.

Looking a bit ragged and smelling of a night soaked in too much alcohol and sweat, Áelfwînë joined in the conversations at the table. He found some happiness in their fellowship, and though the hardships still weighed heavily on his mind, in this moment, he could relax with the simple joys of good company.

# THE HIGH MAGE COUNCIL

As THE COMPANIONS DINED below, Ándrôniüs and Órynë traveled through the corridors of the second level of the Hall of Mages. This area was markedly different from the vibrant, welcoming halls below. Here, the décor was more austere, reflecting its purpose as an administrative wing; white marble floors, bookshelves filled with historical and governmental texts, and a noticeable lack of artwork. Their footsteps echoing off the walls, the two mages walked briskly toward the end of the corridor as the marble transitioned to black before ending at a pair of obsidian doors.

Ornate and vibrant, the doors stood as a formidable barrier, exuding an aura of mystery. Each polished slab of obsidian gave off a reflective sheen that captured and distorted the flickering light from the sconces lining the corridor. Silver and gold inlays traced the edges of the carvings etched into the doors, highlighting the detailed craftsmanship and adding a touch of brilliance to the imposing entrance.

Massive iron handles, shaped like soaring phoenixes, jutted out from the center of each door, their eyes embedded with small, glittering gemstones that seemed to watch anyone who approached. Enchantments reinforced the nearly invisible hinges, ensuring the doors could withstand any magical or physical force.

As Ándrôniüs and Óryně approached, the doors seemed to resonate with a palpable energy, tangible in the vibration that rippled through the handles at the slightest touch. Glancing at one another, they each took a steadying breath before reaching out to grasp the cold iron handles, feeling the magnitude of the moment as they were about to plunge into the chamber beyond.

Óryně pushed his door open a few inches, then abruptly pulled it closed, his brow furrowed with concern. He broke the silence, his voice low and serious.

"As the Grand Mage, I must inform you that the other High Mages of Eldôria believe this is a farce. This wasn't supposed to happen for at least. Well, I don't know. It's not an exact science, as you're very well aware. Some elders on the council even suspect something more sinister is afoot. That the *Dark Lord* has a hand in this."

Ándrôniüs froze in place, his eyes widening before he let out a small chuckle.

"My friend, you must have had too much of the drangoon weed last night. We've already discussed that."

"Yes, but there have been some rather recent developments," Órynë replied, his tone grave. "There are those who believe the rumor that is running rampant through the streets. Reports claim that Ancüli has been seen in the city in the flesh! And there are others on the council that seem to believe that Ancüli was once one of us. You as well as I know that is false... but what is even more intriguing is that they truly believe that he has found a way back to Cáelunárra. Even after his banishment to wherever you sent him. In our discussions, they also conveyed that they believe that he and the Dark Lord have in secret discovered a way to mine the aétherium crystals. Or worse, that they may have learned how to harness its powers just as we have done for so long."

"But they'd need the elves' permission to mine it, the dwarves to extract it, and access to the carefully regulated trade where we sell it back to all the races of our land. Our accountants meticulously file and track all of it. That includes who it is supplied to, who transports the crystal, and what it is being used for, and if it has a final destination after that. There's no way that could have happened right under our noses without us catching even the faintest whiff of it," Ándrôniüs stated, his voice laced with disbelief.

Óryně sighed deeply. "If the Dark Lord is indeed involved, things are not as simple as we'd hoped them to be anymore, my friend. However, there is more."

"More?" Ándrôniüs asked incredulously.

"After our meeting last night, something did not sit right with me. I could not sleep. So I went to the Aétherium Repository and spoke with Grônthael, the Head Vaultsmith. I told him my concern, that the Dark Lord might be tied to their arrival. He said he was already on his way to me with a troubling report. Several crystal stores were missing. At first he thought they had been mis-weighed or cut down during refinement, so he marked the entries to find them easily. But the number kept growing, and the records stopped making sense. Then the rumors reached him, and both of us grew uneasy. So we did what anyone would do when faced with news like that."

Órynë paused and scratched his chin.

"Speak plainly, my friend," Ándrôniüs cut in at once. "You're not making much sense... this isn't making much sense."

"I know I am not."

"Then explain!" Ándrôniüs urged his friend the Grand Mage. "I am your friend; you can trust me with such things."

"But first... I promise and rest assured, this was handled with complete confidentiality."

"How is anything in that place confidential?" Ándrôniüs said even more bewildered at the fact his friend the Grand Mage would know better than trust the vaultsmiths and registrars. "You know how those smithies and registrars are; tongues like an unkempt wildfire."

"Let me finish, please. You see, Grônthael and I made the Vültzëmaegár—"

"The Vültzëmaegár?" Ándrôniüs questioned, bewildered.

"Yes. Yes, my friend," Óryně stated impatiently, waving his arms about.

"Okay. Okay. My apologies. Continue."

"He sent out a call to summon the remaining dwarves and Aétheric Registrars. They worked into the early hours of the morning, and it seems we are missing nearly one hundred-fifty swálthëz of aétherium. It's all unaccounted for, Ándrôniüs. It just vanished. That is surely enough to bring ten sets of champions to our lands," Óryně said tiredly, rubbing his temples as though hearing the news for the first time all over again.

"And who all knows about this?"

"Grônthael, you and I."

"And the registrars and other vaultsmiths?" Ándrôniüs pressed further.

"When Grônthael and I made the Vültzëmaegár, we agreed their memories would be wiped. They will not remember what we discovered if asked. I assure you that."

"Anímaí Labyêsk?" Ándrôniüs said, his voice laced with shock at the charm his friend had used, completely aware of the implications behind it. "That spell is only to be used for—"

"I know! I know, my friend. We can move only forward now. But fret not, we are looking into it further. However, there is more."

"Even more?" Ándrôniüs echoed, utterly flabbergasted, his mind reeling as each new revelation from the Grand Mage stacked atop the last, threatening to unravel his composure right before the momentous deliberations ahead.

"Yes, more," Órynë said, rolling his eyes at his friend's childish reaction. "See, I fear we cannot trust all who sit upon the council. That is why this new information mustn't be divulged to anyone except you, the dwarf, and I. It is important because, as I said before, there are those I feel who are playing both sides of the war. Nonetheless, we shall find out soon enough. But we know nothing for certain about the aétherium, our new chosen ones, the Dark Lord, or even these rumors of Ancülí. The council is in a state of uproar over it all. Most think these five are imposters. However, I believe we should proceed with the tests. You know these newcomers best, so when and if we get to that point, make the proposed tests sufficiently rigorous, testing our so-called chosen ones even if it means limb or..." He paused, his eyes darkening. "Life. If it's known that we tested them harder than those in the past, the council may just set aside its hesitation on the matter. Together, I believe we should show the council that we are also skeptical of these five."

Shaking his head, his features hardening with determination, Ándrôniüs said, "I am not doubtful one bit of these five, and I certainly will not sacrifice what I believe to be our best chances so quickly. I have no doubt the Allfather's hand is in this selection.

And as his Seer, I will assign them tests I know they can pass, but that will still allow them to prove themselves." He paused momentarily, his lips trembling. "They must remain unscathed, Órynë."

Rolling his eyes slightly, Óryné nodded, familiar with his oldest friend's quirks. Deciding not to press him further, he simply stated, "Very well. But we must tread carefully. The fate of all Arcánüs Májörá may very well depend on the outcomes of these tests."

A silent understanding passed between them before they turned and pushed open the black doors, stepping forward to face the other High Mages, their resolve steeled for the difficult path ahead. The weight of the doors caused the hinges to wail, revealing the council chamber beyond.

They entered the room, a semicircular, multi-tiered ascending council chamber filled with a few hundred men and women of all colors and races from the boroughs of Eldôria. Intricate murals lined the chamber's walls, and tall, arched windows filtered beams of sunlight, casting a radiant glow on the polished marble floors. Rows of ornately carved wooden benches lined each tier of the chamber, where the High Mages sat, their expressions a mix of anger, fear, and confusion. At the front of the room stood a grand podium, flanked by two colossal statues of ancient mages, their stone faces stern and grandiose.

The sight was magnificent but unsettling, as the room was booming with violent voices of accusation, denial, and furiosity. High Mages were arguing with each other, throwing papyrus papers, scrolls, and quills. Chaos had taken root among them, and an evil presence festered in the room. It took hold of all those who were in attendance, resulting in an utter lack of decorum among the most prestigious citizens of Eldôria.

Ándrôniüs and Óryné felt the malevolent presence in the room, a darkness unlike anything they had ever encountered in these hallowed chambers. The deep corruption they feared was manifesting. If they did not get control of the gathering soon, surely blood would spill in the sacred council chambers of the mages.

Amplifying his voice with magic, Órynë shouted, "Silence!" The word reverberated through the chamber, quaking across the congregation. The walls trembled, and the cacophony of voices instantly ceased. For a moment, the malevolent presence recoiled, allowing clarity to return.

"This unseemly display serves no purpose. Are we not civilized men and women? We have been endowed with the duty of guiding our citizens through these troubled times. We are here to find solutions, not tear each other apart," Órynë continued.

Stepping forward, Ándrôniüs's presence commanded their attention. "We understand your fears, but this is not the way. Despite being under-prepared, the chosen ones have arrived nonetheless, and it is our duty to guide them. Our unity is essential; otherwise, all hope is lost."

A tall, stern-faced mage with deep brown eyes stood up from the front row. "Ándrôniüs... Órynë... do you truly believe these are the chosen ones? This timing is inapt; the signs have been unclear. And now, with these... these rumors of Ancülí. Here! In this city! And need I remind you of the attack on our seer just outside our walls. How can we trust this?"

Órynë met the mage's gaze steadily. "Vûlët, you know better than anyone that the timing of the chosen ones' arrival was never intended to be exact. We cannot control the whims of fate. If the Allfather commands it, the Allfather will make it so. Our duty is to test them, guide them, and ensure they are prepared for the darkness that lies ahead. The presence of evil we felt just now could very well be an indication of the Dark Lord's interference in these proceedings because he is also unprepared for another assault and seeks to divide us. We cannot let that deter us."

Another mage, a woman with dark hair and emerald robes, spoke up, her voice shaking with emotion. "What if this is a trap? What if the Dark Lord has planted them to deceive us? Why haven't you answered the pleas from the citizenry of Cáelunárra about Ancülí's return?"

Ándrôniüs responded firmly. "Líllíët, we will know soon enough. The tests will reveal their true nature. If they pass, as Órynë said earlier, 'The Allfather commands it', but if they fail and perish in the Coliseum, then surely this could be the involvement of the Dark Lord. But we must give them a chance. We owe it to the people of Cáelunárra to see this through. As far as Ancülí goes, these are just rumors. I understand the worry, so I'm meeting an eyewitness tonight to find out what really happened and will share the truth with you. I will see if this is in fact Ancülí, or some drunken fool's ramblings at a pub."

The murmurs of dissent subsided as the High Mages listened to the words of two of the most respected mages of the age.

Feeling the mood settling, Órynë continued, "Our focus must be on unity. The Dark Lord thrives on our discord. We must not give him that power. If we are weak, he will prevail to our certain destruction."

At his words, the remaining discomfort in the room eased.

Then a mage from the back row, older and with a long silver beard, stood up. "On that note, let us proceed with the declaration of the tests. I agree with our seer. Let us see if they truly are the chosen ones."

Órynë nodded in agreement with the mage from the back row.

Hearing their fellow mage call on them to begin. The High Mages slowly retook their seats, regaining a semblance of control despite the lingering tension. Ándrôniüs and Órynë exchanged a look, knowing they had only just begun to navigate the treacherous path ahead. They stepped into the circle in front of the podium, ready to face whatever challenges the council would bring forward as it convened.

As Óryně opened his mouth to start the deliberations officially, another figure stood, commanding everyone's attention. He was a tall man, his skin deep and cool like wet earth after nightfall, and cunning green eyes that seemed to cut through the chamber. Dressed in rich purple robes, only his eyes were visible until he unraveled his face covering, exposing his stern expression.

"And what are these tests to be, Ándrôniüs?" he demanded, unconcerned that he was speaking out of turn, his green eyes flashing with anger. "The last time you held the tests, they passed effortlessly. We all know what happened then, but if you have forgotten, hidden away in your manor in the woods. The war raged on across all our land. Given you and your predecessors' continual failures, I question your line's competence in choosing champions. I'm unsure if the men of Âldâmûr can endure another wave of genocide. The great mountain kingdom of the northeast; Brâldôr and its dwarven halls built upon them, were nearly all raised. Even here! In our own realm, Eldôria burned! The mage republic cannot handle another incursion from Mûrríëthíêl. I think it pertinent and I call on my fellow brethren and sisters, that here and now we call for a new Harbinger of the Tests, Guardian of the Fates, Seer of the Enigmas," he declared grandiloquently, his voice growing louder and more emphatic with each title, echoing through the chamber.

Ándrôniüs, his face taut with dissatisfaction, shook his head. "No, no, Xándriel, I do not think that is prudent at this time. There are too many unknowns. A change in our leadership now would send us reeling into turmoil, especially with the Chosen already here. This no doubt would give our enemy the opening he needs to destroy us."

Xándriel's voice rose to a shout, reverberating off the chamber walls. "We must hold a vote! The great annals of our people's state, if even one of us is unsure of your position as Seer of the Enigmas, and of Órynë's as the Grand Mage, a vote must occur." He opened his arms wide, sweeping them across the room. "Come, come, a show of hands. We have talked in secret; I know the inner workings of your minds."

As Xándriel's gaze scanned the room, several mages hesitantly raised their hands. Xándriel's lips curled into a snarl. "That's it! A vote!"

Ándrôniüs, his patience dwindling, angrily retorted, "Xándriel, bite your tongue! This is not the—"

"TIME!" Órynë's voice rang out, firm and commanding, as he interjected over Ándrôniüs, his finger pointing upward while he paced about the room. His tone dispelled the lingering squalls between the two, leaving a momentary silence. "Never has there been a vote of no confidence in recorded history, and that's been well over five ages. Dare you tip the scale? Dare you tempt fate? Dare you cast aside these chosen ones? Dare you give the upper hand to the Dark Lord? I shall not allow this vote. What has transpired has unfolded, and the tides of uncertainty are here. We must not weaken the very fabric of the Republic! Lest we forget, the realms of men are split with no faith in their king. He sits upon his throne, shrouded in gluttony and drunkenness, overtaxing his subjects for his indulgences. All the while, the dwarves hoard their wealth in their mountain fortresses. The lÿëch... those cowards. They dare not breathe the air above their swamps. And don't get me started on the elves."

Feeling chastened, those who had previously supported Xándriel retreated into their seats until he stood alone. Sensing the tides of favor shifting, the discontented mage reluctantly sat back down in his chair with a resounding thud and spiteful sigh.

Braving the silence, a tall woman with sharp features and a commanding presence arose from her seat. Her robes were deep blue, embellished with stark white embroidery that caught the light. Her name was Márrisol.

"Let us proceed with Czârrûp's motion to begin these deliberations," she declared, her voice steady. "But if one dies in these tests, I say we leave this land to its own devices. The mages must go into hiding, crossing the great sea back to Aûllíâtënärrä, the land of our forefathers. In our retreat, we will allow this new dark age conjured by the Dark Lord to scourge the land, leaving all who remain here at the mercy of his evil."

The room fell silent for a moment before all the council members gave their agreement, their voices echoing through the chamber in a chorus of 'ayes'.

Órynë nodded, acknowledging her words. "Thank you, Márrisol. Though I see no reason for us to discuss returning to our ancestral homeland."

A man of great stature with a peppered beard, his eyes a dark brown and a scar across his face, stood up next. "Órynë, I, like many of my fellow mages, would rather not see another war rage on and our seed wasted, staining the very earth with the blood of our youth, our sons and daughters. And for what? I feel as if we have no other choice but to return to Aûllíâtënärrä. I know I'm already packing my castle at Tweed and readying my ships.

My people are ready. The sentiment is mutual among most of my brothers and sisters here. What say you? Will you not join us?"

A low rumble of agreement spread across the congregation as many acknowledged the desire to avoid the seemingly inevitable conflict and loss facing them.

Órynë scoffed, slamming his fist on the podium. "Nâttûâllâ, you would leave our allies to deal with this evil on their own? Would you abandon our allies to Ancülí and the Dark Lord, leaving them to be slaughtered? Since when do we mages, the mighty Áírrmá, abandon all hope and practice cowardice?"

Xándriel, undeterred, interjected over both Nâttûâllâ and Órynë, his voice full of conviction and sarcasm. "I think that is precisely what he is saying. I think the decision has been made for you. But if we are to move forward with this charade; Ándrôniüs, pray tell. What are these tests?"

The uncertainty in the room was unmistakable as all eyes turned to Ándrôniüs, waiting for his response.

Órynë, breathing a sigh of relief that they had finally reached this point, cocked his head and shifted the focus toward Ándrôniüs, his tone puzzled but commanding. "Yes, Ándrôniüs, what are the tests you feel they must complete? You've spent the better half of a fortnight with them."

Ándrôniüs took a deep breath, hoping to exude confidence. "Ethan is brave, driven, and naturally charismatic. His friends look to him to take the lead. But his relentless sense of entitlement can cloud his judgement. Still, that same fire makes him an ideal opponent for a gorlock."

The room erupted in gasps of shock.

"A gorlock?" Xándriel laughed mockingly. "Are you trying to murder him? We might as well turn this land over to the Dark Lord before we even start. Everyone, get their affairs in order. We must prepare the ships for Aûllíâtënärrä."

"Xándriel! Stay your tongue," Órynë commanded, his voice sharp. The other mage receded back into his chair, covering his face once more.

Rolling his eyes at his colleague, Ándrôniüs continued, "Indeed, a gorlock. In a duel. But not only shall he fight and defeat this creature, he must also learn a spell and use it during his test." A clamor of murmurs echoed through the room, the council members exchanging worried glances.

Márrisol stood up, her voice laden with concern. "But surely he is not one of us. What is it you hide from us on the council?" Xándriel uncovered his face, sharply stating, "Indeed, I share the sentiment of Márrisol's statement. What do you hide from us? And if he is not one of us, and he is not of this world. Then how? How can he produce magic?"

Joining Xándriel, Nâttûâllâ stood up with him and stated with conviction, "If the boy truly possesses the ability to wield and harness magic, then he is akin to Ancülí, whom we all brought here to serve our purposes. These are treacherous waters we tread. Have not we learned from the past? From the age before? This is surely the work of the Dark Lord. I again ask you to give us permission to return to Aûllíâtënärrä, Órynë. First, there was Ancülí. Now this... this Ethan. This entire thing is surely of the Dark Lord's doing. He surely uses these chosen ones as his disguised minions, those who were delivered so graciously to our lands."

Sensing the growing tension and feeling uncertain himself, Órynë asked, "Is there something you are not telling me, Ándrôniüs? How can Ethan possess and use magic?"

"Would you all allow me to explain before shouting over one another?" Ándrôniüs replied, "And to you, Nâttûâllâ, quit sowing the seeds of uncertainty. If only your father, the mighty Sûníö, were here to see your spinelessness. And Xándriel, this most certainly, includes you too. Tighten those lips before I suture them closed. Now, as far as the boy Ethan is concerned. The chances of him being somehow connected to our world is next to impossible. However, there is something about him, his presence. It is reminiscent of the old men of this land, the Olmâ, before they became corrupted with power, riches, vanity, and hearsay. I could be wrong, but maybe there are people in his world like we once had before the first poisoning of men in the initial war for our lands. Maybe his kin suppressed their magic and kept it hidden from the world they inhabit. As such, I think this is a fitting task for our young Ethan."

Hearing the break in Ándrôniüs's words, Líllíët wiggled her way into the conversation. "The Olmâ? Then that would mean he is from Cáelunárra, and surely a plant by the Dark Lord."

A loud scoff escaped Ándrôniüs's mouth. "Did you not hear anything I said... I merely *referenced* the Olmâ. I did not *call* him one of the Olmâ. We have seen different manifestations of magical races throughout Arcánüs Májörá's existence. It is possible something similar has happened in their world. Again, he is not an Olmâ, for all those who want to waylay these proceedings further."

"I too am skeptical; my esteemed members of the Vaerônthíloch. But with incredulity in our hearts or not, we must proceed. Let us take a vote on the appropriateness of this test," Órynë declared, silencing the room. He struck his gavel on the podium and proclaimed, "I, as the Grand Mage, make the first motion that Ethan shall fight a gorlock and must use magic, if able, during the test. All in agreement, say, aye."

In unison, the council members voiced their agreement, but beneath the chorus of 'ayes' lurked a tremor of uncertainty; an undercurrent of doubt at the likelihood of success.

Órynë looked at Ándrôniüs, took a deep, steadying breath. "Now, my friend, continue with the declarations."

Straightening his back, Ándrôniüs stood tall, his voice level as he spoke. "Ryan, with all his remarkable qualities: his strength, agility, and sharp mind. I have foreseen that he must face the dwarven prince in a duel and have him submit to his power. He must earn the respect of the dwarves by defeating their prince."

Out of the corner of his wandering eyes, he caught a glimpse of Xándriel beginning to rise from his seat. Órynë's voice cut through the air. "Sit down, Xándriel. You're out of place."

Audaciously, Xándriel uncovered his face once more. "Am I, Órynë? The dwarves are not keen on anyone, not dwarven, let alone someone with particular complexions." He gestured emphatically at his skin. "And if I am not mistaken, the boy... Ryan, is it?"

Órynë and Ándrôniüs nodded in confirmation.

Continuing, Xándriel said, "He shares the same color of skin as

l. The dwarves, they shudder at it for some reason, or they simply are a wretched people for their barbaric views."

Vûlët stood as well, seconding Xándriel's statement. "Though I do not share the same complexion, my children are mixed because of my wife's kin, and the dwarves that trade with us at Tôrthävn always look down upon them, like lesser beings."

Ándrôniüs responded calmly, "Xándriel. Vûlët. You may be correct in your assumptions, but this dwarven prince is more keen on the ways of elves, men and mages. While yes, the scars of the traitorous ones run deep with many of his people, he is a proud atheling and will not allow himself to be defeated by the faults of these assumptions you two have muttered. The actions of a few dwarves should not discount the whole of a kingdom. We can't be sure, so let's allow Ryan the chance to prove himself against the fierce warrior prince."

Xándriel maintained his stance, his tone firm. "If we set aside that aspect, Ándrôniüs, your plan has merit. But simply defeating the prince isn't sufficient. He must kill him. You know the ways of the dwarves. Only through bloodshed will they offer respect to someone who isn't one of their own."

Raising an eyebrow in disgust, Ándrôniüs retorted, "Is bloodshed truly necessary, Xándriel? This fight is not about respect. This fight is about the boy proving he can overcome a formidable opponent. I thought someone of your stature would be smarter than a fly drifting across the open sea, searching for a dung heap that does not exist. You seem far more eager for violence than the rest of us. Are you sure you are not an agent of the Dark Lord?"

Xándriel, unfazed and resolute, turned to Órynë. "Let's settle it with a vote. Óryë, why don't we put it to the council?"

Óryně, not wanting to cause more discontent, ignored Ándrôniüs's plea for no bloodshed. Ensuring the council's focus, he declared, "Very well. Ryan will fight the dwarven prince in a fight to the death. All in favor, say, aye."

The room echoed with a unanimous "aye," sealing the decision.

"Well... there you have it. The young man's fate is decided," Óryně said, speaking in a tone of weary finality, as though the matter had dragged on long enough and he was eager to move on.

Ándrôniüs took a deep breath, trying to bury his distaste with the decision the council had just made, then continued, "Jake. I believe it fit that he to be tried in combat. Though this is a greater test and he will be tried at a greater capacity."

A small, stubby mage with rat-like features, thick square glasses held together with a tape-like substance, and a deep, crackly voice stood up. "Greater than Ethan's?" he asked, his eyes squinting through the thick lenses.

"Yes, Thórnwyn," Ándrôniüs affirmed. "I've been steered to give him the hardest test of all. Jake shall face a dracónyx."

Xándriel let out a booming laugh. "Ha! Are you sure you believe in these chosen, Ándrôniüs? You seem to be setting them up to fail. We might as well shackle ourselves and march straight to Kharzonov! Facing that monster will surely be his end."

Looking visibly concerned, Órynë turned to Ándrôniüs. "I must agree with Xándriel. Are you certain this is the task we wish to set before the boy? It feels... heavy with consequence. Survival is certainly unlikely."

Ándrôniüs scanned the room, his tone sharp. "Well then, does anyone have other suggestions?" The room fell silent, save for the faint sounds of sniffles and coughs.

"No? Well, I would like to remind the council that I do not create these tests on a whim. There is much thought, contemplation, and searching within the Ísëphëlŷ stone to be done prior to bringing the tests before the council. And though I wish to propose less deadly tasks today, I must follow the guidance shown to me, as it offers the superlative path forward toward peace for our land," Ándrôniüs confidently proclaimed.

Breaking the silence that followed Ándrôniüs's declaration, Thórnwyn stood once more. "If our Seer has deemed this task prudent, perhaps we use the adolescent beast that the Dracónyxáushká hatched last season. They could not tame it, and maybe it's time to dispatch the creature?"

Xándriel scoffed. "A *dracónyx* is still a *dracónyx*, Thórnwyn. It *hardly* make's a difference."

Órynë turned to Ándrôniüs. "What are your thoughts?"
Nodding thoughtfully, Ándrôniüs mulled over the proposal.
"Yes... Thórnwyn's suggestion holds merit. Xándriel is right; a dracónyx, whether old or young, is still quite the formidable beast. We will of course arm Jake with drakescale armor and weapons to give him the best chance. The adolescent dracónyx hasn't matured, making its fire less potent and less likely to kill him. A more fitting challenge, wouldn't you agree?"

Silence filled the room once again, and Ándrôniüs concluded, "Then it's settled. A dracónyx it is!"

Órynë hesitated for a moment, then spoke authoritatively. "All in favor of the battle with a dracónyx?"

The council's response was once again in unison but filled with a wavering and unsettling tone: "Aye."

The gravity of the decision hung heavily in the air as the council members processed the potential implications of Jake's test.

Ándrôniüs took another deep breath before addressing the council once more. "Now, Emily! She is small but fiery. A very proud and willful young woman. Well-educated, a true bookworm. A woman after my own heart. If only she were a mage." He paused, amused by the shocked gasps and scandalized expressions from the council members, before continuing with a chuckle. "I speak in jest. I am married, and furthermore, the girl is many hundreds of years too young for me; her purpose in the prophecy is already established. Anyway, I digress. She must retrieve the Goblet of Îgnîs Sápíëntíá from the lair of a glimmer gremlin."

"A fitting task! Though I want that goblet back regardless of the outcome of this test, Ándrôniüs. It has immense value to me." Órynë paused, allowing the council members to absorb the information. "All in favor of the glimmer gremlin?"

The mages of the council nodded in agreement, their voices surer as they responded, "Aye!"

Ándrôniüs continued, his confidence growing as he saw the council's eagerness and was more ready to accept Emily's test. "Each of these tests is designed to challenge their strengths and push them beyond their limits. It is only through such tests that they will truly understand their capabilities and be able to fulfill their roles in the prophecy."

Xándriel cleared his throat loudly, interjecting. "You're forgetting one, Ándrôniüs. You've stated four, but what about the fifth? There is a fifth, isn't there?"

Stuttering, Ándrôniüs replied, "She... she has already faced enough. Hannah is like a delicate flower in a summer drought. She took quite a head knock when facing the Shadewalkers, when they tried abducting them on their first day in our world. I believe that is a fitting enough task. Don't you all think so?"

The council muttered, their voices a mixture of doubt and consideration.

Márrisol stood up, her expression firm. "The prophecy is very strict, Ándrôniüs. Every chosen one must face their—"

"We cannot make exceptions, not even for one who may or who may not have been injured in a mere scuffle. We've all been through worse. Our former chosen have no doubt been through worse. Their predecessors still fought. Every single one of them! The prophecy demands it!" Xándriel said, cutting Márrisol off sharply.

Ándrôniüs, his voice trembling slightly with unease but determined, spoke. "Though Hannah appears fine, Câllirrhöe, my healer, warns that while the outside may look repaired, the internal damage to her brain will take time to heal. I fear pushing her further might lead to irreparable harm. Can we not show some leniency in her condition?"

After his comments, a brief pause ensued, and an eerie silence befell the council chambers. A bitter feeling took root among them as the council wrestled with their thoughts on the issue.

Suddenly, a loud voice from a man in the back broke the silence. He was tall and broad-shouldered, with a stern face framed by a red beard. His mesmerizing hazel eyes gleamed with intensity under his thick, furrowed brows. Draped in dark red robes detailed with intricate gold embroidery, he carried himself with confidence.

"I am with Xándriel, Ándrôniüs," he declared, his voice resonating through the chamber. "We must test her."

Xándriel stood back up. "Thank you, Sûl. I'm thankful for our friendship and your voice of support in this matter."

A chorus of "ayes" began to fill and echo in the chamber one by one. Sûl raised his hand, gathering the attention of his fellow council members, then gestured with his palms downward to silence the room.

"Despite her condition, whatever this test is, it must be fitting," Sûl continued, his voice unwavering. "I think we all will agree."

The 'ayes' echoed again, more forcefully this time, solidifying their collective decision.

Órynë stepped forward, his gaze sweeping over the assembly. "We must adhere to the guidelines given to us about the prophecy, but we must also consider the well-being of our chosen ones. Ándrôniüs, do you have a task that might challenge Hannah without pushing her beyond her current physical abilities?"

Ándrôniüs's mind raced. "Yes, perhaps a task that tests her intellect and resolve rather than physical endurance. She could be required to decipher some ancient texts from the renowned library in the Elven Embassy here in Vâloríâ or even here at the academy? It is a task that requires keen insight and mental fortitude."

Puzzled by his friend and colleague's words, Óryně replied, "There are countless ancient texts, my friend. Some languages used in those archaic leather-bound books are unfamiliar to me. I know how much you value your books and the knowledge they offer, but time has lost some languages entirely. Surely you're referring to something more recent?"

"How about a proposition for the young woman to decipher the words of the ancient language of Luthéllon? The language of the elves? Maybe she needs to learn it... understand it... recite it. How does that all sound to everyone gathered here in this hall?" Ándrôniüs said.

The members of the esteemed body, the Vaerônthíloch, exchanged glances, murmuring amongst themselves.

Aggressively slamming his fist upon the back of the bench in front of him, Xándriel bellowed, "No! This is insufficient. You know they must face a more in-depth ordeal." He looked around with arms wide open, gesturing for others to stand. "Don't you think so, my fellow council members?"

Silence befell the chamber again. Many felt pressured and unsure. They knew a test was a test, regardless of the contents and strenuous ordeals required of that test. Despite a tradition of increasingly rigorous physical tests, they all knew they shouldn't provoke Xándriel. A few raised their hands warily in support.

Márrisol stood up. "Xándriel, you know there is no such law. The prophecy's guidelines state they must be tried, nothing more, nothing less. Shadewalkers have indeed already tested her twice, and she lived to tell the tale, or so we've heard. However, to further magnify the encumbrance of her task, I propose we isolate her. How about this even: why not sequester all of them? Emily at the Hall of Mages, the three boys trained and housed at the Grand Barracks, and this... Hannah at the Elven Embassy." Looking around the gathered assembly, she continued, "All in favor of Hannah's test and this additional element being added to the tests, raise your hands."

Excluding a few here and there, most raised their hands, almost in defiance of the task that Xándriel was trying to impose on the council about the chosen. After a quick look at Órynë by Márrisol, the Grand Mage spoke.

"Well, I think that this test for Hannah is sufficient," Órynë said, pausing for effect. "All in favor."

A moment of hesitation followed before the council, almost unanimously, responded, "Aye."

Ándrôniüs nodded, relief washing over him. "Thank you. I believe this will be a suitable test for her. But the sequestration of all? Is that really necessary? They are still new to this world and draw strength from each other."

"Another vote on the separation of the chosen as they prepare for their fates," Órynë proclaimed.

The vote passed quickly, with most voting in favor.

Órynë surveyed the room once more before moving to stand behind the podium to his right. "Now that we have concluded the test deliberations, and this council has ratified them on this, the thirteenth day of Thŷndréll, in the year three hundred fourteen of the eighth age, I, Órynë, the Grand Mage of the Republic of Eldôria, hereby conclude these discussions. Unless there are other matters to discuss?" A long pause befell the council, then he continued. "No? Then all in favor?"

"Aye," everyone agreed in unison, except Xándriel who shoved his way across the knees of his fellow council members, heading for the stairs and then to the podium where Ándrôniüs and Órynë stood.

"This will not be the end of this, Óryně," Xándriel snarled, shaking his finger in the Grand Mage's face. "Your seat will be mine when they fail; then, this foolishness in these chambers will cease. I guarantee the Republic will collapse under your leadership. I will decide who the next chosen are to be and they will liberate us from the Dark Lord." He then pushed off the podium, leaving the firm stand shaking as he turned on his heel and stormed through the obsidian doors, disappearing in a huff of rage.

A great relief washed over the council members as Xándriel seemed to take most of the negative feelings with him. Chatter broke out around the room as the High Mages discussed the proceedings and the events to come.

Many of the mages began to leave, shaking both Ándrôniüs's and Óryně's hands as they exited. After everyone had left and silence ensued, Óryně turned to Ándrôniüs. "Do you really believe that these common folk we know nothing about can, in fact, complete these tests?"

Ándrôniüs smiled at Óryně. "Perhaps this is exactly what we needed. Not knowing who our champions would be. In the past, we've always selected them ourselves, trying to control fate. We've lied to the people, claiming they were sent here by the gods. But maybe this time, the gods, even the Allfather, truly sent them. As for the tests, I only presented what I have seen to be. Who am I to change or question what the gods or the Allfather have already set in motion?"

Óryně rubbed his chin thoughtfully. "I suppose you may be right, but I believe that someone here will report to the Dark Lord about the events that have transpired here today. We must remain vigilant, Ándrôniüs."

Placing a reassuring hand on his friend's shoulder, Ándrôniüs said, "Indeed, Óryně. We must."

Gesturing toward the exit, Óryně said, "Shall we? We must inform the chosen of the tasks they will face. Over the next week, give or take a few days, these tests shall take place. There isn't a moment to waste."

As they walked out the doors, Ándrôniüs spoke up. "I'd like to inform them of their tasks and leave you to less trivial matters, Óryně. With your blessing, of course."

Óryně looked at him with confusion as they entered the hallway. "Are you sure? It's always been the responsibility of the Grand Mage to inform them."

"Yes," Ándrôniüs stated as he glanced down the hall and saw Xándriel waiting at the far end. "I believe you have other matters to handle," he said, gesturing with his head toward the seething figure.

"Indeed, you may be correct," Óryně sighed. "I give you my blessing to inform the chosen of our decision."

Making their way to the end of the hall, they approached the mage.

"Xándriel, what is it?" Óryně inquired.

"I must converse with you alone about this absurdity," Xándriel snarled, his face contorted with anger.

"I shall take my leave, Óryně," Ándrôniüs said, bowing to him before exiting the hallway and retreating down the stairs to the main gathering place in the Hall of Mages, where Ethan, Ryan, Jake, Emily, and Hannah waited rather anxiously with Ísolde and Áelfwîně.

# THE TESTS UNVEILED

HIS STEPS PURPOSEFUL YET measured, Ándrôniüs made his way toward the group scattered about the hall. Ethan, Ryan, and Jake were engaged in animated conversation with Áelfwînë, whose spirits seemed to have lifted considerably since Ándrôniüs last saw him. Their laughter reverberated through the grand hall; it was a comforting sound that contrasted with the events of the meeting he had just taken part in.

Turning his attention to Ísolde, Emily, and Hannah, Ándrôniüs observed the three women sitting together, sipping the finest pine nettle tea from Pinemarsh Manor. He meandered closer, finally settling into a chair beside Ísolde and placing a gentle hand on her shoulder.

"Well, that ended far quicker than I expected," Ísolde said, genuine bewilderment in her voice. "I warned them this sort of thing can drag on into the wee hours of the night, sometimes even stretch into days or weeks."

Meeting her gaze, Ándrôniüs let out an exasperated sigh. "It felt more like an age than just a few hours."

"That bad?" Ísolde said sympathetically.

"Yes, dear... Xándriel is quite dissatisfied with Órynë and I. He has gained quite the voice since becoming the Grand Exchequer of the Treasury of the Republic. There was even talk of returning to Aûllíâtënärrä. He even called for an Orrûvanëthalë. But though some were reluctant, the council ultimately ignored his remarks, and the deliberation of the tasks of their tests consumed the floor."

"Oof, that terrible, terrible man," Ísolde said, turning to the rest of the group. "Xándriel is not one to ever cross, children."

"Wait... what about the tests?" Áelfwînë cut in with a low grumble, leaning forward. "Was there a filibuster? A recess? Did the process stall somewhere? Something feels off. Nothing in those chambers moves that quickly. Tell us everything."

"Declared. Voted upon. Ratified," Ándrôniüs said triumphantly.

Ethan, who had been eavesdropping from afar, left his seat and paced closer. He stopped behind Emily and Hannah, placing his hands on the backs of their chairs. His eyes were filled with anticipation.

"Now that that's done, do we *finally* get to hear about the tests now? The prophecy?" he interjected fervently. "Or, is there more wasteful waiting around?"

Ándrôniüs sighed and smiled wanly. The old mage looked quite drained, the toll of the meeting still painted across his face. "Yes, Ethan, you will hear of them soon enough. This is a pivotal moment for all of us, and it means we are one step closer to ridding Cáelunárra of the evil that has plagued it for so long."

"When?" Ethan pressed.

Ándrôniüs rolled his eyes and turned square with the boy. He tried to keep the burning desire to slap the boy buried deep down. However, Ándrôniüs took a deep breath and steeled himself and allowed a few more moments of quiet to pass before answering.

"That is not important right now. What is though is what we talked about earlier, now Ethan, do you remember the specifics of yours and Hannah's encounter this morning in the alley near the market?"

"What is this about Hannah and Ethan in an alley?" Ryan said jokingly, followed up with a smirk as he and Jake joined the group.

"Did you two rekindle your high school fling?" Jake added.

Ándrôniüs rolled his eyes again, then palmed his face.

"Bleh... Don't remind us of that, Ryan. It's repulsive," Emily said, rolling her eyes in disgust.

Ryan looked at her, eyes wide and slightly surprised by her increasing distaste for the two.

"Whoa there, Em," Jake said as he watched her once calm demeanor turn sour in an instant.

"Oh, come on! Don't act all innocent like you're not sneaking off every single night. Seriously, at all hours! And with... you know who... At least you're actually getting what you want," Emily snapped, her voice brimming with jealousy and frustration, the bitterness dripping with every word.

"I'm not getting what I want, Emily! I don't know what you're on about!" Hannah said, rolling her eyes in dissatisfaction at her lifelong friend.

Before the conversation could drift further, Ándrôniüs interjected. "Children stop! We've got no time for this squabbling. Have you no manners? Or are you five incapable of holding your tongues behind those lips? And most certainly, I have no idea what's going on with you all, but it needs to stop here. And Jake! Sneaking off at any hour of the night is not safe, even here in this great city. It would behoove you to stay indoors after sunset."

Ryan, wanting to get one last line in before Ándrôniüs went off on another tangent about something, nudged Emily's shoulder and said, "I mean, if they're having fun, we might as well, too." He finished with a wink.

Misunderstanding his playfulness for a serious advance, Emily looked at him even more displeased, as she had been friends with Ryan for nearly ten years and did not view him that way in the slightest.

"I'd rather not... thanks," Emily said, stepping back a pace with a sharp side-eyed roll.

"What did I say children, enough!" Ándrôniüs said, rubbing his temples. "Now, where were we?"

"Well, why can't we talk about An—?" Ethan started, getting cut off almost immediately.

"Not right now, Ethan! I said we'd discuss it later! Oh, my days," Ándrôniüs said, looking up to the ceiling of the Hall of Mages. "Allfather, please give me strength!"

There was a brief pause as the teenagers realized that the old mage might have been stretched too thin in what they thought was just witty banter between the five of them, something they did regularly back home.

Overwrought with the multitude of responsibilities weighing on him, Ándrôniüs stood up and took a deep breath, trying to steady himself, and letting his frustration out in a long exhale. Closing his eyes, he started muttering under his breath.

Concerned, Ísolde placed a comforting hand on her husband's arm. "Are you well, dear?"

Ándrôniüs took another deep breath, still trying to suppress the emotional turmoil inside him. "Yes, dear. It has just been a long morning, with much yet to be accomplished this day. I just need a moment in silence... to piece together the next steps."

The room fell silent as everyone absorbed Ándrôniüs's words. While they were eager to hear what they'd be facing soon, they allowed the old mage this moment to breathe. Their acquaintance had been brief, but he had defended them with his life, given them refuge at his home, and escorted them across Eldôria, all the while trying to maintain his sanity and his role in whatever transpired next. The seriousness of the situation was undeniable. Despite the unease gnawing at the pits of their stomachs, they could only watch and wait until he revealed the next steps.

Ándrôniüs took many minutes to pace back and forth in the hall before finally coming to an abrupt halt at the door and gesturing for the group to join him with a sweeping motion.

"Let us walk," he said, his voice steady and confident once more.

One by one, the group rose to follow. Before he opened the door to the Hall of Mages, Ándrôniüs looked back.

"Once outside, we must not speak of the tests. We are going somewhere quiet, where we can discuss these matters in more depth, without prying ears."

"Why?" Ethan asked, his tone tinged with intrigue.

Ándrôniüs thrust the door open, and thunderous applause erupted from the crowd outside. People cheered, waving banners and clapping in celebration. White smoke billowed from the central spire atop the Hall of Mages, curling into the sky like a beacon for all of Vâlorîâ to see, while white smoke also emanated from pipes in the street, permitting it to lazily drift through the crowd.

Turning to Ethan, Ándrôniüs said, "That is why, Ethan."

"Why is there a crowd?" Ethan asked, his curiosity undeterred.

"The council's decision to ratify your tests has been announced to the city," Ándrôniüs explained as he led the friends from the hall. "The Archbishop climbs to the highest spire and starts a fire, releasing white smoke to declare that the chosen have arrived and are being prepared for the tests."

The celebratory crowd parted as they made their way through, cheers and applause echoing in their wake. Gradually, the bustling energy of the town market, which Ethan and Hannah had visited earlier that morning, faded into quieter streets. The uneven cobblestone paths guided them through white-walled passages, past vibrant shops with colorful displays, quaint houses, and beautifully crafted buildings; a side of Vâloríâ they had yet to explore.

After some bobbing and weaving, the tight streets gave way to a large open area. A breathtaking sight rose before them; a towering tree at the heart of a circular building, its massive roots intertwined with the structure itself. Water cascaded down the granite walls, shimmering in the sunlight as it flowed over the smooth stone. The building's design, a harmonious blend of the earth's creations and architecture, seemed to embody peace itself. Meticulously maintained gardens surrounded the area, with trimmed hedges and vibrant bushes enhancing the serene, awe-inspiring atmosphere.

Ándrôniüs gestured toward the grand building. "This is the Elven Embassy," he said. "We are the last race to remain cordial with the elves, though it is only a flicker of an ember now. Few elves reside here, but inside is a magnificent library. It holds records from every realm: Eldôria, Illithría, Brâldôr, Âldâmûr, the Blackmire Marsh, and even Khạrzọnọv. These lands were once all elven, before the other races came and the elves ceded and ultimately retreated to the great Illithrían Wood."

As Ándrôniüs spoke, the group stood in quiet awe, marveling at the sight before them.

He paused briefly, taking in the breathtaking sight alongside them before turning his focus back to the task at hand. "This way; to the walls of Vâloríâ we go," he said, his voice even.

The group followed, their spirits enlightened by the beauty of the Elven Embassy. Leaving the building behind, they made their way toward the imposing city walls and guard towers of the east gate, identical to the one they had entered upon their arrival in Vâloríâ.

The massive gates, constructed of heavy oak reinforced with iron bands, groaned under their own weight as the city guards slowly pushed them open. The sound of gears turning reverberated through the stone walls, a deep, resonant hum that marked their departure from the safety of Vâloríâ. Clad in gleaming armor, the guards nodded respectfully to Ándrôniüs and the group as they passed through.

"Safe travels, chosen ones," one guard said, his voice reverent.

Another guard, wearing a kind smile, added, "May the light of the Allfather guide your path."

Ándrôniüs smiled faintly, shaking his head. "Our rendezvous is only to the edge of the wood. We will be well within sight and earshot of the city. No long journey today, gents."

The guards exchanged confused glances before one stammered, "Our apologies for the misunderstanding, Seer."

"You're only doing what you were trained to do. No harm done," Ándrôniüs replied, his tone calm and reassuring.

The first guard stepped forward and handed him a small banner intricately woven with the emblem of Vâloríâ. "Wave this on your return as you approach the gate, so we know you're a friend, not a foe. Few re-enter through this gate once they leave. This road has been all but forgotten, with only a few elves from time to time passing through on occasion."

Ándrôniüs took the flag, examining it briefly before handing it to Ryan. "Thank you. May you always be blessed."

The guards nodded in acknowledgment.

Leaving the safety of the city, they followed a cobblestone path that gradually gave way to a narrower dirt trail flanked by tall grasses, vibrant wildflowers, and shrubs. The path curved gently as they walked, revealing a distant tunnel formed by the interwoven branches of ancient trees. Though not directly on their route, the hole in the forest stood prominently ahead, marking the edge of the dense forest stretching beyond it. The deep woods lay just down the path they were following.

As they walked, Emily's curiosity got the better of her. "Where are we going?" she asked. The others agreed with her statement in their own ways.

Ándrôniüs glanced back, offering a reassuring smile. "Just to the edge of the wood. There were some stumps I used to study at during my time at the academy. It's the perfect place to share the details and gravity of the tests you will face in the coming week."

Assuaged by Ándrôniüs's words in response to Emily's question, all of them nodded. A few steps further and the aforementioned stumps came into view, each varying in size and species. Though having aged much since Ándrôniüs's youth and a bit more overgrown with the life of the earth, it was indeed a quaint and quiet spot, perfect for one who would want to study or have some peace and quiet from the world. Birds chirped from their trees, frogs croaked from the nearby pond, squirrels rustled in the underbrush searching for acorns, and a cool breeze with a slight nip brushed against their faces.

Pointing to the stumps, wordlessly instructing them to take seats, Ándrôniüs gave them a moment to get settled before speaking. He smiled and intertwined his fingers at his waist.

"Now, Ethan, Ryan, Jake, Hannah, and Emily, we must discuss these tests. They will not be easy; I can promise you that. We must consider the possibility of death, as with any grand quest."

Ethan's eyes widened in shock. "Death?" he said, his voice trembling. While he had unrelentingly demanded information on this very topic, that fatal word made him regret his zealous actions.

Ándrôniüs nodded solemnly. "Yes, death. Now, who wants to hear about the tests you will face?"

The group exchanged slightly stunned expressions. This was the moment they had been waiting for; the time when they would finally discover what was required of them. However, this sudden revelation of death rattled them to their cores. These were no longer just mere tests. The significance of their presence in this world and what was at stake was becoming more evident. Death or serious injury could genuinely befall them before they fulfilled their destinies and their hopeful mission to return home. The magnitude of this realization set in, causing queasiness within their bellies.

They knew the familiar comforts of their world and the simplicity of their past lives were far behind them. With the ever-present burden of destiny being thrust upon them, leaving each of them feeling a sense of irrevocable responsibility.

"What? Has a wayward spell tangled your tongues?"

"Huh?" the group all said disjointedly together.

"'Tis a figure of speech," Ándrôniüs said with a kind smile and snicker. "I find it surprising; especially you, Ethan, the one always champing at the bit to get answers. Yet on the precipice all of you are as still as a shadow waiting to be seen under a new moon."

"What in God's name are you talking about?" Ethan asked, as he had become more confused with the similes that the mage was using. "Look, Ándrôniüs, we're just afraid. We came here against our will. We're wrapped up in this prophecy we do not understand. You treat us as if we are some sort of saviors. We're just five young adults who want to return home and be done with this nonsense. So, of course, hearing we could face death in a test we did not want nor ask for is a little unnerving."

The other four nodded in approval.

He nodded his head emphatically, and again the old mage smiled, blankly even, as if the expressed worries of the five and Ethan's words passed through one ear and out the other.

"There is no need to dwell on the past at this moment in time. We must all move forward. You must complete the tests, and rid the world of the darkness, most importantly the Dark Lord Mûrríëthíêl. Once those requirements and possibly more are fulfilled, then maybe there will be a discussion on how we get you home. So, on that note; who wants to hear what they will face?" Ándrôniüs replied.

The five turned their heads and looked at one another, rolling their eyes and shrugging their shoulders.

"Sure," they all said again disjointedly.

Ándrôniüs stood before them for only a moment longer. His

eyes pierced into each of theirs, as if searching their souls for any sign of doubt. While he saw it at the forefront of their minds, he did not become discouraged at the prospect they were truly unready. He maintained his steady gaze, and in that moment, they knew there was no turning back now. The tests awaited, and with them, the fate of Cáelunárra.

Taking a deep breath, Ándrôniüs turned to Ethan. "You will face a gorlock in combat. This creature is formidable, and you must not only defeat it, but also learn and use magic during the battle."

A puzzled expression took hold on Ethan's face. He looked around at the others, voicing what everyone else was thinking. "A gorlock?"

Ándrôniüs nodded, his expression serious. "Yes, Ethan, a gorlock."

Ethan scratched his head. "Okay? A gorlock?" He paused, seeing Ándrôniüs didn't understand his confusion. "And what is a gorlock?"

Ándrôniüs's eyes widened slightly. "Oh, heavens, my apologies for the misunderstanding. You must have other sorts of beasts in your world. A gorlock is... well, it'll be a tough opponent. The gorlock stands just over eight feet tall and has thick, matted fur that can be difficult to penetrate. It has fiery red eyes and venomous fangs as long as your forearm. Its claws are sharp enough to rend steel, and a roar from one at times can paralyze the minds of the bravest of warriors."

The stunned look still present on everyone's faces morphed into incredulity and panic as Ándrôniüs spoke. Their minds started racing about Ethan's chances of survival against such a monster.

Ethan's face turned pale with terror. "Are they trying to kill me? I don't even know how to fight! And what do you mean magic? I don't have magic!"

Raising a calming hand, Ándrôniüs's face softened. "I understand your fear, and I can't blame you for feeling this way. But know this: you can defeat the gorlock. We will train you, not just in combat, but also in using magic to help you."

Ethan, his face still pale but with a hint of pink returning, exclaimed, "How do you know I can do magic? I've never done anything magical in my life."

Speaking with quiet conviction, Ándrôniüs said, "I'm not entirely sure, Ethan. It's just a feeling I have... a sense that there is something more to you... no, no. Inside of you. Something powerful. It's been waiting to be awakened."

"A feeling! You're basing this on a feeling! Risking my life for a feeling! All on a whim that I might be able to do something... magical?" Ethan exclaimed.

"Calm yourself, my boy," Ándrôniüs said in a soothing tone. "I will be there every evening to oversee that you receive the best training."

Ethan took a deep breath, his hands trembling slightly. "I don't know who's crazier right now: you, for suggesting this, or me, for even considering that this is even remotely possible." He glanced at the mage, searching the man's face for something: certainty, or maybe a hint of doubt."

"I know it's hard for you to understand, my boy. Just try to understand. Lay down your sword. Suppress that hesitation. Trust the process even. And in that you will discover more about yourself than you ever knew," Ándrôniüs said with an urgency.

Ethan paused for a moment. He was unsure of what to say. His mind raced with anxiety. Ethan drew in a long breath and let it out, settling himself. He lowered his head and did it again, before raising his head and looking back to the mage's empty gaze. "I'll do it. Just know this isn't blind trust. I'm doing it because I have to, not because I think you're right." He paused, his jaw tightening. "But Ándrôniüs... I sure hope you know what you're doing."

Ándrôniüs placed a reassuring hand on Ethan's shoulder. "I have faith in you, Ethan. You are stronger than you think, and with the right training, I know you will succeed. Believe in yourself."

Turning away from Ethan, Ándrôniüs locked eyes with Ryan next. "You have an immense task ahead of you, too. Like Ethan, you also will be tried in combat. Though with a less intimidating opponent."

"Oh, thank goodness. What do I have to fight?" Ryan said, letting out a sigh and feeling slightly guilty that he was relieved that Ethan had the harder task.

Ándrôniüs's expression turned serious. "Not a what, but a who. You will face The Dwarven Prince of Brâldôr."

"I thought you said it was going to be a creature... You know something easier to fight?" Ryan's eyes widened in disbelief.

A loud chuckle escaped Ándrôniüs's mouth. "Ryan, my dear boy, I never said it would be easier. It just will not be something as dangerous as a gorlock," he said, glancing at Ethan before refocusing on Ryan. "Prince Ûrvákënák is the first in line to inherit the Kingdom of Brâldôr, which lies in the mountains to the northwest. He never backs down from a challenge and has never lost a fight in a skirmish. Well... at least not to my knowledge. The council has deemed this to be a fight to the death."

Ryan's face went tight with shock. "Death? You mean I have to kill someone. I've never killed anything in my life," he exclaimed, his breaths coming quicker, more shallow with each word. His head spun, and he dropped it into his hands.

Emily interjected, her voice trembling with a mix of fear and frustration. "I think I see a trend here, Ándrôniüs. I don't think we're keen to know any more."

Ándrôniüs raised his hand reassuringly. "Everyone, listen to me. These tests are designed to push you to your limits, to reveal the true strength within you. We will ensure you are as prepared as you can be in the time that is afforded to us."

Clearing his throat, he continued before any more spirals of doubt could stir in their minds. "Jake, you will have one of the more daunting tests," he said and paused, knowing he would have to moderate his next words. "You will face no man or beast that dwells on the ground. You fight the fearsome dracónyx."

The perplexed expression on Jake's face deepened with each word. "I'm up for the fight, Ándrôniüs, but like Ethan, can you explain what in God's name a dracónyx is?"

Ándrôniüs, knowing that Jake's test was the most likely to end tragically, weighed each word before speaking.

"A dracónyx is a reptilian-like winged creature that dwells high in the mountains, rarely seen by mortal eyes. It's covered in dark scales that shimmer with an almost metallic sheen, making it difficult, not impossible, to kill."

Jake's face paled as he absorbed the description. "Yeah... I'm pretty sure you just described a dragon. It certainly seems that the High Mage Council is just trying to kill us at this point, guys."

"Dragon?" Ándrôniüs said with a shake of his head slightly with confusion. "Nevermind... as I've already said, I have faith you will be victorious. The goal of these tests is not to kill you, but to strengthen you. You each have a real chance to overcome these challenges, pass the tests, and emerge triumphant. If you apply yourselves in the training, we will provide to you. You will rise to take your place among those who came before you."

Turning, he spotted Emily leaning against one stump, steadying herself from a sudden bout of dizziness. The tension in her posture betrayed the trepidation that filled her at hearing her friends' assignments. Stepping toward her, he gently took her hands and helped her to steady her feet, then drew her into a quiet embrace. As she tucked a strand of hair behind her ear, his voice softened. "My sweet Emily... your test will be to face a glimmer gremlin."

Emily pushed off Ándrôniüs, putting distance between them. "A glimmer gremlin?"

"Yes, yes. A glimmer gremlin," Ándrôniüs confirmed, sensing her confusion. He continued, "A glimmer gremlin is a rather large, elusive creature that thrives in darkness. Its skin shimmers with a faint, eerie light that seems to shift and vanish in the shadows, making it nearly impossible to see. Despite its size, it moves swiftly in the dark. Though it appears blind because its eyes are rather large and reflective, it can see in complete darkness. You will navigate its lair, not fight it, to retrieve the Goblet of Îgnîs Sápíëntíá hidden deep beneath the city."

Emily's eyes widened in terror. "Underground in the dark? I'm not sure I can do that. I'm claustrophobic and even more terrified of the dark."

Ándrôniüs looked puzzled. "Claustro-what?" he asked, puzzled. Shaking his head before she could respond, he continued, "Emily, this tests everything about you. Obviously, the Allfather knew this. Though his wisdom may not be apparent now, the Allfather knows all of you and your weaknesses, which he can transform into immense strengths. This includes you, Ethan. And you, Jake. And you, Ryan. The Allfather wants to see if you can overcome your deficiencies before setting you upon a more treacherous path. It doesn't have to be perfect, or pretty, or won fairly; you just have to complete it."

"And me?" Hannah interjected softly as she stood up, bracing herself to hear about the terrifying ordeal that awaited her.

"Hannah, my dear," Ándrôniüs said endearingly, his eyes softening as he looked at her. "You will have no simple test. Though the council shone favorably on you because of your recent injuries from your encounter with the Shadewalkers."

"What does that mean?" she asked, her voice filled with apprehension.

"The council has deliberated and decided that your test will be one of pure knowledge and willpower. You must learn the Elvish language sufficiently to convey a message to all at the Coliseum on the final test day. You will decide the fate of this entire ordeal if the others are successful, of course. This will ensure that the secrets of the prophecy may be revealed to you all."

Hannah's eyes widened. Her heart pounded, not from fear, but from disbelief. "Learn the Elvish language in a week? And convey a message to the whole Coliseum?"

Even as she spoke, Hannah's gaze drifted to her friends—each facing monsters and peril—and the knot of dread that had been tightening in her chest loosened. Her task might be daunting, but at least it wasn't deadly. A small spark of relief kindled, followed by guilt that she was avoiding the physical ordeals her friends would be facing.

Ándrôniüs nodded solemnly. "Yes, Hannah. The Elvish language is ancient and complex, but it holds the key to understanding the deeper mysteries of our world. The elves will judge your progress and determine if you are worthy."

Her mind raced with the enormity of the challenge, but she met his gaze and squared her shoulders. "I will do my best, Ándrôniüs," she said, her voice steady despite the uncertainty gnawing at her.

Ándrôniüs placed a comforting hand on her shoulder. "I have faith in you, Hannah. I feel as though you are quite ready for this test. I would even go so far as to say this is a fitting task for you. If I'm not mistaken, you were about to undertake something similar in your world."

A quaking silence befell their minds. Though none had spoken of Hannah and her mission to Switzerland in the coming months, they had no doubt of what he was referring to.

She whispered inaudibly, "How do you know that?"

He gave her a merry wink and full-faced smile. "Because I am the Seer of the Enigmas, my dear. Trust that your coming tests are no mere coincidence."

"Now, what do we do? When do we start?" Ethan spoke, eager to move forward now that they had been told about their tests.

"I should have known there would be more questions from you," Ándrôniüs said with a chuckle, feeling slightly more tolerant after their discussion.

Eyes wide open and still reeling, Ryan added, "I mean... Ethan is right. Like... do we start tomorrow? In a few days? Or weeks?"

The mage looked at each of them fondly, and though he was terrified for them, he simply smiled and said, "The tests will be administered over the course of this week. Tomorrow is the opening ceremony at the Coliseum, where you will be presented to the public. The first test will occur the following day, in the evening. But we will worry about that tomorrow. First, we must head back into the city and run one last errand before we partake in dinner and rest. In the morning, the real work begins."

# THE FIRST FAREWELL

THE SUN STARTED ITS dip beneath the mountains, casting a warm golden glow over the land as the sky transitioned into vibrant hues. In contrast, the sky to the north was stark black as towering thunderheads gathered. Birds settled into their nests, while squirrels and other small creatures scurried back to their dens. The world seemed to quieten as all creatures sought their places of comfort.

Noticing the gathering clouds, Ándrôniüs turned to the group. "It would seem that the weather is turning, children. Let us return to Vâloríâ before we end up drenched."

They all nodded in agreement and began making their way back up the cobblestone path. As they walked, Ándrôniüs handed Ryan the small banner that he'd forgotten near the stumps. With a subtle gesture, he encouraged Ryan to raise the flag high above his head, signaling their return.

"Ryan, higher! Wave it around," Ándrôniüs commanded.

Ryan obliged, raising the Vâlorían banner above his head and waving it as if it were in a heavy windstorm. The guards in the tower laughed, and even Ryan's friends chuckled as he led the group to the gate. Ándrôniüs couldn't contain himself any longer and began laughing uproariously. Ryan, realizing the jest, now thoroughly embarrassed, stormed several paces ahead, still holding the flag high, but waving it less exuberantly.

At the entrance, the same guards who had opened the gates for them met them. Still chuckling at Ryan's little display, they allowed them re-entry into the city. A chill took to the air, and the once-inviting breeze turned into a nagging wind, whipping the girls' hair and skirts and nearly blowing everyone over with large gusts that swept through the streets.

Returning the way they came, the group soon reached the Elven Embassy just as a light mist slowly started to fall, the sun having inched ever closer to disappearing behind the mountains in the east.

Ándrôniüs came to an abrupt halt in the gardens in front of the embassy. "This is where we must say goodbye to Hannah. Her test will begin tonight. Please, make your goodbyes prompt," he said.

"What exactly do you mean?" Ethan asked, his brows furrowed.

"This is where the sequestration begins," Ándrôniüs replied.

"I thought you said we'd face these tests together!" Ethan huffed in a bout of rage.

"Ethan, those words never left my lips," Ándrôniüs said as calmly as he could. "You made an assumption. These feelings are of your creation. You disappointed yourself. Unfortunately, this is how the council... well, how the Allfather directed these tests to be administered, *through* the council. But you should know that Hannah will spend the next week here, ensuring she has no contact with the outside world. Or knowing what is happening in the rest of your tests."

Ethan, his tone reflecting the fury inside of him, burst out. "I will not allow this!" He stomped his foot down like a child in a tantrum. "We will not be separated!"

"If you insist on doing things your way," Ándrôniüs said, his voice taking on the firm finality of a parent at wit's end, "then I'll call over the guards and have them escort you to the dungeons where you can wait, in solitude, until the time and date of your test arrives. If that is the path you're willing to choose."

Ethan rolled his eyes, accompanied by an emphatic huff. While he didn't agree with the mage separating him from Hannah, he figured it was best not to push his luck, especially after testing him once already and being warned he'd be tossed off a cliff for it. So Ethan, wanting to hold on to every last moment with Hannah, spoke up before Ándrôniüs could intervene.

"Hannah, are you going to be okay?" Ethan asked.

Giving a confident nod, Hannah said, "Don't underestimate me, Ethan. Sure, I'll miss you guys, but I know we can do this. I'm more worried about you all than myself, honestly."

Emily, though their rising squabbles with one another approached Hannah and gave her a firm embrace.

Ethan standing in the background now, his voice laced with frustration, muttered, "I really don't like this."

Growing weary of Ethan's obstinacy, Ándrôniüs stepped in. "My boy, I understand your concern, but this is the way it must be. I have told you over and over to trust in the Allfather and his plan. And again I say, each of you has his or her own path to follow, and there can be no digression from that path. It is like you refuse to grasp the simplest things. Please try to understand—something, anything—I beg of you, for all our sakes."

As he spoke, a familiar figure approached from down the street, and Ísolde appeared. Her serene presence abated some of the volatile emotions.

"I'll stay with Hannah at the Elven Embassy to assist with her task," she reassured them, her voice soothing. "We'll make sure she has everything she needs. And Ethan, I know how you are. Just don't you worry. The elves and I will take good care of her."

Ándrôniüs smiled, relieved to see her. "I see you found my letter. Thank you, my dear. Your support will be invaluable."

Ísolde hugged Hannah and then turned to the others. "I did. Good luck to all of you. We'll see each other again soon."

Turning to address the group, Ándrôniüs said, "Now, the rest of you hurry along to the Hall of Mages. I need to speak with Hannah privately."

The four friends left, each casting a final, encouraging glance at Hannah before moving out of sight. Ísolde also departed, moving toward the entrance of the grand edifice beside them.

Ándrôniüs turned to Hannah. "Come along, my dear."

Falling into step with him, they started strolling along the path. The cool air and light mist created a diaphanous atmosphere, softening the edges of the world around them.

"Hannah," Ándrôniüs began, his voice gentle yet firm. "Oh, how do I say this plainly without upsetting you?"

She looked up at him, curiosity in her eyes. "What do you need to tell me?"

"I have a vital message from the Allfather for you, but it must be kept completely confidential," he said gravely. "It is something that will help you in the future, once this journey to mend our land truly begins, that being, if everyone passes their tests."

He sighed, trying to figure out the best way to phrase his next words. "You must leave someone behind. And though I know it will tear the person apart, you must follow through nonetheless, for the greater good of everything."

Hannah's intrigue grew. "What is it? And who is this person?"

Ándrôniüs smiled warmly. "Well, first, I must truly say that the elvish language, though difficult, will come naturally to you. That is why the Allfather assigned you this task. Plus, Ísolde knows the language. She will be of immense value to you."

Growing tired of his circumnavigation of the topic, Hannah cut him off, stepping in front of him and grabbing his hands firmly. "Ándrôniüs, please, this is me you're talking to, not Ethan. Please, just tell me what it is I must do."

Letting out a long, troubled sigh, he looked at the ground, then pulled his head back up. Releasing one of his hands from Hannah's grip, he continued their walk along the garden path.

"No, you are right, dear. I'm just trying to be diplomatic about the issue," he said a few strides down the pathway in the gardens.

"So," she replied. "What is it?"

He sighed again.

"Well, I guess there is no easy way to navigate past this. Regarding the prophecy, when the time arises; if you are all successful, of course. When a powerful individual among the elves asks you to do something, you must do it, whatever the consequences may be between you all."

Hannah hesitated. "What if it's something I morally do not agree with?"

Ándrôniüs chuckled softly. "No, nothing like that, dear. When you hear it, feel it, and know it to be something you can follow, you must act on it. This directive from the Allfather is crucial. It will mend the great rift between the realms of humans and elves. If you fail, many will perish at the hands of the Dark Lord and Ancülí."

"Ancüli?" She questioned more to herself as she pondered that name. "That name," Hannah mused. "It sounds very familiar. Why is that?"

"Well, from what I heard about your little altercation this morning, you and Ethan had a little run in with him in the alleyway on the way back from the market," he said, as they kept their walk steady along the garden paths of the Elven Embassy.

Her puzzled face turned into more of a smile as Hannah said, "Oh, yes! What a nice man he was. He came out of nowhere and stopped a man with a dagger from attacking us. Well, sort of. Are you sure this Ancüli is the same one who I hear works for the Dark Lord?"

"Interesting," he said as he scratched his beard. "Interesting indeed. I need to know if he saw you at all? Did he see your face?"

"Well... not really. I mean, I suppose he could have," Hannah said, pausing as the memory resurfaced. Her eyes narrowed slightly. "Ándrôniüs, you never answered me. Is that man the same one who stands with the Dark Lord?"

"It very well could be, my dear. I suppose there is more to this story that I still need to uncover. Still, I am simply grateful you two escaped unharmed from those wretched alley folk and this figure, who may or may not be Ancüli."

"I wouldn't say unharmed..." Her voice faltered, tears welling in her eyes as the memory surged back with cruel clarity. "There was one... he was trying to hurt me. In a way, no woman should be hurt." Her hands trembled as she spoke, and she clasped them together tightly, trying to hold herself steady. "That's why I didn't really see the man. All I remember was that Ethan was thrown to the ground and got well... you saw him. And by the time I helped Ethan up, and we got him cleaned up a bit, the man just told us to tell you he was back and then disappeared as fast as he arrived."

Stopping momentarily, Ándrôniüs turned to look at the magnificent building they had circled while they conversed, and said, "Well, I s'pose that this conversation is more suited for Ethan then. I'm sorry that the riffraff of this city did that to you. I thought I told you all to stay away from the shadows and alleys?"

"Oh, you did. It's just Ethan—" she said, but Ándrôniüs

interjected with a wry chuckle.

He continued, "That Ethan, I tell you. You had best be careful around him. Anyway, we've digressed from the first part of our talk, but somehow found ourselves on the topic of the other point I wished to discuss with you. Do you think, my dear, that you can do what I asked?"

With the enormity of his words sinking in, Hannah nodded. "I'll do my best to fulfill what you ask. Thank you for believing in me. But Ándrôniüs, please tell me the rest."

Stopping to embrace her tightly, he ignored her requests. "You're like the granddaughter I never had. You will do great things, Hannah. I have no doubt."

Growing impatient yet again with his antics, she firmly said, hardening her tone, "Please, just tell me."

Ándrôniüs, regretting what he was about to do but knowing it was crucial, looked her deep in the eyes. "You must be gentle with him. Ethan will not understand. But he is not your path, nor are you his. You must leave him behind. Your destiny leads elsewhere."

Hannah pulled away from Ándrôniüs, turning away from him, her voice laced with sadness as she said, "But I love him. I think... Ándrôniüs, I know he is difficult at times, but he's the only person I've ever wanted."

Turning her to face him, he spoke gently, grabbing her hands. "Listen, Hannah, there is someone out there for you. Their paths will cross with yours, and that will be your future. I don't say things this plainly for just anyone, so believe me when I say, your path is with him and not Ethan. His path will take him elsewhere. You must remember these things I have told you. Now it is time for you to go and fulfill your destiny."

Confusion filled her, but instead of asking the million questions that ran through her mind, Hannah simply thanked Ándrôniüs for his guidance. Giving him a tight hug and a quick peck on the cheek, she turned toward the Elven Embassy, her resolve firm as she prepared to face the coming days.

After Ándrôniüs ensured Hannah had made it safely within the confines of the Elven Embassy, he stood outside, staring at the sky, waiting for the inevitable rainfall to begin. Sure enough, the rain started, one heavy droplet at a time, gradually picking up speed and dropping on his face. He smiled as the rain momentarily washed his worries away.

The other four awaited him, and he knew he must return to the Hall of Mages to prepare them. He looked back at the Elven Embassy for only a moment, knowing that Hannah was in good hands with Ísolde. A sigh of relief escaped his lips as he felt a sense of reassurance, knowing that everything was unfolding as it should, or so he hoped.

As the rain continued to fall, Ándrôniüs took his first steps back toward the Hall of Mages. The rain came down in heavy sheets, soaking through his robes, but he paid little attention to the minor inconvenience. His mind dwelled on the chosen ones, the prophecy, and the trials that would follow their success. The light of day had all but faded, and the storm intensified, with thunder bellowing in the distance as the blackness of night deepened around him.

He disappeared into the dimming twilight along the streets of Vâloríâ as the townspeople lit the lanterns one by one. The flickering lights cast a warm glow on the cobblestone streets, a stark contrast to the tumultuous thoughts swirling in his mind.

# SOULREND

ETHAN, RYAN, JAKE, AND Emily sat comfortably on the couches in the Hall of Mages, having changed out of their wet clothes and now trying to find respite despite the knowledge of their looming ordeals. The room was warmly lit, casting a soft glow on the ancient artwork and polished wooden furniture. The dancing flames in the fireplace across the room crackled softly as the friends patiently awaited Ándrôniüs's arrival.

Áelfwînë, slightly tipsy, was at the table nearby, handling his demons in his own way. His hair was wild and disheveled, sticking out in every direction like a bird's nest. His eyes were half-lidded, struggling to stay open, and he mumbled incoherently between swigs from his flask.

Ethan leaned forward, his elbows resting on his knees, and glanced at the others. "Do you think Hannah can pull this off? Learning an entire language in a week sounds impossible."

Running a hand through his hair, Ryan sighed. "I don't know, man. But it's no more impossible than our fighting monsters and dwarves and winning. This whole situation is insane. Maybe we should just plan an escape and leave. None of this really involves us, so why should we care?"

"Leave? And go where? We're already in this deep. At least here, they will teach us to defend ourselves. Out there, we would have to deal with the Shadewalkers or worse... if there even is something worse than those things. Besides, Ándrôniüs seems to think we have a chance. They wouldn't throw us to the wolves without a plan, right?" Jake said with a disapproving shake of his head.

Sitting with her legs tucked under her, Emily spoke softly. "But what if we fail? What if... one of us doesn't make it? I can't stop thinking about it. I really don't want to lose any of you."

Áelfwînë his mind fuddled, catching bits and pieces of the conversation, raised his flask unsteadily. "You all worry too much," he slurred, his words thick and muddled. "Tests, prophecies... it's all... *hic*... a bunch of poppycock." His head bobbed as he nodded off again, only to jerk awake and take another drink.

Ethan frowned, watching Áelfwînë with concern. "We can't let ourselves end up like that," he said firmly. "I guess we should just stay focused. Jake is right; we don't stand a chance outside these walls. If they believe we can do this, maybe we should, too. I know I question them more than I probably should, but I think it's time we try to have faith... *especially* me."

Leaning back and crossing his arms, Ryan said, "Easier said than done. We've barely had time to process any of this. And training? What training? We've only got a few days to become master fighters or whatever. This is hopeless."

Feeling his previous certainty fade, Jake nodded slowly in agreement, fear welling up inside him. "Ugh... I don't know, guys. I don't know what else we could do, but maybe we shouldn't get involved in this. It's not our fight. Maybe Ryan's right after all. We should just leave."

Emily glanced around at her friends, seeing their doubt and uncertainty, and Ethan, now standing alone. Her heart ached for him. Rallying what little bravery she had left, she said, "Jake, Ryan, we need to pull together for Hannah, too. She's counting on us just as much as we are on her. Not to mention, how would we get her out of there? And then escape the city? Where would we even go?"

She hesitated, her thoughts drifting to Jake and Elârâ, having seen them slipping off together, not to mention the heated kiss she saw them sharing the night prior when she was heading to the privy.

"Jake, don't you want to help Elârâ? I saw you two of you last night. Just think... she could die if we don't step up. And like Ethan said... like *you* said just moments ago, we have to try. They surely have a plan. So get a grip, both of you!"

Áelfwînë, raised his flask again. "To strength," he muttered, his eyes drooping. "And... *hic*... to not losing our minds."

The group shared a small, weary laugh, the conversation easing slightly as Áelfwînë's drunken stupor offered a brief distraction. It had derailed their worries, if only for a moment, especially as Áelfwînë began singing in his inebriation.

"We walk toward darkness... *hic*... darkness is fun... no... *hic*... shush... no, you shush! We're just trying to sleep here, gents... I know, I know! You don't need to tell me... I said *Shhh*." He then slammed his head onto the table, leaving his audience exchanging amused glances. They worried about the guard's mental state but couldn't help laughing.

A loud crash of lightning and thunder burst out overhead, causing them to jump in their seats. The rain intensified and continued to batter the windows relentlessly, and a heavy sense of realization settled over them. But underneath it, sadness took hold.

Ryan stared out the window, his voice soft and filled with longing when he spoke. "I wonder if my mom is worrying about me right now. She used to always say, 'Ryan, you better not get yourself into trouble,' and here I am, in the middle of some sort of prophecy."

Her eyes growing misty, Emily nodded. "I miss my little sister. She must think I've abandoned her. I used to read her bedtime stories every night. Now, I just hope she hasn't forgotten about me."

Wanting to avoid thinking of his family, and the rising emotions he did not want to face in front of the others, Jake tried to lighten the mood. "Hey, remember the time Ryan tried to impress everyone by attempting to juggle during the talent show last year?"

Ryan groaned, covering his face. "Oh man, don't remind me. The baseball team put me up to it when I didn't break the all-time stolen-base record last season."

Jake laughed. "Yeah, yeah! You started off so well, and then you tossed one of those pins way too high. When you leaned back to catch it and tried to correct yourself, you tripped, and the thing came clobbering down on your head. The whole auditorium lost it!"

Growing frustrated, Ryan said, "Come on, Jake, I said don't remind me! I already lived through it once."

Ethan jumped in as Emily chuckled quietly. "Yeah! You said you'd been practicing for months! Although by that display, we all know what you were really up to. You were infatuated with Maegan, or was it Sophie? I can't keep all your exes straight. Obviously, whoever she was took your time away from 'practice.'"

Continuing the roast, Jake said, "You're a star on the field, but sure as heck not on the stage."

Smiling despite all the teasing, Ryan grinned. "Look, I was going to try to save it, but I just made it worse. After I ran offstage, I slipped on the ice covering the auditorium's back stairs, rolled my ankle, and that sidelined me for the next few games."

Emily chuckled softly. "But hey, you definitely left an impression on everyone!"

Áelfwînë interjected, his speech slurred. "You think that's bad? I once... hic... tried to ride a Lívátalon... No, that's not right. I tried riding a Lavatan... No, no. hic... a Líváthánoneon Snaggletooth in the east... hic... but it was just a horse. Kicked me right in the gut. All the lads at the alehouse laughed at me... thought I was crazy."

Áelfwînë's level of drunkenness left them unsure how to react. They grinned bemusedly and couldn't help chuckling a bit. They knew the guard meant well, but they didn't want to encourage his behavior any further. Ethan stood up and took the tankard out of his floppy hand and put it on the table far from him. And then sat back down with his friends. Ultimately, they refrained from talking further until he settled down as he grumbled and looked for his booze before thudding his head against the table and passing out.

Emily's thoughts turned more serious at that moment. She looked at the fire in the hearth across the room. "Do you think our families think we're dead?"

His gaze distant, Ryan sighed. "I hope not. I hope they're holding on to hope, just like we are."

Wanting to bring back the more pleasant mood, Jake grinned as another memory surfaced. "Remember when we got caught sneaking into the city pool after hours? The security guard was furious, but we all escaped, except for Ethan."

Ethan laughed, shaking his head. "Yeah, and I had to do community service for the city for a good month. Good times."

Another sudden loud crack of thunder boomed overhead, and the four jumped out of their seats again. A flash of lightning that spread slowly across the sky, casting eerie shadows in the room, followed the thunder.

"Where is Ándrôniüs? Shouldn't he be back by now?" Emily said as she shivered, pulling her blanket tight around her shoulders.

To their surprise, the mage was awake again, but no less alert and in his stupor, Áelfwînë declared, "I'll go look for him!" He got up, stumbled a few steps, and tripped over the rug, landing face-down on the floor.

Simultaneously, the doors of the Hall of Mages burst open, and Ándrôniüs popped through, drenched like a wet dog, his robes clinging to him and water dripping from every fold.

Slightly startled at his sudden appearance, Emily tried to crack a joke, her voice wavering. "What? No spell to keep you from getting drenched, Ándrôniüs?"

Unfazed, Ándrôniüs replied, "Well, there is, but the best way to deal with stress is to let the water wash it away, not to mention it makes for a refreshing stroll." He walked further into the hall and came across the limp form of his guard, who was snoring, completely passed out on the floor. "What happened to him?"

Unsure what to say, Ryan decided to go with the truth. "He was worried about you and went to find you. Then... well, he didn't get very far."

Ándrôniüs shook his head, a small smile on his lips. "Best leave him be for now. I'm going upstairs to change, and I'll be right back down to discuss the preparations we must get underway. Jake, why don't you go find Elârâ and see if she has anything left over that we can make a meal of? But no dilly-dallying! I know you have eyes for the girl, but I shan't be long."

He disappeared up the stairs, leaving a trail of water in his wake.

Stupefied, Jake said, "How does this blasted mage know

everything?"

"I'm not sure, but it seems he's got eyes everywhere despite being one busy man," Ethan said, scratching his head in disbelief.

"Well, I did slip this morning that you two were sneaking off together," Emily said sheepishly.

"Now you've gone and done it, Emily," Jake said, rolling his eyes. "She wanted to keep it discreet, even a secret. Now, what do I tell her?"

"I suppose it's better she hears the truth," Ethan said, though he wasn't sure the words felt right even as he spoke them.

Jake scratched his head, uncertain of what to say next, before finally muttering, "I guess I'll just tell her tonight. We're going to see a play at the amphitheater."

Emily's eyes lit up. She had always secretly dreamed of seeing a Broadway show or something like it back home, but now, here in a world where such wonders weren't just possible but common—those dreams felt within reach. She squealed with delight. "Ooo! Can I come?"

The boys exchanged puzzled glances, clearly not grasping what was so exciting.

"Uhh... I mean... well—" Jake started, the first to break the silence, fumbling over his words.

Before he could finish, Emily cut in.

"Oh, fine... I'll just stay in my room and read more books," she sighed, rolling her eyes.

"Well, on that note... what are we going to do this evening until I leave to meet up with Elârâ?" Jake asked, obviously forgetting the task that Ándrôniüs had asked him to do.

"Jake, are you serious?" Ethan asked plainly, with a blank expression on his face.

Jake gave him the same blank look back, clearly not picking up his hint.

"Go find Elârâ and see if there is anything left for us to eat," Ethan said firmly.

The room filled with laughter as Jake's face flushed bright red before he scurried quickly from the room.

A few moments passed, and Ándrôniüs returned downstairs

promptly, now in dry robes. He sat down at the table and gestured for everyone else to do the same. As he did so, Elârâ and Jake appeared carrying trays of food. The companions each took their places around the table, picking at the provided meal. Elârâ joined them, sitting close to Jake. Her presence entertained the gathered company as Jake attempted to make conversation with the beautiful young mage. Despite his clumsy efforts, Elârâ giggled, her face also now flushed, and a smile tugging at her lips, clearly not minding his attention.

Eventually, Ryan yelled at Jake to join them on the couches to talk with Ándrôniüs after the meal. The two of them hadn't even noticed that the others had moved, so enthralled with each other. Elârâ cutely waved and winked as she left, leaving Jake looking like a lost puppy. Unable to tear his gaze away from her, he stumbled around the furniture, even tripping once and falling flat on his face over an end table near the couches, earning chuckles from the others.

"Alright," Ándrôniüs began, trying to keep the smile off his face at Jake's display. "We need to discuss your tests and how to prepare for them."

Straightening in his chair, Ethan's expression focused. "What exactly does that mean?"

Ándrôniüs clasped his hands together, his eyes thoughtful. "As you know, Ethan, you are to learn a spell. So, I have brought a spell book for you to peruse tonight. Please pick one that interests you, and we will begin working on it. Áelfwînë will also aid in your training, among other warriors who are among the most esteemed instructors at the Grand Barracks."

Setting the proffered book to the side, Ethan glanced over at the prone form of Áelfwînë still snoring loudly, sprawled out on the floor. "Áelfwînë? If he can't handle his liquor, what makes you think I should trust him? Let alone let him teach me how to be a warrior?"

His face softening with empathy, Ándrôniüs said, "Do not judge a book by its cover. That man has seen many battles. He lost his brother in Áethelwûlf. He is grieving. Once he has a purpose in teaching, not only you, but Ryan and Jake as well, he will find his strength. I will also help in the development of your magic. We will make a mage of you yet."

"Wait!" Ryan said, astonished. "They were brothers?"

"Half," Ándrôniüs said. "Yet their bond was stronger than most full-blooded siblings. From birth, to the academy, then the military, and now as part of my personal guard; they've never been apart, except once... for a very long time, but that is a story for another time."

"That makes me feel even worse for him... for his loss," Emily said in a somber tone.

"Indeed, it is tragic," Ándrôniüs replied. "But such is the way of life... we can only move forward." He turned to Ethan. "Now then, do you believe you're ready for the task?"

"Again, how do you know if I even have that kind of power?" Ethan exclaimed, disbelief coloring his tone. "There's no such thing where I come from. It's all just myths," he added.

"A myth?" Ándrôniüs scoffed, his voice rising in indignation. "A myth... ugh! Humans and their small minds, always dismissing what they don't understand." He waved it off, clearly fighting the urge to dive deeper into the subject, as he often did with discussions.

Ryan, trying to ease the tension, spoke up. "We get that there's magic here, Ándrôniüs. We've seen it with our own eyes. But where we come from, it's all just fairy tales and legends."

Ándrôniüs nodded, his demeanor calming. "Indeed, there are many mages here, and as you said, magic is very real. It flows in the veins of us mages and even the likes of some men. They could all use it if they tried, but here, men think that men who wield magic are evil, and they are wary of our involvement in certain aspects of life. Though that does not stop them from calling every time hordes of gorlocks, goblins, orcs, and all manner of other beasts from Khạrzọnọv come to plague their lands. Again, I'm sorry I have digressed. However," he said, pausing, the room falling silent except for the crackling of the fire and Áelfwînë's snores. "Ethan, I have been studying each of you since you arrived. And that is why—"

"Studying us? Are we some sort of experiment to you?" Ethan

cut him off, frustration bubbling to the surface.

"In some ways, yes... well... *hmm*. Let's not go down that road tonight," Ándrôniüs said, waving the thought away. "Nevertheless, yes, I believe your veins specifically carry magic. I've noticed things about you that give me the smallest inclination that you may be like us."

Ethan frowned, his confusion evident. "Like you? I'm not special. I'm just a human from Utah, not wherever your kind comes from."

"If you say so," Ándrôniüs replied, with a hint of amusement in his voice. "Nevertheless, we will train you. All of you."

Emily interjected, her voice trembling slightly. "Erm, what about me?"

"Oh yes, Emily, you too," Ándrôniüs said. "I've brought the best glimmer gremlin hunter in all of Cáelunárra here to teach you, starting tomorrow. You'll learn how to avoid, sneak, protect yourself, and retrieve the Goblet of Îgnîs Sápíëntíá, an immensely important relic. Órynë will be quite distraught if you do not retrieve it. He had such a fit the other night when I requested it to be used," he added with a chuckle, recalling the memory.

Emily pulled her blanket up to her neck, her voice barely a whisper. "Alright."

Ándrôniüs stood up, stretching his arms. "That is enough for now. Return to your rooms when you're ready. I'll sober up Áelfwînë and return him to the inn. Tomorrow, we will have a breakfast feast before we head to the Coliseum for the opening ceremony, marking the beginning of your tests."

He walked over to Áelfwînë and called out, "Elârâ, could you assist me in returning Áelfwînë to his accommodation at The Wobbly Cock?"

Jake, Ryan, and Ethan glanced at each other and began sniggering. Emily rolled her eyes at their immaturity.

Elârâ paying no attention to them, she walked over and said. "Of course."

Ándrôniüs turned to the group. "Good night, children."

He and Elârâ helped Áelfwînë up and led him out the door, disappearing into the rainy night.

Ethan watched them go, then turned to his friends. "Well, I guess this is goodnight, everyone. Get some sleep. If you can."

They all nodded and made their way toward their quarters, hoping for a few hours of rest before the trials to come in the morning.

Ethan ensured that all his friends reached their dorms before shutting his door, only to remember the spell book he had forgotten in the hall. Silently, he reopened his door and crept down the corridor. The hall was dim, lit only by the flames of the wall sconces.

He spotted the book on the end table where he had left it. Quickly, he grabbed it and examined the cover. *The Mage's Arsenal: Fundamentals of Battle Magic* by Draénôr Jangthôrn was inscribed on the cover in elaborate script. The ornate stitching of bronze depicted a staff engulfed in flames on a black field. Intrigued, he opened it to the first page, where a table of contents listed the spells and incantations.

The author divided the book into three sections: one for wands, one for staffs, and one for wandless magic. As Ethan walked back to his quarters, he mused that wandless magic might be the best option. He would likely wield a sword or some other weapon, possibly even wearing heavy armor, and didn't want to be encumbered by a staff or wand.

Deep in thought, he turned to the section on wandless magic. Just as he passed through the archway to the dormitories, he collided with someone. The impact sent him stumbling backward, his book flying.

Emily hit the floor, bursting into laughter. Ethan lay next to her, momentarily stunned by the collision.

Her laughter was contagious, and despite himself, Ethan chuckled too.

"Are you okay?" she managed between giggles.

"Yeah, that's my fault," Ethan admitted, still a bit dazed. "I lost myself in a book."

"A book?" Emily said, surprise flickering in her voice. "Never thought I'd see the day, or hear those words come out of your mouth."

With a playful grin, she rolled over and straddled Ethan, her eyes locking onto his. He was captivated for a moment, lost in the brilliance of her green eyes; something stirred deep within him in the quiet stillness between them. Emily smiled, brushing a loose strand of hair behind her ear. Ethan mirrored the gesture with a soft smile of his own. Then, slowly, she leaned down and kissed him; her lips warm and deliberate. At first, he didn't mind it. Her lips pressed against his, and all the while, his heart fluttered uncontrollably.

They broke apart for a breath, Emily lifting herself just enough to look him straight in the eyes. She leaned in with a sudden spark of boldness and caught his bottom lip lightly between her teeth before letting it slip free.

"Wow," Ethan said, stunned, his voice unsteady. "What was that for?"

"'Cause," she replied, the word barely above a whisper, her confidence flickering and returning all at once. She hesitated only a moment before leaning in again; their lips met in a deeper, breathless kiss that caught Ethan completely off guard. For a heartbeat, neither of them moved. Suspended between instinct and uncertainty, the moment drew them further in. Emily felt everything she had been holding back over the years pouring to the surface, long-buried feelings pushing past every wall she had kept in place.

Ethan froze beneath the intensity of it, overwhelmed by something new rising inside of him, something he had never felt before with her and could not move. The world narrowed around them, carried by emotions they had never known could be this charged between them. They continued locked in place in a passionate embrace until the image of Hannah appeared in his mind. He opened his eyes, and it was Emily.

Ethan, startled by this, pushed her off of him, causing her to tumble across the floor again.

"*Woah!*" he exclaimed.

Ethan's reaction took Emily aback, confused and embarrassed. "What? Am I not good enough for you?" she asked in a slightly abrasive tone.

Ethan stammered, "No... I... I mean, you are beautiful... I mean, I don't... I'm not sure how I feel about this... see you took me by surprise... wait, wait, wait, wait! Emily, don't be... *Ughhh.*" The sound of her door cut his words off, slamming as he backed away, flustered.

Jake and Ryan opened their doors, yawning as they looked at Ethan, who was picking up his book from the floor near his door.

"What was that about?" Jake asked, rubbing his eyes.

Ethan, still confused, replied, "I'm not sure... I don't even want to talk about it, guys." Ducking his head, he retreated to his quarters, closing the door behind him quickly.

Ryan patted Jake on the shoulder. "Shouldn't you be meeting someone?"

"Who?" Jake said, his face completely plastered with the look of someone confused, as if he was missing the point of Ryan's question.

"Elârâ?" Ryan questioned, wondering if the two had cancelled their plans.

Jake's eyes flew open. He disappeared into his room in a flash. Only moments later did he appear, his clothing all askew as he fiddled with it trying to adjust them in a sense of order, though he had totally forgotten about his and her date that evening, as he left in a frenzy.

"Thanks, Ryan!" Jake called out from down the hallway as he disappeared around the edge of the doorway.

Ryan smiled and returned to his room to find the backs of his eyelids.

Inside another one of the many rooms in the hallway, another sat utterly perplexed. What had just happened puzzled Ethan. Emily had never made an advance on him before, so why now? They had never been particularly close, and he had always thought she was repulsed by him. And what about Hannah? What if Emily twisted this interaction in some way, ruining his chances with Hannah? His mind started swirling with the possibilities.

"Shut up!" he yelled out loud, smacking his face to stop his thoughts from spiraling.

Certain he wouldn't be able to sleep just yet, Ethan distracted himself by reading the spell book. Climbing into bed, he covered himself with the wool blanket and opened the book, its old, creaking spine protesting slightly as he flicked through the thick parchment pages. He scanned the titles, mentally noting each one as he passed.

"Blaze of Embers," he whispered to himself as his eyes moved over the text. A spell designed to conjure a small burst of flames. He considered it for a moment, but moved on.

"Iron Skin," he muttered, which promised to harden the skin into an impenetrable armor. It was tempting, but it didn't feel right.

He flipped to another page. "Lightning's Wrath." It sounded powerful, but something about it felt too advanced for him right now.

He kept searching. A spell called "Shadowbind" caught his attention. He paused, intrigued, before ultimately turning the page.

Finally, he landed on a spell that held his attention: "Soulrend." The name alone sent a shiver down his spine. He started reading the description quietly, almost as if he didn't want the walls to hear.

"Soulrend: A spell of immense power, it channels the caster's energy into a concentrated attack that strikes at the very essence of the target, causing severe internal damage that can be lethal if unchecked. Use with caution; this spell requires great focus, and improper use can leave the caster incapacitated, or even dead."

Ethan hesitated, his eyes lingering on the text. This one felt different, more dangerous than the others. He could almost feel the power of the spell emanating from the page, calling to him.

Dimly, he heard something else calling to him. A voice in his mind. The one he had been fighting since their arrival. The one he had been ignoring. Angry thoughts welled up in him. He slapped his face a little, trying to chase away what he now hoped was his conscience wandering, and not the indiscriminate voice that hid away in the depths of his mind urging him to do unspeakable things.

After a long while of wrestling with it, getting control over it and it subsiding, he looked back at the page of the book and, after a moment of consideration, carefully folded the corner of the page, marking it for later.

Ethan studied the incantation on the page; it was in a language he did not know or understand, although its lettering was similar to what he was used to. Somehow, it made sense to him as his eyes carefully traced each word... trying to grasp the intricacies of the spell. "Sárrícírreân ôhr gô líscënâttén." The description of Soulrend lingered in his mind; its potential power enveloped him. He imagined what it would feel like to wield such a force, to channel that energy and unleash it against an enemy.

The thought was both invigorating and unsettling. He could almost see the spell in action, the way it would reach into the core of a foe, causing immense pain and damage. It was a power that demanded respect and caution. Ethan contemplated the implications of using such a spell, the responsibility that came with it, and the risks it posed; not just to the enemy, but to himself, as the description made clear.

He let the words echo in his mind, turning them over as he considered the kind of mage he wanted to become, if such a thing proved possible. He would return to Soulrend when he was ready, and when Ándrôniüs asked him what spell he wanted to learn. For now, he allowed the book to rest in his lap, his mind still running with illimitable thoughts of the spell.

# A Visitor in the Night

DARKNESS CLOSED IN AROUND him. It swirled like a living storm, dense and choking, folding over itself until the world vanished in a crush of black. The air thinned. An endless void in the pits of hell consumed him. Then he saw it. A pinpoint dot on the horizon, dissimilar to the darkness surrounding him. He chased after it as it moved closer. Then, with a rapid thrust forward, it made progress toward him. He blinked only once. Then light, sudden and blinding. The memory hit without warning. He was back on the plane. The cabin lights strobing violently as his friends screamed, their voices drowned out by the roar of engines failing. Rain lashed against the windows, blurring the outside world into a chaotic smear. Lightning flashed—again and again—painting ghostly images of desperation across the surrounding faces. The aircraft shuddered violently, dropping altitude in a sickening spiral as overhead bins burst open, flinging debris into the aisle. Alarms wailed. Oxygen masks dropped. Someone shouted his name. And then the plane tore apart. A deafening screech of metal filled the air as the fuselage cracked, splitting in two. Cold air rushed in, stealing the breath from his lungs. Gravity lost all meaning. And then came the ocean. A violent slam. The crushing black. Silence.

Ethan jolted upright, gasping for air. His chest heaved as if he'd been underwater. His heart pounded against his ribs, his shirt clinging to him with sweat. Cool night air brushed against his skin, but it did little to soothe the trembling in his limbs. He sat there frozen, struggling to separate the nightmare from reality.

He ran a hand over his face and then through his damp hair, trying to ground himself in the present. The room was dimly lit, a lantern on the nearby table casting shadows along the stone walls as the cool breeze slipped through the cracked window, rustling the edge of the curtain. He scanned the room in disoriented confusion, half-expecting someone to be there. But he was alone.

The others were likely still asleep, unaware of the storm that had just crashed through his dreams. He exhaled slowly, shaking his head in frustration as his heart settled. With a last glance toward the door, he lay back down, the mattress still warm beneath him, and stared up at the ceiling, trying to coax sleep to return at whatever hour it now was.

In the night's stillness, Ethan could not fall back to sleep; the images of that fateful day played over and over in his mind. He lay awake, restless. His mind shifted from his dreams to the events of the day, playing over and over in his mind, and that voice, that familiar voice. He stirred some more. He knew the bed was more than comfortable; the pillows were soft but just firm enough; even the blankets were weighted just right, not too heavy, not too light.

Yet, sleep did not come. He tossed and turned relentlessly.

He sat up in his bed once more, surveying the room. A yawn escaped his mouth, and he ruffled his hair. The only sound was the singular flame crackling inside a lantern on the desk. Standing up, he found the floor of his quarters cool. He hesitated for a moment before committing to leaving his bed. With a thrust of his knees, he stood.

He made his way to his desk, his legs popping with each step. With a firm grasp, he pulled the chair out. Another yawn escaped his mouth as he stretched his arms toward the ceiling. Glancing around, he saw the book the old mage had given him sitting on the wooden desktop. He rolled his eyes and pushed it further up, having no desire to read at this hour.

His mind wandered, and he found himself thinking back to the market. While the entire ordeal in the alleyway was awful, his mind always returned to the stranger from the shadows.

*Why did that voice sound familiar? How could it be familiar?*

Trying to put the issue from his mind, Ethan let his gaze meander around the dimly lit room.

Flickering haphazardly within the lantern, the flame began to spit and hiss as if something possessed it. Ethan became caught up in its dance and then heard the pesky voice in his head again. But this time it was audible, slithering around the room.

"I see you, my son," it hissed.

"Huh?" Ethan said, looking around, trying to see whence the voice came.

"In the fire, my boy. I'm in the flame. Look at the flame!" it beckoned to him.

"In the flame?" Ethan questioned, scratching his head, feeling his limbs growing heavy and his mind fogging over until all he could think was to obey the voice.

"Yes, in the flame, you fool!"

Ethan turned to face it. He narrowed his eyes, certain he had glimpsed something within. Not the lantern itself, but within the mesmerizing sway of the flame. He shook his head hard and rubbed his eyes. He blinked once, then again, and leaned closer, hoping he wasn't imagining shapes born of fatigue at this late hour. Yet there it was: a distinct personage taking form within the fire.

"What are you doing in there?" Ethan asked.

"Look here, boy, just listen to me. There is something I need you to do. Something important that will change the course of history. You are the only one who can complete this task," it said, its tone becoming more hypnotic the longer it spoke.

Ethan looked deeper into the flame and saw a man with long blond hair cascading down either side of his shoulders and a silver mask adorning his face. Black shrouded him as he sat on an obsidian throne surrounded by fire.

"I remember you. I saw you yesterday in the alley at the market, right? And your voice, it's familiar," Ethan said, his voice sounding distant to his own ears and his focus slipping as he lost track of what the figure in the flame was trying to ask him.

"My boy, pay attention. Can you do this task for me?"

"You never told me what it is you want—" Ethan was saying when his door opened.

"Who are you talking to, Ethan?" Ándrôniüs said softly as he entered the room and shut the door quietly. Fine black linen clothed him, with a white sash around his waist.

"Nobody!" Ethan exclaimed firmly as he stood up in his chair, the fog fading from his mind. Unsure of what had happened, he knew that even in this world, hearing voices would likely be seen as crazy, and he didn't want to cause trouble unnecessarily. "I must have fallen asleep in the chair and been talking in my sleep."

"Well, then... keep your secrets," the mage said as he walked over to Ethan's bed and sat on it. "I came to discuss urgent matters. I haven't been able to find one minute of rest this night. My mind races much like yours, I presume. A lot has happened in one short day. The deliberations by the High Mage Council, telling you of your tests, and then the separation that was dispassionately pushed upon you five by them, not me. All that coupled with the memories of my past seems to haunt me tonight."

Ethan took a seat back in the chair. He looked back at the lantern, seeking the man within. There was no one, so he turned to look at Ándrôniüs, puzzled. "Why are you here?"

"Ancülí. He is the reason I am here." The mage said with a stern expression, his face cold and devoid of any emotion.

"What about him?" Still unsure why this late-night visit was necessary, Ethan asked.

"You said that you encountered him at the market. You must tell me everything. From before you met him to when he left," Ándrôniüs demanded, walking to the window so he could look out upon the city.

"Why should I tell you anything, Ándrôniüs? You never tell us anything," Ethan said, standing up.

"I do not have time to assuage your ego. I say again, you must tell me everything," the mage said, turning to face Ethan.

"I think it's best if you leave my room," Ethan said, pointing toward the door.

"I won't ask again, Ethan."

Ethan went to take a step toward the door when Ándrôniüs threw his arms up, and a blast of white light sealed off the room. Ethan grabbed at the door handle and began shaking it, but the door would not budge.

"Help!" Ethan screamed. "Anyone! Somebody! Help!"

"They will not hear you, my boy," Ándrôniüs said, walking back over to the bed.

"Let me out this instance, you old fool!" Ethan screamed.

"Ethan, this is your last chance," he said, oddly calm.

"You can't just lock me in here," Ethan yelled as he lunged forward, fists balled up.

Ándrôniüs side-stepped, sticking out his leg and tripping the boy. Ethan crashed into the side of his bed. "Ethan, stop this. I'm not here to hurt you. I'm here simply to clear up anything that may have happened."

"No!" Ethan said, pushing himself to his knees.

"If you refuse to speak freely, I'll be compelled to take matters into my own hands," the mage said, kneeling down.

"Help!" Ethan screamed one last time, scrambling away from the mage but finding himself cornered against the wall.

Ándrôniüs pressed his hand against Ethan's forehead, and a bright blue light filled the room. Ethan froze, then went limp. With the magic that Ándrôniüs possessed, he lifted the boy into the air, the boy's body dangling in front of him. With one hand, he pressed against the boy's right temple, mimicking the action with his other hand as he muttered under his breath.

"Achlàmen Ythráiál Ophtálinen."

A bright yellow light, warm and inviting, filled the room. The old mage lurched back, his eyes rolling back into his head, his mouth foaming, as he let out a loud scream. He floated upward, lifeless, much like Ethan. They were both suspended in the air for a moment before tumbling to the floor.

In his mind, Ándrôniüs drifted forward, as if flying through an infinite abyss. A brilliant, consuming light appeared, overtaking everything in blinding whiteness.

In the next instant, something unfolded before him, and he hovered as an unseen observer. He had never seen this place, but that did not bother him. He fixed his attention on the people before him. Then he saw it: a man in the room, standing like a memory half-forgotten. Unfamiliar, yet unmistakably known. The middle aged man was holding the hand of a wailing woman. Then a third; a person cloaked in a mask of fabric, a funny hat, and clothes that were blue-green in color, emerged from beneath a linen, holding a baby.

He had barely registered the scene before something thrust him forward again. The man from the vision lay over a casket, desperately clinging to it as it lowered into the ground. A little boy dressed in black stood at his side, sad but not fully understanding what was occurring.

Again, Ándrôniüs was pulled forward, stopping on the floor beside the boy as he cried and cringed away while the room around him was devolving into madness: pounding, the breaking of wood, the sound of fists against walls, and yowling. Then the boy was ripped out from under the bed. His perspective shifted, and Ándrôniüs saw the resulting devastation. From his perch in the room's cornice, he was silently forced to see the boy being beaten by the man. The boy cowered but did not shed a tear as every lash of a belt met his backside.

Just as the boy turned to fight back, unable to bear any more, a force propelled Ándrôniüs forward once again, out of the house and into the night sky. He floated aimlessly, then immense speed hurled him toward the ground. Right as he almost made contact, a light brighter than he could even comprehend overtook him. Then, a warm feeling, as if he was going to be okay, arose in his stomach. With hyper-vision, he saw another moment rise before him: a tender moment by a lake. It was two people he recognized, Hannah and Ethan, sharing a tender kiss under the moonlight.

As he began to understand these visions, that this was Ethan, and the life he came from. Ándrôniüs then saw the plane crash. Being thrust forward once more, he finally found himself in the scene in the alley.

He observed the two degenerates as they blocked the way, a dagger waving through the air. As Hannah was nearly stripped of her womanhood, Ethan fought back. Then, a mask he recognized. The silver mask of Ancülí, cloaked in darkness. The warning given to Ethan and Hannah about his return. Ethan, covered in excrement and his blood, struggling to clear his vision, saw little of what unfolded. Hannah, however, truly saw the visage of Ancülí.

She had lied to him about the encounter.

*But why?* He thought to himself.

Then, just as fast as it all started, he clattered back into his lifeless form in Ethan's quarters, letting out a loud gasp. Ándrôniüs stood up, his legs shaky, nearly unable to support his body. Ethan began whimpering, curling into the fetal position.

"I'm sorry. Please accept my deepest apologies for the trouble I caused. I didn't know," Ándrôniüs said, struggling to maintain his balance as he propped himself up on the side of the bed.

Ethan's words were barely distinguishable. "Just leave me."

"Ethan, there is one more thing I must do. I promise you will not remember a thing."

Though Ethan yelled and pleaded for him to go, Ándrôniüs continued, still unsteady on his feet. Falling to his knees, Ándrôniüs crawled on all fours to the trembling Ethan. He pressed his shaky hand to the boy's chest, and a bright yellow light emitted from his hand.

Ándrôniüs said, "Achlàmen Ythráiál Ophtálinen Fínlïnántë." His tone was low, his voice trembling as he tried to maintain his composure.

Ethan went limp once more, his eyes glazing over. The mage, magic flowing through him once more, found his legs. He raised his hands, lifting Ethan from the ground. He placed him on the bed before allowing the magic to subside. The yellow light left with it. Ándrôniüs then tucked the covers around the boy.

The old mage took a deep breath inward, closing his eyes, grounding himself; steeling himself, even. "Anímáí Labyêsk," he said. It flowed off the tongue, but shallow, as tears ran down his face, his voice weak.

He kissed the boy's forehead and stood there for a moment, watching the lines fade from his features as his body settled into sleep.

"I truly am sorry for everything I put you through. Indirectly and directly."

Ándrôniüs walked to the door and whispered, "Încâttântä Vës Vrûth Elëmân," and a white mist rose from the corners of the room, absorbing into Ándrôniüs's hands. Grasping the doorknob, he turned it before glancing back one last time to where Ethan lay in the bed. Hanging his head, he left.

He walked softly and briskly through the Hall of Mages, one thing on his mind. With a swift raise of his hands, he pulled the hood of his cloak over his head, shrouding himself in darkness and secrets. He pressed firmly on the Hall of Mages doors, exiting the hall and finding himself in a light drizzle of rain.

Under his breath, he murmured, "There is one more memory that needs to be silenced this night."

Then the shadowy silhouette of the mage disappeared into the darkness of the streets of Vâloríâ.

# THE COLISEUM

As DAWN BROKE OVER Vâloríâ, the city was already buzzing with an unusual amount of activity. The streets, normally quiet at this hour, were alive with the sounds of townsfolk bustling along, all while the towers of the Hall of Mages continually emitted wafts of white smoke that drifted lazily through the city. The citizenry had gathered outside the hall once more, their chattering growing louder as they discussed the day's fast-approaching event. The clamor was so pronounced that it roused Ryan from his slumber.

Intrigued by the noise, Ryan sat up. The brief time he had spent in Vâloríâ had led him to expect mostly peaceful mornings marked by the tolling of city bells, the chirping of birds, and the mouth-watering aromas of breakfast being prepared in the kitchens down the hallway.

Stretching, he gingerly placed his feet on the cool floor below. He reached for his trousers. Ryan pulled them on and slipped into his shoes. Once tied, he grabbed a shirt, and made his way to the door. Beyond it, he found the hall quiet, save for the persistent hum of voices. He walked down the corridor, drawn toward the sound.

Reaching the common area, he found Elârâ meticulously setting the breakfast table. She wore her hair in an elegant waterfall braid, and a yellow dress that complemented her skin tone and eyes. She looked up as Ryan yawned.

"Well, good morning, Ryan. How did you sleep?" she asked with a warm smile.

Ryan finished his yawn and stretched again. "Halfway decent. And you?"

Elârâ, intent on her task, replied, "Quite fine, thank you."

Noticing Ryan's lingering presence, she added, "Breakfast won't be ready for another half hour."

"Sorry, I wasn't trying to rush," Ryan said, pausing as the noise outside seemed to rise. "What is going on out there?"

She straightened up and pointed toward the door. "That is the noise of the folk who have gathered from all over Eldôria."

Órynë, who had been making his way quietly down the stairs behind them, added, "Not just Eldôria. I hear that there are travelers from all corners of Âldâmûr, too. There are also rumors of dwarves traveling all the way from Brâldôr to cheer on their prince. Because of your unprecedented arrival, much of the continent is stirring, hoping to gaze upon the chosen with their own eyes."

He wore an elegant outfit for the day's events; his robes were richly colored and intricate.

Elârâ bowed and returned to her duties as the Grand Mage focused his attention on Ryan.

"You five are the talk of the realms. People have gathered to meet their champions," Órynë continued.

"Champions?" Ryan asked, his confusion evident. "I thought we were the chosen ones?"

"Champions... Chosen ones... it's really all the same," Órynë commented flippantly as he walked to the table and retrieved a glass of water and began sipping from it. He cleared his throat and continued. "However, if you aren't successful, you will be nothing but a smidgen of the hope that Cáelunárra so desperately longs to grasp. You like the others, will fade away as nothing more than a legend or tale. Some would even say no more than a whisper on the tides of time or a grain of sand in a sea of dunes." Órynë strode around the room as he spoke, eventually coming to place a hand on Ryan's shoulder.

Uncomfortable with the Grand Mage's touch and unsure of how to react, Ryan pulled away awkwardly, shivering slightly at Órynë's hand. "Uh... alright. No pressure on us, I guess?"

"None whatsoever," Órynë responded, maintaining eye contact with Ryan as he paused. He took a seat in one chair and gestured to the one beside him. "Come boy, sit with me."

Still uneasy with the mage's presence in the room, Ryan reluctantly made his way to the chair Órynë had indicated so as not to be rude to the leader of the republic.

The Grand Mage crossed his legs and folded his arms. "Now, tell me, how did you five get to this land?" he asked, his face serious.

Hesitantly, Ryan lowered himself into the chair. "Ándróniüs didn't tell you?"

"Indeed, he did, but I want to hear it from you," Óryně replied.

Choosing his words carefully, Ryan summarized their journey to this new world. "Well, we had just graduated, and Ethan's dad Lucian was flying us to Fiji as a gift. We hit some turbulence and then crashed into the ocean. When we finally made it to land, we were here. It was kind of surreal."

Óryně's brows furrowed, his countenance darkening as he rose, towering over Ryan. "Likely story," he said, leaning down and planting his hands on the arms of the chair, his gaze piercing into the boy's eyes. "It seems to me that you all have very well-rehearsed stories."

From her place by the table, Elârâ watched the scene unfold, unsure if she should interfere or fetch someone to ease Ryan's nerves. Unmindful of her presence, Óryně continued, "Now tell me, where did you get the source of aétherium crystal to bring you here?"

His face beginning to sweat as Óryně's voice rose with each word, Ryan stammered, "I have no clue what you're talking about!"

Over the mage's shoulder, Ryan saw Elârâ leave the room hurriedly. He silently hoped she was getting help.

Unconvinced, Óryně kept pressing. "One of you must be magically gifted and exceptionally well-trained. You look not over twenty years of age. Other mages take hundreds of years to have that kind of power. Or is one of you of the lineage of the Olmâ? Tell me! Which one of you is conspiring with the Dark Lord?" he demanded, pounding his fist on the chair's arm before moving away, arms behind his back.

The Grand Mage seemed to teeter on the edge of coming

unhinged.

"I don't know what you're talking about, seriously!" Ryan pleaded, his voice trembling with fear and confusion. His gaze darted around the room, searching for some escape from the intense scrutiny and rising aggression of Órynë.

Órynë's face twisted, his eyes blazing with suspicion. "You will tell me everything, boy, or you and your friends will pay!" he shouted, his voice echoing ominously throughout the room.

As his fury mounted, the room seemed to darken, and the walls vibrated with an unsettling energy. The air congealed with a malevolent presence. It was suffocating and sickening. Ryan's chest tightened as he struggled to breathe, feeling the oppressive force closing in around him.

Taking a menacing step forward, the mage raised his hand as if to strike Ryan. Just as Óryně's hand descended, Ándrôniüs burst into the room, his presence like a beacon of light cutting through the darkness.

With lightning-like reflexes, Ándrôniüs caught Óryně's wrist mid-air, his grip unyielding. "You will not strike him, you fool," Ándrôniüs said, his voice steady and commanding.

The room seemed to respond to his authority, the vibrations ceasing and the darkness receding.

"Your mind. How did it come to be poisoned? You, above all, should know that if you show even the remotest weakness, the Dark Lord will lay a seed of doubt in you, and it will fester, like a gangrenous wound. You must hold your composure, my dear friend. Ryan and his friends are innocent of whatever your mind has conjured."

Óryně's eyes widened as if awakening from a trance. He blinked, the rage draining from his face, replaced by a look of horrified realization. Glancing around the room, he gazed upon the aftermath he had caused: books scattered across the floor, parchments floating and falling, china rattling, and the chandeliers above swaying dangerously. His gaze shifted to Ándrôniüs, his expression now one of deep shame.

Ándrôniüs released Óryně's wrist, but his gaze remained fixed upon him. "Regain your senses, my friend. We cannot afford to lose ourselves in fear. You especially of all people. These young ones are our hope, not our enemies."

The Grand Mage took a deep breath, his hands shaking. Órynë adjusted his now askew robes. "My apologies, Ryan," he said hoarsely, his voice barely above a whisper. "I... I fear I may have let my doubts get the better of me. Forgive me." He turned to Ándróniüs, his eyes filled with remorse. "Thank you, my friend, for stopping me. I will take my leave and prepare for the ceremony."

With a final, regretful glance at Ryan, Órynë exited the room, his steps unsteady but purposeful.

Ándróniüs placed a steadying hand on Ryan's shoulder, his eyes filled with reassurance. "Come now, Ryan, let's wake the others and get them ready themselves for the day," he said, his voice calm and composed. He gestured for the boy to follow him back to the corridor where the friends were staying. As they passed through the doorway, Ándróniüs glanced back, offering a nod of gratitude to Elârâ.

Elârâ winked back at him, a warm smile playing on her lips.

The shouting had awakened Emily, and she appeared at her door, still in her chemise, her face marred with concern, too afraid to leave her room. "Ryan? Ándróniüs? Did you two feel that shaking and hear all that shouting?" she asked, her voice wavering slightly.

Ryan opened his mouth to respond, but Ándróniüs interjected swiftly. "Best not to talk about it. Let us not cause a disturbance further than what has already come to pass." His gaze swept over the group now gathered in the corridor.

Ándróniüs's eyes made contact with Ethan's, whose frown betrayed his usual dissatisfaction with the mage's evasive answer. "Now, children, you all really must get ready for the day. Breakfast is nearly ready, and a ceremony awaits us."

With his final word, he turned on his heel and strode back through the hallway, leaving the group to ponder what they had missed.

Ethan, ever impatient, turned to Ryan. "What was all of that, Ryan? You surely can't keep that from us."

With a gentle squeeze of Ryan's hand, Emily continued. "Come into my room. All of us can talk about what happened."

Jake nodded in agreement. "Yeah, man, tell us."

Their calls for clarity pressed down on him, causing him to squirm. Ryan took a deep breath, trying to steady his nerves. "It's... nothing to worry about," he said, forcing a smile. "Let's just get ready. Ándrôniüs is right. We have a big day ahead of us."

He quickly retreated to his room, closing the door firmly behind him.

"Weird," Emily muttered as she turned to the others. "I guess we should do the same? He'll tell us when he is ready."

They exchanged knowing glances before turning back into their own rooms.

A few moments later, Ryan heard the sounds of doors opening and closing in the hallway from within his room. He could make out muffled voices, but the thick doors and polished stone walls obscured any specifics, leaving only distant muffled whispers of conversation. He changed into something more formal. Donning a pair of brown trousers, knee-high black boots, and a silky white tunic. Though he still felt uneasy, he made his way out of his room and into the hall.

An unequivocal feeling of dissatisfaction lingered in the air as he rejoined the group, all gathered together. Trying to ignore it, Ryan searched for anything to settle his anxiety. Gazing around the room, Ryan saw that, unsurprisingly, Jake focused on Elârâ as she continued her morning duty of setting the breakfast table.

Jake had donned his finest clothes, reserved for if they passed their tests. It was an elegant but casual ensemble: a dark green tunic with gold embroidery, a matching cloak, and finely tailored trousers.

Scanning the other side of the hall, Ryan sensed the uneasiness between Emily and Ethan as they sat far apart, not daring to make eye contact. Passingly, he noted Ethan wore a similar outfit to his, though in slightly different shades. Emily wore a dark yellow dress and pulled her hair into a neat bun.

Ethan was also looking about for a diversion, not wanting to invite conversation with Emily. Catching Ryan out of the corner of his eye, he waved him over, unknowingly mimicking Órynë's earlier actions. "Hey, Ryan, come over here."

Ryan hesitated, the memory of his confrontation with Órynë still fresh in his mind. After a few moments, he again reluctantly made his way to the chair beside Ethan.

Forcing a smile, Ryan said, "How are things with you?"

Emily, her nerves settling now that there was another person to talk to, squeezed herself into the conversation. She leaned forward, her eyes filled with concern. "Ryan, seriously, what happened this morning?"

"Yeah, you really should tell us," Ethan added eagerly.

Feeling the burden of their scrutiny on him, he scrambled to concoct a lie on the spot. "Oh, you see, Órynë was upset at some townsfolk for entering the hall. He lost his temper with them. It was quite a sight for sure! Even gave me a little fright. It most definitely explains why I was just too afraid to talk about things. The whole thing was just crazy! I mean, you guys saw me... think of how those poor people felt actually on the other end of his wrath!"

Ethan's eyes narrowed, his skepticism clear. "That's it?" he muttered. "It sure didn't seem like that was what he was yelling about."

Ryan maintained his forced smile. "Yeah... that's all it was. I promise."

Arching her eyebrows in disbelief, Emily said, "Seems fishy."

From across the room, Elârâ again sensed that Ryan needed another rescue of sorts. She turned her attention from Jake to him. "Ryan, do you want to help Jake and I grab the last things from the kitchen for breakfast?"

"Sure!" Ryan screamed.

Seeing that this was an opportunity to escape, Ryan quickly stood up and dodged further investigation by Ethan and Emily.

Elârâ, Jake, and Ryan passed through the doors of the hallway that led down to the kitchens just as Ísolde entered through the front doors of the hall. The crowd outside cheered even louder as they caught the faintest glimpse of the chosen within the hall's confines. The thunderous roar of excitement resonated through the stone halls.

Ísolde, dressed in a vibrant purple dress that flowed like a river of amethyst, made her way gracefully toward Emily and Ethan. As she approached, she lovingly squeezed Emily's shoulder and bent down to kiss Ethan on the head.

"Hello, you two," she said, her voice a soothing melody. "Where is everyone else?"

Rolling her eyes in her signature fashion, Emily said sarcastically, "Ryan is hiding away because of a racket that took place here this morning. He won't even tell us what happened. And Jake. See, your husband *demanded* that Ryan not tell us either." She paused, letting out a small chuckle. "He is too distracted by Elârâ to even know what is going on."

Ísolde responded gently, a smile beginning to cross her face. "Oh? Something happened to Ryan? I will make sure to ask my love later if he knows the details. And if it is relevant, I will share what I learn. Also, did I hear you mention something about Jake and the servant girl here? What of him and Elârâ?"

"Oh, he is just head over heels for her," Emily said with a turgid smirk on her lips.

"Yes, Elârâ is indeed a fine woman, and I can't blame Jake for his infatuation. She is one of the most beautiful and, importantly, *eligible* bachelorettes in the entire republic. Many High Mage families have their eyes on her as a match for their sons. Jake had better be careful. He may draw unnecessary attention to himself."

"I wouldn't worry. He doesn't know his head from his heels," Ethan quipped, earning a giggle from Emily.

Unamused, Ísolde admonished him. "Now, now, Ethan. He's your friend. If things turn sour, and they likely will, he'll need you. Especially considering it's forbidden in Eldôria for a mage and a human to be together. When her father finds out about this fondness brewing between them, he will surely put an end to it. Jake will need someone to confide in when that time comes. If it comes, of course."

Emily frowned. "Well, that's an unfortunate law," she said, Ethan nodding in agreement. "Where we're from, pretty much everyone can marry whoever they want."

Explaining further, Ísolde continued, "It isn't a written law, more a long-held custom. Even so, those who cling to the old ways keep it with strict devotion, her father among them. You see, there are other realms that allow it, though we the mages and the elves; do not. But here, though the mindsets of the elders are changing slowly, it'll be near impossible for Jake with her family and who they are."

Echoing her earlier sentiment, Emily restated, "Again, that's unfortunate."

Ísolde nodded gravely. "Yes, I understand that, but there are customs here that you must learn to navigate. Ignoring them could land you in the gallows, or worse, at the guillotine. I think it is prudent to pay attention to them. This is a new world vastly different from your own, so please be careful. All of you."

Just as Ísolde finished her remarks, Ándrôniüs made his way down the staircase. His attire comprised a long, flowing robe of deep blue, bedecked with elaborate silver embroidery. The high collar framed his wise, weathered face, and his staff, made of dark wood and topped with a glowing crystal, added to his imposing yet familiar appearance.

"Children, children!" he exclaimed, raising his arms happily. "Are we ready to feast on the delectable breakfast that has been prepared?"

Ethan looked up, confused. "The others haven't returned from the kitchen," he said.

Ándrôniüs smiled, a twinkle in his eye. "Well, let's hope your fighting is better than your eyes."

Unnoticed, Elârâ, Jake, and Ryan had returned with pitchers of drinks to complete the prepared meal, placing it on the table.

Ethan and Emily made their way to it, eager to sit among their friends and Elârâ. The food looked and smelled divine, a feast fit for royalty. Ándrôniüs made his way to Ísolde, embraced her, and they walked arm in arm to the head of the table where they took their seats.

They passed dishes around and across the table as they filled their plates.

Taking a bite of her toast, Emily flared her eyes at the flavor that greeted her tastebuds. Ethan nodded in agreement after he took a large bite from a melon of sorts. Ryan, per usual, was stuffing his face with all the sustenance that he could reach. His indulgence obviously meant it was more than acceptable to him. While Jake watched Elârâ intently, he ignored the food, drinks, and conversations at the table.

Ándrôniüs raised his glass of juice. "To our champions over the coming days, may you be victorious and your spirits strong."

He paused and took a very large gulp of the juice. Ándrôniüs then set his glass down and leaned forward, his expression serious. "Today is a day of immense importance. Today, we will open the games. After the opening ceremony, we will sequester you further. We will house Ethan, Jake, and Ryan at the Grand Barracks for their training. Emily, you will stay here and train with Lord Radcliffe from Âldâmûr."

Seeing the usual indignant look that seemed to be permanently marring Ethan's face whenever Ándrôniüs was present, the mage continued speaking before the boy could spout something in defiance of his words.

"Everything will work out as it's meant to. Remember, this separation is only temporary. After you complete your tests, we'll reunite you all here until the next phase of our journey begins. At the ceremony this morning, you will find out who goes first. We will announce the next participant after a successful attempt, and collect you sometime the following day."

A pessimistic voice rang out. "This is all unnecessary. All of it. We are not from this world. None of this should concern us. Ándrôniüs, we just want to go home. I am not even sure we can do everything you are asking of us with the little time we have to get ready. What makes you so confident that we are going to survive?" Ethan asked. The others nodded in agreement, their quiet mutters of doubt reinforcing his concern.

Ándrôniüs met their gazes unwaveringly. "I sure hope you four are better at facing these tests than your utilization of your ears. As I have repeatedly said since the very beginning, I know you can do this because I've been watching you. You are all stronger than you'll ever know. I am putting all my faith in you, and so are all the people beyond these walls. I have no doubt you are our champions, as Órynë conveyed this morning."

Ryan's emotions spiked at the Grand Mage's name, and his brow furrowed at hearing Ándrôniüs use of the word champion. "How? Wait, a minute... you weren't there!"

With an enigmatic smile, Ándrôniüs said, "I am everywhere, while being nowhere at the same time, Ryan. And you all should start accepting this."

Emily shivered slightly. "Ándrôniüs, that is downright creepy."

Ándrôniüs's demeanor shifted from solemn to mirthful in an instant. "Indeed, it is, isn't it, Emily? Now! Shall we make our way to the great Coliseum of Vâloríâ?"

They all shrugged their shoulders in varying ways of approval, though still very wary of his and others' belief in their abilities.

At his words, they all stood and attempted to help clean; however, Ándrôniüs stopped them with a wave. "No need for that. Elârâ, would you and the servants mind handling this?"

Elârâ nodded, smiling warmly. "Of course."

In his haste, Jake fumbled as he passed the plates in his hands into Elârâ's arms. She almost lost them, but he caught the stack of plates that began to slip from her grasp, their skin touching momentarily and his face blushing.

Before turning away, Elârâ gave him a sweet smile. "Thank you, Jake."

Ethan smacked Jake on the back of the head playfully. "Enough, man. Leave the poor girl alone. Let's go. There will be time to talk to her later."

On the way out the door, Jake couldn't resist one last glance at the girl he had become very fond of. Their eyes met, and she smiled, turning bright red before hustling away.

Once the doors closed behind them, the sight of thousands of people in the streets, whistling, confronted the group talking, cheering, throwing flowers, rice, and all manner of trinkets into the air, and displaying an overall expression of gratitude. A joyful riot of color and sound filled the streets;

Banners and pennants fluttering in the breeze lined the path from the Hall of Mages to the Coliseum. The cobblestone streets gleamed underfoot, washed clean by the night's rain. The ancient stone buildings towered majestically on either side of their path.

With the sun shining brightly, a warm glow enveloped the scene, enhancing its vibrant colors.

As they approached the Coliseum, its grandeur became apparent. The Coliseum was an architectural marvel, a testament to the skill and artistry of Vâloríâ's builders. White marble walls, sparkling in the sunlight and lined with statues of legendary heroes and intricate mosaics, towered over them. The massive gates, wrought iron and gilded with gold, stood open, welcoming all with open arms.

Inside the Coliseum, it was even more impressive. The arena floor was nearly a perfect circle, the only imperfection being a raised podium that jutted out into the arena. From this spot, the Grand Mage or others in charge would preside over the events of the coming days. Tiered seating rose high into the sky, each level decorated with colorful banners representing the different realms present: Eldôria, Âldâmûr, Brâldôr, and Illithría.

Áelfwînë greeted them at the entrance, roughly twenty other guards in traditional Vâloríân ceremonial armor made of polished silver standing behind him. He escorted the group to the High Mage seating area, where five thrones awaited them. Each throne was a masterpiece of craftsmanship, made of dark wood and inlaid with precious gems. Master artisans enriched the thrones with detailed carvings of mythical creatures and cushioned them with rich velvet fabrics in deep, regal colors.

The Grand Mage and several other High Mages were already occupying the other seats behind the thrones.

Hannah was already there, standing on the far side of the thrones, and looking every bit the picture of beauty. She wore a flowing silk gown the color of fresh snow and embroidered with silver threads that formed the image of the great tree of Illithría on the skirt. Her long blonde hair cascaded down her back, framing her delicate features. Her light blue eyes sparkled in the sunlight. Two guards flanked her, their long, silvery-white hair and pointed ears marking them as unmistakably elven. Their pasty white skin and light blue and green eyes gave them a paradisiacal appearance. They also wore silky white clothing with the great tree of Illithría.

Hannah moved to approach her friends, but the guards leaned down and whispered in her ears, cutting her off from her attempted conversation.

Ísolde pulled Ethan back as Óryně, his elegant staff in hand, stood up and approached the podium just as Ethan was about to confront the guards and talk to Hannah.

"Today, we gather as citizens from Eldória," he began, his voice echoing through the Coliseum. The crowd erupted in cheers. "From Áldâmûr," he continued, and the cheers grew louder. "Brâldôr," he called, and the clanging of metal joined the cheers. "And Illithría," Óryně said, a more reverent clapping ensuing. "Our reclusive friends from the Blackmire Marsh are yet in their realm, hiding away, but they are here in spirit nonetheless, so says the Lýëch Queen in this letter."

He paused and held up a piece of parchment, then continued, "Today, we gather to commence the tests for our champions and cheer them to victory in this Coliseum, so that we may begin the war against the Dark Lord and seize our lands back from his oppressive grip and end the genocides he commits against our peoples."

The crowds cheering once more reached a fever pitch.

Óryně let the cheers subside before continuing. "First, we have Hannah," he announced. Hannah stepped forward, and the elves respectfully applauded. "She will have the week to learn the elven language and recite it to us." She took her place on the farthest throne away, escorted by her elven guards.

In the background, behind the thrones, a bushy-bearded individual chuckled. "Well, we best head back to Brâldôr now; the elven tongue ain't for the faint of heart," he said, meeting Ándrôniüs's eyes before simmering down as the mage shot him a penetrating glare.

Óryně continued, "We have Ryan, who will fight the Prince of Brâldôr." He pointed toward the man in armor who had just spoken.

Ándrôniüs gestured for Ryan to stand up and meet the prince at the podium with the Grand Mage. Both the prince and Ryan appeared at the same time. The two locked eyes, Ryan's kind, but the prince's full of malice at the sight of his opponent. The Prince of Brâldôr's last act before exiting the stage was to spit on the ground, near Ryan's feet. Then he thundered from the podium and left the Coliseum. Deciding not to play into that spectacle, Órynë instructed the boy to take his place upon the throne next to Hannah.

"We have Jake, who will fight the fearsome dracónyx." Órynë paused, waiting as Jake took the seat next to Ryan. "And Emily, who will enter the den of a glimmer gremlin and retrieve the precious Goblet of Îgnîs Sápíëntíá."

Emily took her throne next to Jake.

"And finally, Ethan will face a gorlock, which we caught terrorizing our lands, which we imprisoned in our dungeons for five summers, and who will now face its judgment."

Ethan took his place next to the others on the remaining throne as the crowd roared in approval.

Órynë clapped along with the crowd. "Tomorrow, we will watch Emily try to outsmart and outwit the cunning and ever so sly, glimmer gremlin! For tomorrow, the tests begin!"

The crowd's roar grew even louder, shaking the very foundations of the Coliseum. The echoes became almost deafening, a powerful symphony of support. Beautiful flowers started raining down from the highest tiers, covering the floor of the Coliseum in a vibrant, fragrant carpet. The people of Cáelunárra, in a collective expression of hope and approval, showered the five champions with their blessings, hailing them as the hopeful saviors of their land.

With a downward motion of his arms, Órynë hushed the crowd. "On that note, let us enjoy the games prepared for us this day. We have the legendary fighters of Thǔczǒjle, hailing from beyond the elven realm across the Ídëní. And their counterparts, the Sinister Seven from Nǔnǔmběycz, who will join them on the arena floor. May these foreign personages, who have so graciously journeyed from afar for our revelry, entertain us completely."

The ceremony and the games that followed went well past the lunch hour, and on until the sun started its descent toward the horizon, and the entire Coliseum floor was dancing in the flames of the torches that lined its walls. As the festivities concluded, Óryně's last words, outlining the succession of events for the coming week, echoed powerfully throughout the Coliseum. The crowd's cheers gradually died down, and the people dispersed.

The elven guards standing beside Hannah wasted no time. With a firm yet gentle grip on her arms, they escorted her away, moving swiftly through the throngs of people.

Ethan's heart pounded in his chest as he watched Hannah being led away. Urgency surged through him, and he fought against the tide of people surrounding him.

"Hannah!" he shouted, his voice filled with desperation as he tried to push through the dense crowd.

Bodies jostled him from all sides, and despite his best efforts, he could only catch fleeting glimpses of her as the elves swept her further away.

The crowd was too dense. The noise drowned out his calls, and the masses of onlookers quickly hid Hannah and the elven guards from view.

"Ethan, stop!" Ándrôniüs's voice cut through the commotion as he grabbed Ethan's arm, pulling him back toward the group. His grip was firm, but there was a glint of understanding in his eyes.

"We must not thwart what has already been set in motion," Ándrôniüs said, his tone both gentle and commanding. "The prophecy depends on it, just as each of your paths will diverge as the days press on."

Ethan's frustration and anger were apparent on his face. He tore his arm away from Ándrôniüs, flushed with indignation. "It's not fair!" he snapped. "She's our friend! She deserves to be with us during this time, not alone and scared with some elves we don't even know."

Emily, standing nearby, crossed her arms and gave Ethan a livid glare. "I'm going to be alone too, Ethan. Are you going to do anything to help me stay with you guys?" Her voice was tinged with frustration.

Turning to Emily, Ethan's expression softened, though it remained edged with frustration. "That's different, Emily," he replied, but his voice lacked the conviction he had intended.

"With Hannah... it's different."

Unimpressed by his response, Emily raised an eyebrow. "Different how? Because you're infatuated to a sickly level with her? Well, guess what, Ethan? We're all worried, we're all scared, and we're all going to be separated in some way."

As Emily's caustic remark hung in the air, Ethan's discontent was clear in his expression.

"Emily, you're my friend too," he began, his voice tinged with a mix of confusion and defensiveness. "But this... this is different. I can't explain it, okay? It feels different with Hannah. I can't shake it. It's not about you or anyone else; it's just... different somehow."

Emily's face contorted at his words. "There is no difference, Ethan. Wake up! We're all tired of your obsession with her. Right here, right now, we are all equal. We've always been equal. You place her on this pedestal like she's some goddess. Its disgusting Ethan. And news flash: she's not. She's no better than any of us." As she continued, her voice softened slightly. "We all care about each other in our own way, but you need to knock this off. *Seriously,* just grow up!"

Jake interjected, trying to stem the eruption of emotion between the two friends. "Ethan, it's alright. We don't have to understand everything right now. We just need to trust the process, even if it means we're distanced for a time. This was inevitable. Here, or back home!"

Ethan sighed, his shoulders slumping as he ran a hand through his hair. "I know, I know," he muttered, his voice low. "It's just... I don't know how to explain it. It's like this gnawing feeling in my gut, like I'm going to lose her, and I can't ignore it." His gaze dropped to the floor, the weight of his emotions pressing heavily on him.

"That would be to the benefit of us all," Emily snarled under her breath, rolling her eyes, her annoyance still evident.

Ándrôniüs, who had been quietly observing the interaction, stepped forward and placed a hand on Ethan's shoulder. "Ethan, your feelings are not unfounded. They're part of your journey, their journey, and most importantly, our journey. But remember, everyone has their role to play, including you. The Allfather has a plan. Whatever you're feeling, it's part of the trial you must face.

The Allfather wants you to trust in him. There will be things that happen to you or others that you won't agree with, but you must respect those decisions and their outcomes."

Ethan looked at Ándrôniüs, his frustration slowly giving way to resignation, though the worry still lingered. "Alright," he mumbled, more to himself than anyone else. "I'll try."

Feeling she might have overstepped, Emily approached Ethan hesitantly. Still uncertain, she wrapped her arms around him.

"We'll get through this, Ethan. All of us. Even if we don't completely understand it now."

Ethan took a deep breath, nodded, and gave one last look to where they'd taken Hannah. "Yeah... I guess we will."

Ándrôniüs spoke up, his voice calm yet insistent. "My friends, we must head to the Grand Barracks, where you boys will receive your training. I promise you I will be there every day to guide you through it. I will not abandon you."

Ethan, still grappling with the whirlwind of events, nodded slowly. "Sure, let's go," he said, his shoulders slumping.

# THE GRAND BARRACKS

As the masses that had filled the Coliseum dispersed, Ándrôniüs led the four of them out through the wide gates. As the crowds thinned, the Coliseum, now quieter, seemed to breathe a sigh of relief. The once-exultant roar had subsided into a gentle murmur, allowing Ethan, Ryan, Jake, and Emily to walk comfortably alongside their guide. Towering behind them, the grand building stood strong, the setting sun illuminating its stone walls and creating long shadows.

Along the streets, vibrant celebrations continued to greet them. The people of Vâloríâ, who were filled with hope and joy, spilled into the streets across the city. Dancers were twirling in elaborate costumes, their movements synchronized to the rhythmic beats of drums. Musicians played flutes and lyres, their melodies weaving through the air and mingling with the laughter and cheers of the crowd. Vendors had set up makeshift stalls, offering everything from roasted meats to colorful sweets, while children ran around with garlands of flowers in their hands, tossing them into the air in sheer delight.

Spices, roasting meat, and sweet pastries perfumed the air, creating an almost dreamlike atmosphere during the walk. An inviting atmosphere of jubilant revelry resulted from the blending of colors, sounds, and smells. The entire city was alive, with the citizens rejoicing, their spirits lifted by the hopeful promise of salvation that these newcomers brought.

After passing through the lively festivities, they arrived at another magnificent sight: the Grand Barracks of Vâloríâ. This structure, like the others they had seen, bore the hallmark of Vâloríân craftsmanship. The barracks stood tall, its architecture both functional and beautiful. The walls were high and thick, made of the same white stone that marked the other significant buildings in Vâlorîâ. Every hundred feet along the walls stood a guard clad in the traditional Vâlorîân armor; gleaming steel with emerald accents. The barracks had the look of a fortress, complete with towering keeps at strategic points and a massive wrought-iron gate that was operated by a system of pulleys and chains.

As they approached the entrance, two guards stood at attention. Both had striking green eyes, black hair, and well-groomed curly beards that framed their stern faces. With synchronized movements, they turned to face each other, took three precise steps back, and unsheathed their swords. The blades glinted in the fading light as they brought them together, forming an arch under which Ándrôniüs and the others could pass.

Inside the walls, the courtyard was devoid of life, but certainly not empty. Archery targets were set up, and they arranged dummies for swordplay practice. An array of weapons lined the walls. The air was potent with the scent of freshly oiled leather, metalwork, and the odorous tang of sweat, a sign of the rigorous training that took place here.

At the rear of the courtyard stood a grand staircase, centered on the plaza, and leading up to an imposing structure that dominated the barracks. The building was another masterpiece of architecture, its rectangular form capped by a towering dome, supported by rows of intricately carved columns.

Like towering sentinels, the huge white doors at the staircase peak gleamed with a marble-like sheen in the soft, fading sunlight. The symbols etched into the doors depicted shields, swords, and mythical creatures, all intertwined in a complex dance, their lines both sharp and fluid. Fierce dragon heads, crafted from dark iron and studded with glittering gemstones, formed the handles; the gems shimmered like distant stars. The doors radiated an aura of invincibility, as if only those deemed worthy could pass through into the sanctum beyond.

As Ándrôniüs guided them toward the staircase, the heavy

doors swung open with a deep, resonant groan. At the top of the stairs, framed by the towering columns, appeared a familiar figure; Thâlôr, the Vâloríân soldier who had come to their aid during the Shadewalker attack just days before. His armor caught the light, and a warm, welcoming smile spread across his face as he descended the stairs to greet them.

"Welcome, my friends, to the Grand Barracks," Thâlôr said, his voice filled with warmth and respect. "It's good to see you all again. I'll be your overseer of your brief yet purposeful training here, along with many others. Now, come, let's get you settled."

Thâlôr motioned for them to follow, and the group ascended the grand staircase. The sheer scale of the structure became even more apparent as they climbed, the towering columns casting long shadows that danced in the evening light.

As they reached the top, the massive white doors were before them and appeared even more imposing up close. Thâlôr pushed them open with practiced ease, revealing the interior of the Grand Barracks.

A vast hall stretched before them, lined with more elaborate carvings and statues of Vâloríân heroes from ages past. The air inside was still, and the scent of freshly polished wood and burning torches filled their nostrils. The ceiling stretched high above, supported by a series of arches that made the space feel both expansive and imposing.

"Welcome to the heart of Vâloríâ's might," Thâlôr said, his voice reverberating slightly in the cavernous hall. "This is where you'll be trained and prepared for the challenges ahead."

Ándrôniüs nodded, his expression serious as he looked around. "This place has seen countless warriors pass through its halls. You will be no different. Embrace your time here, and you will emerge stronger than you ever imagined."

The heavy doors of the Grand Barracks slammed shut behind them with a reverberating boom, and the cool, dimly lit interior enveloped the group.

Thâlôr led the way, his movements sure and steady. He glanced back over his shoulder as they neared a spiraling staircase that led upward, its balusters intricately carved. Placing his hand on it, he prepared to ascend, until he noticed Emily trailing behind Ándrôniüs, her presence a stark contrast to the otherwise all-male group.

Thâlôr's voice cut through the air commandingly. "Ándrôniüs, you of all people should know that the girl cannot come past these steps. The council did not choose her path to be here. Either you stay behind, or the girl will need to remain in the courtyard while we get them settled in. I cannot make any exceptions. Not even for a very old friend."

His words were firm, his gaze unwavering as he removed his foot from the step, his hand falling back to his side.

"Yes... yes, you are right," Ándrôniüs said, and then turned to Emily, his expression softening as he spoke. "Emily, you must wait in the courtyard. I promise I won't be more than twenty minutes, and then we shall return to the Hall of Mages together."

Emily's eyes flashed with frustration, her voice tinged with a mix of anger and fear. "No, I want to stay with you! I don't want to be all alone out there by myself."

Ándrôniüs sighed, his tone gentle yet resolute. "I will return promptly. That is a promise, my dear."

Emily's frustration boiled over, her anger directed not just at the situation but at the unfairness of it all.

"Why do I always have to be the one left behind? This always happens to me," she snapped, her voice shaking slightly as she fought to keep her emotions in check.

Without waiting for a response, she turned on her heel, her movements brisk as she stormed out of the building, the heavy doors closing behind her with a thunderous crash.

Ándrôniüs watched her go, his expression full of regret. He knew it was necessary, but that didn't make her struggle any easier. He turned back to Thâlôr, giving a small nod to signal that they could continue. Thâlôr returned it and resumed his ascent up the staircase.

Winding upward for what felt like an eternity, the staircase seemed endless. They passed landing after landing, each beautified with murals of an ancient, stoic, and resolute warrior in distinctive Vâlorîân armor. Finally, after ascending to the sixth floor, Thâlôr halted, gesturing for them to step onto the landing.

As they moved past him, Thâlôr spoke, his tone firm yet respectful. "Ándrôniüs, take them to the common room and say your farewells. Once you're done, meet me in my quarters at the end of the hall. I'll then show them to their rooms."

Ándrôniüs nodded, his voice tinged with urgency. "Thank you, Thâlôr. I won't be long. Time is of the utmost essence."

With a nod, Thâlôr turned and walked briskly down the hall, disappearing into his quarters.

Ándrôniüs led the three across the hallway, the floor beneath their feet creaking with each step. They entered the common room and found a space exuding both comfort and a warrior's discipline. Sturdy wooden chairs and tables furnished the room, and an enormous stone fireplace crackled warmly on one side. Swords, shields, and other weapons lined the walls. At the heart of the room stood a grand oak table, surrounded by high-backed chairs that seemed to beckon warriors to gather, strategize, and reflect on their training.

The old mage settled into one of the chairs, crossing his legs as he addressed them. "Boys, you must get a good night's rest. Thâlôr and some of the finest knights of Vâlôríâ will be your instructors. These men are veterans of Cáelunárra's greatest battles, having stared into the eyes of the Dark Lord and lived to tell the tale. They are wise, and they are the most qualified instructors in the art of war. I promise you, in the short time we have, we will mold you into capable warriors."

His voice laced with apprehension, Ryan asked, "And if we can't measure up? If we still fail?"

With a grave expression, Ándrôniüs replied, "Then we are all doomed to perish, whether in the coming months or the years that follow."

Jake grimaced. "That doesn't sound good at all."

"Not at all, Jake," Ándrôniüs agreed, his tone grave. "They know precisely what's needed to transform you into the best warriors within the time available. That's why it's crucial that you study, learn, and pay attention. These men will test you, push you, and try to break you down. You must trust in yourselves. While you'll train together every day, each of you will ultimately face your tests alone."

Ethan petulantly interjected. "I still think it's unfair. We should all be together during our training."

Ándrôniüs sighed, his patience wearing thin, though his expression softened. "Unfortunately, that's not how the council and the Allfather see it. The gods speak through us, and this is how the gods have foreseen it. As their followers, we must adhere to their ways, or risk perishing at the hands of the Dark Lord. It is the path laid before us, and one we must follow."

Feeling the weight of responsibility, Ryan remarked, "That's a lot for those of us who have never fought in such circumstances, Ándrôniüs."

"Adrenaline will be your ally, along with the knowledge that if you fail, hundreds of thousands of innocents will die," Ándrôniüs said, his voice devoid of humor.

Jake swallowed hard, his voice shaky. "Well, no pressure there."

Ándrôniüs smiled gently, but his eyes were sincere. "None at all," he said, his tone filled with irony. He paused, taking a deep breath before continuing. "As a citizen of this world, I ask you. No. I *beg* of you! Help save our world and everything that we hold near and dear to our hearts. The last time this happened, we were lucky to survive. Now, I must go. Emily's test starts tomorrow evening, and she must prepare. Boys, do everything with haste and precision. I'll check on your progress tomorrow."

As Ándrôniüs turned to leave, Ethan called out, "What about the magic?"

Pausing at the door, Ándrôniüs glanced back. "What spell did you choose, Ethan?"

With a slight hesitation before answering, Ethan named the only spell that came to mind.

"Soulrend."

He had neglected to review the book Ándrôniüs had given him further, and now, in this crucial moment, he regretted it. The word felt heavy in his mouth, as if even speaking it without understanding its full weight was a mistake.

Ándrôniüs's expression grew serious. "A powerful choice,

Ethan. But are you certain?"

Ethan hesitated before he finally nodded. "Yes, I'm sure."

Taking a deep breath, feeling the gravity of what lay ahead, Ándrôniüs replied, "Very well. But know this... it won't be easy. We'll begin your training after Emily's test tomorrow. Until then, rest. Goodnight, boys."

With that, Ándrôniüs disappeared through the door, the soft thud of it closing behind him echoing through the dim room before leaving them in silence.

As Ándrôniüs walked away, his mind raced with questions. Why would Ethan choose such a dangerous spell? Did he not fully grasp the consequences of his choice, or was he merely playing a game? Or worse, had something started to change within Ethan, something darker that Ándrôniüs had yet to see? The uncertainty gnawed at him as he made his way down the hall. He knew that upon leaving the Grand Barracks and delivering Emily to Lord Radcliffe, he must visit the highest tower in the Hall of Mages and peer into the Ísëphëlŷ stone.

Ethan, Jake, and Ryan sat in the room, their thoughts consumed by the enormity of the task ahead. The crackling of the fire was a constant, almost comforting sound in the otherwise heavy silence. They heard Ándrôniüs's footsteps fading down the hall, interspersed with the faint murmur of his brief conversation with Thâlôr. Though they couldn't make out the words, the tone was unmistakably serious.

They were all lost in thought until the whining door broke the silence. Thâlôr stepped into the room, his presence commanding attention as his gaze settled on Ryan.

"Ryan," Thâlôr began, his voice firm yet gentle. "Come with me. I know it's late, but your training can't wait. Your instructors are waiting for you."

Ryan swallowed hard. He hesitated for a moment, then nodded. "Sure thing, Thâlôr." Rising from his seat, he turned to Jake and Ethan, trying to muster a smile despite his nerves. "I guess I'll see you two later tonight."

Giving a reassuring nod, Thâlôr replied, "Yes, you will. Don't worry. It might be late, but you'll see them if they wait up, that is."

Jake and Ethan exchanged a glance, their usual bravado replaced with a shared sense of unease. "See ya," they said in unison, though their voices lacked the usual lightheartedness.

After they left, Ethan attempted to break the silence. "How are you holding up, Jake?" he asked.

Jake leaned back in his chair, his gaze fixed on the flames in the fireplace. After a long pause, he finally spoke, his voice low. "Overwhelmed," he admitted. "This whole thing is unreal, Ethan. I can't wrap my head around it. Do you actually believe any of this?"

Ethan nodded slowly, Jake's words weighing heavily on him. "Honestly, I don't know, man," he replied, his voice low. "It feels like we're being dragged into something we never agreed to. Sometimes, I keep thinking I'll wake up in a hospital bed from some coma, but this dream just keeps going. And it's starting to feel way too real."

Jake let out a dry laugh. "You're not wrong," he said, shaking his head. "But now you know how the rest of us felt during your late-night summer escapades. We were lucky none of us got caught."

A faint smile tugged at the corners of Ethan's mouth as he recalled those reckless nights. "Yeah," he said softly. "Sorry about that."

Jake's expression softened, curiosity flickering in his eyes as he leaned forward. "Eh, it's fine. Those were some of the best memories I have of back home. But, Ethan, why did you do it? I mean, did your dad just not care that you were out all the time? I swear, sometimes I wish my dad didn't give a damn about my late nights and crazy excursions."

Ethan's smile faded as memories he had buried resurfaced. "My dad was never home, Jake," he began, his voice carrying the weight of years of solitude. "After my mom died on one of their trips, he changed. He'd disappear for weeks, sometimes months at a time. I can't even remember where he went on that last trip after she died, but when he came back, everything was different. He turned to alcohol, became distant, and just threw money at me to keep me happy. It was always just me in that big house, all alone. I just told no one."

His face softening further, Jake's heart ached for his friend. "Ethan," he said quietly, "I'm sorry we never asked."

Ethan sighed, his gaze distant as he scratched his brow, lost in the painful memories. "It happens," he replied, though the pain in his eyes was still evident.

Jake leaned forward, his voice gentle. "If you ever need to talk, Ethan, I'm here. It's never easy to face those things alone."

Though the turmoil in his mind was far from settled, Ethan let out a half-hearted, "Yeah."

He reached into his satchel and retrieved the spell book he'd received. Flipping it open to the page marked 'Soulrend', he tried to lose himself in the ancient words, seeking solace in the focus it required.

As he began reading the lines of the spell, the voice that had been intermittently nagging at him since he had first seen Hannah again at Pinemarsh Manor came to him again. It started its antics with a low guttural growl and distant, inaudible whispers. Ethan was growing tired of these occurrences; he was feeling like he was going crazy.

It was as if the world had gone silent. No other voices. No stray thoughts. No sound from Jake's moving mouth. Not even the crackle of the fire in the hearth. The only thing Ethan could hear was the low, pestering voice whispering in the back of his mind. He did everything he could to shut it out, to silence that sinister presence pressing on him from within.

Jake, sensing the shift in Ethan's mood and noticing how he ignored every question and attempt to keep the conversation going, went quiet, giving his friend the space he clearly needed to process whatever was going on in his mind.

Time seemed to stretch endlessly as they sat there, each grappling with their thoughts and fears. The minutes dragged on, punctuated only by the soft, distant sounds of life in the barracks, the creak of footsteps on wooden floors, indiscernible voices from other rooms, and the occasional gust of wind rattling the windows.

Jake's mind wandered to thoughts of Elârâ, her beauty, the way she made him feel, and how he never wanted that feeling to fade.

Yet the challenge ahead, facing the fearsome beast in his trial, crept back into his thoughts, stirring a knot of anxiety in his chest.

Ethan, on the other hand, was attempting to lose himself in the words from Ándrôniüs's book while fighting the small voice in his mind. The phrases echoed, pulling at something deep inside him. It felt like a presence was calling out, urging him to act. The voice grew louder, more insistent, egging him on, pushing him toward something darker. He rubbed his face and ran his fingers through his hair, trying to shake off the strange pull, but the urge grew stronger. A violent thought crossed his mind. That he could strangle Jake. The voice urged him on, whispering that he had the power to do it. Without realizing it, his hands reached out toward Jake's neck, the impulse almost uncontrollable.

Consumed by his own thoughts, Jake didn't notice Ethan's movements. His gaze was distant, focused on the dancing flames in the hearth, unaware of Ethan's advance. Just before Ethan was about to lurch forward, the sound of the door broke the silence, and Thâlôr stepped into the room again, his expression calm.

Ethan immediately pulled back, his heart pounding, snapping out of the strange trance. Jake looked over at Ethan, confused by his sudden movement. Jake brushed it off, thinking maybe Ethan was just trying to give him a scare; after all, Ethan always had a tendency to do those kinds of things.

"Come, boys," Thâlôr said, his voice breaking the heavy atmosphere. "It's time to get you to your rooms. We've furnished and prepared them for your stay."

Ethan and Jake exchanged a glance, then slowly rose from their seats. Thâlôr led them out into the hallway, the door swinging shut behind them.

"Follow me," Thâlôr instructed, leading them up the winding staircase again, but this time only to the next floor up. The corridor here was identical to the one below, lined with numerous doors. Thâlôr guided them to a T-intersection at the end of the hall, where three doors stood.

"This one," Thâlôr said, pointing to the middle door directly ahead, "is Ethan's." He then gestured to the door on the right. "That one is Jake's, and the one behind you is Ryan's. We have equipped each room with your armor and three weapons: a sword, an ax, and a bow. Choose whichever one you want to master; that will determine your training."

Ethan opened his mouth to comment, but Thâlôr cut him off with a firm hand. "Now is not the time, Ethan," he said, his tone leaving no room for questioning. "It's getting late, and in the morning, we begin your training. It will be mentally, physically, and emotionally taxing. But for now, rest. When the barracks' morning bells ring, get dressed in your armor and come to the dining hall on the right-hand side of the main hall. There, you'll meet your instructors: Vôrmghôr of Ellison, Gründhölm of Óttenäch, and Sãã of Pã Hõã Illïeã Mãhã, another distant realm in our world."

Thâlôr, having completed his instructions, turned and made his way back down the hall, fading into the distance as he descended the stairs. Ethan and Jake stood silently at the doors of their rooms. Neither spoke as the reality of their situation sank in deeper with every moment.

Jake, trying to maintain a sense of normalcy despite Ethan's strange behavior in the common room earlier, offered a small smile, deciding it was time for him to go to bed. "Well, goodnight. I'll see you in the morning."

With a prominent frown, Ethan said, "Aren't we staying up to wait for Ryan?"

Feeling uneasy and not wanting to linger any longer, Jake lied. "I don't think so. I'm pretty beat. I'll see you in the morning."

Ethan nodded, though his voice was distant. "Yeah, I guess so. See you tomorrow."

Both boys retreated into their respective rooms. Now utterly alone, they wrestled with their thoughts and fears. Their integration into this world would truly begin on the morrow, with the fate of an entire world resting on their shoulders.

But deep inside, something stirred within Ethan; a darkness he couldn't quite shake. Though unsettled by the thoughts that had surfaced earlier, he pushed them aside, convincing himself not to dwell on it any longer. For now, he would focus on the many tasks ahead.

# LORD RADCLIFFE

Despite knowing that the three boys were under the best care and training Vâloríâ offered, an unsettling feeling gnawed at Ándrôniüs as he started his departure from the halls of the Grand Barracks. His thoughts were melancholy as he walked past the statues that lined the corridor near the entrance, each one a tribute to a warrior who had once been in the same position as the boys upstairs. But something caught his eye; a tarnished spot in the otherwise pristine opulence of the warriors' hall.

He almost missed the desecration in his haste but turned back, drawn to the many markings carved into the figure. Words like "traitor," "murderer," "liar," and "cheat" marred the once-pristine marble. The eyes of the statue had been blackened, the seal of Vâloríâ scratched out, and the name on the plaque mostly erased. But Ándrôniüs knew who this was. He sighed heavily, placing his hand on the outstretched stone fingers of the statue.

"I'm sorry I failed you," he mumbled aloud, a weight of regret hanging in his voice. "I hope this time... it will be different."

With a final, sorrowful glance, he let go of the statue's outstretched hand and made his way out of the barracks. Stepping into the courtyard, he found Emily sitting alone at the base of the staircase, her face buried between her knees, her body shaking with quiet sobs. Ándrôniüs approached and sat beside her, gently placing a hand on her back, trying to offer comfort. She flinched at the unexpected touch, but when she realized who it was, she leaned into him, seeking comfort.

"I'm sorry," Emily whispered, her voice trembling. "I just don't think I can do this."

Ándrôniüs, his voice soft and reassuring, replied, "Fear not the burden, for none are born ready. Even those who came before you trembled when the mantle was laid upon them. But it is not strength that is first required; it is willingness. And if you will take even a single step forward in faith, though uncertain, the way will begin to reveal itself. For courage is not found in the absence of fear, but in the choice to walk onward despite it."

"Do you really think I can do this?" She asked, wiping away the tears from her face.

"My dear, Emily, you are capable of anything you put your heart to."

"Andrôniüs, I have my reservations about your statement. I'm not brave. I'm not heroic. I wasn't built for these kinds of things."

"You may feel that way. But one thing is for certain, I know your heart. I know what you're—" Ándrôniüs said, but ultimately his words were cut short by a swift and poignant Emily.

"But you don't know me," she protested, her voice cracking. "I know myself. I'm all about my books. I know I'm not strong enough."

She stood up, took a few steps down and looked away, struggling to keep her composure.

"I do know you, Emily," Ándrôniüs said, his tone firm yet gentle. "I've watched you for a long time. There's a strength in you that even you haven't discovered yet. I've seen it."

Emily turned and looked up at him, confusion evident in her teary eyes. "You keep saying these things that make little sense. What do you mean, watching me?" she said. Her voice wavered slightly as she pleaded for answers.

Ándrôniüs sighed, his expression pained. "There are things you're not ready to hear, nor even be able to imagine, let alone comprehend. But trust me when I say you're capable of more than you know. For now, we must get you to Lord Radcliffe. He's been waiting patiently."

"For once," Emily said, her voice edged with desperation, "can you just give me a straight answer instead of being so vague?"

"I'm afraid I can't, Emily. For the prophecy—"

"Screw the prophecy!" Emily cut him off, pushing herself away from him as she stood up in a burst of anger. "Everything is about this damn prophecy! Can't you just tell me the truth for once?"

Ándrôniüs stood up and followed her down into the courtyard. "I wish I could explain it all, but there are powers at play that you can't begin to understand. The last time this happened, when our champions were chosen, I failed."

"Wait? You've done this before and failed?" Emily repeated, her anger faltering as she turned to face him.

With a shadow of sorrow crossing his face, Ándrôniüs nodded. "Yes, I failed. And that failure cost us dearly. But let us walk back to the Hall of Mages. On our way there, I will tell you something I've never spoken to anyone about before."

Emily, torn between frustration and a glimmer of curiosity, nodded hesitantly. "Really?"

"Really," Ándrôniüs confirmed.

The old mage quietly gestured for her to walk with him. Together, they made their way through the gates of the magnificent complex, heading for the Hall of Mages.

Back on the street, the quiet of the city enveloped them.

"You see, when I was a young mage, fresh out of the academy, my father, who was the Seer at the time, came to me and informed me he was retiring to Líoníá."

"Líoníá?" Emily asked, the unfamiliar word rolling awkwardly on her tongue.

"In the common tongue, it is known as the Veil. When a mage reaches a thousand years old, they can choose to pass on willingly or continue living among us. My father was a boy when he met the chosen of that age, when my grandfather, his father, was Seer. He lived through the darkness that consumed Cáelunárra then. And when he was chosen to succeed his father as the Seer, he lived through another calamity. The chosen he was to guide and counsel failed. And after they perished, he lived through utter decimation, then another rebuilding of Cáelunárra, and the reforging of the republic in the hundred-year war that consumed Eldôria after."

"That is a lot to live through," Emily simply stated as the old mage paused in his retelling.

"Well, that is not where it ends, you see," Ándrôniüs continued, his voice lower now, burdened by memory. "Over that long, harrowing life, through two great calamities and the hundred-year war, he watched every one of his sons and daughters perish, all but me. Shadewalkers forced him to watch as they strung up and hanged his wife. He held her lifeless body. Later, he lost his second wife to a sickness that ravaged our lands. And as age crept upon him, he watched his dearest friends fall one by one, taken by the sword, by illness, or by the weight of time itself, until none remained."

"I am so sorry to hear that." Emily said as she placed a hand on his forearm, trying to comfort him.

"Thank you, Emily," Ándrôniüs said, looking down at her before continuing. "As you can imagine, he grew weary of this life, and, after getting his affairs in order, he chose to pass through the Veil. One of the last things he did was choose who would assume his duties as the Seer of the Enigmas. I was in my study one day when Lady Elówŷn, the Grand Mage at the time, came to see me. She had received a letter from my father with instructions to pass the sacred Ísëphëlŷ stone into my custody as the new Seer. At the same time, she informed me that it was time to try to find the new champions, to help guide them on their journeys. I was still grieving my father's departure, but I was profoundly proud that he would pass that duty on to me, especially in my youth. And so, I went to my father's Órcráculum. I was very much afraid, like you are now. It was an immense responsibility. I momentarily glanced into the stone, the visages of children from across your world and others coming into view. But I could not bring myself to look fully at the visions it was showing me. Not yet."

Ándrôniüs paused as they approached a grand fountain. The fountain was like everything in this great white city, immensely grandiose. Depictions of angels played instruments upon clouds as water shot out from the top and cascaded down the majestic sculpture before trickling into the pond at the fountain's base. He stood there silently for several moments, observing the golden fish drifting lazily through the water, overcome with the immense feelings that speaking of his past evoked.

Emily approached him, then grasped his arm one more time. "But did you?" she asked.

"I did," Ándrôniüs replied, his voice heavy with regret as he gestured for them to continue walking. "However, in my youth, I thought I could outsmart the gods. See, I chose only four champions from your world and added a fifth from ours, believing I could control the outcome and finally end the darkness that had plagued us for so long. I wanted to be the one to fulfill the prophecy, to rid this land of its curse once and for all. But I fell to my pride. My arrogance—my hubris—unraveled everything. The champions withered like dying roses, and another terrible genocide swept through our lands. The realms of Âldâmûr, Brâldôr, the Blackmire Marsh, and Eldôria barely held their ground while the elves retreated and cowered in their woods. Despite insurmountable losses, we rallied, we fought back, pushing the darkness behind the gates of Khąrzọnọv. But the cost..."

He paused, turning to Emily as they passed through the now empty market. He took her hands in his; his eyes filled with sorrow.

"Therefore, I must be vague, why I can't give you all the answers you seek. I gave them theirs on a silver platter. They failed because, in my youthful arrogance, I sought to wrest fate from the hands of the divine, speaking of things that should have remained unsaid. And with that, I failed once, and I can't afford to fail again."

Emily, shaken by his confession, nodded slowly. She could see the deep scars of guilt and sorrow in his eyes.

"I'm sorry, Ándrôniüs," she whispered, her voice soft but sincere. "I'll try to do my best moving forward," she added.

Ándrôniüs offered a small, sad smile. "I promise I will not fail you, or Cáelunárra, again." Suddenly, his expression shifted, startled. "Oh! Would you look at that? We're here."

Emily looked up and saw the Hall of Mages standing before them, its towering spires cutting through the night sky. They had been so consumed in their conversation that neither had realized how far, nor how quickly, they had walked.

"We must hurry and get you to Lord Radcliffe," Ándrôniüs urged, guiding her through the entrance.

Once through the grand doors, Emily felt a wave of relief wash over her as the familiar sight greeted her eyes. However, a man she had never seen before stood in the hall. Ándrôniüs, on the other hand, seemed to recognize him immediately, his eyes lighting up with excitement as he nearly dashed forward to greet the newcomer.

The man was strikingly tall, with long black hair pulled back into a ponytail, save for a few strands that framed the right side of his chiseled face. Brown leather armor, embossed with a scene of two rearing horses and their spear-wielding riders poised for battle, covered him. Sturdy leather greaves and a sheathed longsword hung at his side. The hilt peeking out from beneath a rich red cape that flowed down his back protected his legs.

"Lord Radcliffe, my apologies for our tardiness," Ándrôniüs said, his voice full of vigor as he clutched the man's hand.

Lord Radcliffe smiled, understanding in his eyes. "No need to apologize, Ándrôniüs. I know how swiftly time seems to move these days."

"Indeed, it does, my friend," Ándrôniüs replied with a nod. "It feels as if we're sprinting through it now, rather than merely walking."

"So, are you my pupil?" Lord Radcliffe said as his eyes settled on Emily.

Emily, who had been lingering near the door, finally stepped forward, her steps hesitant. "Yes, that would be me," she said, her voice firm despite the uncertainty she felt.

Lord Radcliffe's eyes narrowed slightly. "Lord or sire, please," he corrected gently. "And what is your name, young lady?"

Slightly irritated by the formality, Emily couldn't resist a touch of sarcasm. "Lord," she began, emphasizing the title with a smirk, "my name is Emily."

Slightly taken aback, he turned to Ándrôniüs, his bushy eyebrows raised and a hint of amusement in his voice. "Is she serious? Did she just—"

Ándrôniüs sighed and apologetically responded. "Unfortunately, yes. But I ask for your patience. She is a remarkable student, though she can be quite... willful."

Lord Radcliffe chuckled, nodding in understanding. "Ah, strong-willed, I see. Well, Emily," he said, turning back to her, "we don't have time for that. In time it will serve you well, but I'm here to teach you, not belittle you or deal with childish antics. Now, follow me."

Without waiting for a response, Lord Radcliffe began his ascent up the staircase.

Emily hesitated for a moment, glancing back at Ándrôniüs, who offered her an encouraging nod.

"Believe in yourself, as I believe in you, Emily," Ándrôniüs said softly, his eyes filled with confidence. "Hurry along now."

With a deep breath, Emily followed Lord Radcliffe up the stairs. They ascended another flight, arriving at a hallway that was clearly designed for scholarly pursuits. Shelves overflowing with scrolls and books lined the walls, and someone had neatly arranged several sturdy wooden desks along them. Soft candlelight cast a warm glow over the room, and the faint scent of ink and freshly pressed parchment filled the air.

Lord Radcliffe led her to the front of the room, gesturing to a desk where an old, weathered book lay open. "Please have a seat," he instructed. "This book is about the glimmer gremlin, your opponent. We have much to cover, and very little time. What I have learned over a lifetime, I must somehow impart to you in what only feels a few hours and to your disadvantage. But fret not, we will work deep into the night, and after breakfast in the morning, we shall continue. Then, I will escort you to the Coliseum, where you will face this creature."

Emily sat down, her heart pounding, realizing the enormity of the task ahead.

"Now, read," Lord Radcliffe ordered.

Sitting in her chair in the dimly lit study, she quickly flipped through the pages, trying to absorb as much information as possible. She skimmed the details of the glimmer gremlin, determined to understand the creature she was about to encounter. The room was quiet, save for the rustle of pages and the occasional crackle from the burning candles that had melted halfway down, their light fading as the night wore on.

Lord Radcliffe, still as sharp as ever despite the late hour, watched her with a keen eye. "Good, you're reading with purpose," he remarked, breaking the silence. "You'll need every bit of that knowledge if you're to survive the test ahead."

Looking up briefly, she nodded before diving back into the text, mumbling, "The glimmer gremlin appears to be blind, but in the dark of its burrow, it can see perfectly. Its hearing is also unparalleled. It can detect even the slightest vibration upon the ground, and it can smell you from hundreds of feet away."

"That's right. And that's why you'll need to be clever. Mud from inside the burrow, or even the creature's own excrement, will mask your scent. But remember," he added with a wry smile, then winking at her, "walking around in the nude might just do the trick if you don't mind the draft."

Emily made a face, half in disbelief at his words. "I'd rather not, thanks."

He let out a cheerful chuckle, clearly enjoying her discomfort. "Well, if you're not keen on that idea, just ensure you avoid any heavy perfumes or soaps the morning of your test. You don't want to give yourself away before you even get close."

Though the hours dragged on, Lord Radcliffe deemed it prudent to lecture on further, touching on the other dangers that awaited her. "The glimmer gremlin is hideous. Its scaly skin is covered in warts. It has barely any hair attached to its leathery hide. It has large white eyes that are clouded with cataracts. And a nose that would make a troll envious. Not to mention its forked tongue that lay seemingly paralyzed out of its mouth, tasting the air for any sign of you. And don't forget the spiked tail; it oozes poison from its tips."

Emily shivered involuntarily. "Lovely," she muttered, trying to keep her voice steady. "And if I make a sound? How loud is too loud?"

Lord Radcliffe's expression grew serious. "If you make any sound aside from the hunters' steps, I'll instruct you on tomorrow, along with the deep, shallow breaths needed to survive... it will find you. And it will strike you down and feast upon your body. These creatures relish the taste of human flesh. For them, it's a delicacy they rarely get to enjoy."

"And the goblet?" She asked, trying to focus on the goal to avoid hyperventilating.

"It will be deep in the burrow's heart, likely surrounded by eggs, but nonetheless in its nest. If you're lucky, the creature won't be hovering nearby. If not... well, you'll need to act quickly. On the way into the den, light your way with faelight spider blood if necessary, but beware; its blood can signal the start of a mating ritual, attracting the males. You see, the female finds the spiders and kills them. She then coats herself with the luminescent blood. She then extrudes the poison from her spiked tail and also lathers that onto her skin. The poison-blood concoction is like a perfume a young lady like yourself uses to attract men to you."

Emily's eyes widened. "So, basically, I could lure them right to me?"

Lord Radcliffe snapped his fingers and grinned. "Now you're getting it."

She sighed, sensing a hint of impossibility in the task ahead. Nearly spent, the candles flickered, their flames nearly lifeless, as she fought off the drowsiness. To keep her mind alert, she asked, "Is there anything else I should know?"

Lord Radcliffe paused, considering her question. "Only that you should trust your instincts. They'll keep you alive as much as any knowledge I can give you." With that, he called out, "Elârâ!"

His voice echoed through the quiet halls, startling Emily, who hadn't expected him to shout.

Within moments, Elârâ appeared at the door.

"Yes, my Lord?" She said.

"Take Emily to her room," Lord Radcliffe instructed. "She'll need every bit of rest she can get before tomorrow."

Elârâ nodded and offered Emily a kind smile. "Come along, let's get you to bed."

Emily stood, her legs feeling heavy and unsteady as she followed Elârâ out of the study. The walk to her room was quiet. When they arrived, Elârâ opened the door and ushered her inside.

"Try to rest. I've put clean linens on the bed, a fresh chemise for you to sleep in, and prepared a warm bath, should you choose," she said.

Emily nodded. Though she knew finding sleep would be scarce, she laid down, her mind racing with everything she had learned from her text and Lord Radcliffe. The image she had formed of the glimmer gremlin, based on the descriptions she had read and heard, hovered in her mind. Its scaly skin, warts, and those haunting, cataract-covered eyes replayed over and over in her thoughts. She could almost feel the dampness of the underground burrow, the walls closing in as she imagined herself creeping through the dark, guided only by faint shimmers of light from the faelight spiders. The thought of covering herself in mud or the creature's excrement made her stomach churn. And what if she missed the goblet? What if she made a noise and alerted the creature? The anticipation of the test caused her chest to swell with a growing sense of panic.

Unable to bear her racing thoughts, Emily decided she needed to calm her nerves. Rising from the bed, she walked to the small bath that she had previously ignored. The warm water beckoned, and she quickly undressed, sinking into it with a sigh of relief. The heat soothed her mind and body, easing the tension in her muscles and quieting the whirlwind of thoughts.

Relaxing into her soak, fatigue gently lapped at the edges of her consciousness the longer she sat, the water enveloping her like a comforting embrace. Bubbles floated lazily on the surface, their sweet scent filling the air, bringing a sense of tranquility. For a brief moment, Emily allowed herself to let go, her body and mind gradually unwinding from the strain of the day.

As the water lost its warmth, Emily reluctantly stepped out of the bath, dried herself off, and slipped into the clean chemise. She climbed into bed, pulling the blankets up to her chin. The room was quiet and still, shrouded in the deep stillness of the night.

Finally, sleep claimed her, though it was restless and filled with fragmented dreams of dark tunnels and lurking shadows. The event of the test lingered even in her sleep, a constant reminder of the challenge she would face tomorrow.

# THE SECRET PACKAGE

THE DARK TUNNEL SURROUNDED her, and the shadowy figure of the glimmer gremlin crept closer, claws extended, ready to strike. Her heart pounded, the enormity of what lay ahead gnawing at her core, as her subconscious clung to the terrifying image of the creature about to tear her apart.

Suddenly, a loud banging echoed in her dream, resonating through the tunnels as the glimmer gremlin lunged for her. The impact of the sound caused her to jolt, but not wake from her night terror, her mind struggling to surface from the nightmarish vision. Her heart raced faster, the fear now spilling over into her awakening thoughts.

It was as if the creature itself was pounding at her door as another series of three sharp bangs reverberated through her room, dragging her into the present. She awoke with a gasp, her breath coming quickly and shallow. The anxiety from her dream lingered, intensified by the realization of what today meant; not just for her, but for each of her friends.

"Emily, wake up!" Lord Radcliffe's voice came from behind the door, followed by another knock. "It's time for breakfast and then our lessons."

The familiar voice brought Emily back to reality, but the fear from her dream remained. She could feel the knots in her stomach tightening with every passing second, the stress building to a level she had never experienced before. Her entire body felt constricted, as if she were on the verge of breaking under the force of it all.

Another set of oppressive, resounding knocks echoed through the room. "Lady Emily, wake up, or else I will have no other choice but to break down this door despite your state of dishabille!" Lord Radcliffe's voice boomed, startling her even further.

She sat there, petrified. Though alert, she remained frozen, unable to move, as if she had become one of the many statues lining the Hall of Mages and the streets of Vâloríâ. Her heart pounded so fiercely it felt as though it might burst from her chest.

Just then, she heard Lord Radcliffe yell, "One!" and the urgency in his voice snapped her out of her paralysis.

"I'm awake, I'm sorry!" she called out, leaping from her bed and running to the door, her chemise barely clinging to her form and leaving little to the imagination. She swung the door open, facing Lord Radcliffe, who stood impatiently outside.

"I'm here. I'm sorry again; I was stuck in the worst nightmare," she began, but Lord Radcliffe quickly interrupted.

"Lady Emily," he stammered, clearly flustered as he averted his gaze. "Please cover yourself. The impropriety! I have daughters your age."

He fumbled with the clasp of his cape, hurriedly trying to unfasten it to offer her some modesty.

Realizing her state of undress, Emily felt her face flush with embarrassment. Though technically she was covered, her shoulders were clearly visible because of the oversized gown, and the sheer fabric of her nightgown revealed more than her others. She knew it was indecent given the circumstances. She chuckled awkwardly, took the offered cape, and draped it over her shoulders to cover herself.

"My apologies, Lord Radcliffe," she said before retreating behind the door, only her head peeking out.

"Are you covered?" Lord Radcliffe asked after a moment, still shielding his eyes.

Emily shook her head slightly, a smile tugging at her lips. "Yes... I am even slightly hidden behind the door."

Lord Radcliffe risked a peek through his fingers and sighed with relief. "Oh dear, thank you. My wife would have me hanged if she ever knew my eyes inadvertently saw another woman in her nightclothes. I insist, Lady Emily, that you please take more caution when answering doors in a state of undress."

"I'm sorry, it won't happen again," Emily assured him, her embarrassment fading to a dull blush.

Lord Radcliffe composed himself and continued, "You must get ready. I've brought some functional clothing and armor for today's test and the training we'll do beforehand. Ándrôniüs also wishes to speak with you during our morning meal before he heads to the Grand Barracks to assist with Ethan's training."

Still feeling slightly embarrassed, scolded, confused, overwhelmed, and anxious all at once, Emily smiled and accepted the proffered bundle of material before replying softly, "I'll see you in a few minutes."

With a racing heart, Emily moved quickly. She forewent her usual morning bath, opting instead to splash cold water on her face and quickly wet her hair. She brushed through the damp strands, then skillfully braided them to keep them out of the way for the rigorous day ahead.

She laid out the clothing Lord Radcliffe had provided so she could see the entire ensemble. Supple yet sturdy leather, dyed a deep chestnut brown, formed the armor. The craftsman crafted it for mobility, reinforcing the seams with stitching to provide durability without sacrificing flexibility. Protecting her vital organs while allowing free movement, the form-fitting cuirass hugged her torso. Intricate patterns of leaves and vines, a subtle nod to the natural world, embossed the leather, offering both beauty and resilience.

She dressed quickly, admiring the mobility and comfort of the apparel. As she adjusted the armor, she slid on her glasses, the familiar weight on her nose grounding her in the moment's reality. She caught her reflection in the mirror; a figure both familiar, yet not. She was still Emily, but now she looked like a warrior, someone preparing for a task of immense importance.

Taking a deep breath, she stared at her reflection, willing herself to believe in the words she murmured under her breath, "You can do this."

With a last glance at the room, she steeled herself and stepped out the door, making her way to join Lord Radcliffe and Ándrôniüs. As she walked through the corridors, the mantra repeated in her mind, growing stronger with each step, "You can do this, you can do this."

When she arrived at the dining area, the enticing aroma of breakfast greeted her, and she saw the table set by the diligent hands of the Hall of Mages servants and Elârâ. With a warm smile, Ándrôniüs took in Emily's appearance. "Dear, don't you look lovely. Like a rose, so elegant yet ready to strike with its many thorns; protecting itself from any danger that dares approach."

Lord Radcliffe nodded in agreement. "Indeed. I knew that armor would suit you well. It seems to have brought out both your strength and grace."

Gaining confidence from their remarks, Emily returned their compliments with a smile.

"Thank you, gentlemen." She took her seat across from them at the table, helping herself to a few muffins from a bowl, some slices of fruit, and a glass of fresh milk. "Ándrôniüs, I understand that there is something you wanted to talk to me about?"

"Yes, yes. One second, dear." Ándrôniüs said, thinking of something and scribbling something down on a piece of parchment at his side. The minor derailment of his train of thought caused him to trail off, steeping himself in further thought about whatever it was he was keeping notes on.

Emily's eyes drifted to Lord Radcliffe, who also seemed to be lost in thought. With a sarcastic throat-clearing, Emily prompted, "Ándrôniüs, tell me?"

Surprised at her bluntness, Ándrôniüs quickly tried to swallow the mouthful of pastry he had been enjoying, coughing slightly as he cleared his throat.

"Ah, yes, my dear," he began, his tone more serious now. "It's important that you listen closely to Lord Radcliffe. I know I've said this before, but it's absolutely imperative. Everything he teaches you comes from years of experience. He has slain over five hundred of those creatures in his lifetime. He knows exactly how to deal with them. But tell me, Lord Radcliffe, wherever did you get them?"

Lord Radcliffe chuckled, with a modest smile on his face.

"Ándrôniüs, you're too kind. The number is only four hundred ninety-two, to be exact. But I brought two of them with me from the far reaches of Âldâmûr to Vâloríâ. They were meant to be studied here, but with the test upon us, the mages saw fit to use them for the purpose of this task instead."

Emily interjected a question, one that had popped into her mind. Without hesitation, she asked. "How do you transport one of those creatures?"

"With immense care, tact, and most importantly the utmost security," Lord Radcliffe replied. "If we had failed, we would have been nothing more than a meal for those two beasts. They are now confined deep beneath the city, within the Coliseum, where you will need to delve into the lair they've likely carved out. Unfortunately, I don't know the layout of these tunnels. I'm not permitted to assist you with the test beyond your training, so you will venture in blind."

Ándrôniüs nodded. "The same goes for me. However, here is an illustration of the Goblet of Îgnîs Sápíëntíá."

He handed Emily a piece of leather parchment inscribed with an intricate drawing of the goblet.

The art depicted the chalice with a broad, flared rim, adorned with ornate carvings of intertwining vines, and small, shimmering stones set in its base. To Emily's surprise, the parchment seemed enchanted, displaying the goblet with remarkable clarity, as if she were seeing the real thing.

Emily studied the illustration closely.

"Thank you," she said. Ándrôniüs placed a reassuring hand on her shoulder.

"As I've said many times. I believe in you and what you can accomplish today. I'll see you on the victory stand this evening, my dear," Ándrôniüs stated optimistically.

With those ultimate words, Ándrôniüs finished his milk, the liquid clinging to his beard and mustache, leaving a faint white residue. He set the cup down with a soft clink, rose from the table, and nodded to Lord Radcliffe, his movements laced with a sense of urgency. Emily watched him go, making his way out of the Hall of Mages, a knot of apprehension tightening in her chest.

Her mind was like a whirlwind; she was now left alone with Lord Radcliffe again for the remainder of the day. There would be no familiar faces to offer comfort, no friends to help calm her anxiety, no Ísolde to ease her worries with kind words, and no Ándrôniüs to provide the steadying presence she had come to rely on secretly. She was left with only the teachings of a man she felt she could trust, but the briefness of their acquaintance left her feeling unsettled as the task ahead filled her with worry.

Emily's eyes wandered around the Hall of Mages, searching for something, anything, to anchor her fraying nerves. But all she saw was the back of Elârâ, disappearing down the hall, her arms full of dishes and the remnants of the morning meal. Emily forced herself to take a deep breath, willing herself to believe that everything would be alright.

When she turned her gaze back to Lord Radcliffe, she found him lost in thought, his eyes distant as he sipped on his glass of milk. There was something about the quiet intensity of his presence that brought her a surprising sense of calm.

Gathering her resolve, she broke the silence, her voice steady despite the storm within her own mind. "Lord Radcliffe, what will we be doing this morning? Are we back to the books? Or do you have something else planned?"

Lord Radcliffe drained the last of his milk from his cup, slamming it down with a resonant crack. "Yes!" he said with a smile. "Well, stand up. Aren't you ready?"

Slightly startled by his abruptness, Emily simply responded with a nod.

Lord Radcliffe gestured toward the grand doors of the Hall of Mages. Emily found herself nearly jogging to keep up with the lord's long, purposeful strides.

As they weaved through the crowded streets, which seemed to flow like a river toward the heart of Vâloríâ, Emily noticed they were heading in the opposite direction from the crowds.

"Why are we heading out of the city?" She asked, her curiosity growing.

He glanced down at her briefly, but continued striding along determinedly. "Because that's where you will train today," he replied, his tone firm.

Emily's unease deepened. "So, not in the books?" she asked anxiously, having hoped to put her mind to work strategizing how to outwit the glimmer gremlin.

Shaking his head, a slight smile playing on his lips. "Not today. Last night's lessons will suffice. Do you remember what we discussed and what you read?"

"For the most part, I do," Emily answered, though her words were tinged with uncertainty.

"Then you should be ready," Lord Radcliffe said, his voice filled with quiet confidence.

"Ready?" Emily scoffed, clearly not sharing his certainty. "How can I be ready? I've barely been taught anything."

They reached the city gates, where Lord Radcliffe paused briefly. "Yes, Emily, you are ready. If you are indeed as Ándróniüs describes you, that single lesson about the creature will suffice. But fortunately for you, it won't be your last," he said confidently.

Emily, feeling no more reassured than before, muttered, "If you say so."

"I do," Lord Radcliffe replied firmly. "I must trust in the gods' plan for you."

After exchanging a few words with the guards, Lord Radcliffe led Emily through the towering gates of Vâloríâ and into the vast farmland beyond. The city walls towered behind them, casting long shadows across the land as they followed its curve out of sight of the gate.

"Out here, near the edge of the city, is a burrow once occupied by a glimmer gremlin," Lord Radcliffe explained. "I will show you what to look for—signs of these creatures, faelight spiders, and much more. It is imperative that you stay close and pay careful attention to the details."

Emily's anxiety was manifesting; her breathing was coming shallower, jitters filling her body, but she forced herself to respond steadily. "Thank you for doing this for me. I'll try not to let you down."

Lord Radcliffe chuckled softly, his expression lightening. "Of course, Lady Emily. When I first heard you had all arrived,

I assumed it was some sort of elaborate hoax. But when Ándrôniüs's messenger sparrow reached me while I was on assignment in a remote village, asking for my help, I knew I had to answer the call."

Emily offered him a quiet smile, her eyes soft with gratitude. There was a sincerity in Lord Radcliffe that reassured her, a quiet sense that she was in the presence of someone truly honorable. She said nothing, letting her thoughts drift in silence as they walked along the outskirts of the city. The path eventually led them to a bend in the wall, where the earth had given way. A massive hole yawned before them, nearly as tall as Lord Radcliffe himself and wide enough to fit three ox carts side by side.

Her heart pounding as she stared into the depths of the tunnel, Emily muttered, "I don't know what I expected, but this wasn't my idea of a burrow."

Lord Radcliffe nodded. "A glimmer gremlin is quite large. They have been known to fill the entire burrow from side to side. You'll need to be quick on your feet. Their sheer size could crush you if you're not careful."

Emily swallowed hard, her anxiety returning full force. "Oh boy, that makes me want to do this even more," she muttered acerbically.

"You'll do just fine," Lord Radcliffe reassured her with a smile. "Now, follow me."

"But... no torch?" Emily asked, apprehension creeping into her voice.

Lord Radcliffe shook his head. "To whose advantage? Do you not want to learn the way I did? The same way you will need to succeed this evening, or shall I make it easy?"

Emily sighed, acknowledging the lesson he was imparting. "Fair enough."

"Let's proceed." he stated firmly.

The two of them descended into the burrow, the air growing tainted with musk as they ventured deeper underground. Residue dampened the floor, and cobwebs lined the walls. A foul stench filled the tunnel, causing Emily to gag, her reflexes barely able to contain the emesis that tickled the back of her throat.

Lord Radcliffe turned to her, his voice low and steady. "Yes, it's foul, but if you vomit, you will—"

"Die? Yes, I see a trend here," Emily cut him off, a hint of acid in her tone.

He chuckled softly. "No need to get snippy. I'm just trying to teach you."

She rolled her eyes, but he did not see it, thankfully.

Continuing deeper, the entrance faded completely into the darkness behind them. Their eyes adjusted slowly to the dim light, the walls occasionally shimmering with the glow of faelight spiders that scurried away from their presence. The bioluminescence flickered, making it hard to maintain steady vision in the bowels of the den. Rocks, bones, and debris littered the uneven ground, forcing Emily to focus on every step, and her breathing grew heavy.

Lord Radcliffe, sensing her rising panic, spoke calmly. "Best learn to calm that ticker of yours. The pounding will—"

"It will lead to death. Yes, I know," Emily interjected again, her voice trembling. "I'm just afraid of small places."

His amusement evident in his voice, Lord Radcliffe said, "This is small? Try being me in here, hunched down while you walk with ease."

Having that perspective in her mind, Emily felt her anxiety begin to dissipate. Her heart rate slowed as she realized that, despite her fear, she had an advantage.

"See? There you go," Lord Radcliffe encouraged. "Find the good things. Find happiness in the dark. Move slowly and confidently. Breathe in through your nose and out through your mouth; it will help calm you. Hold on to whatever you can, because at the very sight of one of these beasts, you'll surely shudder. I know I still do from time to time."

Emily nodded; their faces were now close enough to be visible in the dim light. "How do I know if I'm close to one?" she asked, her voice barely a whisper.

"You'll know because you'll either run into it; if that's the case, hold your breath, do not move, and hope it doesn't retaliate. But if it's awake and senses you, the spaces between its scales will begin to shimmer with a blue bioluminescence from the faelight spiders it feasts upon. The taint in its blood causes the glow," Lord Radcliffe explained.

"And what does that mean?" Emily asked, her voice trembling again.

Lord Radcliffe's tone was grave. "It means run for your life."

Emily, overwhelmed, quickly changed the subject in a desperate attempt to ease her nerves. "And how do I know I'm in its den, and where I can find this goblet?"

Lord Radcliffe slowed his pace, beginning to move away from Emily, softening his voice. "We are in its den now. This one burrowed straight in and didn't build any offshoots. You'd only be so lucky if that were the case tonight. Feel around with your feet until you come to what feels like a berm made of dirt and rocks, but it will feel loose, like a dune. That's how you know you're near its nest."

At the conclusion of his words, a heavy silence fell, broken only by the persistent ringing in her ears. Emily's eyes strained, struggling to pierce through the oppressive darkness that enveloped her. The occasional flicker of light from faelight spiders provided brief, ghostly illumination, casting eerie shadows that danced along the tunnel walls.

Panic surged through Emily as she frantically searched the dark. "Lord Radcliffe? Where are you?"

But there was no answer. The silence closed in on her, amplifying her fear. Her breathing quickened, her heart raced, and tears blurred her vision as she realized she was alone. She tried to calm herself, but nothing worked. Finally, she sat down, succumbing to her misery, sobbing in the dark.

Then, a thought pierced through the fear; that her friends were counting on her. They needed her to succeed. She couldn't fail them. Emily found the strength to stand up, brush herself off, and carefully begin to feel around with her feet, searching for the telltale signs of the berm Lord Radcliffe had described. After what felt like an eternity, she found it; a slight give in the ground, the sensation of sand slipping beneath her boots. She knelt down and ran her hands over the loose earth, feeling the subtle contours of the nest.

Suddenly, out of the darkness, a hand grabbed her shoulder. Emily screamed at the top of her lungs, her heart nearly stopping. Lord Radcliffe burst into laughter, the sound echoing throughout the burrow.

"How dare you! I thought you left me in here!" Emily shouted, her voice a mix of anger and relief. She barely stopped herself from lashing out at the man.

Still chuckling, Lord Radcliffe spoke between fits of laughter. "You learned, didn't you? You found the nest, didn't you? And the prize... yes, I think you did! And you did it all on your own."

Emily, grudgingly realizing the truth in his words, nodded. Lord Radcliffe had been teaching her to rely on her training, his words, and her own instincts. She would be alone in the tunnels during the test, and this was his way of preparing her.

"Thank you, Lord Radcliffe," she said, her voice filled with genuine gratitude.

"It was my pleasure. I have full faith in you. Now, as we walk back, I will teach you how to tread lightly within the burrow so that you will not call attention to yourself," Lord Radcliffe said.

"Sounds good to me!" Emily said emphatically.

As they made their way out of the burrow, back toward the open air, Lord Radcliffe began telling her the secrets of the hunter's stalk, making her practice as they walked until he could not make out her steps in the darkness.

Gradually, a small pinpoint of light appeared. They kept their stride toward the light, exchanging merriment and his divulging other useful tidbits that would assist her later. Emerging from the darkness into the sunlight, the contrast between the dark, stifling tunnel and the bright, open fields was almost blinding.

They returned through the gates where the city was alive with activity, the cacophony as the people prepared for the event that night almost overwhelming Emily.

Upon reentering the Hall of Mages, they found Ísolde waiting for them; her face lighting up with relief when she saw Emily.

She rushed forward, wrapping the girl in a tight embrace. "Oh, Emily, I'm so glad you're back! I've been worried sick."

Emily, comforted by the warmth of Ísolde's embrace, allowed

herself a moment of peace. "I'm okay," she whispered.

Leaning in close, her voice barely above a whisper, Ísolde mumbled, "Emily, I have something for you. But you must promise not to tell Ándróniüs or Lord Radcliffe. I'm certain it breaks some sort of rule within this prophecy, but dear Hannah insisted I give this to you." With a warm smile, she handed Emily a small rolled-up parchment, delicately tied off with a pink ribbon. "Now, dear, best of luck! I will see you tonight."

Emily's heart raced as she took the parchment, the package far heavier with meaning than with substance. She quickly slid it into the small space between her bust and leather armor, hiding it from view. Her worry intensified because of the secrecy of the moment, but the joy of knowing her friend was thinking of her mitigated it.

She hugged Ísolde back tightly. "Thank you!"

Ísolde, her blue dress flowing gracefully as she moved and her hair pinned up in elegant waves, gave Emily a reassuring smile. "I have no doubt you will be triumphant tonight." With a final flutter of her gown, she exited the room, leaving behind a lingering scent of lavender.

Lord Radcliffe, who had observed the exchange from a respectful distance, stepped a few paces forward. His voice was steady, almost reassuring. "Emily, it is time for you to go study some more, calm your mind, and return for lunch. We'll discuss things further before heading to the Coliseum for this evening's endeavor." With a wink, he turned and ascended the grand staircase, his presence fading as he disappeared from view.

As soon as he was out of sight, Emily felt a surge of urgency. She sprinted down the corridor toward her room, her feet barely touching the ground in her haste. Bursting through the door, she slammed it shut behind her and rushed to the small desk and chair by the window. Her hands trembled slightly as she reached for the hidden parchment, carefully pulling it from beneath her armor.

Delicately, she untied the pink ribbon and slowly unrolled the paper, her eyes eager to uncover whatever secret message Hannah had sent her. A handkerchief sewn closed around the edges fell out, and she picked it up as she read the letter intently.

*"My dearest friend, Emily,*

*How I miss you. Being apart from you all has been more difficult than I imagined. I miss each of you equally, yet in different ways that seem to tug at my heart. The isolation has only made my anxiety grow, but knowing you are out there gives me strength.*

*My head is nearly healed now, and I believe I will have fully mended it by the time we see each other again. The elves have been kind; they're not as distant as they seem. I think people simply misunderstand them. Their food is incredible, and Ísolde has been so much help, though I fear they're starting to realize she understands their language. I worry they might pull her away from me, but for now, she remains close. I've been learning so much here; about the past, present, and future, as well as the language. You would adore this library, Emily; it's a treasure trove of knowledge, the kind you've always loved to explore.*

*But I know this letter is getting long, so I'll get to the heart of why I'm writing. Enclosed with this letter is a small package containing a powder. The elves insisted I give it to you as a last resort, in case you find yourself in a situation where you have no other way out. When thrown and upon impact, it will release poisonous dust particles that will paralyze the glimmer gremlin, giving you precious time to escape. Don't worry though; it's not toxic to humans, so it won't harm you.*

*I know you will do great, Emily. I believe in you with all my heart. I can't wait to see you again, to hear all about your adventure, and to share our stories. Stay safe!*

*Love you, with all the best wishes, Hannah"*

Emily felt a warm embrace, not physically, but deep within her heart, as she read Hannah's letter. The reassurance that her dear friend was looking out for her, even from afar, brought her a profound sense of comfort. It meant the world to her, knowing that despite their distance and separation, she had her back. She carefully slid the enchanted powder back into the hidden space within her bust. She knew how crucial it would be to keep it safe, close, and ready, should the worst happen.

She then walked over to her bed, bringing the book about the glimmer gremlin with her. Settling into the bed's soft embrace, she opened the book and read. It didn't take long for the words to start to blur, the trials of the day having wearied her mind. Despite her best efforts, her eyelids closed, and sleep claimed her.

# INTO THE DEN

When Emily awoke from her adventitious nap, she frantically scrambled out of the bed. There was a *tap, tap, tap* resounding through her room, and she fretfully looked for the source of the noise.

In her sweep of the room, she spotted a bird sitting on the sill outside her small window, pecking at the glass pane. Emily raised a hand to her chest as though she could force her heart to settle its pounding rhythm.

She glanced at the window again and noticed the change in lighting from when she had entered her room. Hurriedly, she adjusted her attire and retrieved her glasses from where they'd fallen on the floor during her nap. As she opened the door, her breathing quickened, and she flushed with embarrassment, realizing she had missed lunch and her afternoon training session with Lord Radcliffe. As she rushed out, she glanced back as she secured the door, only to turn and find herself face to face with her stern instructor.

"I'm sorry, Lord Radcliffe," Emily stammered. "I don't know what came over me. I just passed out. There is no excuse, I know."

Lord Radcliffe's expression softened slightly. "Our afternoon lesson was hardly indispensable to your survival. It was more about defensive strategies for situations without an escape. I'm confident you will manage without it. Now, let's hurry to dinner."

Emily nodded, but was hesitant in her reply. "How are defense strategies not important?" she asked.

He regarded her with a measured look, a smirk playing on his lips.

"I didn't want to bring it to the others' attention in the hall earlier, but I know what was given to you by Hannah. I only wish Ísolde had delivered it somewhere... well, more private."

What you have is Efálállinôus root powder. You see, the elves wouldn't have had access to it; they dare not venture into the scrublands of Khạrzọnọv along the borderlands. The plant thrives only in the high alpine glacial zones of the Zọlgụlzięr Mountains, near the Eastern Pass.

They wouldn't have come across it unless I'd given it to them. First to pass to Hannah, and then to you through Ísolde. I'm not sure what Hannah wrote, but this much is clear: use it only when there's no other way out. I promise you, you need not worry," he said with a wink.

"Besides, I have something else; a present of sorts for you in the main hall where we'll be dining. It'll be another tool at your disposal once you receive it. Then at that time we will discuss everything further... if time permits, of course."

Emily smiled and lunged forward, wrapping her arms around him. They held each other for only a moment. She would keep the entire secret locked away in her mind, never to be spoken of. She had been reluctant at first, but she knew now she could trust Lord Radcliffe, because he would go to such lengths to provide her with help. Gratitude welled up within her, quiet and resolute. No one would ever know; not about the invaluable help she received, nor the small thing hidden now beneath the armor she wore.

She released him and took a small step back, smoothing the front of her armor as if nothing of consequence had just passed between them. Lord Radcliffe did not linger on the moment. They turned on their heels and made way for the main hall. Once inside, he came to the table and looked at her. He then turned toward the table, the scrape of a chair against the floor cutting cleanly through the quiet and restoring a sense of order to the room.

Lord Radcliffe pulled out a chair for her, guiding her to sit before gently pushing her toward the table. He then circled to his seat, settling in as Elârâ brought out their meal—a simple yet delicious spread of greens, vegetables, a perfectly roasted bowl of potatoes, and a slab of venison seasoned with aromatic spices that teased the senses. They ate swiftly but with a decorum befitting the evening.

Once they had finished, Lord Radcliffe gestured toward the package that had been silently calling to Emily since she sat down. "That is for you," he said, his voice filled with warmth.

Emily, unable to contain her excitement any longer, reached for it. She carefully unwrapped it, feeling the slight weight of it in her hands. When the paper fell away, it revealed a small dagger sheathed in a sleek black leather sheath. Her eyes widened as she pulled free the blade, revealing a golden hilt embellished with rubies at its three points. The craftsmanship was exquisite, the blade both beautiful and deadly.

"This is remarkable," Emily breathed, awe and gratitude filling her voice.

His gaze softened with pride and a hint of sorrow. "It belonged to one of my daughters, before the sickness took her from us many years ago. You remind me of her, Emily. I felt it fitting to give this to you; for both its beauty and its purpose."

A lump rose in her throat as the significance of the gift pressed down on her. Without thinking, she stood up and rushed to Lord Radcliffe, wrapping him in a tight embrace. "I'm so sorry about your daughter," she whispered, her voice filled with emotion.

Nearly brought to tears, he patted her back gently. "Now," he said, his voice steadying, "secure that on your hip. We must head to the Coliseum."

*** 

Despite having seen it before, the Coliseum remained an awe-inspiring sight as Emily arrived for her test. The air buzzed with anticipation, the energy of the crowd palpable as the last few stragglers filed into the massive structure.

At the entrance, a familiar figure greeted them—Áelfwînë.

"Emily," Áelfwînë called out, his tone resolute as they approached him. "Your task may not be easy, but I believe in you. I know you will be victorious tonight."

Though self-doubt lingered, she managed a quiet, "Thank you."

Áelfwînë leaned in slightly, his voice dropping as he added, "Oh, and Emily; left, left, right, left, right, right." He winked; his words were cryptic yet laden with a meaning she had yet to grasp.

Emily's mind rushed to decipher what he had just told her, trusting that the guard had her best interests in mind. As they continued on their way, she kept repeating the directions under her breath, hoping that her mind would commit them to memory. The mantra echoed in her thoughts as she followed Lord Radcliffe through the masses of people; her focus was so intense that she barely noticed that they were swiftly moving through the crowd with ease.

They joined Órynë, Ándrôniüs, Ísolde, and other dignitaries in an enclosed box just above the arena walls. The crowd erupted into cheers at the sight of Emily, the sound reverberating through the Coliseum like a storm bellowing in the night.

The arena had been transformed. Massive boulders dotted the landscape, and the dark, menacing entrance to the glimmer gremlin's burrow yawned ominously at its center. Emily's heart lumbered in her chest, each beat echoing louder than the last. The darkness of the burrow drew her eyes, and she felt sweat forming on her palms as the world shrank to a pinpoint.

Lord Radcliffe, sensing her preoccupation, turned her to face him. His eyes bore into hers with a fierce intensity. "Emily," he began, his voice low but steady, "you are far more capable than you know. This test will not break you, but will reveal what we all know lives within you. I've no doubt you'll face it with the strength the prophecy speaks of. And when the time comes, you'll do more than endure... you'll rise. Trust in your heart, trust in your instincts, and most importantly, never second-guess your gut. It will lead you to the right place every time."

Emily hugged him tightly, whispering a heartfelt "Thank you" before turning to face the crowd. Lord Radcliffe gave her one last nod of encouragement before exiting the box.

Órynë stood up, his arms stretched wide as he addressed the crowd with fervor. "Before we begin, let us give another round of applause to the Skëphthäúm tribe. They have graced us with a visit from the ice lands to the north, far across the great sea. Their majestic and truly mystical performance stirred my senses quite vigorously. And if it had that effect on me, I could only imagine it did the same for all of you. Now, once more, let us honor both their perilous journey and the breathtaking artistry they have shared with us."

The crowd erupted once more in applause, this time louder and more spirited. Cheers carried across the grand arena as whistles pierced the air and chants of admiration rose from every corner. Some stood to their feet, clapping with fervent enthusiasm, their voices blending into a wave of celebration that filled the night with energy and life.

Órynë raised his hands, signaling for quiet. The roar of the crowd gradually softened, voices trailing off into murmurs until a respectful hush settled over the arena.

"Citizens of Eldôria!" he shouted, his voice now carrying clearly across the hushed crowd. "Âldâmûr!" A renewed wave of cheers erupted. "Brâldôr!" The clash of metal rang out as soldiers raised their weapons in salute, their cheers joining the chorus. "And Illithría!" Though softer, the applause that followed still carried pride.

Órynë let the sounds fade before continuing, his voice strong and unwavering. "Today, we come together, united in purpose, to witness the beginning of a great test. Emily, our smallest champion, yet no less mighty in heart, will descend into the caverns below; the home of the glimmer gremlin. Let us raise our voices in support. Will you all join me in cheering her on as she steps forward to face her fate?"

The Grand Mage gestured for Emily to descend the stairs into the arena. The crowd roared again at the sight of her, their cheers shaking the very ground beneath her feet. Emily glanced back at Ísolde and Ándrôniüs, who were holding hands and wearing supportive smiles. With a deep breath, she stepped forward, feeling the ground rumble as the creatures below stirred from the commotion above. Perturbation tightened its grip on her once more, but she looked back at the stage one last time, catching Lord Radcliffe's wink and reassuring smile from the stands where he had taken his seat.

Emily inhaled deeply, reminding herself that this was for her friends, for the survival of all these people who were counting on her to succeed. She walked ever closer to the entrance of the burrow. Resting her hand on the cold dirt wall, she peered into the dark abyss before her. The roar of the crowd faded into the background as she took one last glance at the world above, then, with a final breath, stepped forward and disappeared into the den of the glimmer gremlin.

# EMILY'S TEST

To Emily, it felt like time had ceased to have meaning once she had cautiously ventured into the deep darkness that consumed her. She heeded her training, ignoring every urge to turn back and concentrating on her breathing and steps. Though the light from the world above still shone at her back, the entrance was fading; the glow growing dimmer with each passing moment. The air grew heavier with every step, her breaths becoming shallow and labored.

The stench of decay hung in the air, so pungent she could almost taste it. Dull shimmers of faelight spiders scurried across the damp, porous walls. She couldn't tell if the crowd above had quieted or if she was simply too far below to hear their distant roars.

The silence was oppressive, broken only by the occasional trickle of water and the sound of her own strained breathing, which she fought to control. A low ringing rang in her ears, adding to the overwhelming sense of isolation. Her legs were weary from trudged through the muck, the ground beneath her feet growing softer and more treacherous with each step. She hoped it was just mud, but she couldn't be sure because of the foul smell that filled her nostrils.

A sudden chill swept through the tunnel, biting through her clothing and sending a shiver down her spine. Emily pulled her hood tight around her head, trying to ward off the cold. The faelight spiders' glow faded, leaving her in almost complete darkness. She reached out instinctively for the walls, but the reassuring touch of the earthen wall was gone.

The tunnel had widened, the walls now too far to reach. Anxiety gripped her as the ground beneath her started trembling, the muted sounds of clicking, grinding, and groaning reverberating from deep within the earth.

Dim lights appeared ahead, offering a small but welcome reprieve from the darkness. Emily hurried toward a large rock she could make out against the cavern wall, seeking shelter. The lights weren't from torches but from clusters of faelight spiders, their bodies casting a ghostly glow as they scurried across the walls and ceiling of the enormous chamber.

Fear tightened its grip on her chest. She had never felt this claustrophobic, this trapped. The sight of the spiders, their tiny legs moving in frantic unison, sent chills down her spine. She could even feel them crawling around her, their tiny bodies brushing against her skin. She fought the urge to scream, knowing they were harmless yet unable to shake the deep-seated fear they stirred within her.

But why were they running? What could drive them into such a frenzy?

A deep rumble resonated through the cavern, followed by the unmistakable sound of something large scraping against the earth. A deafening screech filled the air, causing Emily to freeze in terror as she tried to cover her ears. But it was futile; the shriek penetrated her fruitless attempt to block it out, too powerful to be muffled. She opted to press herself tighter against the rock, praying it would shield her from whatever was approaching.

After a few moments, she mustered the courage to peek over the top of the rock, the residual light from the scattered spiders illuminating the massive form moving in the tunnel ahead. The creature pulled itself into the chamber with a sickening scrape, its immense bulk filling the space. The faint bioluminescence from the faelight spiders revealed the creature's rough, scaly hide, and the eerie blue glow that emanated from the spaces between its scales.

The glimmer gremlin, twice the size of any creature she had ever seen, lumbered into the cavern, its clawed hands plucking spiders from the ceiling and stuffing them into its grotesque mouth. The sound of its feeding was nauseating, a wet, slurping noise that echoed off the walls.

Her hands searched frantically, brushing against the silky bodies of the arachnids as they climbed, crawled, and scurried over her. In her search, she found a small ledge behind her.

Seeking to distance herself from the creature, she moved upward, inching along the narrow ledge. Her feet barely found purchase on the slick, uneven surface. Every step was a test of her courage, pushing her beyond her limits, but she persevered.

The ledge ended abruptly at the entrance of another tunnel branching off the cavern, to the left of where the glimmer gremlin had entered. The beast had settled down, its body emitting a low, rumbling snore that rebounded through the cavern. Emily peered over the edge, unable to see the ground below. She was out of options and knew she only had one thing she could do. Turning back was not an option, so she knew she had to jump and take her chances to get into the tunnel below.

Taking a deep breath, she leapt off the ledge into the darkness. Down she fell. Her ankle struck a large rock as she hit the floor, sending a jolt of pain through her leg. She let out a muffled cry as she tumbled into the mud on the floor, the thick, cold sludge enveloping her. Despite the pain radiating up her leg, Emily lay still for a few seconds before risking a look back at the slumbering creature. To her horror, its scales were glowing again as it stirred. Her cry had awakened the creature.

Emily dragged herself along the ground, her limbs heavy as the soupy mixture clung to her with every movement, weighing her down. The glimmer gremlin's snout, with its glowing cataract-covered eyes, studied the tunnel entrance, tasting the air as it searched for her. She forced herself to remain calm, smearing more mud over her body in a desperate attempt to mask her scent. Her heart pounded, each beat echoing in her ears as the creature's bulk filled the tunnel. She did everything to calm her heart, bringing its intense pounding under her control.

The glimmer gremlin inched closer, its breath hot and fetid, filling the narrow space with a nauseating stench. Emily held her breath. Every muscle in her body tensed as the creature advanced. Her fingers clawed at the mud, trying to pull herself forward, but it resisted, pulling her back as if trying to deliver her to the beast.

Just when she thought the creature would surely find her, the wall beside her suddenly gave way. The mud shifted, revealing a narrow opening into another cavern to her left. Without a moment's hesitation, Emily crawled through the gap, desperate to put as much distance between herself and the monster as possible. The mud sucked at her legs, slowing her progress as she struggled to move. She could hear the creature behind her, its massive body slowly slithering through the tunnel, relentless in its pursuit.

Emily gritted her teeth, now pushing forward, wading through the dense mud with every ounce of strength she had left. She fought against it, her arms and legs burning with travail as she forced herself deeper into the cavern. The sound of the glimmer gremlin's labored breathing grew louder, its snout close enough that she could feel the heat of its breath on the back of her neck. The fluttering light of the faelight spiders reappeared, casting eerie, shifting shadows on the walls as they ran away.

Emily's mind raced, replaying Áelfwînë's words: "Left, left, right, left, right, right."

At that moment, it suddenly hit her. Those words were not superfluous. Áelfwînë in all his kindness, had given her a map of the den. Looking around, her eyes scanning desperately for a way through, she spotted two tunnels in the dark leading out of the current chamber and deeper into the den. She had to act quickly.

She crouched low, her fingers frantically searching the mud for anything she could use as a distraction. Her hand brushed against a small rock held captive in the mud's grip. She grabbed it, clutching it tightly.

In the process, Emily's arm had become trapped as she dug around, and she frantically tried to free it. Panic set in as she started hyperventilating, her body flailing in desperation. With one last yank, her arm came free with a loud pop, and a sharp yelp escaped her lips. A loud snarl and a series of grunts carried from deep within. Then something ground against the stone. She knew what it was; the glimmer gremlin shifting within the tunnel, preparing for one thing only: to strike. She knew she had dislocated her shoulder. The glimmer gremlin lunged forward, its shimmering scales lighting up its terrifying face, pushing through the hole she had just come through, and causing the wall to crumble.

With all the strength she could muster, she took the rock from her other hand and hurled it over the creature. The rock clattered and bounced off the walls into the cavern whence they both came. The creature whipped around, its massive body slamming into the walls as it charged toward the noise. Mud flew everywhere, splattering against Emily as she pressed herself against the wall, struggling to avoid being crushed in its wake.

As the glimmer gremlin disappeared down the tunnel, Emily took a moment to control her breathing. She struggled to her feet, her body shaking from fear. Freeing herself from the mud once more, she began running as fast as she could down the right tunnel. Her breaths came in ragged gasps, her chest heaving as she forced herself forward, wincing in pain as the movement jostled her arm. She had completely disregarded her training at this point. It felt picayune in this moment. She wanted more than anything just to get to the den as fast as possible.

The tunnel narrowed, forcing her to squeeze through the tight space. Behind her, the sound of the creature's snarls diminished, but the memory of its pursuit lingered, spurring her to move faster, hoping she would soon escape the dark depths of this lair.

Emily's pace eventually slowed as the initial burst of adrenaline receded. The glimmer gremlin was no longer in immediate pursuit, giving her a brief moment to gather her thoughts, but the oppressive darkness of the earth around her made every step feel like an eternity.

The walls started shimmering again, with the glow of arachnids scurrying along. She recited the remaining directions in her head like a mantra—"Left, right, right"—over and over to keep her nerves in check. These were the last directions she needed to follow, her final steps to the goblet.

She paused for a moment, took off her hooded cloak, and rolled it up tightly to use as a gag, something to bite down on. She secured it in her mouth, grimacing as the taste of mud, like rancid milk, coated her tongue. Readying herself, she reached down with her right hand, grabbed her left arm, and yanked down with all her strength to reset her shoulder. With a loud pop that echoed through the tunnels, it slipped back into place, relieving her of the pain and leaving behind only a dull ache. She then unrolled her cloak and refixed it to her body.

She looked around in the muted light that was being provided by the remaining faelight spiders. She saw the next left turn quickly, followed by the right, almost as if the tunnels were ironically guiding her straight into the monster's lair.

Pressing on, she felt the cold seep into her bones as the minutes stretched into hours. A ghostly light bathed the next cavern she entered, as if daylight had somehow seeped miles beneath the surface. The glow came from what seemed like billions of faelight spiders, their tiny bodies illuminating the vast space in a macabre display of life amidst the darkness.

Emily allowed herself to rest again briefly, leaning against the icy wall, her body shaking with fatigue. But then, she felt it. The earth trembled around her, a reminder that the glimmer gremlin was still out there, lurking in the shadows, waiting. She fought to keep her destructive thoughts at bay, forcing herself to focus on the task at hand. Five tunnels presented themselves; one on her right, four to her left. She knew that her path lay to the right.

She was so close, she could almost visualize the Goblet of Îgnîs Sápíëntíá, its intricate details etched into her memory. She pushed forward, determined to make it through this ordeal. But doubt threatened to take hold in her mind; while she had been lucky this far, she knew that her luck would not last forever.

Seeking comfort, her hand instinctively reached down her shirt, searching for the small package of Efálállinôus root powder, only to find it gone. Panic flared in her chest. Without the powder, her chances of survival plummeted.

She let out a defeated sigh, but had no choice but to keep moving. The tunnel walls became her guide as she dragged her hand along them, the rough texture of it wearing her fingers raw. On her next step forward, suddenly, there was no floor beneath her feet. She fell, feeling weightless for a brief moment, before she came crashing down onto the rocky floor below.

As her breathing became labored, her sight dimmed; a tingling sensation spread through her body before she lost consciousness.

\*\*\*

Emily awoke with a gasp as faelight spiders began fluttering across her face. She frantically brushed them off. Her chest heaved; her heart pounded. Her body aching, she sat there trembling.

Time stretched on as she gathered enough strength to move forward. Haltingly, she groped along the rocky floor in the dark, her fingers finally brushing against something soft and delicate as she searched for the walls.

A surge of relief washed over her as she realized she had found the nest. She pulled herself closer, her heart racing with a mixture of hope and dread. Reaching forward, her hands brushed against something cold and metallic. She wondered if it was the goblet. Emily at the moment convinced herself it was. The ribbed texture of the goblet sent a jolt of relief through her. She brought it close to her face, trying to make out the details, but her eyes strained fruitlessly in the darkness.

The ground started rumbling once more, a warning that the glimmer gremlin could be nearby. Emily's fingers traced the elongated stem of the goblet, feeling the wide bowl at the top. Was this the Goblet of Îgnîs Sápíëntíá? She held it in her hand, but doubt gnawed at her. Something told her to check the nest again. She remembered Lord Radcliffe's advice—to trust her gut—and searched around.

Almost immediately, her fingers brushed against another object. Another goblet, perhaps. Panic set in. There were two goblets. What if there were more? What if these were decoys placed to confuse her?

The rumbling grew louder, and she could hear the distinctive clicking, grinding, and groaning of the glimmer gremlin. There was no telling if it was under, above, or inside this very chamber with her as the sound resounded through the hollowed-out passages of its warren.

Frantically, she searched the nest, kicking at the ground to see if there were more areas concealing more goblets that she might need to find. But with each desperate kick, rocks loosened and clattered against the walls, sending reverberations through the cavern. The sound of the glimmer gremlin was nearing, getting louder, likely drawn by her frantic efforts, but her desperation made her careless.

Finding only the two, Emily tied the goblets to her side, their metal clinking softly as she secured them. She drew her dagger, feeling its reassuring weight in her hand.

Pressing herself against the wall, she retraced her steps back to the ledge from which she had fallen. Reaching up, she cursed loudly as she realized she was too short to pull herself up. Desperate, she was feeling along the wall when she hit something that rebounded back at her. She reached forward, feeling a rough, twisted, twine-like object. Her hands ran up and down the length of the item, and she realized it was a rope.

She grasped it firmly with both hands and began climbing the wall, her feet pressed against it, pulling hand over hand as she ascended from the den of the beast.

As she reached the lip, she knew the glimmer gremlin would likely be nearby, drawn by the sounds she had inevitably made. She waded back through the thick muck of the tunnel, forcing herself onward, the goblets clinking at her side.

To her relief, she did not encounter the monster as she backtracked—left, left, right, left, right, right—until she found herself in the first cavern she had entered. While she had passed through the tunnels unmolested, the sounds of the glimmer gremlin had never given way. They relentlessly pursued her, no doubt following the clinking of the goblets.

Portent sounds echoed through the surrounding tunnels. She could hear it clicking, groaning, and screeching at repetitive intervals, as if it were communicating with something else. As the thought occurred to her, Emily froze in her tracks. A memory flashed in her mind; Lord Radcliffe's words from one of their conversations—"I brought two".

Her mind raced with panic once more as she remembered those words, the mental turmoil mirrored with another increase in her pulse and breathing. She now realized that she had been extraordinarily lucky to have made it this far with only meeting one of the monsters. Stopping beneath the lip of the wall where she assumed she had hurt her ankle, Emily listened, the dull pain in her leg competing with her still twinging shoulder. One of the creatures was still in tow, its distinct sounds reverberating through the tunnels.

She began searching with her fingers brushing against the ground, searching for a rock or anything she could use to throw down one of the tunnels as a diversion, so she could make her escape. Surprisingly, she found a rock, but it was firmly stuck in the ground, and only budged slightly. As she struggled to pry it free, her hand brushed against something soft, fabric-like. Her heart skipped a beat. Could it be? Emily grabbed it. She held it up to her face, trying to make out what it was in the darkness.

Hope sparked within her as she clutched the small package, praying it was the powder she had lost. Stuffing the package into a pocket, Emily refocused, redirecting her newfound excitement to working the rock free. It loosened just as she felt a fetid breath against the back of her neck. Then came the feeling of something wet and bristly against her skin.

She turned slowly, her heart pounding, and there it was. A glimmer gremlin, with its scaly skin glistening in the dim light, its eyes clouded with cataracts yet still piercing through the darkness. Its forked tongue flicked out. Emily shuffled away from it slowly. She held her breath, daring not to breathe. Her heart beat erratically even as she tried to calm it, her nerves causing it to leap and bound.

Then, with a swift motion, the creature moved forward, but stopped again within inches of her. The creature's massive nostrils flared as it sniffed, trying to pinpoint the location of its elusive prey.

Placing the rock softly back onto the ground, she clutched her dagger tightly, pointing it at the creature's face, ready to strike if it lunged. But the beast hesitated, confused by her scent masked by the mud. Its monstrous form blocked the only way out. She was trapped. Stepping back, Emily's foot caught on the loose stone, sending her sprawling to the ground, the goblets clanking against the floor. The glimmer gremlin screeched, the sound bouncing through the cavern, as another rumble shook the earth. Something else was coming.

The faelight spiders scattered, illuminating the scene with their eerie glow. From a tunnel, a glimmer gremlin emerged, its grotesque form filling the remaining space, leaving Emily no escape. Their massive bodies blocked every route, trapping her between them and the cavern walls. As they began wildly sniffing around, their forms jostling against each other and growing more agitated with each passing moment, panic surged through her.

Emily pressed herself against the wall, edging closer to the opening she had come through, hoping for a miracle.

But then disaster struck. The goblets slipped from their binding, clattering to the ground with a metallic clang. The creatures whipped their heads toward the sound, their snarls reverberating in the confined space. She gasped instinctively, covering her mouth with her free hand, her heart hammering as she fought to suppress the scream that threatened to escape.

In their movements, they formed a tiny gap; far too small for her to squeeze through. The glimmer gremlins began scratching at each other, their anger and frustration building as they struggled to locate her in their frenzy. In her desperation, Emily remembered the soft pouch she had found earlier, the one she hoped contained the paralyzing powder Hannah had sent with Ísolde.

The goblets continued to clink together as the beasts fought, and Emily knew she had to act quickly. She reached into her pocket and grasped the object within. With a prayer in her heart, she hurled the pouch straight at the creatures. It exploded in a cloud of dust, filling the cavern with a noxious fume. The glimmer gremlins screeched in agony, their massive bodies thrashing as they tried to escape the poisonous dust. But the tight space worked against them. They lodged themselves in the cavern, their limbs flailing helplessly.

One of them collapsed against Emily, its enormous arm pinning her to the ground. The weight was crushing, trapping her beneath its immobile form. A wave of temporary relief washed over her as the creatures fell still, succumbing to the effects of the powder as Hannah's letter had described, but panic quickly followed. She reached down, searching for the goblets, only to remember they had come loose and tumbled somewhere in the dark cavern.

Now she did not know where they were. She felt her emotions surge; so close to victory, yet suddenly all felt lost. Her predicament was dire: the goblets were missing, likely buried under a monster, and she couldn't tell if the creatures were only temporarily paralyzed or if they were finally defeated.

Frantically, she began feeling around with her hands, searching for anything. Her fingers brushed against a leather tassel; could it be? She grasped it, pulling it back to her. The clang of metal filled the air. Pressing it to her face, she felt the familiar texture of a goblet followed by another. Her hands confirmed it. They were the goblets she had lost, miraculously close by. Re-securing the goblets to her side, she felt relief, hoping one was the one she'd been tasked to find.

But now, she needed a way out. Futilely, she pushed against the arm, trying to wiggle herself free, but it was to no avail. Feeling the grip of her dagger still in her hand, she realized she would have to cut herself free. The thought sickened her, but there was no other choice.

With trembling hands, Emily gripped her dagger and began slicing into the creature's thick, rubbery flesh. The blade dug deep, and warm blood oozed over her fingers as she cut through muscle and tendon. Then she faced the bone. She started hacking at it with her dagger, each blow a desperate bid for freedom, chipping away at the bone little by little. Finally, with a sickening crunch, the bone gave way, and the weight shifted slightly. Emily pushed the limb off of her and took a deep breath.

Emily scrambled out from under the beast's arm, slipping in the blood and mud as she pushed herself through the narrow space between the paralyzed creatures. Jagged rocks tore at her exposed clothes beneath her armor, cutting her skin and sending sharp bursts of pain through her body, but she kept moving. Her body was slick, the goblets clinking at her side as she finally pulled free, collapsing onto the ground with a clatter.

Emily, without hesitation, took off in an explosive sprint, her entire body throbbing with pain, but she didn't care. She had to get out. The tunnel stretched on, the light ahead growing brighter with each step. Her pace quickened, turning into a full sprint as the sounds of the crowd reached her ears, muffled at first, then clearer as she neared the surface. The once comforting light now seemed harsh and blinding after so long in the dark, but she did not falter.

A thunderous roar from the crowd greeted Emily as she burst from the tunnel's mouth. They gasped and cheered at the sight of her—covered in the blood, mud, and the remnants of her struggle deep within the earth. Her chest heaving, she raised the goblets high above her head, a symbol of her hard-won victory.

Lord Radcliffe, Ándrôniüs, Ísolde, and Órynë rushed toward her, their faces a mix of relief and pride.

"Emily!" Lord Radcliffe shouted, his voice carrying on the waves of the cheers. "You did it!"

Ándrôniüs reached her first, his eyes wide with astonishment. "I knew you had it in you, Emily. I never doubted it for a second!"

Embracing her tightly, soiling her beautiful dress, tears streaming down her cheeks, Ísolde said, "I am so glad you're safe."

Órynë retrieved both goblets from her and inspected them, ensuring one of them was the Goblet of Îgnîs Sápíëntíá. The first he did not recognize. But when he saw the second, he turned to the crowd and shouted, "Behold! The victor of the first test! Let us all feast and celebrate the bravery and strength of Emily, who has brought honor to us all!"

The Coliseum erupted in cheers. Emily managed a smile, the first genuine smile she had felt in what seemed like days. Despite the muck and blood covering her, she felt a sense of pride and accomplishment. She had done it. Against all odds; she had survived.

Again, Órynë's raised his hands, commanding silence and reverence for the champion before them. "Let this day be remembered as the triumph of courage and sheer willpower," he declared, his voice filled with pride. "Emily has faced the depths of darkness and emerged victorious. Let us bring today's events to a close and celebrate the strength that dwells within us all. No matter your size, you too can accomplish the impossible."

Emily stood at the center of it all, the pressure of many days slowly lifting from her shoulders. Her heart swelled with gratitude and pride as she looked back at Lord Radcliffe, Ándrôniüs, and Ísolde, all of whom had believed in her when she had doubted herself.

Lord Radcliffe, ever the stalwart mentor, stepped forward, his ceremonial armor gleaming under the fading light. "Come, Lady Emily," he said with a soft smile. "Elârâ awaits you in your quarters. She'll help tend to your injuries."

*** 

Emily entered her room to find Elârâ waiting patiently in a chair, her face lighting up with relief the moment she saw Emily. "Oh, you survived!" Elârâ exclaimed, her voice trembling with emotion.

Smiling widely, despite the implication to the contrary, Emily said jubilantly, "I did!"

Elârâ's eyes widened as she noticed the bloodstains on Emily's armor, skin, and matted with the mud in her hair. "Oh my, is that blood yours?" she asked, her voice tinged with concern.

"Some of it, maybe," Emily replied with a slight chuckle. "But most of it belongs to that thing I had to cut through to escape."

Approaching, Elârâ inspected her with gentle touches. "Turn around. Let me help you with your armor."

Emily hesitated, feeling a bit embarrassed and unused to such help. "I can undress myself. You don't have to."

Elârâ smiled reassuringly. "It is customary for the victor to have someone bathe them, Emily. Don't you worry; my eyes are for someone else, not you."

Feeling a wave of relief, Emily obliged. Elârâ carefully unfastened the laces of Emily's leather armor, letting the leather breastplate fall to the ground. She then moved to Emily's boots, loosening them and guiding Emily to sit as she pulled them off. When Emily stood again, Elârâ helped her behind the vanity screen, where she assisted in removing the rest of her clothing.

Elârâ pointed to the bath, already filled with warm, fragrant water and a layer of bubbles. Emily climbed in and sank into the soothing embrace of the water as Elârâ began to gently scrub the grime from her body. The warmth seeped into her aching muscles. Elârâ worked with care, washing Emily's legs, arms, and torso before moving to her hair, which she submerged under the water, allowing the muck to melt away.

Once Elârâ finished, she drained the tub and refilled it with fresh water, giving Emily a moment to relax. "I'll return in ten minutes to help you get dressed," Elârâ said softly.

"No, that's fine," Emily replied, her voice barely above a whisper. "I'll dress myself. Thank you for your help."

Elârâ smiled and turned to leave, but before she could go, Emily's voice stopped her.

"Elârâ, who do you have eyes for?" Emily asked, well aware of the answer but seeking confirmation for her friend's sake.

Blushing, Elârâ closed the door, walked back toward Emily, and took a seat by her. "Jake," she admitted shyly. "He's the type of person I've always dreamed of, but my father would surely never allow it."

"Maybe in the coming days, you'll have a say in it, Elârâ," Emily suggested with a hopeful tone.

Even though Elârâ smiled, Emily saw that the smile was forced, and her genuine emotions were evident behind her facade.

"Only if my father perishes, but I do not wish that. I love him dearly, despite our differences. However, that is a colloquy for another time. I really must go. I must ensure the staff is ready for your celebratory feast. I'll check in on you soon," Elârâ replied.

Elârâ shut the door behind her as she left the room, leaving Emily alone with her thoughts. Her mind shifted to reflect on the events of the day. She marveled at her survival, recalling the darkness of the caverns and the terror of facing the glimmer gremlins. The overwhelming sense of victory settled over her like a warm blanket.

It all felt surreal.

# HEROES OF THE PAST

THE NEXT MORNING, IN a room across the city, Ryan sat at his small desk, half-heartedly leafing through some parchments. He had been awake for some time, his stomach in knots, knowing this would be the day he faced the warrior prince. By the stream of light beaming down through his window, he tried to focus enough to read, hoping to take his mind off the coming test, but to little avail. A knock on the door broke through his spiraling thoughts.

"Ryan, are you awake?" a familiar voice called out.

Recognizing Ethan's voice, Ryan forced himself to respond. "Yeah, man, what's up?"

Ethan's voice softened with concern. "Can Jake and I come in?"

Ryan sighed and muttered, "Sure, why not?"

The door slowly swung open, and Ethan and Jake crowded into the room. The space was small and sparsely furnished; a soldier's quarter, more or less. A narrow bed pushed against one wall, and a simple wooden desk cluttered with parchment and a few candle stubs sat under a small window. The walls were cold gray stone, and a single armor stand held his gear. The metal was scratched and dented, bearing the marks of the countless others who had trained and fought in it before him.

"Man, you must be freaking out, knowing you have to not just fight, but kill someone today," Jake said, the remark only fueling the *Sturm und Drang* churning in Ryan.

Ethan shot Jake a sharp look, his voice laced with irritation. "Dude, seriously? Did you really have to say that?"

Having stiffened, Ryan tried to stay calm. "Yeah, not the right time or place. At least you're fighting creatures, not a person."

"You're right, man. My bad." Jake winced, regretting his

flippancy.

Before Ryan could respond, five rapid knocks resounded through the room, followed by the door swinging open. Thâlôr entered, his presence commanding immediate attention. He glanced at the three friends, his expression unreadable.

"Good morning to you all. Ryan, your instructors wish to see you before breakfast. Gather your things and get ready for the day." Thâlôr turned on his heel and left, the door clicking shut behind him.

Ryan exhaled slowly, his emotions causing his chest to tighten. "Well, guys, I guess I have to get going. See you at breakfast... I hope."

"Yeah, hopefully," Ethan echoed with feigned optimism.

Jake and Ethan exited the room, heading toward the dining hall.

Left alone, Ryan set about gathering his things, carefully laying them out on the neat bed. The armor, now his, was a perfect fit. As he ran his fingers over the smooth metal, he couldn't help but think of the person or people who had worn it before him, their courage embedded in every inch. He wondered: had its previous occupant died tragically, or had they simply outgrown it? Perhaps they had something more personal made for them.

Outside his door, a basin of warm, perfumed water awaited him. He retrieved it and patted himself down thoroughly; the scent masked the odors of his sweat and grime. With deliberate care, he dressed himself. First the tabard, then the pants and socks. Next, he donned his armor, piece by piece, until steel encased him completely. Each buckle and strap felt like a step closer to the inevitable confrontation ahead. He secured his sword to his side and held his helmet in his hand.

Grasping the doorknob, Ryan turned it slowly, as if trying to delay the inevitable. Steeling himself, he swung the door open and stepped into the corridor.

The morning light filtered through narrow windows, casting long shadows on the stone floors. Ryan's thoughts were a tumult of apprehension at the task ahead, but one thing was certain: by tonight, he would either rise as a warrior or fall in the attempt.

As he descended the seven flights of stairs to the landing of the main hall, his heart pounded with trepidation with each step. There, he found himself face-to-face with the three formidable warriors he had come to know: Vôrmghôr, Gründhölm, and Sāā. Over the last few days, he had learned that each man was a living legend, and their presence alone invigorated Ryan, momentarily suppressing the anxiety running freely in his head.

Vôrmghôr stood at the forefront, a mage of short stature but heavily muscled. Veins pulsed beneath skin that seemed carved from stone. His sharp brown eyes were ever alert, contrasting with the neatly kept beard that framed his stern face. He wore a fitted leather cuirass and battle-worn metal plates that glinted in the dim light, each scar on his armor a silent testament to hard-won battles.

Beside him stood Sāā, a towering figure nearly seven feet tall, his broad shoulders and sculpted build making him a giant among any race. Intricate tribal-like tattoos covered his bald head, winding down his neck and arms. The myriad of scars that marred his body disrupted the symmetry of the tattoos, telling their own stories. Sāā's formidable physique was highlighted by his traditional Vâloríân garb, a simple yet imposing ensemble of dark cloth and leather.

Gründhölm, the last of the trio, was a mage of medium height with fair skin and a face marked by a long scar that ran from his left eye to the right side of his cheek. He had short blond hair, and his blue eyes seemed to peer right through Ryan. His armor was simple but well-crafted, with a heavy cloak draped over one shoulder, leaving the other arm bare to show the mottled burn scars along its length.

Vôrmghôr spoke first, his voice gruff but tinged with a hint of humor. "My dear lad, about time you woke from that slumber," he said, clapping Ryan on the back. "We were thinking we might have to drag you out of bed."

"I'm sure we did him in with that Olympian circuit yesterday. You sure you can do this, boy?" Gründhölm chuckled, shaking his head.

Ever the calm giant, Sāā smiled faintly. "Gents, he learned from us; the Grand Marshals of Vâloríâ's legions. You know he can do this."

Vôrmghôr's eyes narrowed slightly as he turned to Sāā. "I never said he couldn't, did I?" he shot back, his tone defensive.

The giant laughed deeply, a rumbling sound that echoed through the hall. "Now, now, little one," Sāā teased, patting Vôrmghôr on the head as if he were a child. "Settle down. We wouldn't want the little man to throw a pother."

Ryan couldn't help but chuckle at the playful antagonism between the three warriors. It was clear they were bound by a deep respect for one another, even though they would taunt each other numerous times throughout the day.

Knowing they could go on for some time, something he had become quite accustomed to, Ryan tried to steer the conversation back on track. "What training do I have today with you all?"

Vôrmghôr, abandoning his brief stare-down with Sāā, turned to Ryan with a serious expression. "Nothing today, lad. It's a day of rest. You've learned well and been one of our best students in recent times."

"Indeed. I'd conscript you into the Vâloríân army as a lieutenant if I could," Gründhölm said in agreement.

Sāā leaned in, his towering presence almost overwhelming. "Just remember, you can beat this prince. He is just a man, much like you. But smaller. More dwarf-like, well, just a dwarf, not a man. Anyway, you know what I mean. You have as much of a chance to strike him down as he does you. I have no doubt you will give him quite a match today."

Not at all sharing their confidence about the situation, all Ryan could mutter was, "I hope so."

Gründhölm's voice took on a more serious tone. "There is no hope. There is only doing it and fighting until you are spent on the field of battle. Even if you fall, the Allfather will graciously accept you into his halls, as long as you have expended every ounce of your being fighting to win."

"But I am not ready to die," Ryan said, feeling an icy shiver run down his spine.

"No living being; man, mage, elf, dwarf, whatever Sāā may be," he said, shooting a jest at his friend, "is truly prepared to die."

Vôrmghôr's expression softened slightly as he added, "Every man yearns to experience the world and draw his last breath knowing he's fulfilled his purpose. But let's set death aside for now."

He approached Ryan, lifted his chin, firmly grabbed his hands, stared into his eyes, and said, "When you defeat him—and I know you will—grant him a warrior's death. When he's down and you see the fear that no doubt will be in his eyes, allow him to grab his weapon; let him embrace it. It's the dwarven way. To deny him that would be the greatest dishonor."

"I'll make sure it's honorable," Ryan said, his jaw tightening as he absorbed the gravity of Vôrmghôr's words.

Sāā also gave him a supportive pat on the back, his voice gentle despite his imposing size. "Indeed, make it honorable. It's about respect. After tonight, they'll sing songs about you."

"Are you sure there's nothing else I should be training today?" Ryan asked, almost longing for the distraction from the looming confrontation.

Vôrmghôr exchanged glances with the other two warriors before shaking his head. "I don't think so. Anyone else?"

Both Gründhölm and Sāā shook their heads.

"So, what do I do in the meantime?" Ryan asked, trying to keep his voice steady.

Sāā grinned. "Eat breakfast, train some if you'd like, come in for lunch, and then meet in this hall. You'll then be escorted to the coliseum for your fight."

Ryan bowed to the three warriors, a gesture of deep respect that they returned with nods of approval.

As he turned to leave, Gründhölm called out after him, "And tell those two friends of yours that once they're done eating, they need to meet us on the staircase in the courtyard. We begin their daily training immediately after they finish their breakfast."

Ryan left them as they made their way outside. He paused at the base of the stairs, contemplating whether to return upstairs and change out of his armor. The heavy metal plates and tight leather straps felt excessive, almost out of place for something as simple as breakfast. But the thought of climbing seven flights of stairs quickly dissuaded him. With a resigned sigh, he turned down the hallway to his right and headed toward the dining hall.

As he entered, the smell of fresh bread and cinnamon filled his nostrils; a welcome contrast to the stale air of the barracks. The dining hall buzzed with the sounds of warriors enjoying their breakfast, voices mingling with the clatter of cutlery against plates.

He spotted Ethan and Jake at a table near the far end of the hall, their plates piled high with a breakfast designed to fuel warriors. Thick slices of salted ham, boiled eggs, hearty porridge, and dense bread slathered with butter. A plate loaded with the same hearty meal had been prepared for him by his friends. Ryan approached the table, his armor clinking softly with each step.

Ethan looked up as Ryan sat down. "So, any training for you today?"

"Yeah, they've got me fighting Vôrmghôr after breakfast," Ryan said, straight-faced. "*Without wasters.*"

Jake's eyes widened, his face a picture of disbelief. "Are they trying to kill you before you even make it to the Coliseum? You've heard the stories about him, haven't you? If you're using a real blade... that's not good."

"I'm just kidding, man," Ryan chuckled, shaking his head. "No, today's a rest day. They told me to take it easy, maybe do some light training if I feel like it. But no grueling circuits today."

Ethan leaned back, stretching out his sore muscles. "Lucky you. I wonder what they've got planned for us after that insane session yesterday."

Groaning in agreement, Jake said, "Yeah, my quads are killing me after that run from the Grand Barracks to the inlet, and then swimming across to Tháldrüm and back. They're really trying to break us down, aren't they?"

Ryan rubbed his shoulder, wincing slightly. "Just your quads? Everything hurts on me."

With a mischievous grin, Ethan reached under the table. "You think you've got it bad? Check this out." He pulled off his boot and sock, slamming his foot onto the table. His pruned, pale skin emitted a funky smell.

Recoiling in disgust, Ryan heaved. "Ethan, that's revolting!

We're eating here!"

Jake burst out laughing, though he quickly added, "Yeah, man, put that thing away before we all lose our breakfast."

The three friends laughed together, the sound easing some of the unease that had been lingering since the day began.

Once they had finished their meal, Ryan stood up from the table, wiping his mouth with the back of his hand. "Hey, before I forget, the gents want you two in the courtyard for training. They didn't say what you'd be doing, but they told me to tell you to be prepared."

Ethan looked less than thrilled by the prospect. "Great, just what I need after yesterday. C'mon, Jake, let's go get ready for another day of getting our asses kicked."

Jake nodded, though he looked equally resigned. "Yeah, well, if we don't see you before the fight tonight, good luck, Ryan. *Seriously.*"

The three of them exchanged brief but heartfelt embraces before parting ways.

Returning to his room, Ryan methodically removed his armor, placing each piece back on the stand with care. Once he was down to his tunic and trousers, he fastened a leather belt around his waist and pulled on a pair of well-worn boots, their leather soft from use.

He headed back downstairs, feeling the need to stretch his legs and clear his mind before the activities of the night to come. He descended the steps, making his way to the foyer of the Grand Barracks.

The statues, tall and imposing, each carved with exquisite detail, capturing the essence of the warriors they represented, drew his gaze. Ryan moved among them, tracing the names engraved on the plaques at their feet: Ibrahim, Hiroshi, Cormac, Áslaug, Mikhail, Jacques. But when he reached the seventh statue, he paused.

Someone defaced this one with a ferocity that made it unrecognizable. Deep, jagged scratches marred the stone, obscenities covered its surface, and the plaque that once bore the warrior's name had been so violently desecrated that only the letter 'C' remained discernible. The mutilation of the statue was so extensive that it seemed to echo the disgrace of the figure it depicted.

Nearby, an eighth podium stood conspicuously empty, raising a silent question: why had someone left it unfilled, and who, or what, was to occupy it?

Ryan turned his attention back to the defiled statue, his thoughts swirling with questions. Why was this one marred while the others stood untouched? What had this warrior done to deserve such a fate?

Lost in thought, Ryan didn't hear the footsteps approaching until they were nearly on top of him. He turned to see Thâlôr, dressed in a white tunic clasped with a circular seal of Vâloríâ on his right shoulder. His hair flowed down his back, giving him the appearance of an ancient statesman. The warrior stopped beside Ryan, his gaze fixed on the defaced statue.

Ryan had been wrestling with a question since the first time he entered the foyer, and he decided now was the time to ask it. "Thâlôr, who are these people?"

Thâlôr smiled faintly. "That's a good question, Ryan. Walk with me," he said, leading Ryan to the statue on the far left.

They stopped in front of the figure. The statue before them depicted a man in traditional Persian garb from the dawn of the empire, his form tall and noble. He wore a long flowing robe embroidered with patterns of lions and eagles. A wide, belted sash wrapped around his waist, and a sheathed scimitar rested against his hip, hinting at his warrior status. His beard was long and carefully groomed, and a tall, cylindrical helmet adorned his head, resembling those worn by his ancient kings. His face bore a fierce yet regal expression, forever frozen in stoic dignity.

"This is Ibrahim, one of our first champions," Thâlôr began. "He came to us from a land called Persia, in your world. Ibrahim was a prince before he came here, but he was chosen and brought here to fulfill a different destiny. He fell in the Battle of Lôríthíl near the south gates of Khạrzọnọv. He perished at the hands of the Dark Lord, who smote his head from his body on the battlefield after an unrelenting duel. Ibrahim succumbed to death only after losing all those who fought alongside him. His death marked the beginning of the first darkness."

Stepping to another statue, Thâlôr said, "This is Hiroshi, a blade master from Ishida. Though he did not claim the ultimate victory, he ended the Dark Lord's mortal form, only to fall moments later to a gorlock coming to the aid of his master. His last stand at the Siege of the Eastern Pass marked the start of the second darkness."

The statue depicted Hiroshi in full samurai armor, standing proud and defiant. His Kabuto, a helmet bedecked with the intricate crest of a dragon, sat high on his head, while his face exuded a calm and resolute honor. His kimono underneath bore symbols of loyalty, sacrifice, and the legacy of his people. In one hand, he gripped the hilt of his Katana, the blade just beginning to emerge. At his waist, the wakizashi rested as a reminder of the bushido code he followed. The statue radiated both the heroism of his victory over the Dark Lord's mortal form and the sorrow of his fall moments later.

Continuing to walk down the line of statues, Thâlôr started recounting the histories of those that remained.

"The people still speak her name: Áslaug of Veðrvangr, Shieldmaiden of the North, daughter of winter's wrath and the iron tide.

Alongside her stood four renowned warrior-sisters: Brynhildr the Bright-Eyed, Sigrún Wolfborn, Hervor of the Broken Blade, and Freydís Bearblood. People remember their names, carved into saga and stone, not just for grace, but for the ruthless beauty of their furious, breathtaking, wild, and merciless nature; like the sea.

It was they who taught our legions the arts of shieldwall discipline, axe-rotation, and thunder-charge formations. Many of the war doctrines we hold sacred were first spilled from their blood and fire.

And yet, even their brilliance could not hold the tide at Côrcaemán. One by one, they fell. Not in retreat; but in defiance. Their fall marked the collapse of our five legions, shattered on those obsidian fields.

But Áslaug did not falter. Even when all ranks broke, banners tore, and command was lost, she alone charged at and through the throngs of darkness. With blade in hand and a war-song on her lips, she carved ruin into the dark tide; felling hundreds, and breaking the backs of two enemy generals before the shadows overwhelmed her.

Some accounts even claim that warriors of old forged forward with her, guiding her through to the end. But her death was not the end. It was the price.

Though Côrcaemán plunged us into darkness, it also shattered the Dark Lord's armies so completely that neither side would recover for an age. The field was ash, but from it rose a reckoning. The Sixth Age ended there. With five fallen maidens. Our world forced to begin again."

Ryan and Thâlôr shuffled a few steps in complete silence before stopping in front of another statue; a man.

"This is Jacques. Like the others, he wasn't born in these lands. He came to us from the far west; across the ocean, he said. A fur trapper from the high plains, where the Apsáalooke once walked and his people, the French, called it *les terres hautes*. He wandered into our world young, quiet, and dangerous in the way only men who've survived too much can be. But he didn't come here to hunt. He came to unite us. And he did.

Before the Republic was even a dream, he brought together the fractured kingdoms of men, the stubborn halls of the dwarves, and even the scattered hosts of the elves. It was he—Jacques of Languedoc—who forged the banner we all hope to march beneath one day: a united Cáelunárra.

The Battle of Amüngdráng claimed his four counterparts; Jacques stood alone. But he didn't stop fighting. Forty-three years he gave to us. Through siege, betrayal, famine, and false peace. He stood with us until the very end.

At the Siege of Läcküllôrra, high in the mountains of Brâldôr, the Dark Lord unleashed a new weapon. A powder that exploded on impact. When it struck the fortress, it turned stone to ash. Jacques was standing on the wall. He was gone in an instant. Nothing left of him but the whisper of his name on the wind.

The dwarves rebuilt, but the loss was too deep to bury. Entire clans—men, women, children—burned because of the Zâwxînê, those traitorous dwarven kin who opened the gates from within. Dwarves, just like them in the east; same look, same blood, just darker-skinned. Once staunch allies, turned bitter rivals.

So don't be surprised, Ryan, when the dwarven prince meets you with fire behind his eyes. It's not hatred. It's a memory. And memory runs deeper than stone in these mountains.

But remember this! Jacques' death bought us time. Enough to bleed the Dark Lord's armies dry! Don't let that be for nothing."

Once Thâlôr finished his monologue about Jacques of Languedoc, he gestured for them to move down the line.

"Mikhail came from the time of Novgorod. A war general, hardened by frozen campaigns and border raids—made of iron and winter—and the most promising champion ever seen, a reassurance after the tragic defeat of Cormac the age before.

When Mikhail first arrived in our lands, he was beset by all manner of dark beasts on the journey to Vâloriâ. He kept himself, his companions, and a group of refugees safe for nearly fifty years until the High Mage Council could locate them and provide aid. His heroic actions and the ease with which he completed his test brought hope to all who heard of his exploits.

But it was not to be. A fortnight after completing their tests, someone wiped out Mikhail and his counterparts. They were on their way to Shí Lû Dürr, the seat of the High King of Âldâmûr and the gathering point for the forces amassing to fight. But on the road, just after crossing the River Tynnëmynnwn, they were caught out.

Vränkëphlét the Deceiver was the one entrusted to guide them. A mage of our own. One of our councilmen. And a double agent. He succumbed to the Dark Lord's madness, became a Shadewalker, and slaughtered them all."

Thâlôr's head bowed, lines of sorrow etched into his face.

"The location of the betrayal and slaughter of Mikhail and the four other champions of that age is unknown; lost to the sands of time. The elders of the Áírrmâ still alive dare not speak of it. So heavy is our shame that one of our own was responsible for so much destruction. They've done all they can to erase it from our oral history.

But scrolls remain. Books are hidden. Stories whispered.

Ammón Cúrr it is known as now. The place of betrayal and treachery. After that came the most brutal of all the wars against the darkness. The plague. The famine. The destruction left behind. None like we've seen before; or since. The forces of darkness tore through the land like rot through root."

Finally, they reached the defaced statue. Ryan stared at it, the silence between them heavy with unspoken words.

"And who is this?" Ryan asked, his voice hushed.

Thâlôr's expression darkened, his tone growing more somber. "We do not mention his name. Though he performed great deeds and was expected to lead us to lasting victory, he abandoned all that is light and good. He became an agent of the Dark Lord, betraying his allies, his brothers. He poisoned the minds of mages, dwarves, men, and elves, driving a wedge between the four kingdoms of Cáelunárra and the republic. His sown rifts may never heal. Some say he came from your world; others believe he was born in ours, as he used the teachings of the mages to commit unspeakable acts. No one knows for sure. But we do not speak his name within these hallowed walls because to do so would give power to the darkness he left behind and bring dishonor to those who gave up everything to protect Cáelunárra."

His gaze lingered on the defaced statue. The significance of Thâlôr's words pressed on Ryan's chest. "Then why keep his statue here if he was so wicked?"

Thâlôr turned to Ryan, his eyes intense and unwavering. "This statue teaches us, reminding us that even the mightiest minds can be swayed, and that even those destined for greatness can still fall. It warns us that there is no room for weakness within these halls. The champions of Cáelunárra are not merely warriors; they were and are a final bastion against the darkness that hungers to devour us all."

Swallowing hard, Ryan felt the implications of Thâlôr's words sinking in. "How do I know if I'm strong enough? How do I know if I'm ready for all of this?"

Thâlôr watched him solemnly for several moments. "Cormac the Brave," he began, his voice heavy with reverence, "was one of our most unlikely champions. A man of frail build who had lost a leg and was blind in one eye. Fear was his constant companion, and yet, it was this very man who nearly brought an end to the darkness that has plagued Cáelunárra."

Thâlôr placed a hand on Ryan's shoulder, his grip firm yet comforting, as if anchoring him. He walked him toward another of the statues on the right side of the walkway.

The statue before them portrayed a man of humble yet unyielding presence. Cormac stood tall, despite the frailty in the subtle thinning of his frame. A carved wooden prosthetic replaced his left leg. His right eye, sharp and focused, stared ahead with determination, while a weathered patch covered his blind left eye. Dressed in a simple cloak and worn tunic, his humble origins were evident. In one hand, he held a staff, more for support than combat, but the grip of his fingers suggested it had seen many battles. His face, though lined with age and hardship, radiated a quiet bravery that spoke of his enduring spirit.

Thâlôr's eyes seemed to darken as he spoke about the sculpture. "Two thousand years ago, in the Third Age, Cormac led a force that none have since matched. He brought together men, elves, mages, dwarves, and even the reclusive lýëch, uniting them in an assault on the Dark Lord's stronghold, Vragmọr. They reached the very walls, those cursed walls, and rock by rock they started to break them down, inching closer to what could have been the salvation of our world."

His voice grew quieter, yet more intense, as if he could see the scene unfolding before him. "But just as victory seemed within their grasp, the Dark Lord unleashed a horror none could have foreseen... a toxic gas swept through the battlefield, a vile mist that choked the life out of every living being in its path. Cormac, and nearly every warrior of fighting age, perished that day. Their bodies lay strewn across the battlefield, their final breaths taken not by sword or spear, but by the insidious fumes of the Dark Lord's malice."

He paused, letting the gravity of the tale sink in. "That day marked the end of an era, plunging us into a new age of darkness. Cormac had come closer than anyone before or since to defeating the Dark Lord, but in the end, it simply was not enough. His legacy is a reminder of how close we came, and how devastating the cost of failure can be."

Thâlôr's eyes met Ryan's. "Cormac's strength was not in his body, but in his heart and his belief in something greater than himself. That belief carried him further than any other, and it is that same belief that you must hold on to as you face your own trials. For in this world, it is not strength alone that will save us. It is the courage to stand, even when all seems lost."

Ryan nodded, understanding dawning on him. "I see. So it's not about being perfect, or even the best; it's about believing in something worth fighting for."

"Exactly," Thâlôr said, his voice softening. "And as for the empty podium," he continued, gesturing to the vacant space, "it stands as a reminder that one of you—Hannah, Emily, Ethan, Jake, or even you—could become the savior, the Champion of Champions. Or, like those before you, you could become another whisper among the winds of this world. But know this: one or more of you will take their place here," he said and pointed to the empty podium, "for better or worse."

Ryan looked at the empty podium, a sense of foreboding settling in. "That's a lot of pressure," he muttered. "I feel like we're destined to fail, or at least most of us are."

Thâlôr's expression remained unreadable. "There is that sentiment among the people of this world, yes. It's why some have stopped believing in the prophecy. The darkness never seems to subside, and it continues to consume the souls of those who join the Dark Lord and those who die fighting him. It is a constant battle, one that never seems to end."

Ryan sighed. "It's the same in our world. I just wish I could make a difference there."

Thâlôr's grip on Ryan's shoulder tightened slightly. "Then use that desire to make a difference here. This is your home now, and our people could use that ambition. The people of this world need you. I have faith that you will defeat the Prince of Brâldôr tonight and usher in another victory; a step closer to the prophecy being fulfilled and bringing peace to Cáelunárra after many ages of suffering."

Looking into Thâlôr's eyes, seeing the conviction there, Ryan said, "I hope I can do that for this world."

Thâlôr nodded, a small smile playing on his lips. "There is no hope, only action, remember that. Now, I must attend a meeting with the High Mage Council; they have requested an audience with me, their Grand General. Please, enjoy your rest. You will need it for your fight."

Thâlôr turned and left through the barracks entrance. Ryan watched him go, his mind swirling with thoughts and doubts. He stood alone in the grand foyer, staring up at the statues that stood high above him. The history they represented overwhelmed him, each one making him feel insignificant.

As he gazed at the defaced statue, Ryan couldn't help but wonder what kind of warrior he would become. Would history remember him as a hero, or would his name be lost, just another casualty in the endless cycle of war?

* * *

Ryan returned to the courtyard of the barracks after a long walk through the streets of the city. There, he focused on honing his form, practicing his stances, refining how he would shield himself, and perfecting his attacks. His movements were deliberate, enough to get his blood pumping and his mind sharp, but not so intense as to exhaust him before the evening's challenge. Feeling sufficiently prepared, he ate a light meal before he ultimately planned a visit to the barracks' hot baths; a sanctuary where warriors went to soothe their aches after a day of rigorous training.

The hot baths were a marvel in themselves. Steam rose in thick, curling tendrils, vented out through the narrow windows near the high ceiling. Artists decorated the walls with intricate mosaics depicting scenes of valor. The water was warm, infused with minerals that eased his muscles and soothed his mind. Ryan closed his eyes and allowed himself to sink into the relief the baths provided.

He had lost track of time while soaking in the heat of the

water, working its magic, when a servant approached. The young man, dressed in simple but clean attire, bowed respectfully before speaking.

"Ryan, it is time. The evening draws near, and you must prepare yourself."

His heart fluttering with a mixture of nerves, Ryan gave a nod to the young man, acknowledging the servant's words. "Thank you."

The servant bowed his head and left. With a reluctant sigh, Ryan lifted himself out of the comforting heat of the bath. He dried off with the provided towel, its soft fabric a small comfort against the chill that now nipped at his skin. Wrapping the linen around himself, he gathered his belongings and made his way up the barracks stairs to his room.

Once inside, Ryan's gaze fell upon his armor, polished and gleaming in the dim light. He began the ritual of dressing, arming himself to meet the Prince of Brâldôr.

With a last glance around the room, he reached for the door; the wood creaked softly as it swung open. The moment he stepped through, the door closed behind him with a resounding thud, echoing through the now-empty room. All that remained was the sound of his armor clinking softly with each step as he descended the stairs.

At the bottom awaited Thâlôr, Vôrmghôr, and Áelfwînë.

Ryan approached them, his heart thumping loudly in his chest. Drawing nearer, he tried to calm his breathing, but deep down, his apprehension gnawed at him.

Thâlôr was the first to speak, his voice steady and reassuring. "Remember, everything will be fine. Trust in all that we have taught you. Tonight, you must focus. Muster every ounce of bravery that you can, for the Prince of Brâldôr will rely greatly on brute force to break you down. Outmaneuver him, and victory will be yours."

His voice wavering, Ryan replied, "I'll try, Thâlôr. I'm... scared. I keep running through everything in my mind, but it's like the closer we get, the harder it is to focus."

Vôrmghôr nodded in understanding, stepping forward with a look of encouragement. "Fear is good. Fear means you still care whether you live or die. The ones who don't feel it? They're reckless and lose their edge. They're always among the first to fall. And besides, boy, you have trained hard. As I said earlier, no pupil who has walked through those doors in the last age has been as strong as you. You have the skills, and you have the heart. The prince may be stronger and more experienced, but strength alone does not win battles. Use what we have drilled into you. Keep your movements quick, your mind sharper than his blade."

"I'll keep that in mind, Vôrmghôr. I just... I hope I don't freeze out there," Ryan said, his reservations beginning to lift with his instructors' encouragement.

Áelfwînë stepped forward, placing a comforting hand on Ryan's shoulder. "Everyone tends to freeze, Ryan, but remember this; you are not alone. The Allfather watches over you, as do the spirits of those who have fought before. They are with you now, and they will be with you on that floor."

Finding some comfort in their presence, Ryan said, "Other than saying I'll do my best, I have no other words to say."

"Well, on that note! Let us offer a warrior's blessing over the lad," Vôrmghôr said, looking at the others.

The three men gathered around Ryan, their hands resting on his shoulders.

Thâlôr led the prayer, his tone reverent. "Allfather, we ask for your blessing over Ryan as he steps onto the Coliseum floor this night. Grant him the strength and wisdom of those who have gone before, guide his hand, and steady his heart. We ask that you send Vâlgârd to be with him in every swing, every block, and every movement, that he may lay another brick on the road to fulfilling the prophecy and bringing victory to these lands."

Ryan closed his eyes, focusing on the words, trying to absorb the strength they offered. The echoes of their prayer filled the dimly lit hallway as Thâlôr completed the blessing.

Thâlôr then gestured toward the door, a solemn expression on his face. "We will watch from the stands among the people of these lands. We will be there when you are victorious and bring great honor to these walls."

"Thank you, all of you. I'll do my best to honor everything you've taught me," Ryan said, trying to sound confident, even if it was only to lift his own spirits.

Áelfwînë took Ryan by the arm and led him through the hall, past the statues of warriors who had fought and fallen before him. The cold stone eyes of the statues seemed to follow them as they walked, a silent manifestation of the bravery required to stand where Ryan would soon stand.

# RYAN'S TEST

As the citizenry and those from abroad once more filed into the Coliseum for the second night of events, the air was alive with a perceptible sense of merriment. Music played from all corners, mingling with the sound of laughter, cheers, and applause. The prelude to the night's main event was a comedic routine that jested at the Dark Lord, humorously depicting his inevitable defeat.

Torches lined the Coliseum, their flames casting a flickering light on the red tapestries that hung between them, adding warmth to the pristine white walls. Dignitaries from all corners of Cáelunárra took their places in the stands. Ándróniüs and Ísolde, accompanied by Óryně and his wife, settled into their seats, along with the brothers, sister, and parents of the Prince of Brâldôr and the esteemed members of the High Mage Council.

A person in drab attire approached the Grand Mage and whispered into his ear, informing Óryně that all the dignitaries had arrived; he then rose from his seat and went to the staircase leading to the podium that jutted out into the Coliseum.

He raised his hands. The crowd quieted, the hum of conversations gradually fading.

"To our entertainers tonight, thank you," Óryně began, his voice echoing through the vast space. "It was a much-needed prelude to lighten the mood. You may take your leave and find your places among the crowd!"

A round of applause followed as the performers bowed and quickly left the Coliseum floor, their departure marked by a sense of anticipation of what was to come.

Once they had exited, Óryně continued, his voice imbued with the gravity of the night. "Tonight is important for us all. This is another spoke in the wheel that ensures our prophecy is fulfilled, putting the best warriors forward. Tonight, we have the honor of witnessing a fight to the death between the Prince of Brâldôr and Ryan, one of our chosen."

The crowd erupted in cheers; the noise swelling like a tidal wave.

Órynë waited patiently for the cheers to subside. "Though the blood spilled tonight may be innocent, whoever succumbs to their fate will not have died in vain. This is to ensure that our chosen are indeed the chosen of our prophecy. We must also extend our gratitude to King Orthôrjárl and Queen Whëlzôrná of Brâldôr, who have come to Vâloríâ, accompanied by their other children. Tonight, we will either celebrate their son's victory or honor his sacrifice."

Cheers and the clashing of metal erupted from the Brâldôrian section of the Coliseum, the sound reverberating through the stands in agreement. Óryně waited for the din to die down before raising his voice again.

"Champions, you are called to fight in the Coliseum!"

The crowd remained hushed, the anticipation heavy in the air. The sounds of chains and gears beneath the arena floor echoed throughout the quiet confines of the walls. Two large holes opened up on either side of the large circle, and two figures slowly emerged. The crowd erupted in a deafening roar as the figures rose into view.

The prince took one step forward and raised his arm in the air with a guttural roar, invigorating the other dwarves in the stands. A towering mountain was etched onto his breastplate; his armor was forged from the strongest Brâldôr steel. His helm, adorned with three imposing horns, featured a long steel piece that covered and ran snugly down the ridge of his nose, casting a shadow over his fierce eyes. Strapped to his arms were two small, square shields. Though short in stature, the prince exuded the confident presence of a seasoned and formidable warrior.

"Ryan and Ûrvákënák, approach the middle of the arena and exchange the customs and courtesies for this fight," Óryně's voice rang out again.

Ryan and Ûrvákënák moved to the center of the arena. A bow to the crowd preceded their facing each other. Their eyes locked in a tense, unyielding stare. They bowed to one another.

An immense uneasiness washed over Ryan, the magnitude of what was about to happen crashing down on him and making him feel faint.

"Take your places," Órynë commanded.

Ryan and Prince Ûrvákënák turned and took twenty measured paces in opposite directions, the crowd buzzing with anxious whispers as the clinking of their armor filled the air. Ryan counted silently in his mind—*seventeen, eighteen, nineteen*, and finally, *twenty*. He stopped, placing his hand on the hilt of his sword, his heart fluttering in his chest.

"Let the fight begin!" Óryně declared, with multiple resonant, bellowing horns sounding to mark the occasion.

The Coliseum erupted once again in an explosion of cheers, shouts, and the pounding of feet and weapons against the stone tiers. Ryan and Ûrvákënák turned to face each other, drawing their weapons. Ryan unsheathed his longsword, while Ûrvákënák reached behind his back with both arms, drawing two dwarven short axes, twirling them in his hands.

The crowd's cheering quieted as their focus turned to the two beings below. Ûrvákënák let out another guttural scream, a primal roar that silenced the Coliseum and sent a shiver down Ryan's spine. The sound was raw, filled with the rage and ferocity of a warrior. As the scream carried through the air, Ûrvákënák launched himself into a mighty sprint toward Ryan, his short axes gleaming in the torchlight. The intensity of the scream and the sudden charge stunned Ryan, hitting him full force with the reality of his situation.

Hyper-focused on the prince barreling toward him with terrifying speed, Ryan froze, his body momentarily paralyzed by the overwhelming surge of adrenaline. The world around him seemed to blur as he fought to free himself from the panic and brace himself for the inevitable skirmish thundering toward him.

The dwarven prince's armor clanged with each step, creating

an almost surreal slow-motion effect. He was mere seconds away from collision, and Ryan instinctively raised his shield. Ûrvákënák, with another battle-hardened roar, leaped into the air, bringing his ax down in a powerful arc. The impact was nearly catastrophic. Steel clashed against steel, sparks flying from the sheer force of the blow, and the blow knocked Ryan flat on his back. The numbing shock from the strike coursed through his arm, the pain so intense that he let out an involuntary scream, his vision momentarily blurring.

With a merciless sneer, Ûrvákënák planted his boot on Ryan's neck, the pressure cutting off his air, while his other foot pinned the boy's hand, preventing him from using his sword. Ryan's fingers twitched, straining desperately toward the hilt, only to be met with the immovable force of the prince's weight.

Ûrvákënák's voice boomed across the Coliseum, dripping with disdain. "This is your champion? This is your chosen one?" He spat the words at the crowd, his voice rising in scorn. "Mages, is this the best you could call upon to face me, the Prince of the Dwarves?"

The crowd fell into a hushed silence, the gravity of the moment sinking in as the fight seemed to end before beginning. Ûrvákënák pressed harder on Ryan's throat, savoring the helplessness in the boy's eyes and causing him to gasp like a fish out of water.

Bending down, the prince's voice dripping with venom. "Your blood is not worthy of my ax." With an irrevocable act of contempt, he spat in Ryan's face, then raised both axes high, preparing to deliver the finishing blow.

But just as the prince began his triumphant bellow to the heavens, a surge of adrenaline pulsed through Ryan's body, reawakening his fading senses. His vision cleared, and with newfound clarity, he saw a vulnerability in Ûrvákënák's armor; an unprotected gap between his legs. Desperation fueling his actions, Ryan mustered all his strength and drove his knee upward into the prince's groin, the metal of his poleyns making brutal contact.

Ûrvákënák's scream of agony was visceral as he crumpled to the ground, clutching at his injury. Gasping for air, Ryan scrambled to his feet, his lungs burning with each labored breath. He struggled to regain his feet, his limbs weak and trembling like a newborn fawn's.

The prince began to recover, staggering to his feet, and Ryan rushed forward and delivered a fierce kick to Ûrvákënák's torso, sending his shorter opponent rolling across the arena floor. But the move, though successful, was poorly judged. Ryan's strike inadvertently brought him within reach of one of Ûrvákënák's axes. With a desperate lunge, the prince seized the weapon and lashed out, striking Ryan's foot with the blunt end of the ax.

Pain exploded through Ryan's foot, the protective armor barely absorbing the force. He screamed again, the sound raw and ragged, as Ûrvákënák rose, the prince's resolve burning hotter than ever. Reacting on instinct, Ryan kicked up granules of sand into the prince's face, momentarily blinding him. Seizing the opportunity, Ryan scrambled to reclaim his sword and hastily re-secured his loosened shield.

Ûrvákënák, incapacitated by the sand and clawing at his eyes in a panic, desperately searched for his lost axes. Ryan circled him like a predator. He kicked the axes further away that the dwarf could reach. A surge of confidence washed over him, and Ryan couldn't resist taunting his opponent and the dwarves in attendance.

"Brâldôr, is this the best you can conjure as your future king?" His voice, dripping with mockery, reverberated across the arena, inciting a wave of boos and curses from the Brâldôrian section.

The taunt was not just directed at Ûrvákënák, but also at the Brâldôrian dignitaries and their royal family. The family of the prince gasped, feeling the tide of the fight shift ominously and recoiling at the audacity of what they thought were unwarranted words.

Ûrvákënák's fury ignited at the insult. His rage boiled over as he cleared his eyes. Snot and dust smeared across his face as he roared in anger, the veins in his neck bulging. "Dare you dishonor and mock my people? My title? Those will be the last words you ever utter, you bastard!"

The prince charged Ryan, who braced himself, raising his sword in a defensive stance. But Ryan's lack of training and inexperience in dueling betrayed him. He struck prematurely, leaving himself defenseless. Ûrvákënák, with a warrior's precision, parried the strike and slammed into Ryan, their helms clashing with a force that sent both men crashing to the ground, concussed and dazed from the violent collision.

The arena fell into a tense silence; the crowd held its collective breath as the two combatants lay on the cold stone and dirt floor of the Coliseum as they struggled to regain their senses. They lay there for several long moments, ears ringing and heads pounding. Ûrvákënák was the first to stir, pushing himself up onto his knees. His hands braced against the ground as he fought to steady his breathing, each inhale and exhale a battle of control. Slowly, his vision cleared, the double images merging back into one.

With a guttural roar, he directed his outrage at Ryan, pausing between each word, his voice seething with contempt. "You... are... not... worthy... to... be... killed... by... my... ax!" His words dripped with animosity; the words mirrored by the raw hatred in his eyes.

Seeing Ryan still struggling, crawling desperately in search of his lost sword, Ûrvákënák seized him by the shoulders, his grip like iron. With a powerful thrust, he flung Ryan backward, slamming him onto the unforgiving floor.

"Again, boy, I say you are not worthy of staining my axes with your filthy Zâwx̃înê blood!" Ûrvákënák snarled, towering over the boy like a vengeful god. He reached down, lifting the protective visor of Ryan's helm, exposing his weary, bloodshot eyes.

"This is your end, boy," Ûrvákënák hissed, his voice low and deadly. He raised his fist high above his head and brought it crashing down, unleashing a barrage of concussive blows against Ryan's face and helm. Each strike was like a hammer against an anvil, the deafening impact resounding through the Coliseum as the crowd felt the tide shift back in favor of the Prince of Brâldôr.

Ryan's world shrank to the size of a pinhole; his vision swam in a haze of pain. His eyes welled up, but he clenched his teeth, refusing to let the tears fall. Each blow sent shockwaves of agony through his body, his ears ringing, his vision blurring, the line between reality and hallucination beginning to blur. His consciousness teetered on the edge of darkness, the world around him fading as he strained to hold on, knowing that with every strike, he was one step closer to oblivion.

The world spiraled, his head snapping to the side from yet another brutal blow. He thought his eyes were playing tricks on him when he caught sight of four sets of feet amidst the relentless assault. Blood streamed from his eyes, nose, ears, and mouth. It mingled with the sweat and tears that he could no longer hold back, but he forced his gaze upward. Four familiar faces stood above him—Cormac, Hiroshi, Ibrahim, and Áslaug—each clad in their Vâlorîân armor, standing as ghostly figures in his delirium.

Cormac, his voice firm, spoke first. "Ryan, this world needs you. Get up!"

"Do not allow yourself to succumb to these injuries. You are stronger than this," Áslaug said, her tone fierce and commanding.

Hiroshi pointed urgently. "Ryan, look!"

Ibrahim, seeing Ryan fading, knelt beside him and screamed into his ear, his voice cutting through the fog of pain. "Ryan, wake up! Cáelunárra needs you! Now, look!"

The four ancient heroes pointed to something across the Coliseum.

Through the haze, Ryan turned his head, his grasp on reality swirling as he saw that Ûrvákënák had briefly left him. As he staggered toward Ryan's sword to deliver the final blow, Ûrvákënák turned his back. Ûrvákënák had raised his hands in premature celebration; his breath was labored, and his chest heaved with each gasping inhale. He bent down to retrieve the weapon, confident that victory was his.

Cormac reached out, his spectral hand glowing faintly. "Ryan, take my hand," he urged, bending down closer to him.

In his altered state, Ryan reached out instinctively, his hand connecting with the ethereal light. A surge of adrenaline flooded his veins, revitalizing him. Before he even realized what was happening, he was upright, his body moving with almost supernatural speed and precision. It felt as if he were being carried by an unseen force, his feet barely touching the ground as he closed the distance between himself and the prince. With a swift, powerful kick, Ryan struck Ûrvákënák square in the face. The impact was devastating, sending the prince reeling backward as blood gushed from his mouth and nose. Ûrvákënák blinked uncontrollably, his vision swimming as blood oozed from every orifice of his head. Ryan, fueled by an unstoppable force, tore off his helm and hurled it to the ground. The sound of the helm hitting the stone reverberated through the now silent Coliseum.

Ryan placed his foot on Ûrvákënák's neck, staring down into the prince's eyes, now wide with the realization of his own impending fate. Seeing a weapon nearby, Ryan picked it up. It was one of the prince's ax's.

Desperation laced the prince's voice as he gasped, "My ax, boy, my ax!" He reached feebly for his weapon lying nearby, while Ryan held the other ax firmly in his grip. The crowd watched in breathless silence, the arena charged with an unbearable anticipation. Ryan nudged the ax on the ground into the prince's trembling hand; everyone watched. Ûrvákënák grasped the weapon with all his remaining strength, bringing it close to his chest, his eyes squeezed shut to prepare for the fatal strike that would end his life.

Ryan, his face stern, leaned in closer until their faces were nearly touching. "Open your eyes, Prince," he commanded. The words hung heavy in the air as Ûrvákënák hesitated, then slowly obeyed, his eyes locking onto Ryan's.

At that very moment, a blood-curdling scream pierced the stillness, reverberating throughout the silent Coliseum.

"No, not my son! Please spare him!" The voice, raw with anguish and desperation, recalled from the stands.

Ryan's gaze shifted to the source of the plea, his foot still pressed firmly against the prince's throat. The Brâldôrian section of the Coliseum erupted with cries, and soon a unified chant filled the arena: "*Spare him! Spare him! Spare him!*"

The other sections joined the dwarves in their plea to spare the prince. Hearing these unified pleas, Ryan hesitated. He lifted his foot from the prince's throat and looked up at the devastated faces of the King and Queen of Brâldôr, along with Ûrvákënák's siblings, their expressions also unmistakably filled with fear.

Órynë, sensing the shift in the crowd, stood up. He stepped up to the podium, raising his hands to calm the rising tide of voices. "This is the way, great people of Cáelunárra. This is the command of the High Mage Council."

The Coliseum's crowd protested his words vehemently; defiance erupted.

A voice rang out from the stands. "He bested the prince. Let the prince live!"

Another person exclaimed, "No blood should be spilled!"

Órynë's voice grew sharp with frustration. "Ryan, deal your blow, or the prophecy will be rendered moot!" he shouted, his tone steeped with urgency.

But the discontentment and dudgeon grew louder, reverberating throughout the arena in direct opposition of Órynë's command.

Óryně turned in desperation to Ándrôniüs. "What do we do? This is the way! Blood must be spilled!" His voice was frantic.

Approaching the podium calmly, Ándrôniüs's presence commanded attention. "Unless the crowd demands otherwise," he replied. "You know the rules of the Coliseum, the ways of Vâlgârd. If the people speak with one voice, it is as if all the gods themselves have spoken. Only then can we alter the test, for the gods live in all of us, not just you and me."

Ryan, still circling the Prince of Brâldôr on the floor of the Coliseum, saw Ûrvákënák rise to his feet, clutching his ax, ready to fight to his last breath. Ryan squared up to him as the crowd's boos and pleas for mercy swelled into another deafening roar. The hostility between the two warriors was unmistakable, each waiting for the other to make a move.

Back at the podium, consumed by rage, Óryně felt darkness creeping into his mind, one he did not recognize. He knew what it demanded—*kill Ándrôniüs*. The voice whispered relentlessly, and Óryně reached into his pocket, his hand wrapping around the hilt of a small dagger. He looked into Ándrôniüs's eyes, uncertainty gnawing at him. The voice grew louder, more oppressive, urging him to take the life of the mage before him. But instead of giving in, Órynë fled the stage in fury, unable to bear the defiance of the crowd.

The crowd's disesteem reached its fever pitch, and Ándrôniüs astonied by the sudden withdrawal, having no other choice, stepped forward as the next most senior mage, arms outstretched.

The crowd quieted.

"This day, the Allfather has spoken through all of you. The gods have heard your pleas. The test has been redressed. Thus, on this day, no blood will be spilled. The Prince of Brâldôr has been defeated."

The crowd erupted into cheers as flowers rained down from every tier of the Coliseum, littering the ground in celebration of Ryan's victory. He tossed the prince's ax on the floor and picked up his own weapon, sheathing it with a gigantic sigh of relief.

But the celebration was short-lived.

"No... No.... No!" Ûrvákënák screamed, his voice laced with fury. Even in his concussed state, he staggered toward Ryan, driven by a blind rage.

The crowd shrieked in shock as Ándrôniüs shouted, "Stop him!"

Guards flooded the Coliseum floor, racing toward the two warriors.

Ryan, hearing the clattering of armor, turned just in time to sidestep and trip the charging prince, sending him tumbling to the ground. Ûrvákënák lost his grip on his axe, but with the other hand, he retrieved the one Ryan had discarded. Ryan, acting on instinct, kicked the prince's hand and unsheathed his own weapon, ready to deliver the fatal blow.

"Stop! You have won, Ryan!" the lead guard shouted, his voice filled with urgency.

Ryan wanted to strike the dwarf down, his mind a storm of galimatias, every thought pulling him toward violence. The gasps rising from the stands and the maenadic cries from the dwarven delegation only fed the frenzy building in his chest. Then, a hand closed around his sword arm in the air, firm and urgent, pulling him back from the edge. He looked around at the faces watching him, the magnitude of their duty to stop him settling on him like a stone.

And with the guards now surrounding them, his lowered sword in one hand, Ryan reached down with his free hand to grasp the prince's hand and pull Ûrvákënák to his feet, his grip strong and unyielding as he lifted the ponderous dwarven warrior from the ground. Towering over him, Ryan locked his eyes onto the prince's, intense and unrelenting. He bent down once more and retrieved the prince's ax. With a calculated move, he slammed the ax into Ûrvákënák's chest. Not to kill, but to force it into his grip, ensuring the prince understood that his life was being spared.

"Your own blood is not worthy of your ax, prince," Ryan said, his voice cold and final. He spat a mixture of blood, mucus, and saliva on the ground near Ûrvákënák's feet before turning with a limp, wobbling from side to side, taking short and uneven strides away, escorted by the Vâlorîân guard. As they led the two warriors from the field on separate paths, the crowd remained silent, their rivalry unresolved.

Ándrôniüs's voice echoed through the now-hushed arena. "And with that, we concluded today's events. Ryan is the victor. Tomorrow, Jake will face the terrifyingly magnificent dracónyx. Rest assured, each of you will be safe. We will cast a protection spell to encase the arena, ensuring you can witness the battle without harm. Now, go home, *enjoy* your feasts, and rest well. We will see you on the morrow!"

The crowd, reassured by Ándrôniüs's words, cheered once more. The enthusiasm in the air was apparent as the people of Cáelunárra, their hearts still pounding from the spectacle they had witnessed, slowly filed out of the grand arena.

As they exited, the Coliseum's once-vibrant energy dissipated, leaving a profound stillness. The memory of the battle and raw emotion seemed etched into the ancient stones. With the last spectators gone, the grand arches stood in silent vigil. The torches that had flickered brightly now dimmed, casting long shadows as the sun set. One by one, the flames sputtered out, leaving only the faint scent of smoke and the soft crackle of embers.

As darkness consumed the arena, the only sound was the whisper of the evening breeze. The Coliseum, a monument to countless battles, now stood in silence, its stones bearing the invisible scars of the day's events. The echoes of triumph and defeat would forever linger, even after the last torch had gone out.

# ELARA'S VISIT

THE MORNING LIGHT DANCED through the small windows of the study, casting pale rays across Jake's face, offering little comfort from the thoughts that wandered in his mind. The angst had been building for days. His training, though vigorous, did not exhaust him enough to clear his mind of the nagging disquiet that bit at his subconscious. Though one thing was front and center in his mind, that today was the day he would battle the fearsome dracónyx.

He tried to reminisce about the few intense days of training under his belt; days filled with grueling lessons in tactics, archery, swords, axes, and heavy weapons. Each session at the Grand Barracks had pushed him to his limits, with rigorous defensive drills led by seasoned warriors. From sunup to sundown, his days were long and punishing, beginning with a brutal Olympian circuit every morning.

Today he had awoken earlier than usual and had taken it upon himself to do the run alone. Afterwards, instead of sitting in his small, barren room, he attempted to be productive and asked the head librarian for a book about his foe. As he scanned the words of the literature, he sipped from a vial of Vígorrést Draught, which he had saved for this morning instead of taking it before he went to bed the night before.

The draught had been brought to him each night. It was a godsend, leaving him mostly recovered, with only minor aches from the previous day's grueling endeavors.

On this morning, Jake felt a mix of emotions. He was content in knowing he had prepared as much as he could, but the knowledge that he was about to face what could only be this world's equivalent of a dragon clawed at the back of his mind.

The uncertainty surrounding his friends' fate gnawed at him; he hadn't seen Ryan return to the barracks, though the distant roars from the Coliseum the night prior had filled him with hope. Rubbing his eyes, Jake stood up from his chair, letting out a loud yawn. He looked around the room, not sure what he was searching for. He knew he needed to tend to his armor before he took to the Coliseum to undergo his test, so, with a stretch of his arms high in the air, he pushed in his chair and returned the book to the librarian and went upstairs to his room.

Once there, he marveled at the entire ensemble that made up his armor. He stood for only a moment and then bent down to grab a rag from a drawer under his desk. He began with the breastplate, rubbing it to give it a polished shine.

The entire aggregation of drakescale armor was a masterpiece of craftsmanship. Forged from the scales of a dead dracónyx, the armor gleamed with a dark, iridescent sheen, each scale meticulously shaped and riveted to interlock perfectly with the next. The scales, treated through a secret alchemical process, were nearly impenetrable, capable of withstanding the crushing force of a dracónyx's tail or the searing heat of its fiery breath. A layer of insulating material lined the armor beneath the scales, offering another layer of protection against the extreme temperatures. This armor was designed to keep him safe, though it did not make him invulnerable; death was still a possibility if the beast were to employ its bite. Then, and only then, would the beast render the armor useless.

As Jake stood there in his room, contemplating the battle ahead, the sudden creak of the door startled him, breaking his concentration. He quickly turned to investigate the disturbance.

Jake was greeted by the sight of Elârâ. Elârâ wore a beautiful verdant gown and intricate braids, elegantly enhancing her already stunning appearance. But it was her eyes—those captivating green eyes—that drew him in, filling him with a yearning no woman had ever given him.

"Elârâ!" Jake exclaimed, his heart leaping as he pulled her into his arms. He held her tightly, savoring the warmth and comfort of her embrace. But he felt her trembling, something she never did.

It was only then that he realized something was wrong.

Gently lifting her chin, guiding her eyes upward to meet his gaze, he asked, "What's wrong?"

Pulling herself into his embrace once more, Elârâ buried her face against his chest, choosing silence over speech as emotion surged through her. Then, without a word, she rose onto the tips of her toes and did something she never had before. She kissed him. Not a timid, fleeting brush of lips, but a deliberate, soul-stirring kiss. For the first time, she led. Her mouth moved with unspoken longing, a fire long held at bay now set free. It was not just affection. It felt as if it was a declaration. And though the world around them seemed to blur, in that moment, nothing else existed but their fierce and tender communion.

Jake smiled, his heart swelling with affection, and asked softly, "What was that for?"

Tears kept falling from her eyes, even more so than before, streaming rapidly down her face.

She turned, leaving his pleach to sit on the edge of his bed, her gaze dropping to the floor. "You know what's wrong, Jake. Don't play coy. You know our love, it's forbidden."

His heart, thinking the unimaginable was about to happen, started pounding with forlornness. "Then let's run off!"

"Where?" Elârâ shot back, her voice rising as she rubbed her eyes, trying to hold back the flow of tears. "There's nowhere the Dark Lord doesn't have eyes. He watches the Marsh, Brâldôr, Âldâmûr, Illithría, and even here in Eldôria with his spies."

"Then let us take a ship to anywhere else. There's got to be somewhere other than here where his reach cannot find us. I don't care about this prophecy. I care only for you," Jake pleaded, dropping to his knees at her feet. He clasped her hands in his, his voice thick with emotion.

Looking down at him, the sadness deepened. "No, Jake, you *must* care. You're no coward. You must fight and fulfill your destiny."

"This isn't my destiny, Elârâ. This is some tall tale that I've been dragged into, and I don't want any part of it!" Jake's voice broke with frustration.

Elârâ's voice softened as she shook her head. "This isn't a tall tale, Jake. And that's why my father is right. This could never work... humans and mages. It's just too much."

His heart sank to a depth he could not comprehend. He was afraid of what she would say next. Still, he foolishly asked, "What are you trying to say?"

She leaned forward, kissing him once more, then gently brushing the hair from his eyes. "There are *suitors*, Jake. My father is meeting with them all day before we go to the Coliseum to watch you tonight. He says that this could never be, and I *must* marry one of them. He told me that the only way he might even consider the idea of you is if you are victorious tonight."

Jake's eyes burned with determination as he gripped her hands tighter. "Then I will win for you tonight. I swear it."

Elârâ couldn't help but let out a small laugh through her dejection at his fierce resolve. "Oh, Jake, you know it will take more than that. My father will create trial after trial for you, while, on the other hand, he'll accept a dowry from some far-off mage who's probably six times my age."

"Why is that funny?" He asked, affronted by her laughter.

"It isn't, not really. It's just... I love everything about you, even your determination that knows no bounds," she replied, her voice trembling.

His voice was soft, but insistent. "Elârâ, we don't need their permission. Let's just be one together. We can marry in secret, and then nothing could tear us apart."

Her expression darkened as she shook her head. "It's not that simple. The Grand Mage himself must avouch it, even with my father's blessing. That's unlikely, Jake. Órynë is very much like my father and particularly inflexible about such things." She paused, her voice dropping to a whisper. "But there is another way."

Jake's heart quickened. "What is it? You must tell me. I will do almost anything," he said, his voice filled with resolve.

With intensity in her eyes, Elârâ slowly began unbuttoning the top of her dress, each button revealing glimpses of her freckled skin as it came undone. Leaning in close, she whispered in his ear, her voice trembling with desperation, "Make sure I'm no longer worth the bride price. To them, I'll be nothing more than used merchandise, easily cast aside for someone they deem more deserving. My father will then have no other choice but to accept you."

Though momentarily tempted by her vulnerability, Jake reached out with trembling hands and gently stopped her from revealing anything more, his fingers brushing against hers as he carefully buttoned back up her dress.

"No, Elârâ," he murmured, his voice soft but firm. "I simply can't."

Her eyes flared as she pulled away from him, her breath hitching with emotion. "Am I not enough? Am I not *beautiful* enough for you?" she spat, her voice trembling. "Any man would take me as *his* prize, as a *trophy*, and boast that they made a woman of me. Yet you dare not? Do you not want me?"

Jake's heart ached as he responded, his voice filled with pain. "It's not that, Elârâ. I just believe we should wait until we're married. You deserve that."

Tears streamed down Elârâ's face as she spoke, her voice laced with bitterness. "Well, then my father says you must cut the head off the dracónyx and tear out its still-beating heart. Present it to him at the Coliseum, in front of everyone. Only then will he have no choice but to consider our wishes. And even then, he says it's *highly* unlikely."

Without waiting for a response, Elârâ stood up, hastily fixing her dress and wiping away her tears. She glanced at Jake one last time, her expression a mix of unadulterated love and stomach-wrenching despair, before turning and slamming the door as she left the room. Jake was alone in a whirlwind of paralyzing confusion after the door slammed shut behind her.

Her words magnified the pressure of the challenge that awaited him. The dread of facing a fearsome dracónyx now mingled with his feelings for Elârâ, making it almost impossible to think clearly. He had just turned down the woman he loved deeply, a decision that he had not fully come to terms with yet. The enormity of impressing her father, a task he felt ill-prepared for, combined with the looming prophecy he neither believed in nor wanted to be a part of, was overwhelming.

He took a deep breath, trying to gather his thoughts as he undressed, preparing to wash himself before he headed to breakfast. Just as Jake unbuttoned the top button of his shirt, three loud knocks shattered the silence, pulling him from his momentary reverie and sending his mind spinning once more.

Annoyance surged through him, and he snapped, "Who is it and what do you want?"

The door creaked open again, revealing Thâlôr, his expression calm yet concerned. "Are you alright, Jake? Is there anything you need?"

Jake sighed, wiping his face with his hands, trying to pull himself together. "Not that I can think of, but thanks for asking." His voice had softened, but the irritation still lingered beneath the surface.

Studying him for a moment, Thâlôr's eyes were thoughtful. "Was the visit from Lady Elârâ not what you had hoped for?"

Jake rolled his eyes, the emotions of the morning still raw. "I'm not even sure where to begin, Thâlôr." He paused, lowering himself into the chair near his desk. "Was I wrong to deny her? Was I wrong not to follow through with her advances? Should I have just... done it?"

Sensing the broil in Jake's mind, Thâlôr sat on the corner of the bed. "Now, don't take this the wrong way. Some people would, but these thoughts are all my own. You see, in my experience," he began, his tone light, yet carrying a hint of wry wisdom, "and in my many years upon this land, I have learned that if you do something, a woman says she wants, you'll be wrong. Well, mostly... anyway... And if you do something she doesn't want, you're more than definitely wrong."

He paused, choosing his next words carefully as he stood up and peered out the small window.

"Women are funny beings. But, nonetheless, they are our partners in life, and like a minefield, we must walk a fine line. While also being there to love, care, and, most importantly, comfort. I'm not even sure how it all works. I've failed three times now. I guess what I'm trying to say is: you're young. It's fine. Elârâ is just overwhelmed because of the unfairness that women of her status are subject to here. Unlike men of power and status, they don't get to choose who they love; the fathers arrange their futures only for their own piety and clout."

He clasped his hands behind his back, his gaze distant. "In the end, it's best to be an honorable man. I believe you were honorable in your actions. But ask yourself: did you bend your morals? Did you compromise your beliefs? Did you stay true to yourself? And did you stay true to her in your beliefs? If yes, then you did the right thing... the *honorable* thing."

Jake, feeling a sense of justification but still nonetheless uneasy about the situation, nodded slowly. "Yeah, I guess you're right."

Turning to face Jake, Thâlôr's eyes were gentle yet firm. "It's best not to dwell on things that have passed, for they have passed, and they cannot be unwrought. We can only look to the future and focus on the decisions we have control over in the present and the days ahead." He offered a reassuring smile. "Now, let's go enjoy the delectable pastries in the dining hall and spend a little time with Ethan before you take on that monumental task this evening."

Jake felt a small sense of amelioration from Thâlôr's words. He grabbed the door for Thâlôr, and they both left the room, heading down to the dining hall.

While making their way down the stairs and through the winding corridors, Jake's thoughts drifted to his friends, and he turned to Thâlôr. "So, I guess it's safe to assume that Ryan passed?"

Thâlôr nodded, and with a hint of pride in his voice, said, "With flying colors. Though I'm sure he'll be feeling the extent of his fight today. He was dealt some pretty nasty blows. But yes, he was victorious."

A wave of relief washed over him. Jake was ecstatic at the news of Ryan's victory, which meant Emily had succeeded as well. Knowing his friends had faced their tests and emerged triumphant provided a glimmer of hope.

As they neared the dining hall, the warm, inviting aroma of freshly baked pastries and spiced drinks welcomed them. The hall buzzed with activity, filled with warriors and trainees, all preparing for the day's duties.

Entering the dining hall, Thâlôr spotted Ethan sitting alone at a table, a heap of food in front of him. He gestured for Jake to join his friend while he went to fetch some food for both of them.

Noticing his friend approaching the table, Ethan offered a smile. "Hey man, how're you doing this morning?"

Jake sighed as he sat down. "Been better. My mind's wrapped around so many things, I just can't think straight."

His expression turning more serious, Ethan leaned in slightly. "Anything you'd like to get off your chest?"

Shaking his head, a resigned look washed over Jake's face. "There's nothing I can do about it. Just have to take it day by day." Though anxiety clung to his voice, he let out an oddly timed chuckle and added, "That's if I survive the night."

"Don't say that!" Ethan exclaimed, the burden of Jake's words hit him hard, his own fear about his own ordeal flaring. He sighed, then continued, "Well, I'm here for you if you need me." He paused, glancing over at Thâlôr, who was approaching with two modest plates of food. Hurriedly, Ethan asked, "Have you heard anything about Ryan?"

"He passed. Which means it's my turn tonight. How's training with Ándrôniüs?" Jake asked, trying to change the subject.

Ethan rolled his eyes, a grin tugging at the corners of his mouth. "The old man's a crackpot—"

Before he could finish, Thâlôr reached the table, setting down the plates with a knowing smile. "That 'old man' is wiser than any other I know," he remarked, his tone both admonishing and affectionate.

Letting out a bark of laughter, Ethan said, "Yeah, yeah, I know. He's just... intense."

Thâlôr chuckled as he sat down across from them. "Intense, yes. But that intensity has kept him alive all these years. You could learn a great deal from him if you'd *actually* pay attention. In many battles, he has been instrumental in leading the mages to victory. He's just as capable there as he is in his books." He paused, sliding a plate of pastries toward Jake, then took a bite from his own before adding, "Today's training will be different."

"Different how?" Ethan asked, curiosity piqued.

"Vôrmghôr, Gründhölm, and Sãã have been called away to investigate a potential attack in Âldâmûr. It's urgent and requires their expertise. They could be gone for many days, weeks, or months," Thâlôr informed.

"That'll put us behind in training," Ethan remarked, concern creasing his brow. "Does that mean we get more time to train, then? Or, are we delaying the tests?"

Jake added, "I mean... Ethan is right. What does that mean for us?"

Thâlôr turned to Ethan first. "You'll be training with Ándrôniüs today, focusing on your magical abilities. And I want you to take it seriously, Ethan. This isn't the time for laziness or childish games. Ándrôniüs may be odd, but he's a master of his craft. You have natural talent, but you're only scratching the surface of your potential. It's time to dig deeper."

The usual lightness faded from Ethan's face, the gravity of the situation settling in. Tomorrow, he would face his own trial against the gorlock—if Jake survived his test tonight.

Turning to Jake, Thâlôr continued. "As for you, Jake, you'll have a day of rest, just like Ryan did before his test. Use this time to gather your thoughts; prepare yourself mentally, physically, and, most importantly, emotionally."

"Great... *more* time in my head. That's never a good thing for me," he grumbled.

Thâlôr chuckled softly. "No, it's never easy for any man, but don't dwell on the conversation we had this morning. Focus on being in the present. Visit the pools below the barracks, take a walk through the city, or beyond the walls, near the farms and fields you passed when you first arrived, or find peace in one of the city's many gardens. The choice is yours, but remember, this day is about *centering* yourself."

Pushing back from the table, ready to leave, Thâlôr added, "If there's nothing else, I'll let you be."

Jake hesitated for a moment before calling out as Thâlôr walked away. "I do have one question before you go."

The mage paused, turning back with a curious expression.

"What is it?"

His worry apparent in his eyes, Jake asked, "How am I supposed to defeat a dracónyx with just a sword?"

With a knowing smile, Thâlôr offered one last reply. "You'll be surprised by the tools you'll have at your disposal when the time comes." He winked, then added, "And remember that you have something to fight for. Something to live for." With that, he turned on his heel and departed, leaving Jake and Ethan to ponder his words.

Ethan leaned in, his voice filled with curiosity. "What do you think he meant by that?"

"Sorry, Ethan. I just need to go," he mumbled, grabbing a few pastries from his plate before turning for the exit.

Surprised by the sudden shift in his friend's demeanor, Ethan called after him. "Hey, where are you going? We still have time to do something before I start my training for the day!"

Jake paused at the door, his voice strained as he responded. "I just need some time to myself, okay?"

Without waiting for a reply, he left.

* * *

After spending a few restless hours meandering through the streets of the city, Jake found his way back to the gates of the Grand Barracks. Crossing under the archway into the courtyard, he noticed Ándrôniüs and Ethan in the midst of a training session. Ethan appeared to be struggling.

Dark red and black energy swirled around his hands. With a burst of effort, Ethan discharged a smidgen of the energy, which ricocheted off the dummy. However, his assay didn't truly cause any substantial destruction. As Jake watched, Ethan stormed off, frustration etched on his face, with Ándrôniüs quickly following, urging him to concentrate and keep practicing.

From where Jake stood, he couldn't help but chuckle to himself. That was classic Ethan; always letting his temper get the best of him and quitting before truly giving anything a fair shot. Shaking his head, Jake headed inside. The doors creaked open as he pushed them; the sound ricocheting throughout the silent hall.

Just inside the main hall, he paused, taking a moment to marvel at the craftsmanship of the seven statues before him. Though he had passed by them many times, today they felt different. Their empty eyes seemed to follow him, judging him. Perhaps it was because of his doubts about the prophecy, his disbelief at the nonsense being thrust upon them, or his reluctance to face his test tonight against the dracónyx. Or maybe it was something more, something he had no knowledge of. A shiver ran down his spine, but he brushed it off and continued up the stairs, two at a time, to the seventh floor.

When he reached his door, Jake noticed a letter lying near the threshold. Bending down to pick it up, he recognized the emblem on the seal; a profile of an ox with a manor in the background. It was the mark of Elârâ's father, Frânícê. But what caught his eye was the small purple flower pressed into the wax—Elârâ's favorite. A smile tugged at the corner of his lips; this letter was from her.

Jake entered his room and sat down at his small wooden desk, the weight of the missive heavy in his hands. His heart skipped as he carefully broke the seal, the parchment feeling as though it carried the answers to a world's worth of decisions. Taking a deep breath, he unfolded the letter, his eyes scanning the familiar handwriting:

*Dearest Jake,*

*I wanted to apologize for my actions this morning. Even more so than ever, I find myself wanting to be only yours. You protected me from myself and my destructive thoughts. You truly value me as a person, and that is why I want to spend all my life with you. Though this letter may be of some relief, because I no longer blame you and instead respect your decision, I must tell you my father has accepted a tentative offer from the High Mage of Silverthorne for his son Éamon.*

*I only write to you to tell you this because now, and truly only now, you must be victorious tonight. You must cut out the heart, as I said earlier. Approach my father in his seat and cast it at his feet. You must proclaim your love and declare that you wish to marry his daughter Elârâ. This is the bride price, the heart of a dracónyx—the most valuable thing any mage can receive. If you do this, he will have to forego the other offer and accept yours, as you are the mightier suitor because you killed a dracónyx, a feat he will have witnessed with his own eyes, and you delivered its still beating heart to his feet. No mage can deny that request, regardless of the race of the one who brought it to him.*

*I beg of you, Jake, win not for the prophecy, not even for Cáelunárra, but for me. Secure my freedom, loose the chains of my pedigree, so we can be married.*

*All my love, Elârâ*

Jake's hands trembled as he finished reading the letter, the words burning in his mind. Elârâ's plea, the urgency of her request, crashed over him like a tsunami. He knew what he had to do, but where could he even begin? How could he undertake the Herculean task of facing the dracónyx and then delivering its heart to a man who might still deny the most valuable dowry in all the land?

He could see her in his mind's eye; Elârâ, the woman who had become something he could not live without, living in a world where her choices were stripped away, where her future hung in the balance. The image of her being forced into a marriage with Éamon, a man she did not love, twisted his insides. The idea of her freedom being snatched away ignited a fire within him, a fire that he hoped would fuel him in the coming battle.

The stakes had never been higher. This wasn't just about the prophecy; it was about the life he wanted to create in this world. He had to succeed. He had to claim the heart of the dracónyx, not for glory or for the prophecy, but to save the woman he had come to love from a life she didn't want.

Jake folded the letter carefully, placing it back into its envelope. He knew he wanted to carry that letter with him during the fight tonight. Folding it once more, he slid it into a pocket on the inside of his armor.

# JAKE'S TEST

"Jake! Jake! Jake!" The familiar voice rang out, accompanied by pounding on the door.

"What is it, Ethan?" Jake called back groggily, pulling himself out of bed to let his friend in.

As Jake swung the door open, Ethan practically burst into the room, his face alight with excitement. "I did it!"

Jake yawned, his brain struggling to understand what his friend was trying to convey. "What did you do?"

"The spell!" Ethan exclaimed, his eyes wide with a mix of disbelief and triumph. "I did it, I really did it! Ándróniüs instructed me. *Well*, more like pushed me to find something deep within. Something that was dark, but that was tied to something good. I don't really understand the old kook and his ramblings. But anyway... that's how I was able to channel the magic, to make the spell actually come out of my hands. I guess I have magical abilities, after all."

He paused, his expression dimming slightly. "Though it was short-lived... he said it wasn't powerful enough, but still; I took off the head of the training dummy, Jake! I did it!"

Jake's confusion slowly gave way to understanding, a grin spreading across his face. "That's amazing, man! I'm glad you could do it. Just... don't get your hopes up too high. Tonight is going to be tough. I don't know if I have it in me."

"Sure, you do. I just wanted to share the news before Thâlôr and Ándróniüs came to get you. Technically, I'm not even supposed to be here," Ethan said, flashing a quick smile. "Good luck tonight, man. I wish I could be there with you."

"Yeah, me too," Jake replied, still shaking off the remnants of sleep.

Ethan hesitated at the door. "Well, I'll see you. Hopefully, we'll all be at Hannah's test in a few days and then finally be done with this. And maybe then we'll get some answers about how to get home!"

"I wouldn't get your hopes up for anything, Ethan. Even if everything goes right," Jake reminded him.

"Well, aren't you in a chipper mood," Ethan said, giving Jake an odd look before closing the door softly behind him.

Not long after Ethan's exit, three sharp knocks landed on the wooden door.

"Just come in," Jake called out, still stretching.

Ándrôniüs was the first to poke his head through the doorway. "Jake, are you ready?"

With a grim smile on his lips, Jake turned to address him. "As ready as anyone could be, I guess."

Thâlôr stepped into the room after Ándrôniüs, making the space feel even smaller with all three men inside.

Glancing at Jake, Thâlôr said, "Yes, you are. How was the rest of your day?"

Jake shrugged. "Uneventful, yet eventful... as you probably know."

Thâlôr chuckled, his deep voice filling the room. "Indeed, I do. Well, we come bearing good news."

One eyebrow arched in curiosity. "Good news? Am I finally off the hook for this nonsense?"

Ándrôniüs scoffed, shaking his head. "Boy, this isn't nonsense, and you know it. I can't believe you still deny that there's something more going on after everything you've seen."

Raising a hand to calm his companion, Thâlôr said, "Ándrôniüs, it's okay. It took me a hundred years before I believed."

Ándrôniüs grumbled in agreement, then shifted his tone. "The good news is that tonight, you'll have some powerful tools at your disposal. You'll be armed with a dragonspike ballista, crafted by the same blacksmiths who forged your armor. You'll have three shots—*only three*—as the aétherium crystal heads are rare and difficult to procure. We could only manage to get these for you. Additionally, you'll have an array of drakebinder ballistas equipped with wýrmwéb shots. These weighted nets incapacitate the dracónyx, at least temporarily, until it frees itself."

Ándróniüs placed his hands on Jake's shoulders, his gaze intense. "I believe in you, my boy. Even if you don't believe in all of this, I believe you have a greater purpose to fight for. My intuition tells me so." He finished with a wink.

Thâlôr's eyes met Jake's. Only the two of them knew about Elârâ's visit earlier that morning, so how could Ándróniüs know?

"Yes, indeed you do, Jake," Thâlôr added, his voice firm. "Now, let's get you ready."

With practiced precision, Ándróniüs and Thâlôr began preparing Jake for the battle ahead. They had him doff his shirt, leaving him bare-chested in the cool room. Ándróniüs moved to the side, shaking out the garment draped over his arm. He carefully held it up for Jake to see, the material shimmering as it caught the light.

"This," Ándróniüs began, his voice reverent, "is an émberweave mantle. It is a protective garment woven by the Naïads. You may remember Câllirrhöe; when I foresaw that this would be your task, I instructed her people to create it, knowing that you would be the one to face the dracónyx. It's made from the silk of salamanders from the ponds near my home, combined with the fibrillae of the aquatic plants that grow there. This is no *ordinary* cloth. The essence of fire and water, light and shadow, imbues it, making it both a shield and a symbol of the elements themselves."

Jake stood in awe as Ándróniüs draped the mantle over his shoulders. The fabric was almost translucent, yet it shimmered with an ethereal light. As the mantle settled around him, Jake could feel its weight; not in a physical sense, but in the significance it carried. This was a gift from a world he barely understood, yet one that seemed to recognize him as a part of its destiny.

The lore, the history, and the intricate connections between people and places all felt like a dream, as if he had lost himself in a coma in some foreign hospital back home. And yet, the touch of the émberweave against his skin was undeniably real.

Ándrôniüs and Thâlôr continued to ready him, securing an émberweave belt around his waist, followed by matching socks and gloves. The material, soft yet resilient, seemed to pulse subtly. Next, Thâlôr retrieved a pair of greaves, their surface shimmering. The sabatons, which fit snugly over Jake's feet, followed these, crafted with precision and strength. Next, Thâlôr secured the cuisses for the thighs and the poleyns for the knees.

They placed the cuirass over Jake's chest; it fit snugly against his muscular frame. Vambraces, gauntlets, and a large kite shield completed the ensemble. The armor, while sturdy, maintained a surprising level of flexibility because of the interlocking nature of the scales.

Jake secured the helm to his side with a leather strap, allowing him to carry it in on his hip as he made way to the Coliseum.

After securing the final piece of armor, Thâlôr picked up a long, wrapped bundle he had placed on the bed upon arrival. With care, he unraveled the blanket, revealing a great sword with a serrated blade that gleamed with a dark, ominous sheen.

Thâlôr handed the sword to Jake. "This is Dŷrnîêth. It is the blade of my people. My kin, the first Lord of Süïl, is the namesake of the blade. I traveled back there to retrieve it for you. This sword has slain over a hundred dracónyx during the First Age battles with the Dark Lord. It was wielded by my father, his father before him, and those beyond. Now, I pass it on to you, Jake, as I have no offspring, nor shall I ever. May it guide you to victory."

Jake gazed at the blade in awe, a lump forming in his throat at the underlying meaning of the gift.

Ándrôniüs, noting the late hour, urged them along. "Jake, Thâlôr—we must hurry. The Coliseum awaits, and destiny is calling."

Ándrôniüs, Thâlôr, and Jake stood in a tight triad, looking into each other's eyes. They nodded in solemn accord. One by one, they filed through the door, leaving yet another room in the Grand Barracks empty. Another chosen warrior had begun his test, never to return to these hallowed halls. Ethan was the last of them left in the Grand Barracks, the final one to face his fight.

Down the stairs and through the gate they went, past the guards, and into the bustling streets of Vâloríâ. Though many of the city's citizens had already made haste to the Coliseum, eager yet anxious to witness Jake's battle against the dracónyx, some remained lining the streets. They waited for him to pass, flicking white paint to mark him with vibrant dots that stood out against the dark drakescale.

Jake's breathing grew heavier as they drew closer to the Coliseum, its enormous structure looming over the shops and houses they passed. As they reached the great fences of the Coliseum, Áelfwînë intercepted them.

"I will escort the boy to the chamber," Áelfwînë said.

Thâlôr and Ándrôniüs nodded, parting ways with Jake, and making their way quickly to the High Mage Council's seating area.

Jake turned to Áelfwînë. "I guess it's time, isn't it?"

Áelfwînë nodded, his expression stern yet supportive. "Think back to everything we warriors taught you from the day you arrived at the barracks. Do you recall that first night when I told you to be light on your feet, to serpentine, and to be quick and agile?"

Responding with a simple nod, Jake said, "Yes."

"I know there's a lot on your mind, so let me remind you: the dracónyx has an enormous head with widely spaced eyes. Because of that, it can't track you all that well if you keep to serpentine movements. But if you run at it straight on, it'll be able to focus and land direct hits. Keep moving, stay quick, and never let it get a clear shot at you," Áelfwînë advised.

"I'll do my best," Jake replied, trying to steady his nerves.

Áelfwînë rested his hands on Jake's shoulders, looking him directly in the eyes. "I have no doubt you will. Now, we must make our way to the warriors' chambers."

He gestured toward the Coliseum, and they began walking through the crowd toward the hallowed walls. "Once inside, you'll be alone until they hoist you into the arena. You'll have a minute to get your bearings. There are obstacles—giant rocks and boulders—that you can use for cover, as well as many weapons to aid you."

They reached a door, and Áelfwînë opened it, guiding Jake

inside. "They will hoist up the dracónyx, and the fight will begin. It may stay on the ground or take to the skies in a fury, trying to escape."

As Jake stepped into the dimly lit chamber, Áelfwînë secured the door behind them. "From within here, you'll hear its cries, its breathing, and the scratching on the walls. But fret not, Jake. You are protected down here. On the floor of the arena, the beast will not be able to escape. Just remember, because of a shield protecting the crowd, the dracónyx flames will be even more powerful."

Jake, his voice shaky, stuttered out, "Th... th... thank you."

Áelfwînë gave him a reassuring wink before slamming the door shut, leaving Jake alone with his thoughts. The darkness of the room pressed in on him, and the sounds of the dracónyx reverberated through the stone walls. Taking a deep breath, Jake untied his helm and secured it on his head. He then took a seat on a nearby chair, preparing himself mentally for the battle that would soon begin.

*** 

The Coliseum bustled with energy, though there was no precursor to the fight between Jake and the dracónyx. A tense silence hung in the air, a stark contrast to the usual roar of the crowd, as the dire circumstances of the evening weighed heavily on everyone present.

Ándrôniüs made his way to the stand with Thâlôr, his eyes scanning the gathering crowd. He noticed with growing concern that Órynë was absent, nowhere to be found. He began inquiring of those around him where the Grand Mage might be, but no one had any answers.

So they waited.

The crowd grew uneasy as time passed, the sun beginning to set and leaving the floor of the Coliseum lit only by the flickering light of the torches. The setting sun painted the sky in hues of red, pink, and purple, adding to the foreboding atmosphere. Below, the dracónyx began bellowing from the deep pit of the Coliseum, slamming itself against the hatch that held it captive.

With no other recourse, Ándrôniüs stood up, assuming Órynë's place, and addressed the crowd. "My good people of Eldôria, Âldâmûr, Brâldôr, and Illithría. I ask that you forgive our Grand Mage in his absence. He must be under the weather and forgot to inform someone of his ill-timed delinquency. I will perform his duties as we gather together to witness a fearsome battle. Man versus beast, to the death. Tonight will either be a night of astonishing victory or one that will forever linger in our minds as another tragedy. But let that not be the case! Tonight, Jake, our champion, our chosen one, our victor, will smite the mighty dracónyx on the field of battle, paving the way for our future tests with Ethan and the gorlock, and Hannah as she recites the beautiful language of the elves. Now! Let the battle begin!"

The crowd erupted in cheers, the sound of clanking armor and weapons rebounding through the grounds of the Coliseum.

Jake was hoisted up, rising until he stood alone on the floor of the arena. Around him lay massive boulders, some towering like multi-story buildings, others riddled with holes, and some too small to offer cover. Four ballistae were positioned in a square within the Coliseum, aimed skyward.

Suddenly, the entire Coliseum shook with an intensity that felt like a minor quake. Shrill bellows and screeches filled the air, their intensity almost deafening. The loud clunking and clicking of gears echoed as the massive hatch of the Coliseum opened, releasing the fearsome creature into the arena; it then took off into the sky. The dragon-like beast triumphantly screeched as it escaped, but its flight abruptly ended midair when it slammed into the invisible shield above the Coliseum.

With a resounding quake, the dracónyx landed, sending a tremor throughout the grounds, and drawing gasps of awe and terror from the crowd. Fire blasted into the air, raining ash from the sky and filling the arena with thick, acrid smoke. The dracónyx's massive leathery wings unfurled, creating a windstorm throughout the Coliseum, and amazed all present with its terrifyingly majestic sight.

The torrent of wind slammed Jake to the ground, an immediate demonstration of the power he was about to face.

The dracónyx towered over the Coliseum floor, its presence

dominating the space. Its massive head was the most fearsome part of its body, broad and angular, with a crown of jagged horns that jutted out like barbed spears. The creature's eyes, glowing a malevolent shade of crimson, seemed to pierce through the smoke, searching for its prey. Sparks and embers danced from its wide nostrils with each breath, the fiery heat of its lungs illuminating the scales along its snout and jaw.

Its neck was long and sinuous, coiling with the strength of a creature born to crush and strangle. As the dracónyx craned its neck around the towering boulders, its scales shimmered in the torchlight, reflecting hues of deep black, red, and green.

The armor-like scales were thick and nearly impenetrable, each one layered and interlocked to form an almost invincible shield. Despite the bulk of its head and neck, the torso seemed almost disproportionately small, a stark contrast to the other parts of its body.

Four long, muscular legs supported the creature, each ending in massive claws that curled inward, sharp as razors and capable of slicing through stone. Those claws scraped against the floor of the arena as the beast prowled, leaving shallow gouges in the stones. Its wings were vast, leathery membranes that stretched tight over a frame of bone and sinew. When fully extended, they seemed to blot out the sky, each flap sending gusts of wind that whipped through the arena and stirred the dust and ash into a chaotic storm.

But the most dangerous part of the dracónyx was its tail. A long, razor-like appendage that whipped and lashed with deadly precision. It ended in a spade point, edged like a blade, and capable of cleaving through armor and flesh with terrifying ease. It swayed back and forth, a deadly pendulum that hinted at the creature's lethal power.

The monster let out a bone-chilling roar, its voice reverberating through the walls of the Coliseum. Flames shot from its nostrils as it snarled, the sound like the crackling of a great furnace. Its breath was hot and suffocating, filling the air with the stench of sulfur. The beast's gaze locked onto Jake, its eyes narrowing with cruel intelligence as it spotted him crouching behind a boulder.

With terrifying speed, it lunged forward, its powerful legs propelling it across the arena in a ground-shaking charge. Its neck snaked forward as its jaws gaped open, revealing rows of jagged teeth dripping with saliva. The creature's wings flared, adding momentum to its charge, while its tail whipped behind it, the spaded tip slicing through the air with a menacing whistle.

Jake barely had time to react as the monstrous beast bore down on him, the ground trembling beneath its weight. The dracónyx was a force of nature, an unstoppable juggernaut of fury and flame, and it was coming for him with one intent: to destroy.

The battle was a chaotic blur. Jake was tossed and thrown like a rag doll, slammed into the ground and the unforgiving stone walls of the Coliseum. His body ached with every impact, and his breath came in shallow, labored bursts as he fumbled through the fight, petrified by the sheer power of his foe.

Jake ran from boulder to boulder, trying to escape the relentless pursuit. His sword, Dŷrníêth, was knocked from his grasp, skidding across the stone floor, out of reach. Panic set in as he realized he was weaponless against the malevolent beast.

Searching desperately for the next boulder to shelter behind, Jake realized his frantic evasions had brought him closer to another weapon. Glancing quickly at the deadly creature stalking him, he dashed for the ballista. When he reached it, his hands fumbled over the controls as he swung it around, aimed, and fired. It was a wŷrmwéb ballista, and the netted projectile encapsulated the dracónyx head. The creature winced and thrashed, its claws tearing at the net, trying to free itself. It clawed and scratched until finally, with a roar of frustration, it ripped the net away and took off into the sky.

During its struggle, Jake saw his chance. He sprinted toward Dŷrníêth. Grabbing the hilt with both hands, he turned to face his foe, which was now circling above, searching for him. He dashed toward a cluster of boulders, hoping to use them as cover.

It swooped down, searching, as Jake caught a glimpse of the three aétherium crystal spears still intact in another ballista. The dragonspike ballista. They were his best hope of bringing the beast down. But before he could make a move for it, an inferno of flames erupted from the beast's maw, engulfing the ground around him. The heat was unbearable, and Jake screamed in terror as he dove back behind the rocks for cover.

His mind raced as he recalled the tactic his instructors had taught him. Gritting his teeth, he made a dash back toward one of the wýrmwéb ballistae, zigzagging through the rocks, leaping over some, and ducking behind others as the dracónyx's gaze followed him from above. He reached the ballista just as the beast swooped down again. Jake grabbed hold of the ballista and fired it off, the net wrapping around the Dracónyx's face once more.

The creature crashed into the ground before him, the impact of it slamming both Jake and the ballista into the side of the Coliseum. He was thrown clear of the beast's flails, his body aching from the impact. Miraculously, he was still alive; his armor, specially crafted for tonight, had taken most of the damage, though every muscle screamed in agony. Pulling himself up, Jake watched briefly as the creature struggled to free itself from the net. In its frenzied attempt, one of its grotesque claws inflicted a deadly wound, blinding itself in one eye.

Knowing he had only moments, Jake sprinted back toward the dragonspike ballista. The dracónyx, now half-blind and enraged, reared onto its hind legs, exposing its chest. Summoning every ounce of strength, Jake aimed the ballista and fired the first aétherium crystal spear. The spear flew true but struck the dracónyx in its remaining eye as it bowed its head, blocking the shot from hitting its chest. The beast bellowed in pain, fire spewing from its mouth as it thrashed in agony.

Seeing the creature wounded, Jake grabbed Dýrníêth and charged toward the beast, both hands gripping the sword tightly. The dracónyx flailed in pain, trying to dislodge the spear. As Jake neared it, the beast's massive foot caught him, sending him flying backward once more and crashing hard onto the stone floor. Jake groaned but forced himself to his feet.

The beast shrieked, a sound that echoed through the Coliseum as it thrashed in blind fury. Jake wasted no time. He rushed forward with Dýrníêth and slashed at the creature's wings, hacking through flesh and bone until nothing remained but tattered sinew. The beast flailed on the ground, its tail whipping violently, sending Jake flying into a boulder.

Bruised and bloodied, Jake knew he had to end it. He pulled himself up and retrieved one of the aétherium crystal spears from the dragonspike ballista. He kissed the blade of the spear and charged back toward the beast. With the spear in one hand and Dŷrníêth in the other, Jake charged at his foe. The blind beast thrashed in pain, rolling onto its back and exposing its underbelly once more. The crowd's roar grew deafening as Jake ran up the creature's tail, across its massive body, toward its chest. He stopped where the heart lay, directly between the front legs of the terrifying creature.

With a last burst of strength, Jake raised the spear high into the air before driving it down into the beast's heart. The dracónyx let out one last, earth-shaking bellow as fire erupted from its mouth, engulfing the entire floor of the Coliseum in flames. The beast thrashed violently, throwing Jake and screeching deafeningly.

The fatally wounded dracónyx lay defeated on the floor of the Coliseum, struggling for breath. Jake retrieved Dŷrníêth, no longer fearing the creature. He walked swiftly toward its head, bowing under its massive horns, and placed a hand on its neck.

"I'm sorry for taking your life; you're truly a magnificent beast," Jake whispered, feeling a pang of sorrow for the creature.

With an ultimate act of mercy, Jake raised Dŷrníêth over his head and brought it down with all his might, severing the beast's head in one clean strike. The crowd erupted in cheers as Jake stood, raising the blood-drenched sword high in the air, proclaiming his victory.

But there was still one task left. The true reason he had foughtto win Elârâ's hand in marriage. Jake rushed to where the spear lay embedded in the dracónyx's heart. With Dŷrníêth, he sliced off the lance, leaving the spearhead within the heart. He then cut open the beast's chest, revealing the massive, waning heart, its beats slowing. It was bright red and nearly the size of Jake's torso.

As he struggled under the weight of the heart, the crowd's cheers faded, wondering at his strange behavior. Ándrôniüs's voice rang out across the field of battle, his words meant to bring closure to the event, to declare Jake the victor. Jake's wildly beating heart drowned out Andrôniüs's voice.

Jake narrowed his vision, sharpening his focus only on where Frânícê—Elârâ's father—was seated with her and two other men, presumably the High Mage of Silverthorne with his son, Éamon. With labored steps, he approached the edge of the wall; the heart held high. The crowd, sensing something significant was about to happen, ended their conversations and attempts to leave and fell into stunned silence as Jake pushed the heart up and over the wall, letting it fall at Frânícê's feet.

Frânícê, a weak and frail-looking man who only carried the illusion of power, recoiled in surprise. His pale, thin face twisted in confusion, his wiry frame shaking as he stood. His small, beady eyes darted nervously between Jake and the heart, his mind struggling to comprehend the scene before him.

"What is this, boy?" Frânícê demanded, his voice uncertain.

Jake, wiping the blood from his face, met his gaze with steadfastness. "Sir, I love your daughter, Elârâ, and she loves me. You cannot deny that we belong together, nor deny this bride price I bring to you. I ask for your permission to marry her."

Frânícê's thin lips curled into a sneer. "This is forbidden—humans and mages—its simply diabolical!"

His voice hardening, Jake said, "And yet, she chooses me, not some young man who has accomplished nothing in his life."

Feeling all eyes upon him, Frânícê's voice crackled in his attempt to control the situation. "But he is a mage, nonetheless! I shall not allow this to happen!"

"Not even after I've proclaimed my love for her and brought you a bride price worthy of her?" Jake challenged, his eyes blazing with resolve.

Spitting in his face, Frânícê caustically snarled, "Indeed, you mere slug."

Jake's mind raced, desperation creeping in as his thoughts became fleeting and frantic. How could he win over Frânícê? Would he have to force his hand? The memory of that morning flashed before him, Elârâ, willing to do anything, throwing herself at him, desperate to secure their future together. Though nothing had happened between them, barring a few innocent kisses, and though he didn't want to lie, he knew there was no other way.

Narrowing his eyes, Jake said, "Then you force my hand, sir. She is no longer innocent. This morning, she visited me in my chambers, and we consummated our marriage, conducted in secret."

Frânícê turned to Elârâ, his face pale with horror. "That is not true! Elârâ, *tell me* that it is not true."

Elârâ stood, her voice calm but firm. "Father, it is true. You forced us to do this. This was our failsafe. I will not marry a man I barely know and do not love."

Rage filled Frânícê's eyes. "And this human, this lowlife man-scum, is he any better? He has only been in our land for what, a few weeks? And you have known him for a few days at most? What can he truly offer you, the daughter of one of the oldest families in the Republic?"

"That may be the case, Father, but I will not marry a man who only seeks a seat on the council once his father is gone. Jake knows me. He has courted me. He is a good man. Any woman who is human, mage, elf, or dwarf would be fortunate to have him as a life partner," Elârâ said fervently, tears beginning to fall down her rosy cheeks.

"Guards! Arrest this man! I do not care if he is a champion of anywhere, least of all this charade of a prophecy. Guards!" Frânícê yelled, ignoring the sincere pleas of his daughter.

Anticipating this reaction, Thâlôr had already positioned himself near the stands where Elârâ, her father, and the others were seated during the fight between Jake and the dracónyx.

He stepped forward. "Guards, remain at your posts. I can confirm this, Frânícê. I saw her enter his quarters this morning."

Frânícê's face twisted with anger and disbelief. "And why did you not stop her, Thâlôr? You dare defy your own blood?"

Remaining calm, Thâlôr's voice was unwavering. "Because I am the one who performed their marriage, Frânícê. Here is the certificate, signed by the Grand Mage himself! All must believe and see it."

He held up the parchment for all to see, the seal of the Grand

Mage clearly visible. The crowd murmured in shock, their disbelief evident as they looked upon the folded document that validated Jake's and Elârâ's union.

Frânícê's face turned a deep shade of red, his anger boiling over. He turned to Elârâ, trembling with fury. Without warning, he lashed out, striking her across the face. "You are no daughter of mine, you *swine!*" he spat.

Before anyone could react, Jake was upon him. Rage surged through Jake's veins as he grabbed Frânícê by his long, graying hair and threw him to the ground, his foot pressing down on Frânícê's neck as he grasped the hilt of Dŷrnîêth to draw it.

"Apologize, you fool! How dare you strike any woman, let alone her, your own *daughter*! How dare you *defile* her with your own hand!" Jake thundered, his fury reverberating through the Coliseum.

Frânícê gasped for breath, his hands clawing at Jake's armored boot, but the pressure was relentless. The attendees stood in a stunned silence, the crowd watching in horrified fascination.

Sensing that Jake was on the verge of committing murder, Thâlôr quickly intervened. He grabbed Jake's arm, pulling him back with a firm but gentle grip. "Jake, there is no more we can do. You have won your bride. She is yours and you are hers. He is defeated, and so is the dracónyx. We must move on."

Jake hesitated, the fire of anger still burning in his eyes. But as he looked at Elârâ, her face reddened with the imprint of a hand. The rage ebbed away, and he removed his booted foot.

Now free from his captor, Frânícê stood shakily, straightening his clothes, his pride shattered. Without another word, he stormed out of the Coliseum.

Thâlôr wasted no time. He turned to Jake and Elârâ, his voice urgent. "We need to leave. The situation is delicate, and we can't afford to stay any longer."

Without waiting for a response, he hastily escorted them out of the Coliseum, weaving through the winding corridors past onlookers too shocked to speak. They moved quickly through the streets, past the Grand Barracks, and finally arrived at the Hall of Mages. The heavy doors swung open, and Thâlôr guided them inside. The atmosphere within was calm and secure, a stark contrast to the events in the arena they had left behind.

Thâlôr ensured the doors closed behind them, his face serious. "Here, you will be safe. No one can harm you while you are within these walls."

Still trying to catch his breath, Jake looked at Thâlôr with a mix of gratitude and confusion. "How did you know this would happen? How did you know to be ready?"

Stepping forward, Elârâ rested her hand on Jake's arm. "Thâlôr is my eldest brother, Jake. He knows our father better than anyone."

Jake's eyes widened in realization. "Wait... you two are..."

"Yes, Elârâ is my younger sister. And as her elder brother, I see fit that she marries you. I mean especially after those two acts of bravery in the Coliseum; I know she will be well tended after with you as her husband. You have my blessing." Thâlôr cut him off gently, his voice softening as he added, "However, the records will not show that this marriage happened today. We should keep this a secret until you two are officially married."

Clattering with Thâlôr, emotion welling up within him, Jake embraced him. "Thank you, Thâlôr, for everything. For this, for the training, and for believing in me."

Thâlôr returned the hug, a rare smile breaking through his stern demeanor. "You have proven yourself worthy, Jake. Not only to marry my sister, but to continue the legacy as the Lord of Suïl. Once my father passes, you and Elârâ, once wed, will take your rightful places on the throne and, with our family's sword, Dŷrnîêth, you shall lead it into the light, bearing the offspring to continue our line. Elârâ and I are the last of our family, and I cannot produce an heir. Now, please, get some rest, both of you. Tomorrow, we will face other challenges."

With those words, Thâlôr took his leave, exiting quickly through the doors of the Hall of Mages. Left alone, Jake and Elârâ turned to each other, their eyes meeting with a shared understanding. They had overcome the odds; they had won her freedom, and now, they had each other.

Jake pulled Elârâ close to him, his voice soft as he spoke. "I love you, Elârâ."

Elârâ smiled up at him, her eyes glistening. "And I love you, Jake."

In the silence of the empty hall, they kissed passionately, a moment marking the true beginning of their future together, even amidst uncertainty.

# THE STORMS WITHIN

AT THE DAY'S EARLY turning, on the morning of Ethan's test. An oppressive inquietude marked him. Sleep eluded him, with only fleeting moments of shallow rest punctuating the long hours of darkness. The absence of his friends, who had always been a source of comfort, amplified the isolation within the drab confines of his room. The solitude brought forth an eerie stillness, the kind that seemed to stir dormant fears and the shadowy memories that lurked in the depths of the mind; an inner tempest that now sought to take hold.

The uncertainty surrounding his friends' fates loomed over Ethan like an oppressive shadow. Jake's outcome remained a mystery. There had been no news of failure, leaving only speculation. Had he succeeded, or was the lack of information some orchestrated cruelty? The ambiguity pressed upon Ethan's thoughts, adding to the unease that already clung to him.

Turbulent and malicious thoughts churned relentlessly, their significance fueling the solicitude that clouded Ethan's mind. Among them was the persistent presence of that small, insidious voice; an ever-watchful adversary, seemingly biding its time to reclaim dominance. It was clear that this voice sought to stage its return, probing for cracks in Ethan's resolve. Though he had managed to suppress it thus far, the question hung over him: how much longer could he endure this before it broke through?

Ethan sought refuge in positive thoughts, turning to the idea of rekindling his relationship with Hannah. Yet even this hopeful notion spiraled into a series of unrelenting questions. What about Emily's unexpected advance? What had driven her to act that way? She was just as beautiful as Hannah, but his heart had always belonged to the latter. And what of Hannah herself? Was she still the same person he loved? The questions deepened, shifting to his father. Would he be proud to see his son again, to embrace him as he had during Ethan's childhood before his mother's death. And, more pressing still, what if he failed the test? Would he even survive to find out the answers? These fleeting glimmers of hope were fugacious indeed, giving way to a relentless tide of doubt and self-interrogation that pulled him further into his unease.

Ethan lay motionless, his mind a turbid whirlpool of thoughts, while the hours dragged on with an almost malicious slowness, as though the night itself sought to prolong his suffering. Time seemed to warp and stretch, each passing moment feeling as interminable as the last. Beyond the confines of his room, the world stirred. The first rays of dawn crept over the mountains to the east of Vâloríâ, their soft, golden light threading through the small window like a gentle promise of reprieve. The light brushed his face with a warm, tender touch, its brightness gradually pulling him from his sleepless torment. His heavy-lidded eyes blinked against the invading light, his body aching from the weight of his restless night.

The remnants of the prior evening's training clung to Ethan's form. His muscles ached from the rigorous drills overseen by the barracks' trainers, and his parched throat hinted at a night spent in heedless frustration. The morning light poured mercilessly through the small window of his room, indifferent to his longing for sleep, its unrelenting glow a stark contrast to his forespentness.

Ethan tossed and turned in his bed, struggling to find comfort. The pillow he pressed over his head did little to block out the encroaching daylight, and the mattress beneath him, while serviceable, failed to provide solace. Each attempt to shield himself under the blanket was thwarted as the fabric, too short to cover both his head and feet, left him exposed to the cool morning air. His frustration mounted with every failed effort.

Frustrated, he sighed deeply and rolled onto his back, his fists slamming down onto the bed in exasperation. The world was against him, even in the simplest of comforts.

"I guess I'll get up now," he muttered to himself, the resignation heavy in his voice.

Ethan heaved himself into a sitting position, his gaze drifting across the dimly lit room. His eyes lingered on the book of spells Ándrôniüs had given him days ago, still untouched on the desk. With a resigned sigh, he dragged himself to the chair, pulling it out noisily before collapsing into it with exaggerated effort.

Ethan opened the book to the contents page, flipping through it with mechanical precision. Page after page turned, his actions increasingly impatient, though the spells within again failed to capture his attention. With a sharp motion, he slammed it shut and shoved it aside. It slid across the desk and tumbled to the floor; the thud resonating in the quiet room, punctuating his mounting frustration.

Anger rose inside him, and he knew he couldn't stay in this room any longer. He stood up, intent on getting out, but halted as he realized he didn't know where to go. He didn't feel like encountering anyone, and even at this early hour, there were likely to be people about in the more public areas.

For several minutes, he paced furiously around his room, much like a caged lion. The solution came out of the blue. The pools beneath the Grand Barracks was likely to be empty at this hour. Hopefully, he could use the mineral-rich hot baths to rest his worn mind and aching muscles. He gathered the things from his accommodation and headed off to the basement of the grand structure.

However, once he arrived, he noticed someone had firmly shut the pool's doors, and no servants were nearby to attend to the patrons. Generally, the doors were open throughout the days and nights as recruits, guards, and many more who called this place home came to relax.

Ethan turned to leave as he thought it would be better to depart than make entry into the pools. He had learned his lesson that one time in high school and did not want to repeat that again. Though as he turned on his heel, he heard something.

Ethan, being all too curious, investigated. Pulling on the handle, he expected it to be locked, but the door opened despite its whining hinges, and he slid in unnoticed. Once inside, he was in the wardrobe room, where the patrons would strip down to their loincloths before entering the pools.

Talk and laughter filled the space, the source hidden within the mist over the pools. He placed his belongings in one of the many wardrobes along the wall and removed his nightshirt, leaving himself in only a loincloth. The voices grew louder, though their words remained indistinct, cloaked by the dense fog that shrouded the pools.

The water came into view from time to time as the steam eddied around the space, the air thick and rendering the surroundings hazy. Voices drifted through the mist, distinct now: Áelfwînë, Thâlôr, and Ándrôniüs. Unbeknownst to them, Ethan lingered nearby, positioning himself behind a pillar near the staircase, his form obscured by the swirling vapors.

Unaware of their eavesdropper, Áelfwînë said, "Ándrôniüs, do you really think he could be the one?"

"I assuredly believe so. I've watched him all his life," Ándrôniüs responded, his tone serious.

Thâlôr interjected, his voice skeptical. "And how have you watched him?"

Áelfwînë nodded in agreement, echoing the sentiment.

With a hint of mystery, the older mage said, "I am the Seer of the Enigmas. You know that power is vested in me, and no one else. It is my duty to observe those from other worlds and bring them here to face these tests, to fulfill the prophecy, to defeat the Dark Lord." Stumbling over his words, Ándrôniüs quickly added, "When the time is right, of course! *Strictly* under the guidance of the council."

Thâlôr's tone sharpened as he eyed Ándrôniüs with suspicion. "So, are you denying that you brought them here early? There is talk among the republic's elites that you have grossly abused your power."

A clamorous scoff escaped his mouth, and Ándrôniüs looked visibly taken aback. "What are you accusing me of? Such an act would be treasonous without the approval of the High Mage Council and the blessing of the Grand Mage. I can do nothing but watch from my tower, such as it has been since the beginning of time when the Allfather bestowed this responsibility upon my family."

Áelfwînë leaned forward, his interest piqued. "But... surely you could tell us if the boy is the one?"

"Ándrôniüs, could you not share just a little information?" Thâlôr added.

"You know these secrets are merely for the Council. I have bewrayed too much already. However, what I can tell you is that I believe so. Although I could never view his father in the stone. So, ultimately, I cannot confirm. It appears the father knew I was searching for him all these years. I'm certain he enshrouded himself, masking where he is. Though I could never be certain. Alas, I follow my gut, hoping that he *is* the one, so we can end this once and for all," Ándrôniüs said, trying to maintain a veil of mystery.

The skepticism persisted in Thâlôr's mind, causing him to ask, "So, you just watch whomever, whenever?"

Ándrôniüs's response was evasive, his voice taking on a cryptic edge. "In a sense, yes, but also no."

Áelfwînë continued to press further, showing persistence. "But if he is the son, it would mean... what exactly? Is it for this prophecy, or is it something else the High Mage Council has been working on?"

With a knowing look, a smirk tugged at the corner of Ándrôniüs's mouth. "Ah, the son of someone great and powerful... Or perhaps not. Who's to say? The Council has many plans, many prophecies to fulfill. One now. Another for five hundred years hence. Does it matter which one? The lines often blur, my friends, and not all paths are as straight as they seem. Whether this boy—whoever he is and wherever he may come from—will eventually be the one to fulfill it, I cannot say. It may not even be one of these three. It ultimately could be one of the two girls, as the prophecy has no requirement for the one who is to save this world. What I can say for certain is that, eventually, the Council, the Grand Mage, and the Seer will choose a champion who will bring peace to this world; again, whether that is now or many eons in the future is unclear."

Thâlôr let out a frustrated sigh. "There you go again with your ambiguous yet somehow candid answers."

Ándrôniüs chuckled softly, clearly enjoying the game. "Why settle on one path when there could be many? The future is a tapestry, and I simply weave the threads as they come. Whether it is in fact this boy that is destined for greatness or simply a pawn in a larger scheme, only time will tell."

Áelfwînë exchanged a glance with Thâlôr, both of them trying to piece together the puzzle that Ándrôniüs had laid out before them. "So, whose son is he, then? And why is it so important?" he asked, his voice laced with curiosity.

Once more, Ándrôniüs tilted his head slightly, his eyes narrowing as if considering how much to reveal. "Ah, now that would be telling, wouldn't it? Perhaps he's the son of a hero long forgotten... or perhaps the offspring of something more sinister. I ask you, does it matter? The prophecy will unfold as it should, and the boy will play his part, willingly or not."

Thâlôr shook his head in exasperation. "You're impossible, Ándrôniüs."

Ándrôniüs simply smiled, his expression inscrutable. "Possibly. Or perhaps just prudent."

A sudden clatter broke through the mist as Ethan slipped, trying to get closer and in the process knocking into an urn full of linens, drawing their attention sharply. All three turned toward the source of the noise. Thâlôr was the first to react, moving swiftly to grab the figure emerging from the fog. Locking the intruder in a headlock, he demanded, his voice full of authority, "Who are you?"

Gasping for air, Ethan struggled to speak, barely managing to squeak out a few words. "Thâlôr, it's me! It's Ethan!"

Recognizing the voice, Thâlôr quickly released him, causing Ethan to stumble back onto the stone floor. "My apologies, Ethan," Thâlôr said, reaching out to help him up. "You can't just sneak in on people during private conversations like that, though."

Áelfwînë, his tone a mix of annoyance and amusement, added, "Yes, it's well known within these halls that when the baths' doors are closed, they are closed for a good reason."

Ethan pushed himself upright, massaging his side where he had landed. "I see that now," he muttered. After a brief pause, he turned his gaze to the three of them, the question escaping him before he could stop himself. "What were you talking about, anyway?"

Ándrôniüs, however, was far less amused than his companions. His eyes narrowed, his voice sharp and cold. "That is no business of yours, boy. You should be asleep at this hour. Now, Thâlôr, Áelfwînë, I take my leave. Do as you see fit with the snoop."

Ándrôniüs turned and left, and the atmosphere in the room shifted, leaving a lingering uneasiness in his wake. Ethan stood frozen, his expression betraying a sense of isolation. For days now, Ándrôniüs's temper had seemed shorter, his patience thinner. To an observer, it might have appeared that he was losing interest in guiding Ethan, though the reasons remained unclear.

Thâlôr's steady voice broke through the silence. "Ethan, we know you meant no harm. Come, sit with us, and join us for breakfast in the dining hall this morning when we finish."

"Then we'll begin some last-minute training on your abilities with Soulrend," Áelfwînë added.

Ethan, affronted, asked, "I don't get a day of rest like the others?"

His tone light but firm, Thâlôr responded, "Rest? Do you think that rest is something you're deserving of?"

"Why wouldn't I be?" Ethan shot back, a hint of dissatisfaction creeping into his voice. "The others got it."

Áelfwînë's response was stern. "But did you take your studies and training here seriously?"

Hesitantly, Ethan replied, "As serious as I thought I should."

Thâlôr leaned back into the pool, a small smile playing on his lips. "Then you have your answer," he said, sinking deeper into the restorative waters.

Ethan, still feeling agitated, snapped, "What is my answer?"

His eyes flashing with a warning, Áelfwînë responded. "Do not take that tone with us, boy. Now come sit, relax and let your mind empty. Only then will you have clarity. Ethan, I know what hides in the darkness of your mind. It is the same that hides in mine. Now, I insist! *Sit.*"

Confused and increasingly panicked, Ethan realized that defying Thâlôr and Áelfwînë would only lead to harsher treatment during his training. Resigning himself to their command, he stepped into the pool. Thâlôr lightened the mood by playfully tripping Ethan, sending him face-first into the water with a splash. Laughter erupted from Thâlôr and Áelfwînë, filling the chamber with echoes of mirth.

Ethan surfaced, sputtering as he brushed the water from his face and wrung out his hair. He turned to face Áelfwînë and Thâlôr, a smirk forming on his lips as the last traces of his anger faded away. With a resigned sigh, he turned back around and waded through the warm water until he reached the far side of the pool, directly opposite them. He took a seat, submerging himself up to his chin in the soothing water.

The laughter from their earlier antics had subsided, replaced by a quiet sense of relaxation. Thâlôr and Áelfwînë had also settled into their own spaces. The three of them formed a silent triangle, each on his side of the pool.

Ethan leaned back against the smooth stone edge, allowing the steam to curl around him like a protective veil. The bubbling warmth of the mineral-rich water worked its magic, easing his muscles and, more importantly, his mind. He closed his eyes, surrendering to this rare moment of peace.

Across the pool, Thâlôr and Áelfwînë were similarly at ease, having found their places of quiet reflection. The warmth of the water enveloped them all, and for a while, the silence between them was neither awkward nor tense; each person lost in their thoughts.

As the minutes passed, the worries of the day seemed to dissipate into the mist, carried away by the soothing embrace of the hot springs.

Eventually, the three finished soaking in the baths, the steam and warmth having worked to ease both body and mind. They exchanged nods of mutual understanding before rising from the pool. Moving toward the wardrobes lining the bathhouse entrance, they retrieved their clothes and dressed in silence.

As they ascended the staircase leading to the main hall, the quiet stretched between them until Ethan broke it.

"What were you all talking about earlier?" he asked, his voice cutting through the stillness. "Who's this son you mentioned? And what's this prophecy really about?"

Thâlôr and Áelfwînë exchanged exasperated glances, their expressions tightening as they struggled to respond.

Thâlôr finally spoke, his tone evasive. "It's not something you need to concern yourself with, Ethan. There are many prophecies, and not all are meant for us to understand just yet."

Knowing no bounds, Ethan pressed on. "But if it involves me or the others, don't I have a right to know?"

With a hint of amusement in his eyes, Áelfwînë smirked. "You're always so eager for answers, boy. But sometimes, it's best not to know everything at once. What we discussed is beyond your concern... for now."

"Beyond my concern? How can that be when I'm in the middle of all this?" Ethan's frustration was undeniable as his face became rigid, his mouth twitching with the effort to hold back an outburst.

Thâlôr sighed, attempting to steer the conversation away. "Prophecies have a way of revealing themselves. Whether it's you, someone else, or no one at all, things will unfold as they must. And that time is certainly not now."

Before Ethan could push further, they reached the main hall, where the enticing smells of apple cinnamon porridge and freshly baked bread wafted through the air.

Eager to avoid talking about this subject further, Thâlôr said, "Let's eat before we talk any more about things we don't fully understand."

The three of them entered the dining hall. Loaves of crusty bread, bowls of steaming porridge, and wooden platters filled with butter and preserves filled one long table. Simple pewter plates and wooden spoons were laid out, accompanied by goblets for water and ale. The setting was rustic, yet hearty. They gathered their fill and took chairs near the exit of the hall.

"So, this prophecy... does it really involve us? Or is it something else entirely?" Ethan asked, trying once more to pry answers from his companions, seeing as they were wrapping up their meal.

Thâlôr and Áelfwînë exchanged another look, this time one of mild irritation.

Áelfwînë spoke first, his voice firm. "Ethan, *ENOUGH!* We've told you all we can for now. The rest will come in time."

Finishing his last bite, Thâlôr nodded. "We're not trying to hide things from you, but there's no point in telling you what even we don't fully understand. Focus on what's in front of you... your training, your preparation."

Áelfwînë quickly finished his last bites, eager to escape with Thâlôr from Ethan's persistent questioning.

Standing up, Thâlôr looked down at Ethan. "Finish up and meet us in the courtyard for training. We'll be waiting."

Ethan watched as they left the hall, their words leaving him with more questions than answers. He took a few more bites of his food, his appetite diminished by the unresolved queries in his mind. When he finally finished, he hurried after them.

Ethan pushed open the heavy doors of the Grand Barracks and stepped outside, hesitating at the top of the staircase down into the courtyard. A chilly drizzle, begun while they were in the pools underneath the barracks, lightly soaked the stone underfoot.

Thâlôr's voice, sharp and biting, boomed across the courtyard. "Ethan, down here! Now!"

A sudden carking gripped Ethan, his stomach churning and mind racing. Had he pushed them too far with his questions? A knot of anxiety contorted his stomach as he realized that this training session might be far more brutal than any he'd faced before. Readying himself for whatever was about to happen, he took a deep breath and descended the stairs. The rain remained light as he approached Thâlôr and Áelfwînë, who stood waiting in the center of the courtyard, their faces set with steadfastness.

Áelfwînë's voice carried a hint of sarcasm as he addressed Ethan. "I hear your Soulrend is weak. That's good... it's a spell born from the darkness, one we wouldn't wish even on our enemies. Is there anything else you'd like to practice? Or are you willing to tempt fate with it?"

Surprised, Ethan said timidly, "Soulrend is dark? Why didn't Ándróniüs tell me?"

Mimicking Ándróniüs's mannerisms, with a slight twist to his words and a smirk, Thâlôr replied, "He seems to think, in his professional opinion, that you've had little happiness in your life, which is why you chose it. He believes that the darkness in you is your greatest ally. If used correctly."

Ethan, growing more uneasy, shook his head. "I'm not evil."

Áelfwînë's tone was sharp as he cut him off. "We never said you were. Stop putting words in our mouths."

Now thoroughly unsettled, Ethan muttered, "I guess I'll just *shut up*."

Thâlôr nodded, his expression stern. "That would be wise. Now, see that training dummy over there?" He pointed to the wooden figure across the courtyard. "Render it useless."

Ethan's anxiety flared. "I can't just do it on the spot. I'm not in the right headspace for this."

Stepping forward, Áelfwînë's eyes narrowed with a menacing glint. "Then I'll just have to get you there."

Without warning, the warrior raised his hand and backhanded Ethan across the cheek, sending him sprawling onto the cold, wet stone.

At the moment of impact, the sky seemed to mimic the violence. The rain, which had been a mere drizzle, suddenly intensified, falling in heavy sheets as if the heavens were responding to the blow. The cold droplets stung as they struck Ethan's skin, mingling with the pain from Áelfwînë's strike.

Ethan looked up, shock written across his face. "What was that for?"

Thâlôr's voice cut through the downpour, cold and commanding. "You're not in the right *headspace*? What does that even mean? What if you're attacked? Ethan, listen to me. You're part of a real life-or-death situation. It's time to grow up! It's time to take things seriously! It's time to become a man! In order for you to use Soulrend, you must be able to channel your deepest and most painful memories. You must taste the darkness and its bitterness. You must be one with it, angry enough that you could take our lives; but with benevolence grant us mercy."

Grabbing Ethan by the collar, Áelfwînë hoisted him to his feet as the rain poured down even harder, turning the courtyard into a treacherous, slick surface. "I say again, boy! Destroy that training device."

When Ethan hesitated again, Áelfwînë swept his legs out from under him, slamming him back onto the unforgiving stone.

Ethan cried out, his voice raw with desperation. "STOP! You two, stop!"

Hovering over him, with his expression unyielding, Thâlôr was a shadow in the storm. "We'll *stop* once you learn to wield Soulrend correctly."

He grabbed Ethan by the hair, yanking him upright once more. "Now, again, render it useless."

Ethan's heart drubbed with a confounded mix of wode and despondency, his breathing shallow. The rain drenched him to the bone, but he barely noticed. His tears mingled with the relentless downpour, indistinguishable in the deluge.

Memories of a past filled with violence flashed through Ethan's mind; echoes of cruel words and the sting of harsh blows. Each memory, sharp and fragmented, fueled the darkness that lingered in his soul. It was a darkness not easily understood, but one that now clawed its way to the surface, fed by the pain and anger that coursed through him.

Ethan stood unsteadily, his body trembling beneath the weight of emotions he struggled to control. The storm above continued to reflect the turmoil inside him, its fury intensifying as if the very sky shared in his torment. Thunder rumbled through the air, shaking the ground, and a jagged bolt of lightning suddenly split the heavens. The flash lit up the courtyard in strobe-like bursts, casting eerie shadows across the slick stone. For a brief moment, the storm seemed to pause, revealing the depths of Ethan's inner struggle and his face contorted with anguish.

"NOW!" Thâlôr ferociously yelled.

Startled by his demand, throes and forlornness intagliated into every line of his face, Ethan assumed the defensive stance Ándrôniüs had drilled into him. With one foot planted firmly behind the other, his knees slightly bent as though ready to spring forward. His arms hung at his sides, but they were tense, every muscle in his body coiled tightly, like a spring wound to its breaking point. He closed his eyes against the onslaught of rain, forcing himself to breathe deeply, to focus on the boiling cauldron of anger roiling within him.

Images of his father's face emerged in his mind's eye; cruel, mocking, and unyielding. The memories of the pain, the humiliation, the helplessness all surged forward, like floodwaters breaching a dam. These were the memories he had tried to bury, to forget, but now they burst free with terrifying intensity, fueling the dark energy gathering within him.

With a primal scream that cut through the roar of the storm, Ethan unleashed a force unlike anything he had ever experienced. It was raw, unrefined, and terrifying in its power. Red and black mist swirled around his hands, thick and malevolent, an almost living entity. The mist coalesced, growing denser, darker, and more menacing, until it surged forward in a powerful wave as he raised his arms toward the training dummy. The air itself seemed to warp and crackle with energy, as if Ethan's emotions were twisting into the very fabric of reality.

The energy exploded from him with a ferocity that took him by surprise, a tangible manifestation of the darkness he had kept locked away for so long. The wave of power ripped through the courtyard, a tsunami of rage that obliterated the dummy in its path. For a moment, that dark force seemed to consume the entire world, leaving nothing but the searing red and black mist pouring from his hands.

But just as quickly as the power came, it vanished, dissipating into the stormy air as if it had never been. The mist faded, leaving behind only its fury and the devastated remains of the training dummy, now reduced to splinters and ash. The sudden release of energy left Ethan staggering, his vision blurring as the world tilted precariously around him. His strength, so formidable just moments before, seemed to drain from his body, leaving him hollowed out and spent.

The storm continued to rage around him, but to Ethan, it was all distant, muted, as if he were hearing it from the bottom of a deep well. His legs buckled, and he felt himself falling, the cold, wet stone rushing up to meet him. Before he could hit the ground, strong arms caught him, preventing him from collapsing entirely. Thâlôr and Áelfwînë had rushed to his side, their faces pale and worried as they lowered him gently to the ground.

Ethan's breathing was shallow; his body was limp and unresponsive. The darkness within him, momentarily unleashed, had taken its toll, leaving him unconscious in their arms, a reminder of the fine line between control and chaos, between the light and the dark that battled within him.

Above him, the two trainers exchanged glances, the realization that they might have pushed him too far in their efforts to draw out his power sinking in. The two men crouched beside him, shielding him from the worst of the rain, their expressions a mix of concern and something else, perhaps fear of what they had just witnessed, of the raw, untamed power that had nearly consumed the boy before them.

"Could it be?" Thâlôr murmured, the question laced with both awe and dread.

"I think it could," Áelfwînë replied, his voice a mix of disbelief and urgency.

"We must fetch Ándrôniüs and Câllirrhöe," Thâlôr said urgently. "If he stays in this catatonic state, he will have to forfeit, and all will be lost."

"I'll get them," Áelfwînë responded, turning quickly and sprinting toward the gates, then on toward the Hall of Mages.

Thâlôr looked back at the wall, now tarnished with a blackened scorch mark where the spell had made contact, eradicating the training dummy. Luckily, a protective spell on the walls of the barracks had kept the destructive force from causing more damage. He picked up Ethan's near-lifeless body. A shiver ran down his spine as he realized he had never seen a spell with that much raw and uncontrolled power before. He had trained hundreds, if not thousands, of Vâloríâ's soldiers, and never had anyone wielded such power; not even him. But Ethan, in his adolescence and with his limited training, was more powerful than he had ever imagined a mage could be.

Carrying Ethan up the stairs and into the hall of the Grand Barracks, Thâlôr laid him beneath the towering statues of the past champions of Cáelunárra. Minutes passed as he watched over Ethan, trying to rouse him back to consciousness. He rubbed his knuckles against Ethan's sternum repeatedly, but no response came despite his persistent attempts.

As the minutes turned into nearly a half-hour, Ándrôniüs, Áelfwînë, and Câllirrhöe appeared, pushing open the heavy doors of the barracks. The sound of the storm raged outside, with lightning flashing and heavy rain pouring down, casting ominous shadows across the hall. Ándrôniüs stormed in. His presence filled the room with an ominous weight, the air crackling with the same intensity as the lightning that flashed beyond the barracks walls.

His anger barely contained, Ándrôniüs turned on Thâlôr and Áelfwînë. "What did you two do?!"

Thâlôr, still shaken by what had transpired, immediately spoke up, his voice carrying a mix of urgency and guilt. "Ándrôniüs... Ethan, he used Soulrend and... this."

Câllirrhöe glided gracefully over to where Ethan lay. Despite the situation, she retained her ethereal elegance, her flowing form barely touching the ground as she knelt beside Ethan. Gently, she lifted his eyelids, her delicate hands checking for any signs of life. Her serene expression faltered as she noticed the faintness of his breath.

She squeaked in alarm, her usually calm demeanor breaking. "He is fading!"

Ándrôniüs, his anger still barely contained, said, "Again I ask, what did you two do?!"

"Nothing... I mean... we pushed the boy, as you instructed, to inflict fear and push him to reach the full potential of the spell," Thâlôr said, stepping away from Ethan's side cautiously.

His eyes narrowed, suspicion lacing his words, Ándrôniüs demanded, "And how did you do that?"

Áelfwînë, visibly uneasy under Ándrôniüs's gaze, reluctantly confessed. "We may have pushed too far. We used the old ways of training, inflicting pain on the boy, methods reserved only for those who need an extra push to reach their potential."

With a storm brewing in his eyes, Ándróniüs's expression darkened further. "No, you did not. You know those ways are forbidden! Too many of us were lost to the Dark Lord because of those practices."

Defensive, but aware of the gravity of the situation, Áelfwînë protested weakly, "I know... but he was recalcitrant. You know how the boy can be, Ándróniüs."

With a tone of exasperation, Thâlôr added, "He kept asking questions about the prophecy and the identity of the boy that we were discussing this morning. Things he should not be privy to."

Ándróniüs's face twisted with fury as he spat his words. "And you thought it prudent to abuse the boy? Do you not know what lies within him? Did you not understand why I didn't push him? I've repeatedly told you confidentially that you must gently coax his power, not force it. Because of his past and the torment he's endured, he could become a danger to us all."

"I apologize, Ándróniüs. This is not what we intended." Áelfwînë's guilt was evident in his voice.

Câllirrhöe interjected urgently, her voice cutting through the argument like a blade. "Ándróniüs, we must get him to the infirmary immediately. I'll need to perform a miracle if we're to have him to a full recovery in time for tonight."

As Áelfwînë and Thâlôr moved to help pick up Ethan, Ándróniüs snarled in anger. "You two have done *ENOUGH!* He is in our care now."

With a strength that belied his age, Ándróniüs heaved Ethan's limp body over his shoulder and swiftly followed Câllirrhöe as she led the way down the winding stairs to the infirmary. Thâlôr and Áelfwînë stayed behind, pondering how they might have better handled the situation.

# CALLIRYSIS ELUMIRAE

Rushing down the stairs, Ándrôniüs moved with surprising agility, his years seeming to fall away as he hurried through the dimly lit halls of the Grand Barracks. They reached a set of double doors and upon entering, the sight of the room; pure white struck Ándrôniüs, almost as if they had stepped into a realm of light. The walls, the floor, and the very air itself seemed to glisten, evoking a celestial, almost heavenly atmosphere.

Câllirrhöe turned to Ándrôniüs as he set Ethan upon a bed, her expression grave. "Ándrôniüs, I need these ingredients: aéthërial dew, lünáris petals, sŷlphrót essence, crystalized wéilwrót, and thrälfáylaín nectar. Please hurry. You can find these at any apothecary in Vâloríâ."

Without a moment's hesitation, Ándrôniüs blasted back through the double doors, leaving Câllirrhöe alone with the unconscious Ethan.

Quickly, she started setting up her workstation. She deftly arranged beakers, a mortar and pestle, and vials, each item delicate and perfectly sized for her small hands. Unsure of how long it would take Ándrôniüs to return with the necessary supplies, she sat down, her tiny fingers tapping nervously against the table. Time seemed to pass slowly, each minute feeling like an eternity as she watched Ethan's skin lose its color, his lips turning a sickly blue.

As her miasmic thoughts darkened, pulling her toward sorrow, the doors burst open with a thunderous crash.

"I have it all!" Ándrôniüs gasped, thrusting the ingredients onto Câllirrhöe's workstation. "I have everything you asked for!"

Câllirrhöe immediately began sorting through the bag,

muttering to herself, "All here, thank you, Ándrôniüs."

"What are you making?" Ándrôniüs asked, trying to mask the fear in his voice.

"Cállïrŷsis Elúmiráë," she replied, her tone heavy with the seriousness of the situation.

Ándrôniüs gasped, his face paling. "Is he that near death?"

Câllirrhöe nodded solemnly, her eyes never leaving her work. "Indeed, Ándrôniüs. I fear he may be beyond my expertise, but I will give it my all. Now go, you must go do what you do best to prepare for his test in case I am unable to revive him in time."

Feeling the immense pressure, Ándrôniüs's anger flared once more. He stormed out of the infirmary, leaving Ethan's fate in Câllirrhöe's capable hands. His mind raced as he hurried back through the barracks.

Was it possible to salvage the prophecy? If Ethan couldn't fight, would all their efforts be wasted? As the Seer of Enigmas, he would need to weave a new path, one that could still lead to the prophecy's fulfillment, despite this monumental setback.

Ándrôniüs's thoughts were a cyclonic furor as he rushed into the main hall where Thâlôr and Áelfwînë awaited. When he entered, objects in the surrounding area began to rattle and shake.

He bellowed with fury. "YOU FOOLS! Ethan is on his deathbed! Do you know what this means?"

The two looked at him blankly. They dared not answer.

"DO YOU?" Ándrôniüs pressed with a furious snarl, so close that his spittle sprayed them.

They still did not answer, lowering their heads, averting their gazes, clearly ashamed.

"Of course not, you fools! That means this is all for nothing. You two have eradicated the only chance we had. We were so close to the eve of this all being completed. You two are as mindless as a conscripted foot soldier fresh to battle. What have you to say for yourselves?"

Thâlôr and Áelfwînë, taken aback by the raw anger radiating from Ándrôniüs, were speechless. A crepuscular darkness filled the room, weighing on their chests, as the very walls seemed to tremble in response to Ándrôniüs's vehemence. They had never seen him like this before, and the reality of their actions settled heavily on their shoulders and in the pits of their stomachs.

Áelfwînë was the first to break the silence, his voice barely a whisper. "What would you have us do?"

His eyes blazing, Ándrôniüs snapped, "One of you must fight in his stead if he cannot."

Thâlôr, his voice shaking, asked, "But what about the prophecy? His failure to fight will prevent the prophecy's fulfillment."

His voice cold and biting, Ándrôniüs snarled, "But you two dullards didn't think about that when you nearly killed him this afternoon!"

As the room continued to quake with Ándrôniüs's fury, a small crowd gathered outside the hall, drawn by the commotion. Thâlôr, noticing them, urgently whispered, "Ándrôniüs, there are people... this must not be discussed in front of them."

Ándrôniüs turned, his gaze sweeping over the onlookers. His expression darkened further as he muttered under his breath, "Fâräzŷenn Sâccûtrëâ Vûrrë Mŷëlûrn Ëltë." The words grew louder and louder, filling the room with a resonant chant until the crowd became eerily still, their movements slowed to a crawl, as if they were snails. Thâlôr and Áelfwînë felt a strange sensation wash over them as the spell's influence caught them, aware but disconnected from the near-frozen world around them.

Snapping back to the moment, Ándrôniüs grabbed both Thâlôr and Áelfwînë by their shirts, his grip ironclad.

Áelfwînë, desperation in his voice, volunteered. "I will fight. Stop, Ándrôniüs... I will fight in his stead. It was I who struck first; I offer my life in his place."

His voice as cold as the storm outside, Ándrôniüs commanded, "Then you must enter the Coliseum and fight in his stead. You must not utter a single word. None shall know it is you. You must fight in his place. I, being the Seer, will go to the fane in the Hall of Mages and strike a bargain with the Allfather, even if it costs me my life. He and I will work together to weave a new path forward because of your carelessness."

His face pale with fear, Thâlôr shouted, "But wouldn't that surely turn Áelfwînë? You know the scars he bears! We cannot sacrifice him."

Turning his anger toward Thâlôr, Ándrôniüs snarled, "Then that is his price to pay if he cannot control the darkness that *festers* within him."

Thâlôr, defiant but fearful, exclaimed, "No! It simply must not be that way!"

"Then shall you fight in both their stead?" Ándrôniüs demanded.

"No. I cannot." Thâlôr, his resolve crumbling, shook his head.

Ándrôniüs, a cold smirk forming on his lips, turned back to Áelfwînë. "Then let's see what kind of mage Áelfwînë truly is, and whether he can overcome the darkness that seeks to reclaim his heart and mind. He was once one of them. Let us see if he truly gave up their ways."

Without another word, Ándrôniüs stormed off, heading back to the infirmary to assist Câllirrhöe. Thâlôr and Áelfwînë remained in the darkened hall, the burdensome atmosphere lingering even after Ándrôniüs left.

"We must ready you, my friend," Thâlôr said, his voice heavy with regret. "I'll summon the blacksmiths to make the necessary adjustments to Ethan's armor, ensuring it fits you perfectly, to keep your disguise intact."

As swiftly as Ándrôniüs had disappeared, he suddenly returned, realizing he hadn't lifted the enchantment he had cast. Muttering, "Sÿërrë Sâccûtrëâ Azjŷërríc," he reversed the effects of the spell, and the onlookers outside his spell resumed their normal pace, unaware of the secret conversation that had just taken place. Ándrôniüs cast one last glance over his shoulder, his eyes burning with intensity. "And if either of you speaks of this to anyone, for any reason, I will see that both of your heads are smitten from your shoulders for your treachery and loose tongues."

With that final portentous warning, Ándrôniüs vanished down the stairs, heading back to the infirmary, leaving Thâlôr, Áelfwînë, and the gathered crowd in stunned silence, each person filled with questions and fears about what had just transpired. The darkened hall, now quiet, was heavy with the weight of impending decisions and the consequences that lay ahead.

\*\*\*

The hours dragged, and the storm raged on, unleashing its fury with unbridled intensity. Inside, the atmosphere was equally tempestuous, charged with anxiety and fleeting thoughts of what lay ahead.

Thâlôr worked with unwavering focus, preparing his dearest friend for the battle that might yet come. Though Áelfwînë's frame was larger than Ethan's, their builds were close enough to maintain the deception.

Stories below, the suspense was unmistakable. Ándrôniüs, usually so composed, now sat with his head buried in his hands, his heart heavy with the weight of his potential failures. Across the room, Câllirrhöe had enlisted the aid of several other Naïads, their presence adding a shimmer of divine light to the otherwise somber space. They worked in quiet synchronization, their hands moving with practiced skill as they prepared Ethan's lifeless body. They had cut away his clothes, leaving him in nothing but his loincloth as they tended to him with a mixture of magic and alchemy.

Câllirrhöe, her delicate hands steady, ground the ingredients meticulously, the sound of the pestle against the mortar ringing around the space. She added water in careful increments, her magic subtly heating and cooling the beakers and vials as she swirled the mixture with precision. The potent herbs and mystical essences created a heady, life-pulsing aroma that filled the room.

Finally, the tonic was complete. She wiped the sheen of sweat from her brow and held up the vial of Câllïrŷsis Elúmiráë to the light.

The liquid within was mesmerizing. A shimmering, empyreal gold that fluttered with silver flakes, like captured stardust swirling in the small glass container. It was a sight to behold, a concoction of immense power, and yet it was barely more than a gulp for any human, mage, dwarf, or elf alike.

"It is ready," Câllirrhöe whispered, her voice barely above a breath.

Ándróniüs stood, his once vibrant form now tinged with a grayness. He approached Ethan's still body, his heart breaking as tears welled in his eyes. This could be the end; not just for Ethan, but for everything they had just begun to fight for.

He leaned over Ethan, his voice hoarse with emotion. "If you can hear me, boy... live. Please, live. I'd give my life in exchange for yours if I could."

Câllirrhöe's voice was gentle as she approached him, sensing the depth of his sorrow. "Would you like to administer it?"

Ándróniüs shook his head, his tears falling freely now. "No... I leave it to your expertise. I will take my leave. I must prepare the Coliseum."

"Will you not stay?" Câllirrhöe asked softly, her tone tinged with understanding. "I know he reminds you of the boy you lost to the Dark Lord all those years ago."

Memories of his past flooded back with painful clarity. "I am too close to this again. I really must go," he said, his voice trembling. As he walked to the door, his hand lingered on the frame. He turned back, his eyes filled with unspoken pain. "Please, take good care of him."

With that, Ándróniüs left, his departure heavy with the burden of his own regrets. Câllirrhöe turned her attention back to Ethan, her heart aching for the boy caught between life and death. She flew over to his face, her tiny body landing gently on his cheek. With meticulous care, she administered one drop of the Câllïrŷsis Elúmiráë every ten seconds, the liquid shimmering as it touched his lips. This was a painstaking process, one that would take time and patience, but she knew it was their only hope.

As each drop fell, Câllirrhöe whispered soothing words into Ethan's ear, urging him to fight, to hold on. Urgency filled the room; this small vial of shimmering gold bore the weight of the world. The process was grueling, each second stretching into infinity as Câllirrhöe watched Ethan's color continue to fade, his skin growing colder, his breaths more shallow. Regardless of the time, she persisted, her hands steady despite the growing fear in her heart.

Ándrôniüs, meanwhile, stormed through the halls of the Grand Barracks and out its doors, his mind racing with thoughts of what would happen if Ethan didn't awaken in time.

He moved swiftly through the weather raging around him, as if the very heavens were mourning Ethan's fate. Lightning continued to tear across the sky, followed by the deafening roar of thunder. Streams of rain, mixed with light hail, battered the city, turning the streets into rivers of mud. It was as if night had descended prematurely, the darkness around him ominously tied to the fragile thread of Ethan's life.

Pushing through the crowded streets, the people drenched and huddled against the buildings, sheltering from the elements, became obstacles in Ándrôniüs's path. He moved with purpose, shoving those who didn't move aside, their protests lost to his ears. Anger flared in the crowd, citizens shouting curses in his wake, calling him a fool. But he paid them no heed, driven by the urgency of the task at hand.

The Coliseum was up ahead. The massive structure, so often a place of glory, now stood as a foreboding testament to the battle that would soon unfold. Ándrôniüs crossed the threshold of its gates, entering the grand yet augural building. He made his way to the warriors' hold, a place that now sat eerily empty, save for the distant, bone-chilling sound of the gorlock's roars as it pounded against the walls of its keep. The beast's fury echoed through the stone, reverberating in the air as it awaited its challenger; whether that would be Ethan or Áelfwînë, Ándrôniüs did not yet know.

Standing alone in the turbulence, surrounded by the oppressive sounds of pounding, lightning, thunder, cheering, and shouting, Ándrôniüs felt his mind teetering on the edge of despondency. He paced back and forth, the gravity of the situation bearing down on him. The storm was slowly losing its ferocity; the lightning ceasing its relentless assault in the sky. The thunder became more sporadic, its growls growing distant as the storm waned, revealing an early evening sky tinged with a gentle, inviting orange hue.

Hoping to maintain his innocence and plausible deniability if ever questioned about who fought that day, Ándrôniüs refused to know who would be brought to the hold. With a heavy heart, he opened the door, leaving the empty room behind. He traversed the labyrinthine passages of the Coliseum, descending into its bowels before finding the staircase that would lead him to the main seating area, where he would meet Ísolde and the others. Each step up the stairway felt heavier than the last, and his hand gripped the rail for support.

As he reached the top of the stairs, he paused, peering over the edge into the arena. His eyes scanned the sea of faces until they found Ísolde. Her beauty, even in the dim light of the flickering torches, brought a brief moment of clarity and comfort to his troubled mind. He stepped forward, maintaining the pretense of knowing nothing. He sat beside Ísolde and grasped her hand, his fingers trembling slightly.

She turned to him, surprised by his touch and knowing something was wrong. "I have not felt you grab my hand like this in ages."

"Well, I have missed you, my dear," Ándrôniüs forced a smile, though it didn't reach his eyes.

Looking at him with concern, Ísolde inquired. "Is everything okay at the barracks? It seemed urgent."

Ándrôniüs, a master of deception, felt a sting of guilt. He despised lying to her, but he couldn't burden her with the truth. Not yet.

He muttered, "It was nothing, just a trainee that needed mending beyond my capabilities, so Câllirrhöe is assisting."

Ísolde's expression softened with sympathy. "Oh, the poor child, I hope they live."

The sentiment hit Ándrôniüs deeply, her concern mirroring his own. He replied, looking into her eyes, "Indeed, I do too... for all our sakes."

Sensing the shadow behind his words, Ísolde's voice became tinged with worry. "Please do not tell me it was..."

Ándrôniüs hesitated, the lies feeling like poison on his tongue. "Only time will tell, my dear." He spoke carefully, holding back his true emotions. He hated deceiving her, the one person he treasured above all else, but he couldn't bring himself to reveal the full extent of the peril they faced.

Sensing his inner turmoil, Ísolde reached over and gently turned his face toward her, her eyes searching his. She smiled radiantly, and it seemed to cut through the darkness surrounding him. "I understand. You will tell me when the time is right, my love." She leaned in, pressing a soft kiss to his lips, her warmth momentarily easing the frigid grip of fear in his heart. As she pulled away, Ándróniüs felt his eyes well with tears, the burden of his secrets almost too much to bear.

Though his mind did not have to wait long to be pulled from wallowing in sorrow. Thâlôr approached the stand and took his place beside Ándróniüs.

"The boy is in the hold," Thâlôr whispered, his voice carrying the weight of their shared concern. "We can only hope now that he is fit enough to carry out the task."

Ándróniüs nodded, his eyes dark with worry. "I hope so too, Thâlôr. I do hope he lives to see the morrow."

A deep melancholy settled over them, a heavy pall that seemed to mirror the fracturing dark clouds that still lingered overhead, blowing to and fro. They sat silently, each lost in their thoughts, wondering what the night would bring. Who would emerge victorious, and who would fall?

# THEXAUMILLIER

THE COLISEUM SEATS WERE filled to capacity, leaving only the walkways and staircases for the latecomers to utilize. Despite the unpleasant weather, they all had come to watch the final battle that was promised to them during these tests. The crowd conversed in a hushed manner about the dramatic finish between Jake and the dracónyx from the night prior. All in attendance were hoping, more or less, for a similarly electrifying display between Ethan and the gorlock.

After a while, their thoughts and mutterings shifted into questions about the whereabouts of the director of events, the Grand Mage Órynë. Many of the High Mages that comprised the council and other dignitaries present for the administration of the tests also wondered where he was. His absence had not gone unnoticed the previous evening, and it made his current absence that much more glaring. They all knew this test would be one for the history books of Cáelunárra; a human from a world far beyond their own using magic was an unprecedented spectacle to be witnessed.

In the stands, Ándróniüs was preyed upon by his many thoughts, his somber mood deepening.

Xándriel made his way with the utmost haste to the council seating area where Ándróniüs sat.

He bent low, his face serious as he spoke. "I have an urgent message for you, Ándróniüs."

Surprised by Xándriel's sudden appearance and the distraught look upon his face, Ándróniüs accepted the letter, noting the elegant seal of the Grand Mage. It was an intricate design of silver and gold, depicting a phoenix rising from flames, symbolizing rebirth and enduring power.

But why had Órynë not brought this himself? Why had he not spoken to Ándrôniüs in person? The new questions churned in Ándrôniüs's already turbulent mind.

"Thank you, my friend," Ándrôniüs said, his voice strained. "Will you join us, Grand Exchequer? I believe there are few free seats left."

Xándriel nodded and took an empty seat near Ándrôniüs.

Ándrôniüs stared at the letter, his mind racing with what it could contain. He thought to himself, Could he really handle another calamity at this time?

With a heavy heart, he broke the seal on his knee; the wax falling to the ground. Inside the envelope was a small piece of parchment, which read:

Ándrôniüs,
I must take my leave. I no longer feel fit to lead the Republic. The prophecy no longer holds meaning for me. The timing of this is all wrong, and I am certain the Dark Lord has his hand in it. I know this because he has and continues to try to possess my mind, poisoning my thoughts, my actions, and my very being. His promises of power now tempt me, and I can no longer serve. I am leaving for Aûllíâtënärrä. This means you are now the Théxaumíllíer. My only parting advice is this: do not make the same mistakes I have made. Be impervious to the tricks and ways of the Dark Lord. And if you do feel his ways tempting you, when you recognize them, do not succumb to the darkness, my friend. It may taste oh, so sweet! But indeed, it is bitter beyond anything you can imagine. Know that I will constantly pray for you from the lands of our forefathers.
Órynë

In a numbed stupor, Ándrôniüs rolled up the parchment and tucked it into his pocket. He went to crumple the envelope when he noticed there was something else inside it. He reached in and pulled out a golden key; its beauty was breathtaking. The key was slender and ornate, crafted from pure gold with engravings that swirled along its length. At its head was the symbol of Eldôria, a radiant sunburst encrusted with tiny, glimmering diamonds. Xándriel, noticing the key in his hands, stood up with a flourish. "All hail the Théxaumíllíer! Long live Théxaumíllíer Ándrôniüs. Never have the titles converged with one another. We are *indeed* living in unprecedented times. May you live long and prosper, my brother."

The other mages on the stand, startled at his declaration, also stood up and echoed in unison, their voices rising in a powerful chant; "Long live Ándrôniüs, the Théxaumíllíer of the Republic of Eldôria!"

Following their lead, the coliseum attendees joined in, picking up the chants emanating from the podium.

While this was no calamity, this was not a turn of events he had ever expected, nor wanted. His mind now consumed by this shifting of circumstances, Ándrôniüs could only stare blankly ahead, paralyzed by it all. He now had the immense responsibility of this title and would have to balance overseeing the prophecy and guiding a nation. This responsibility bore down on him, but as the voices rang out around him, a fierce determination hardened within his heart. The night was not yet over, and there was much to be done.

Feeling the burden of this new title and the immense responsibility that came with it, Ándrôniüs stood up with a revived sense of exigency. He was now unprecedentedly the Théxaumíllíer of the land he had grown up in and loved deeply. Every street, every blade of grass, every tree, and every creature from the Great Sea to the forests of Illithría, and from the Sea of Despair to the Fötzë Mountains, was his responsibility. All of it was woven into the very fabric of his soul. He knew he had to usher in a new era for his people, one that would bring hope and strength in the face of the dark times ahead.

With mixed emotions plastered upon his face, Ándrôniüs made his way to the podium that jutted out into the Coliseum.

The storm had returned, with clouds rolling back across the sky, cloaking the land in darkness once more. The only light now came from the flickering torches that lined the Coliseum floor, casting eerie shadows on its ancient stones. As he raised his hands, the crowd fell silent, ending their chants, their anticipation almost tangible.

He scanned the faces before him, the people of Cáelunárra, who had gathered from the farthest reaches of their continent, united by their hopes and fears. Yet in the warriors' hold, he knew only one could emerge: Áelfwînë or Ethan. Could he deceive the entire world, or was he merely deceiving himself, believing that all would be well no matter who fought?

Fleetingly, he realized he had not taken the time to strike a new deal with the Allfather, a regret that tugged at his mind. Could he continue on? Could he find the right words to weave another line on the tapestry he had worked so hard to create?

Taking a deep breath, Ándrôniüs gathered his thoughts, knowing that the words he spoke now could shape the future of all their lands.

"Dear friends and acquaintances of our beautiful Cáelunárra," he began, his voice carrying through the stillness like a clarion call.

"I know you have traveled far—from the reaches of Brâldôr, from Illithría, and from the realms of men—to be here tonight. Yet I come before you bearing *grave* news, but also *laudable* news."

He paused, letting the tension in the air build, before continuing.

"Our Grand Mage no longer believes in the prophecy, and even less so, in you all. He has left this land and all of us behind in a time of uncertainty. But *fret* not! For *I* will lead us into the light. I will lead us to victory. We will exterminate the Dark Lord from these lands with the help of our champions. And like the phoenix on the emblem of the sacred seal of the Grand Mage, Cáelunárra will be reborn from the ashes of the coming war. The coming scourge will unleash itself upon us, our lands, our way of life, our children, our loved ones, and our brothers and sisters in arms. But together, we will rise victorious!"

The crowd erupted into a roar, their voices filling the Coliseum with a fervor that echoed into the night. Ándrôniüs stood tall, feeling the power of their unity coursing through him.

"Now," he declared, his voice rising into the roar, carried by the momentum of the crowd, "let the test begin."

The coliseum held its volume, not erupting further but refusing to settle. The cheers took on a focused rhythm, no longer wild but purposeful. Their voices honored more than just Ethan's courage; they acknowledged the quiet reckoning that had begun for Ándrôniüs, whose path forward would now be watched by all. He knew his responsibilities would only grow from here. Eventually, he would need to appoint a new Seer of the Enigmas; a position that had been in his family for generations. The question gnawed at him: should he consolidate the power within himself until the war with the Dark Lord was won? Or should he pass on the baton to another? He knew Xándriel was right. These were unprecedented times. The Republic had never before seen the title of Théxaumíllíer invoked. Its purpose was true upheaval, not a ceremonial passing of a title or fleeing in the absence of a real crisis.

As he pondered this, Ándrôniüs made his way back to his seat beside Ísolde. Her smile was a beacon of warmth amidst the stormy chaos that surrounded them. The Coliseum was alive. Lightning continued to split the sky as thunder rolled like the drums of war. Beneath the stands, the rumbling of the mechanisms signaled that the platforms were rising, bringing the combatants to the floor. The clash between man and beast, between good and evil, was imminent.

# ETHAN'S TEST

THE PLATFORM CLICKED INTO place, silencing the crowd. All eyes watched as a lone figure stepped onto the wet stone. The warrior in immaculate red and white armor was striking against the flickering torches. His large square shield bore the emblem of a scarlet cross, its polished surface gleaming with a brilliance that reflected the storm's fury overhead. His breastplate, a masterwork of craftsmanship, clung to his muscular frame, exuding an aura of unyielding valor. The helm, with its two menacing horns jutting from either side, concealed his face entirely, leaving only narrow slits for his eyes and mouth. A visage both terrifying and awe-inspiring.

Across the arena, from the shadows of its holding chamber, the gorlock emerged. At nine feet tall, the creature was a terrifying sight. Its skin was a grotesque mix of black and green, marred by warts, moles, and scales.

Sparse, wiry hair sprouted haphazardly from its body, adding to its ghastly appearance. Its eyes, deep, malicious red, glowed with an otherworldly hatred and a burning desire to crush all who stood before it. The gorlock's fangs, long and yellowed, protruded from its twisted mouth, and with a guttural laugh that surged through the entire Coliseum, it mocked the warrior before it.

"You send little man fight me?" the gorlock growled in its broken common tongue, its voice a rasping sneer of contempt.

The words echoed across the stone walls, drawing a mixture of gasps and murmurs from the crowd.

For a moment, time seemed to suspend itself as the two adversaries locked eyes, the static between them undeniable, the very air crackling with presentiment. The Coliseum, with its thousands of spectators, momentarily seemed to vanish, leaving only the warrior and the beast facing each other.

Then, as if triggered by some unseen signal, both combatants exploded into motion. They sprinted toward each other with a speed and ferocity that belied their sizes, the ground trembling beneath the force of their strides. Each step reverberated within the arena, resonating with the promise of a violent collision. The crowd, caught between horror and fascination, watched with bated breath as the distance between the two narrowed in a matter of heartbeats.

The sky, dark and ominous, suddenly blazed with a blinding flash of lightning, casting the entire Coliseum in a harsh, white glare. The combatants stopped as their eyes adjusted to the burst of blinding light. At that moment, the blinding light revealed every detail of the impending battle; the warrior's determined stance, the malicious glee in the gorlock's eyes, and the shimmering red and black mist swirling ominously around the warrior's hand.

With a battle cry that seemed to rise above the storm itself, the warrior swung his sword in a mighty arc, the dark mist coiling and twisting around his hand as he channeled every ounce of his rage into the spell. Everything but the two fighters went still.

Silence fell upon the arena. It was heavy and instantaneous. Then a single cheer. It was hesitant and uncertain, but it cracked the quiet, the stillness. The crowd then erupted. Every mage, man, dwarf, and elf in attendance could not comprehend the enormity of what they were witnessing, but they all knew one thing: no human from their realm should have produced magic. And yet he had. There was no denying it. The dark red and black mist that now swirled around him was proof. An ear-splitting blast ripped through the air as the warrior let loose the magic he conjured, sending it barreling toward the gorlock.

The gorlock, despite its massive size, moved with surprising agility, leaping to the side with a guttural snarl, evading the spell by mere inches. The warrior's sword clashed against the gorlock's club, the impact sending an otherworldly shockwave through the arena, a harsh prelude to the brutality that was unfolding.

Lightning flashed again, illuminating the gorlock's twisted grin as it bared its fangs. It swung its massive club around viciously. The warrior barely raised his shield in time, the force of the blow sending him staggering backward. He skidded on the slick stone floor, and for a brief, terrifying moment, the blow left him defenseless. His shield split in two. The pain in his arm was so immense that the swirling mist of the spell he was trying to conjure sputtered and died out.

But there was no respite.

The gorlock, sensing weakness, roared and charged forward, its eyes blazing with the promise of death. "Now, little man, you die. No match for Dụrgth."

The crowd could feel the beast's intent, its words a wave of malice that threatened to engulf the lone warrior standing in its path. The storm above seemed to reach its fever pitch, the heavens themselves appearing to rage against the violence below, each cacophonous clap of thunder like a drumbeat of doom.

The warrior, melancholy and resolve mingled in his eyes, gripped his sword tighter, his muscles straining against the exhaustion that threatened to overtake him.

But as the gorlock pursued him, inching ever closer, raising its club for a killing blow, something shifted; a stillness, a suspension of time itself. The lightning ceased, the thunder quieted, and the air became heavy with the uncertainty of the moment.

The gorlock's eyes, glowing with unbridled fury, bore down on the warrior, who stood his ground despite the overwhelming odds. For the spectators, the world outside the Coliseum faded away, leaving only the battle that would determine the fate of this lone man against an embodiment of darkness.

And then, in a single, breathless instant, the gorlock brought its club down with all its might.

The scene froze.

With the club mere inches from the warrior's head, the outcome of the clash hung in the balance. The crowd collectively held its breath, each person on the edge of their seat, their hearts pounding in unison with the warrior's, the moment stretching into eternity.

Who would triumph in this battle of titans?

The question lingered unanswered, as the storm outside illustrated the turmoil among those who watched. Ándrôniüs, now standing amidst the throng, felt the weight of the world on his shoulders, knowing that the answer to that question would not just decide the fate of the combatants, but the fate of all Cáelunárra.

Just as the tension reached its zenith, a gale-force wind struck the city with sudden, violent fury. It howled through every street, pried open every window, tore flags from their hoists, sending them fluttering into the darkened sky.

With a gust of wind, every torch in the Coliseum was extinguished, leaving the world in absolute darkness. The arena cut to black. Only the sounds of metal striking wood and the air filled with grunts and yells lingered.

Then two yells. One undeniably human and the other a beastly roar. A sickening crunch as either metal on bone or wood on skull reverberated through the hallowed floor of the Coliseum. Silence followed this grotesque sound. Just silence.

And in that silence, they held their breaths; the battle shrouded in mystery, its outcome hidden from all eyes, leaving them to wonder, fear, and hope in the oppressive, unyielding darkness that concealed the revelation of the test's victor.

# THE MORTHYLITES

OVER THE LAST WEEK, Hannah had awoken each morning in the heart of the Thalirîthion Anvandrë, the elegant elven sanctuary where she had been living, surrounded by the enigmatic beauty of a world that seemed both ancient and mystical.

Despite the elves showing her the utmost respect usually reserved for royalty, the separation from her friends caused her significant anxiety for the first few days. She eventually found solace within her demanding studies, immersing herself in the words, phrases, and rich history of Cáelunárra.

She spent her days being guided by Ísolde and her two elven guards, Mŷthrálôn and Lôrŷnthás. The language of the elves, Luthéllon, was the only tongue spoken within these sacred walls. The common tongue was strictly forbidden unless they were talking with someone who did not know the language. This practice exempted Hannah because the embassy's purpose for her presence was to learn, and she quickly adapted to the new linguistic environment.

The Thalirîthion Anvandrë was a breathtaking marvel, a circular building that seemed to merge seamlessly with nature. At its center grew a majestic tree, its roots entwined with the very structure itself. The tree, eld and wise, stood tall, like a venerable elder full of knowledge.

The elven-made building was uniformly majestic, its stone walls masterfully sculpted to allow water to cascade down in a gentle, continuous flow. Sunlight danced across the flowing water, casting a mesmerizing effect throughout the structure.

Impeccably manicured gardens, with perfectly trimmed bushes and hedges, surrounded the Thalirîthion Anvandrë, adding to the scene's serene beauty.

Inside, the grandeur of the building continued to awe Hannah. The surfaces glistened like silver in the sunlight. The halls within were vast, lined with carvings and arras that told the ancient history of the elves. Hannah mostly spent her time in the Bálárîôn Thárívôr, a grand library containing the elven race's accumulated knowledge. Shelves stretched from floor to ceiling, filled with scrolls wrapped in fine white fabric and books bound in leather. These texts chronicled everything from the elves' first steps in Cáelunárra to the current events that shaped their world.

Luthéllon, the language of the elves, was a challenge unlike any Hannah had faced before. Though it shared a familiar alphabet with the common tongue of this world, its structure and pronunciation were entirely foreign. The words flowed like a river, each syllable heavy with elegance.

Hannah devoted herself to mastering it, spending long hours poring over scrolls and practicing her pronunciation until her voice was hoarse. Ísolde, Mŷthrálôn, and Lôrŷnthás were patient teachers, guiding her through the complex rules of the language, but the frustration of mastering this ancient tongue irritated her, pushing her to her limits.

Despite the challenges, there was a peaceful beauty in Hannah's daily routine. Each morning, she rose with the dawn, the first light filtering through the delicate curtains of her chamber. Dressed in the light, flowing gowns provided by her elven hosts, she would partake in a simple breakfast of fruits and bread before making her way to the Báláríôn Thárívôr.

When her eyes grew tired from reading, Hannah would retreat to the central garden of the Thalirîthion Anvandrë. The garden, shaped like a ring, encircled the grand tree at the building's center. Cherry trees lined the lush lawn, their blossoms filling the air with a sweet fragrance. A clear stream wound its way through the garden, teeming with silver fish and the Naïads who lived among the elves.

In the afternoons, Hannah practiced her recitation with Ísolde, Mŷthrálôn, and Lôrŷnthás. The elven language was as much a song as it was speech, and Hannah found herself entranced by the melodic quality of the words, even as she stumbled over their pronunciation.

Each day concluded with a quiet dinner in her chambers, followed by more study until sleep claimed her.

At the closing ceremony of the tests in the Coliseum, she would recite to the people of Cáelunárra her hopeful mastery of the elven language, as all would gather to witness the culminating oration she would deliver. Unlike the trials of strength, the battles against death, or the challenges in the depths, Hannah's test was unique. It was a test of the mind requiring her to master one of the most revered languages in all of Cáelunárra.

She would be one of the few beings outside of the elven race to accomplish this feat, continuing its legacy. The language was preserved by the elves, even as its prominence faded, like autumn leaves giving way to the common tongue.

Hannah knew that the eyes of an entire world would be upon her as she took part in this multi-day challenge, and the thought filled her with both dismay and tenacity. She was the final testee, and this was her test.

***

The morning of the last test came languidly, the sky tinged with soft hues against the lingering clouds. Though the previous night's storm had subsided in the early hours, a chill remained, along with a dense fog that clung to the land, leaving what was beneath it a mystery.

In the mornings, the inlet of the Sea of Despair and the traders crossing the tidal path from Tháldrüm were usually visible, but the excessively thick fog hid them that day.

Hannah awoke with a mixture of titillation and perturbation eddying in her chest. She sat up slowly; the blanket falling away as she stretched her arms, trying to shake off the remnants of sleep. Today was the day she had been preparing for, the day she would stand before the people of Cáelunárra and prove herself.

Even though she had just woken up, Hannah was a vision of grace and quiet strength. She wore a silk chemise that clung softly to the curves of her body; the fabric flowing like water around her as she moved. She had neatly braided her long, golden hair the previous night, the elaborate weave falling down her back with a few loose strands framing her face. As she turned from her bed to face the window, the sunlight caught her eyes, making them sparkle like aquamarines in the early morning light.

Hannah took a deep breath, steadying herself. Rising from her bed, she walked over to the wardrobe, the soft fabric of her chemise whispering against her skin. She opened the doors, revealing an array of finely made gowns and garments, each one a testament of the elegance and aptitude of the elves.

Her hand hovered for a moment before she handpicked a gown of pale green silk, its fabric shimmering in the morning light. The gown had been a gift from Ísolde, a token of encouragement for the challenge that lay ahead.

With the gown draped over her arm, Hannah walked behind the vanity in her room, where the soft light cast her silhouette onto the wall. Slowly, she let the silk chemise slip from her shoulders, the delicate fabric pooling at her feet.

She donned the pale green gown; the silk flowing softly over her body. Fanciful embroidery adorned the bodice and arms. The dress fastened with a silver belt around her waist, the simple yet elegant accessory cinching the gown and accentuating her figure. Slipping into a pair of soft leather shoes, she made her way to the mirror to fix her hair.

Hannah took another deep breath, allowing the calm resolve she had nurtured over the past few days to settle within her. Satisfied with her appearance and the strength she felt within, she gathered her thoughts, reminding herself she could do this.

With a last glance in the mirror, she turned and walked to the door of her room.

She moved gracefully down the hall, the soft leather of her shoes barely making a sound against the polished stone floor. The Thalirîthion Anvandrë was quiet at this early hour, the only sound the distant trickle of water from the central garden's fountain.

Descending the stairs, she was greeted by the sight of Mŷthrálôn and Lôrŷnthás waiting for her. The two elven guards were as stoic as ever, their silver armor gleaming in the early morning light.

Mŷthrálôn, tall and imposing with his long, silver hair cascading down his back, gave her a nod of approval as she approached.

"Tŷr ílar, Hannah," Mŷthrálôn asked, greeting her in Luthéllon, his voice deep and resonant as it echoed softly through the marble halls. His silver eyes, sharp and observant, met hers.

"Ila sílvâthiël. Valëth ílar." Mŷthrálôn continued, the formal tone of the ancient language rolling off his tongue with ease.

Hannah, standing tall, responded in Luthéllon, her accent still carrying the trace of human origin. "Yes, I am. I'm ready for the day. Are there any further tasks that I must complete?"

Her voice, though steady, held a note of apprehension as she looked between the two guards.

Lôrŷnthás, who was slightly shorter than Mŷthrálôn, but equally dignified with his golden hair tied back in a warrior's braid, stepped forward. His expression softened into a warm smile as he replied. "No, there is not. We simply wanted to wish you the best of luck today."

His voice, though gentle, carried a sincerity that made Hannah's heart swell with gratitude.

His stern demeanor softening as well, Mŷthrálôn gestured down the hallway with a nod. "There is quite the breakfast feast beginning among all those who reside here, in celebration of you completing your task."

Looking up at him, Hannah's brow fluted slightly in confusion. "But I haven't proven myself yet," she said, her voice tinged with modesty.

The thought of being celebrated before she had even been tested seemed premature, almost undeserved.

Lôrŷnthás chuckled softly, the sound like a breeze through the leaves. "But you indeed have proven yourself, Hannah. You came here and are the first human in three thousand years who has committed to learning our language and has done so. You've lived among us, and you've dined with us. You have left your mark on all of us. You have shown us that there is hope for Cáelunárra and the realms of men."

Overwhelmed with a rush of gratitude, Hannah felt her eyes sting with tears. Without thinking, she crossed the space between them and embraced Lôrŷnthás, breaking the ancient code of elven warrior decorum that forbade such familiar contact. But at that moment, the formality didn't matter. Lôrŷnthás, taken aback for only a second, returned the hug with a soft laugh, his arms wrapping around her gently.

"Thank you," Hannah whispered, her voice full of pride.

Mŷthrálôn, though usually unyielding in his adherence to protocol, allowed a small smile to curve his lips at the sight. "We must hurry to the Arathênor," he said, "where we will feast in your honor."

Together, they began their walk through the winding halls of the Thalirîthion Anvandrë. The building was a labyrinth of elegance, each corridor more breathtaking than the last. They passed through grand halls lined with textiles, their colors vivid and lifelike. Each turn revealed rooms where scholars pored over ancient texts, places of worship where soft hymns were sung in Luthéllon, and serene spaces where elves meditated, their minds deeply connected to nature.

As they moved deeper into the building, the air grew cooler, and the lighting more subdued. They descended a staircase that spiraled down into the earth; the walls were lined with carvings of elven lore. Countless generations of elves who had walked this path before her wore the steps smooth.

They arrived at the Arathênor, a vast underground hall that seemed to glow with an inner light. Reverent conversation filled the room, and the air was rich with the scents of the morning feast. Elves of all ages and stations had gathered, their expressions warm and welcoming as they greeted Hannah, each one expressing their gratitude and well-wishes for the journey that lay ahead of her.

The Arathênor itself was a masterpiece of elven craftsmanship. Its ceiling was high and vaulted. Elven families' symbols and fresh flower garlands decorated the ancient oaken tables lining the walls. The centerpiece of the hall was a long table that stretched nearly the length of the room, covered in an array of foods that glistened like jewels on the plates.

The morning feast was a delicate affair, a reflection of the elves' deep connection to the earth. Bowls of ripe berries, their colors vibrant and varied, sat alongside platters of freshly picked apples, their skins shining with dew. Mushrooms, with their caps rich and earthy, were sautéed to perfection, while roots of all kinds were prepared in intricate dishes that spoke of centuries-old recipes. The plates, made of fine porcelain with silver trim, were set with care, and the cutlery was polished to a mirror finish, each fork and knife a work of art in itself.

Hannah's heart swelled with gratitude as she took her place at the table, surrounded by the elves who had become her friends and mentors. The soft chatter of conversation filled the air as the feast began, and Hannah couldn't help but smile as she tasted the sweet and earthy flavors of the elven cuisine.

In her short time with the elves, Hannah had grown to love their rich culture, their way of life, and how seamlessly they existed in harmony with the world around them. Whether the world was in turmoil or as still as a mountain meadow on a summer's day, the elves moved with a grace and serenity that captivated her. She knew she would miss them and the grandeur of the Thalirîthion Anvandrë, the exquisite delicacies they shared, and the profound wisdom they imparted.

After the breakfast feast had concluded and the elves had collectively assisted the servants in clearing the tables, Hannah made her way to the Báláríôn Thárívôr. She ascended the staircase, her thoughts occupied by the upcoming test. As she reached the main level of the Thalirîthion Anvandrë, a familiar figure came into view—Ándrôniüs.

His attire, robes of cream stitched with white cynosure, was more elegant than she had ever seen him wear. Gleaming silver tassels glistened as his tall, stately hat was draped over his shoulder. He stood before a grand painting, his gaze deep and contemplative.

Curious, Hannah approached him, her footsteps light on the polished floor. As she drew near, she gently rested her head on his shoulder, and Ándrôniüs responded by placing an arm around her, pulling her close in a warm embrace.

The painting before them was both beautiful and terrifying. It depicted a great battle, unlike any she could imagine. She had never paid much attention to this one, generally always being hurried from here to there. Fierce creatures with nightmarish forms clashed with men, elves, and dwarves. Dracónyx roared from the sky, its fiery breath rending destruction upon the battlefield. Bodies of friend and foe littered the ground, trampled in the desperate struggle for victory.

"War is a strange thing, isn't it?" Ándrôniüs murmured, breaking the silence.

Hannah lifted her head slightly, her expression tightening as she mulled it over. "What do you mean?"

He sighed, resting his head against hers. "War... it's neither good nor evil. Each side believes its purpose is just. But is war truly just? Is it ever right to wage war for the gain of one? Or is it just to rid the world of something we find abhorrent?"

Hannah considered his words, the gravity of them sinking into her mind. "I've never been a fan of war," she admitted softly. "But sometimes I believe it can be justified."

"Oh, my dear Hannah, no one person loves war. Well... maybe the Dark Lord and his creatures. However, a fickle thing, justification for those wars is," Ándrôniüs said, his voice tinged with melancholy. "But can a war be just if it is fought for liberation? For personal gain? For country? For any number of reasons?"

He paused, as if mulling things over in his mind. "And what if those liberated later betray the ones who freed them? Was that war still just, or did it simply pave the way for more suffering? Thus, the never-ending cycle of greed, death, despair, and rebuilding... for what? To take part in it all over again."

Hannah lifted her head, her expression puzzled. "I'm not sure I follow," she said quietly.

Ándrôniüs gestured to the painting. "This work is called 'The Severing of Valediction.' It tells the story of the Môrthŷl people, a once-prosperous race who lived in the southern reaches of Khạrzọnọv. Their kingdom, Môrthŷlílen, was rich in culture, with its castles towering darkly against the desert skies, built from volcanic rock. They had mastered the art of purifying the waters of the Sâlzhâr Sea to sustain their people. But their decline began with the rise of Mûrríëthíêl."

He paused, his gaze fixed on the painting as he continued. "Mûrríëthíêl enslaved many of them, while others vanished, becoming mere whispers of their former selves. Escapees sought refuge in Âldâmûr, pleading with the united Caucus of Regents for aid. This caucus convened in this very building in Vâloríâ before Eldôria founded the republic. The elves, dwarves, and men joined forces to liberate them, and during that time they began constructing a great wall from the Sâlzhâr Sea to where the southern gate of Khạrzọnọv now sits, to hold back the creatures of the deep that Mûrríëthíêl had twisted into his monstrous army. However, once victorious, the three kingdoms demanded compensation for their losses. The agreed price was the weight of every fallen soldier in diamonds from the Môrthŷl mines, which ran deep beneath their capital, Tôrgráth."

Hannah listened intently, her eyes tracing the battle scene before her.

"But the previous king, King Crôrívrën, succumbed to his wounds. Without an heir, his brother Thrângûnvôr took power. And with that power, King Thrângûnvôr of Môrthŷlílen," Ándrôniüs said, "in his treachery, he sought aid from Mûrríëthíêl instead of paying the agreed price, which he thought was egregious. Mûrríëthíêl, ever hungry for power, agreed, and together they unleashed a new wave of horror upon the three kingdoms. The last stand was here, where the southern gate of Khạrzọnọv now stands. The three kingdoms united, pushed back the darkness, securing a temporary peace, but the Môrthŷl people were annexed into the dark kingdom Khạrzọnọv, and Mûrríëthíêl turned on them, slaughtering every last one, from the youngest child to the oldest elder."

Her voice was barely a whisper as she asked, "And how does this relate to what we were talking about?"

Ándrôniüs sighed deeply. "Well, here we are again on the edge of a precipice, teetering on this edge of war and peace. Sure, there have been attacks between your coming and the last, but a fragment of peace has been there, and total war has been held at bay. But again I say, is war ever truly just? Was this one? Will this war be justified? Are we the aggressors, simply led astray? Or are we really on the side of justice? And can we ever know if any wars are ever justified? Perhaps the answer lies beyond our understanding, only to be revealed when we meet the Allfather himself, on our dreaded day of reckoning."

Nodding slowly, Hannah absorbed the gravity of his words. "I suppose that makes sense. But why are you here, Ándrôniüs?"

Turning to her, a soft smile played on his lips. "I've come to collect you, Hannah. I believe a reunion of sorts is in order."

Hannah's face lit up with excitement; her voice filled with hope. "Will I really get to see them again?"

"In due time," Ándrôniüs said, letting out a hearty chuckle. "You will see them all on the stage, but you must not acknowledge them until your part is done."

Her excitement waned, replaced by a tinge of disappointment. "Well, that was short-lived." She sighed. "I guess I can wait a few more hours. I've waited five days, after all."

Ándrôniüs chuckled again, gesturing toward the door as they began walking, taking their leave from the Thalirîthion Anvandrë. As they stepped through the grand doors, Hannah felt the warmth of the sun fully on her face for the first time in days. She smiled, savoring the light that bathed her, a stark contrast to the filtered sunlight she had grown accustomed to in the garden of the Thalirîthion Anvandrë.

"Now, do you remember what I told you when I left you here?" Ándrôniüs asked, his voice light as they strolled through the bustling city streets.

Hannah nodded. "That when the time arises, if I pass my test, and a person of great power among the elves asks me to do something, I must do it, whatever the consequence may be."

"Indeed," Ándrôniüs replied with a smile. "But what about the other part, Hannah?"

"That I must leave Ethan behind. But the other part, I'm still unsure what that means," Hannah admitted, her brow furrowing in thought.

Ándrôniüs, his hands clasped behind him, walked slowly beside her. "In due time, Hannah, you shall understand. For now, let us enjoy this walk to the Coliseum."

# HANNAH'S TEST

As they approached the Coliseum, lutes strummed and singers' melodious voices filled the air, celebrating the final day of the tests. Stalls lined the streets, with their owners selling a variety of wares. Dancers twirled gracefully in the open squares, their colorful garments billowing around them like flower petals in the breeze. Children ran through the crowds, their laughter mingling with the jubilant chatter of the townsfolk.

They neared the grand gates of the Coliseum, which stood wide open, welcoming the throngs of people who had come to witness the last test.

Before they stepped inside, Ándróniüs gently placed a hand on Hannah's shoulder, causing her to pause.

"There is something you must know about Ethan," he said, his tone serious.

With her heart skipping a beat, Hannah's mind raced with worry. "Did he die?" She asked, her voice trembling, fearing the worst.

Ándróniüs chuckled softly, shaking his head. "No, dear Hannah, he is very much alive. Would I be escorting you to the Coliseum if he had failed or perished? Anyway, he took quite a knock on the head last night. After he delivered the killing blow, the beast dropped its club on his head and knocked him out cold. He has quite a case of amnesia now, poor lad."

"That's a shame. He will hate not remembering that he completed it," Hannah stated.

"I know he hasn't let me forget," Ándróniüs replied, with a small chuckle. "But it's important that we keep telling him he fulfilled his test. I looked into his mind. There's nothing since..."

He paused. "Well, that part does not matter. But since he has no memory of it, he might need to be reminded that he succeeded."

Hannah nodded, understanding the gravity of the situation. "Well, you can count on me to support him."

Ándróniüs smiled warmly at her. "I knew i could at least count on you. Now, let us make our way to the podium and bring these tests to their conclusion. I've had about enough of spectacles for one life."

They walked through the grand entrance of the Coliseum, the noise of the crowd growing louder as they neared the stairs leading up to the seating area. The atmosphere was energetic; the crowd reveling in anticipation that this was the day they would start the next chapter of their world and, hopefully, usher in peace by removing the Dark Lord from Cáelunárra.

As they approached the podium, Hannah's eyes scanned the faces of the crowd, searching for her friends. She spotted them in the distance, each dressed in fine garments befitting the occasion. Even Ethan, despite the bandage around his head and a slight pallor to his skin, looked strong and resolute. Jake, Ryan, and Emily were there too, their expressions a mixture of emotions as they saw Hannah approaching.

Hannah kept silent, her heart aching to run to them, to embrace them after so many days apart. Instead, she maintained her composure; her face a mask of calm as she took her place next to Ísolde, who was seated among the dignitaries. Ísolde gave her a reassuring smile, squeezing her hand gently as she sat down, her heart pounding with the anticipation of the moment.

The Coliseum held a packed crowd to the brim. The torches that lined the walls flickered about in the breeze. As Hannah settled into her seat, she took a deep breath, feeling the enormity of the elven language, the history, and the legacy she was about to carry forward. The final test awaited her, as Cáelunárra watched from the prepared stage.

Ándróniüs made his way to the podium, below which the finishing acts of a Brâldôrian comedic act were underway. The performers, dressed in loose-fitting clothes of flashing colors, executed their final dance steps with a flourish before bowing deeply to the cheering crowd. Their faces beamed with satisfaction as applause echoed through the grand Coliseum.

Ándrôniüs joined in, clapping in unison with the masses that filled the arena. He then stepped forward, his presence commanding attention, and spoke, his voice carrying across the vast space.

"Thank you, thank you, performers. Your retelling of the *Battle of the Bouncing Beards* is always a pleasure," he said with a warm smile, bowing in gratitude to the departing performers.

He paused momentarily, allowing the echoes of the crowd's cheers and clapping to fade as the performers elegantly exited the Coliseum floor. Raising his hands, he addressed the audience once more.

"'Tis a beautiful morning here in Vâloríâ, the calm after the storm. Though the air remains foggy as the darkness retreats from our land, it leaves behind the promise of new growth and prosperity. With every inch the fog retreats, it brings forth new opportunities for life to flourish."

He paused again, his gaze sweeping over the sea of faces before him.

"Like today!" he exclaimed, his voice filled with conviction. "Over the past five days, four of our champions have proved themselves in various tasks set forth by me and the High Mage Council. And now, our last test remains. Hannah will complete our trials, setting loose the prophecy that has long been foretold. That five would be delivered from another world and deliver us from evil. This marks the beginning of our hopeful last stand against the Dark Lord Mûrríëthíêl, our chance to sever the head of the beast that is Khạrzọnọv, and to bring a new light to the land of Cáelunárra, ringing in a lasting peace for all."

Ándrôniüs paused, his thoughts briefly returning to his conversation with Hannah that morning. The significance of the responsibility she carried was not lost on him.

He scanned the crowd, lowering his hands to his side, his gaze intense and thoughtful. As he scratched his scruffy beard, pondering his next words, he raised his arm and pointed toward the people gathered before him.

"Five thousand years," he began, his voice resonating with a deep, solemn tone. "For five thousand years, our people have endured the shadow of Mûrrïëthíêl's tyranny. We have seen our lands ravaged, our loved ones taken, and our spirits tested. But we have also seen the resilience of our people, the unbreakable will to survive, to fight, and to reclaim what is ours. Today, as we stand on this precipice of a new era, we must remember that war, though never desirable, has its place in the great wheel of peace. It is the crucible through which our freedom must be forged."

The crowd listened intently, the gravity of his words sinking in.

"War is a terrible price to pay, and it leaves scars that last lifetimes. But there are times when it is the only path to liberation, the only way to rid our world of the darkness that seeks to consume it. Mûrrïëthíêl's reign of terror must end, and it falls to us, to our champions, to ensure that his evil is vanquished, once and for all."

Ándrôniüs let his words hang in the air for a moment.

"This is *our* time," he continued, his voice growing stronger, more impassioned. "Our time to rise, to take back what has been stolen from us, to light the way for future generations who will know peace because of the sacrifices we make today. Let it be known that we did not seek this war, but we will see it through to its end. And when the dust settles, when the lives of the slain have been numbered, when their loved ones have laid them to rest and grieved their loss, and when the cities have been rebuilt from the rubble of this great terror, we will stand together, united in victory, as the dawn of a new age rises over Cáelunárra."

The crowd erupted in cheers, their voices a powerful chorus of hope. Ándrôniüs stood tall at the podium, his heart filled with both the burden of leadership and the fierce pride of a people ready to reclaim their lands.

Ándrôniüs then gestured for Hannah to approach. She rose gracefully, pacing her way toward the stand where she would share the stage with him, if only for a moment. As she stood beside him, the contrast between them was striking. Ándrôniüs, a towering figure of power and authority, and Hannah, a beacon of grace and hope. He wrapped an arm around her in a warm embrace, kissing the top of her head, and then raised his arm to speak again.

"Hannah," he began, his voice resonating with pride, "the very picture of beauty and elegance. She stands as a beacon that bridges the gap between elves and the other races of Cáelunárra. Over the past few days, she has lived among them in the ever-beautiful Elven Embassy. She has painstakingly studied, word upon word, their language, and now, she will recite it and close these ceremonies, mending the tears of our societal differences, showing that we can unite once more!"

The crowd erupted once more in applause and cheers.

Ándrôniüs leaned down to whisper in Hannah's ear. "I believe in you, Hannah. This is your time to shine."

He patted her on the back before stepping away, receding into the crowd to take his seat next to Ísolde.

Hannah took a deep breath and shuffled fully behind the podium. The crowd fell silent, eager to hear her speak. Her mind flashed back to the first book she had opened, the one that introduced her to Luthéllon with Ísolde's help, and then to the morning's feast prepared in her honor by the elves.

She pulled a small piece of parchment from her pocket, its surface inscribed with the delicate script of Luthéllon. Placing it on the podium, she began first in the common tongue.

"Great people of Cáelunárra, I come today to fulfill my promise to you by speaking the language of the elves; Luthéllon. First, I want to thank Ísolde and my teachers at the Thalirîthion Anvandrë for the many painstaking hours they spent with me as I fumbled, eviscerated, and made a mockery of their language. I'm no showman like Ándrôniüs or the others who have taken this stage, but I wanted to thank you all for being here and believing in my friends and me as we strive to better your world. Now, let me begin with what you all have been waiting for."

She paused, looking down at her parchment, then recited in Elvish. "Illithría, Eldôria, Âldâmûr, Brâldôr, arë Blackmire Marsh. Ílarë var Valorië Cáelunárra. Ílar thalrîn var vathrion far ílar. Ílar ra-thalorin norath var Mûrríëthíêl arë Ancûlí. Ílar ra-vathrion—"

From beyond the Coliseum, a sudden clamor of terrified screams could be heard. The once unified crowd quickly became a sea of worry, heads turning toward the source of the commotion. The tension was unequivocal, with an uneasy murmur spreading through the stands.

Ándrôniüs rushed to the podium, his voice booming as he called for silence.

But as the crowd calmed, his eyes widened in horror. Rising in the sky were fireballs, arching ominously toward the city.

"Trebuchet!" Ándrôniüs shouted, the word hanging in the air like a death knell.

He paused, catching his breath before yelling, "Man the battle stations! To the Grand Barracks! Every man, woman, and child able to fight! Head to the barracks to take up arms! All those who cannot fight, take shelter where you can!"

Horns bellowed from the depths of the city, a dire warning of the attack, though its origin was still unknown. The crowd, once celebratory, now descended into chaos, a frantic scramble occurring as people tried to flee or arm themselves in defense of Vâloríâ.

Ándrôniüs rushed back to where Ethan, Emily, Jake, and Ryan sat, sheltering Hannah with his body, and shepherded them toward cover.

As they ran, a whooshing sound suddenly filled the air, followed by a dark cloud rapidly overtaking the sky.

The fluttering mass resembled birds, but the terror in the crowd revealed the truth: "A midnight volley is upon us!"

The screams of fear turned to cries of pain as the rain of obsidian-tipped arrows and shards of wood fell, striking down many where they stood.

With urgency, Ándrôniüs shouted, "Hit the floor! Crawl, crawl into the depths of the Coliseum!"

They dropped to the ground, crawling over the bodies of the fallen, the blood-soaked floor slick beneath them from the many people not as fortunate as they. The cries of the injured and dying mixed with the relentless thudding of the trebuchet fire pots as they pounded the city.

Jake and Ryan struggled to drag Ethan, who, still dazed and weakened from the events of the previous day, barely comprehended the surrounding siege.

They reached a covered area below the stands of the Coliseum, safe for a moment from the volleys of arrows. The sounds of battle outside still reached them; the pounding of fire pots, the clanging of metal as soldiers took up arms, the distant roars of the enemy. Terror paled Vassilios's face as the Coliseum's caretaker huddled in a nearby corner. He was a small, unassuming man, dressed in quaint, worn clothing that spoke of a simpler life. His eyes were wide with fear, his hands trembling as he crouched low, a pool of urine beneath him.

Catching sight of him, Ándrôniüs yelled, "Get yourself together, Vassilios! We are under attack!"

Whimpering, Vassilios cried, "I cannot fight, Ándrôniüs. I'm too old for this. I've seen my share of war. All my sons have been lost to these battles."

Ándrôniüs scoffed in frustration, but before he could respond, Mŷthrálôn and Lôrŷnthás tumbled down the stairs, narrowly escaping another volley of arrows. In their haste, they collided with Emily, sending her sprawling.

Emily cried out in pain as her face slammed into the stone floor.

"My apologies, my lady," Mŷthrálôn said quickly, helping her to her feet as blood gushed out of her nose, the elves helping to try to stop it.

Lôrŷnthás's eyes remained fixed on them, making sure the girl was alright, before he walked over to the stairs to observe and assess the situation. Fire pots continued to rain down in tandem with the midnight volleys.

Ándrôniüs, his voice thick with urgency, asked, "Do we know who mounted this attack?"

The questions from the group came in rapid succession, each more frantic than the last:

"What is going on?" Ethan demanded, his confusion evident.

"Who would do this?" Jake added, his voice tinged with disbelief.

"But I didn't finish," Hannah said, her voice small, more concerned about her interrupted recitation than the surrounding chaos.

Emily, being more practical, shot back, "That isn't important right now, Hannah. Ándrôniüs, what do we do?"

Jake, remembering that Elârâ was caught up somewhere in all of this, said, "I must find Elârâ because she needs me..." I mean us; we can't leave her behind."

Emily fired back at Jake, her tone sharp. "She'll be fine, Jake. Right now, we are more important. Now, let Ándrôniüs speak."

Feeling a fire burning in his heart, Jake turned his unease on Emily. "No, you don't know if she'll be alright. Ándrôniüs, can we get her? Can I get her? I need to make sure she's alive and at least protected."

Echoing Jake's sentiment, Ryan said, "Yes, we should find her!"

"Silence!" Ándrôniüs bellowed, his frustration boiling over. "This is no time to squabble! There are more pressing issues. I'm trying to think!"

He looked around desperately, his mind racing. He counted the group over and over in his mind in quick succession before realizing someone was missing, and he started crying out. "Ísolde! Ísolde! Where are you, my dear?"

Lôrŷnthás approached him carefully, his arm stretched outward, his hand landing upon his shoulder, his voice heavy with sorrow. "She did not survive, Ándrôniüs. The volley was too much. I saw it with my own eyes."

The world seemed to collapse around Ándrôniüs as he processed Lôrŷnthás's words. His heart felt as if it were being torn from his chest, and a wail of pure agony escaped his lips, a sound so raw and powerful that it sent shivers down the spines of those around him.

His grief quickly turned to rage as he fell to his knees. The ground beneath them trembled as his power surged, the air around him darkening as his anger took hold.

"That is enough!" he roared, his voice filled with fury. "We must win this battle against Mûrrïëthíêl. He has already taken too much from me. My brother and sisters, my son, my friends, and now he steals the love I will never find again."

Breathing heavily, Ándrôniüs turned his gaze to Vassilios, who was still cowering on the ground.

Without warning, he charged at the caretaker, grabbing him by the hair and slamming him against the stone wall.

"Do the tunnels still exist?" he demanded, his voice a dangerous whisper.

"Ow, let me go!" Vassilios whimpered, tears running down his face.

But Ándrôniüs was relentless, slamming the man's head against the wall again.

"Vassilios, do the tunnels still exist?" he screamed, his face mere inches from the caretaker's.

"Yes, yes, they exist!" Vassilios cried out, his voice trembling with fear.

Ándrôniüs released him, casting Vassilios to the ground, where the caretaker curled into the fetal position, trembling.

Turning his burning gaze to the two elven guards, he commanded them. "You will take them to the woods. Do you hear me?"

Mŷthrálôn stepped forward, his expression grave. "That road is forbidden for humans to use."

Ándrôniüs turned to him, his eyes blazing. "I know, but the tidal path is likely blocked by this unseen army. This has to be the work of Mûrríëthíêl and Ancülí. If we go that way, our escape will certainly result in death. And who knows what lies to the south and west. The Kítspäk and Fötzë mountains are too tall for us to escape to, and who knows what may be lying between them and Willowdale and Ellison."

Hesitation laced his words. Lôrŷnthás said, "But if King Ithírmáris finds out we are taking that forbidden path, he will surely have all of us killed."

"Do not fight me on this now!" Ándrôniüs snapped, his patience worn thin. "Once he hears of the desecration of Vâloríâ, he will have no other choice. Have him send aid to the town of Fernwick in Tháldrüm, where I will send our people if Vâloríâ falls. Now, run! Run like you've never run before! Your lives depend on it!"

Mŷthrálôn and Lôrŷnthás began arming everyone from the weapons left behind in the rush to escape the Coliseum walls, shoving swords and shields into the hands of all except Vassilios, who remained huddled in the corner.

Ethan, still trying to make sense of the chaos, called out, "But what about you, Ándrôniüs? Will you not come?"

Already turning away, Ándrôniüs replied, "I will find you at Fernwick in seven days' time. If you are not there, I will come to Éldrath and petition King Ithírmáris to find you all. My place is here with the people of Vâloríâ and those who are its guests. I am now the leader of the Republic, and I must stand firm with our people in this time of trial. The prophecy has now indeed been unleashed."

Lôrŷnthás, his voice laced with concern, asked, "And if we are to be executed?"

As Ándrôniüs slipped into the shadows, he answered coldly, "Use the girl."

The old mage's last words puzzled everyone. What girl? In the confusion, they all exchanged uneasy glances.

Mŷthrálôn and Lôrŷnthás wasted no time, however. Examining the man still cowering and whimpering on the floor, Lôrŷnthás kicked Vassilios, demanding, "Where is this tunnel, coward?"

Vassilios, his face pale with terror, pointed weakly. "Behind me, on the other side of this wall. Find the phoenix and pull the fifth tail feather from the right. It will give way and open a passage."

"Hurry!" Mŷthrálôn shouted, grabbing a torch and leading the way around the corner, the others following closely behind.

Mŷthrálôn ran his torch along the wall, revealing the intricate golden carvings of animals; stags, bears, fish, birds, and more. His eyes locked onto the phoenix with ruby eyes, standing out against the others. Handing the torch to Ryan, who struggled to support Ethan, Mŷthrálôn counted in Luthéllon. "Ón... Túr... Thír... Fâr... Vír."

He glanced at Lôrŷnthás, took a deep breath, and pulled on the tail feather. Gears groaned as they started turning, and the wall slowly gave way, revealing a narrow passage in the floor. One by one, they slipped through, descending into the dank, foul-smelling tunnels beneath the city.

# THE SEWERS

EMILY GAGGED AS SHE found herself waist-deep in murky water.

"Are we in the sewers?" She asked, her voice filled with disgust.

Mŷthrálôn nodded grimly. "It would appear so," he replied, trying to mask his own revulsion.

Everyone was gagging and heaving as they stood in the rancid water, the stench overwhelming.

"We must hurry," Lôrŷnthás urged, reaching for the torch he had left at the entrance. But as he did, a hand shot out from the darkness, grabbing him and sending a jolt of fear through the group.

Vassilios, desperate and tearful, clung to Lôrŷnthás. "Take me, please! Spare me!" he begged, his voice trembling.

Lôrŷnthás pulled him close, saw the lever on the wall, and pulled it, setting the gears in motion once more. He pushed Vassilios back toward the Coliseum, his voice cold. "You are a coward. You should be ashamed of yourself. You're no warrior of Vâloríâ. You've no place with us."

Lunging forward, Vassilios tried to force his way through the closing passage, but he became lodged as the walls closed in on him, crushing his body and sealing the way shut.

Emily shrieked, stumbling backward in the tight space, as Vassilios body jammed in the narrowing gap, bones snapping like dry twigs. Hannah stood frozen, her pale face draining of even more color, eyes locked on the pooling blood trickling down the stone wall. Neither had seen someone die, especially like that. Jake and Ryan turned away with grimaces, jaws tight. And Ethan, still dazed and confused, blinked blankly at the scene, too disoriented to react. The elves exchanged a quick, unreadable look. They had to move. Now.

Turning away, Lôrŷnthás's expression hardened. "We must go," he said, leading the others deeper into the darkness, the echoes of the battle above fading as they ventured further into the unknown.

Deeper and deeper they ventured, each step taking them further from the carnage above, yet closer to an unknown fate. The oppressive weight of the earth pressed down on them, the air growing cooler and damper with each passing moment. Twisting and turning, the tunnel was a labyrinth of shadows and echoes, where the only certainty was the lingering stench of decay and filth. Having been hip-deep and clinging to their skin, the sewage had lessened to a mere trickle.

As they pressed forward, rats and mice, fleeing the devastation above, dropped from unseen cracks in the ceiling, striking them on their heads and shoulders. The rodents scurried through the sewage and tried to grab onto them with their tiny feet, determined to seek refuge from the chaos that engulfed the city above.

Through the small vents that allowed fleeting glimpses of the world above, the group could see the darkened sky, lit sporadically by flashes of fiery explosions. The sounds of metal clashing and the anguished cries of the dying echoed faintly through the sewer tunnels. The very air was putrid with the undeniably potent smell of burning flesh, the scent of bodies turned to ash mingling with the foul odor of the sewers. It was as if the city itself was screaming in agony, each tremor from the trebuchets above sending cascades of dust and debris raining down upon them.

They reached a massive gate, its iron bars cold and unyielding, locked from the inside as if someone had shut it against some ancient terror. The gate was a formidable barrier, standing in stark contrast to the decaying surroundings. It was a relic from another time, its once gleaming surface now pitted with rust and age, but still strong enough to withstand the ravages of time.

Beyond the gate, there was a glimpse of the imposing wood of Illithría. The forest stood like a guardian, its dense, menacing trees standing tall and proud, their branches intertwined to form a nearly impenetrable canopy. The air around the trees seemed to pulse with an ancient energy, as if the forest itself was alive and impassively watching the terror unfolding before it.

"Ryan," Mŷthrálôn called out, his voice a strained whisper that barely broke the oppressive silence. "Hand me your ax."

Ryan handed over the weapon, the weight of it heavy in Mŷthrálôn's grip. With all of his strength, Mŷthrálôn began slamming the ax into the lock. Each strike sent a shockwave through the tunnel, the sound of metal-on-metal echoing like a death knell.

Sparks flew in a dazzling spray of light, briefly illuminating the tunnel before fading back into the shadows. The lock rattled and jumped, groaning under the force of Mŷthrálôn's blows, until finally, with a sharp crack that reverberated through the tunnel, it gave way and fell to the ground with a dull thud.

Mŷthrálôn wasted no time. "Lôrŷnthás," he called over his shoulder, his voice tense and urgent, cutting through the darkness like a knife.

Lôrŷnthás, who had been guarding the rear, pushed his way forward through the group, his movements swift and sure despite the cramped conditions. They spoke quickly, their voices low and melodic.

"Tír nôr, ílar?" Mŷthrálôn asked, his tone sharp with urgency.

"Ílar var arith tharanë vathrion norathrîn. Ílar var thalrîn ithra sílvâthiël arë ílar var faral áylârdâr," Lôrŷnthás replied, nodding in agreement.

The words, foreign to all but Hannah, held a resonance that was felt deep within their bones. Without another word, Lôrŷnthás crouched low, his form melding with the shadows as he disappeared into the ferns and brush that lined the space between them and the wood, vanishing as if the underbrush had swallowed him whole.

Mŷthrálôn turned back to the group, his face a mask of resolve hardened by centuries of battle.

"Wait here. We are going to ensure the path is clear," he instructed, his voice leaving no room for disobedience.

With that, he too disappeared from sight.

Minutes passed, each one stretching out longer and longer.

Breathing shallowly and quietly, the friends huddled against the cold, damp stone walls, listening to the distant sounds of battle. The screams and yells from Vâloríâ were like ghouls, haunting the edges of their consciousness, while the relentless pounding of trebuchets unleashing hellfire against the city's defenses continued in the background, a constant reminder of the danger that still lurked beyond. The wait for the elves' return was agonizing, their distress clear as war drums echoed in the distance, matching the frantic beat of their hearts.

Suddenly, the brush stirred, and the scurrying of field mice intensified as they hurried into the tunnel, across the feet of the five, signaling the approach of something—or someone. The concern spiked as a possible threat drew closer. Gripping the hilts of their swords, Jake and Ryan tensed, ready for whatever might emerge from the shadows. The primal urge to survive clashed with the unknown danger that lurked just beyond their sight.

But then, from the depths of the thick brush, the two elves reappeared, their faces etched with a sense of urgency. Relief washed over the five friends like a cool breeze as they let out the breaths they had been holding, their bodies relaxing, if only for a moment.

Mŷthrálôn turned to Lôrŷnthás, his voice barely a whisper, yet carrying the weight of the world. "Týr arith sílvâthiël?"

Lôrŷnthás, his breath coming in quick, shallow gasps, nodded. "Sílvâthiël," he confirmed. "Sílvâthiël, Mŷthrálôn." He then turned to the five companions, his eyes flickering with the intensity of the moment. "We must hurry. Jake, Ryan, I will take Ethan."

Lôrŷnthás hoisted Ethan over his shoulder with ease. Ethan had grown increasingly dizzy and nauseated, becoming weaker from the exertion he was putting forth in his frail state. Without wasting another moment, the elves turned and sprinted through the brush into the forest, the remaining four friends scurrying in their wake.

They left the sewer tunnels behind, the stench and darkness swallowed by the thick underbrush that clung to them like a living entity, pulling at their clothes and skin as if trying to hold them back. The ground was treacherous as they entered the wood, mottled with thick roots and jagged rocks, everything twisted and intertwined.

Vâloríâ was reduced to plumes of smoke and raging flames, now in their past. The flames and smoke rose high into the sky, casting a fiery glow that illuminated the once-beautiful spires, cathedrals, and towers as they crumbled and fell, disappearing from the skyline like a distant memory. Once vibrant with light and life, the city was now reduced to ashes, undoubtedly destroyed by Mûrríëthíêl and Ancülí.

But the forest of Illithría held its own secrets, and as they disappeared into the deep, dark wood, the group could only hope that those secrets would offer them some protection from the calamity that now reigned supreme.

The shadows of the trees closed in around them, the canopy above blocking out the remnants of the city's burning light, leaving them in a world of darkness and uncertainty, where the only truth was the pounding of their hearts and the relentless drive to survive.

# GLOSSARY

Below is a complete guide to help you understand terms used in my world and how to pronounce them.

***

**Áelfwîne̎** [ah-elf-wee-neh]: (1) Guard of Ándrôniüs.

**Áethelwûlf** [ah-eth-el-woolf]: (1) Guard of Ándrôniüs.

**Aétheric** [AY-thair-ik]: As in Aétheric Registrars. (2) Mages that work in the Aétherium Repository.

**Aétherium** [ay-THEER-ee-um]: (1) Ore found in the mountains of Cáelunárra. (2) Used to imbue many things with magic.

**Aéthe̎rial dew** [ay-THAIR-ee-uhl]: (1) Dew from the aéthe̎rial plant.

**Áírrmá** [ah-EE-rr-mah]: (1) The race of the mages.

**Âldâmûr** [AHL-dah-moor]: (1) The realm of men.

**Allfather** [all-father]: (1) Godly being and creator of all.

**Ammón Cúrr** [AH-mohn KOOR]: (1) The location where the chosen warrior, Mikhail and four others, died by deceit.

**Amüngdráng** [AH-mung-DRAHNG]: (1) The place of a battle in Âldâmûr on the plains of Nôrnvaêr.

**Ancu̎lí** [Ann-choo-lie]: (1) The Dark Lord's servant.

**Ándrônius̈** [ah-ndroh-nee-us]: (1) High Mage of Pinemarsh Manor, Seer of Enigmas, and Théxaumíllíer.

**Apsáalooke** [ahp-SAH-loo-kay]: (1) Indigenous people of the northern plains, known to outsiders as the Crow. Traditionally inhabiting the Yellowstone River valley and ranges of present-day Wyoming and Montana, they were fierce warriors, expert horsemen, and key participants in regional trade and diplomacy during the fur trapping era.

**Áslaug** [OWS-lough]: (1) One of the chosen of Cáelunárra.

**Arathênor** [AH-rah-thay-nohr]: (1) Dining hall in the Thalirîthion Anvandrë.

**Arcánus̈ Májörá** [AHR-kah-noose MAH-yohr-AH]: (1) The world created by the Allfather.

**Aul̂líâtënärrä** [OO-lee-AH-teh-NAH-rr-ah]: (1) Homeland of the Áírrmá (Mages).

**Az'ug̮u̮l** [AZ-oo-gool]: (1) Khą'zǫ'gu̮l word for Shadewalker.

**Báláríôn Tháríŷôr** [bah-LAH-ree-on thah-REE-vor]: (1) Library.

**Bral̂dôr** [BRAHL-dohr]: (1) Homeland of the dwarves.

**Bral̂dôrian** [BRAHL-dohr-ean]: (1) Someone of/from Bral̂dôr.

**Brynhildr** [BRIN-hild-er]: (1) One of the five chosen that fought alongside Áslaug.

**Cáelunárra** [K-eye-loo-NAH-rah]: (1) Continent on Arcánus̈ Májörá.

**Cal̂lirrhoë** [KAL-ir-roe-eh]: (1) Naïad from Pinemarsh Manor.

**Cállïrŷsis Elúmiráë** [CAL-lee-riss el-LOO-mee-ray]: (1) Tonic given to those on the brink of death.

**Côrcaemán** [KOHR-kay-mahn]: (1) A Môrthyl̂íte

city turned by the Dark Lord. (2) Where Áslaug and the other four chosen of the age died.

**Créquhiêvins** [CRAY-WHI-eh-vins]: (1) A type of fly that lives in bogs. (2) It is known for its swarms and stinging bites.

**Crôrívrën** [KROHR-ree-vrehn]: (1) One of the Kings of the Môrthyl̂ people.

**Czârrûp** [czar-roop]: (1) High Mage of Valoríâ.

**Dracónyx** [DRAY-cone-iks]: (1) Dragon-like creature of Cáelunárra.

**Dracónyxáushká** [DRAH-koh-nix-AH-ush-kah]: (1) The scientists and trainers that seek to domesticate the dracónyx.

**Draénôr Jangthôrn** [dray-NOR JANG-thorn]: (1) High Mage of the third age, author, and grand warrior.

**Dŷrníêth** [DEER-nee-ehth]: (1) Sword of the Lords of Su̇íl, known for slaying many dracónyx.

**Durgth** [DOORG-th]: (1) A name of a gorlock.

**Éamon** [AY-mon]: (1) Son of Frânícê, Lord of Silverthorn.

**Efálállinoùs** [eh-FAH-LAHL-lee-nus]: (1) A bush in which its roots are used to help incapacitate glimmer gremlins.

**Elârâ** [el-ah-rah]: (1) Servant at the Hall of Mages.

**Eldôria** [el-DOH-ree-ah]: (1) Land of the mages.

**Éldrath** [EHL-drahth]: (1) Capital of Illithría.

**Elówŷn** [EH-loh-WEEN]: (1) Name of a former Grand Mage of Valoríâ.

**Elyrëndhôr** [EH-leer-EN-dhor]: (1) The celestial dance seen in the northern skies, believed to be the shimmering lights that accompany a fallen warrior's spirit as Válgârd, god of war, carries them to the halls of the Allfather. (2) Considered a sacred omen among elves and often invoked during funerary rites and pyre ceremonies. (3) A universal term used by all races—elves, dwarves, men, mages—recognized as the proper, ancient name for the phenomenon known across the world as the dancing lights of the heavens.

**Émberweave** [EM-ber-weave]: (1) Naïad-made garment that helps protect from heat, burns, and is used in fights against Dracónyx.

**Fötzë** [FUHT-zeh]: (1) Name of mountain range.

**Frânîcê** [FRAH-nee-say]: (1) High Mage of Suïl.

**Freydís** [FRAY-dees]: (1) One of the five chosen that fought alongside Áslaug.

**Fünchâ** [FOON-chah]: (1) Hills in Eldôria.

**Grônthael** [GROHN-thay-el]: (1) The Head Vaultsmith of the Aétherium Repository.

**Gründhölm** [GROOND-holm]: (1) (1) Warrior of Valôriâ.

**Hervor** [HAIR-vor]: (1) One of the five chosen that fought alongside Áslaug.

**Ídeïní** [EE-deh-NEE]: (1) The large river in the southern reaches of the elven realm that separates Cáelunárra from the lands beyond.

**Ígnîs Sápíëntíá** [EEG-nees SAH-pee-ehn-TEE-ah]: (1) Óryneï's goblet that has mystical powers.

**Illithría** [EE-leeth-ree-ah]: (1) Realm of the elves.

**Illithrían** [EE-leeth-ree-ahn]: (1) Someone of the dominion of elves.

**Ísëphëlŷ** [EE-seh-feh-LEE]: (1) A magical stone that allows the Mage to peer in and see past, present, and future. (2) Imbued with pure Aétherium Crystal essence.

**Ísolde** [EE-sol-de]: (1) Wife of Ándrôniüs.

**Ithírmáris** [EE-theer-MAH-rees]: (1) King of Illithría.

**Íthûlíën** [eeth-ool-ee-ehn]: (1) Son of the

Allfather, brother of Thêlímûríër, one of the deities of Cáelunárra.

**Izzârrë** [EES-zahr-reh]: (1) Luthéllon word for Shadewalker.

**Kharzonoy** [khar-zone-ov]: (1) The land of the Dark Lord.

**Kha'zo'gul** [KAH-zoh-GOOL]: (1) The tongue of Kharzonov.

**Kítspäk** [KEETS-pahk]: (1) Name of mountain range.

**Khóâzzë** [KHOH-ahz-zeh]: (1) Áírrmá word for Shadewalker.

**Läcküllôrra** [LAK-ue-lor-rah]: (1) A city in Braîdôr (2) Location of Jacques, one of the chosen's death. (3) A siege led by the by the Zaŵxîneî, forces of the Dark Lord.

**Líllíët** [LEE-lee-ET]: (1) High Mage of Valoríaî.

**Líoníá** [LEE-oh-NEE-ah]: (1) The Veil. (2) The land where the Áírrmá (mages) can willingly go after reaching a thousand years old.

**Líváthánoneon** [LEE-vah-THAH-noh-nee-ON]: (1) A type of dragon with snaggle teeth from the Líváthánoneon mountains in Illithría.

**Loríthíl** [LOHR-ee-theel]: (1) Province in Âldaîmuîr.

**Lorŷnthás** [LOHR-ee-nthahs]: (1) Elf who leads the five chosen into the wood of Illithría.

**Lünáris petals** [LOO-nah-rees]: (1) Petals from the lünáris plant.

**Luthéllon** [loo-THAY-lon]: (1) Language of the elves.

**Lýeïch** [LEE-ehch]: (1) A reclusive race that lives in the Blackmire Marsh.

**Márrisol** [MAHR-ree-sol]: (1) High Mage of Valoríaî.

**Michaud** [mee-SHOH]: (1) Chef on plane from Utah

to Fiji.
**Möchí Möchí** [MOH-chee MOH-chee] (1) Hills in Eldôria.
**Môrthŷl** [MOR-theel]: (1) Lost kingdom of men.
**Môrthŷlílen** [MOR-thee-LEE-len]: (1) Name of someone from Môrthŷlílen.
**Môrthŷlíte** [MOR-theel-ite]: (1) Name of someone from Môrthŷl.
**Mûrríëthíêl** [moo-rree-eth-ee-ayl]: (1) The Dark Lord of Khạrzọnọv.
**Mŷthrálôn** [MEE-thrah-lone]: (1) Elf who leads the five chosen into the wood of Illithría.
**Naïad** [NYE-ad]: (1) A creature known for its healing and craftsmanship.
**Nâttûâllâ** [NAH-too-AH-lah]: (1) High Mage of Valoríâ.
**Nôrnvaêr** [NOHRN-vayr]: (1) A province in Âldâmûr. (2) A place of many battles due to the proximity to the Eastern pass.
**Nŭnŭmbĕycz** [NOO-noo-mbehts]: (1) A land across the great sea.
**Olëstrë** [OH-leh-streh]: (1) A marsh in Eldôria.
**Olmâ** [OHL-mah]: (1) The first race of men who possessed magical abilities.
**Órcráculum** [OHR-KRAH-koo-loom]: (1) The office of the Seer of Enigmas where they do their utmost secret work.
**Orrûvanéthale¨** [OR-roo-vah-neh-thah-leh]: (1) The word associated with the calling of a new Grand Mage and Seer of the Enigmas.
**Orthôrjárl** [OHR-thohr-YAHRL]: (1) King of Braîldôr.
**Óryne¨** [oh-rin-eh]: (1) Grand Mage of Valoríâ.
**Óttenäch** [OH-ten-ahkh]: (1) City in Eldôria.
**Pā Hōā Illīeā Mahā** [PAH HOH-ah ILL-ee-ah MAH-hah]: (1) Homeland of Sāā.

**Sāā** [sah-ah]: (1) Warrior of Vâloríâ.

**Sâlzhâr** [SAHL-zhar]: (1) A great salt sea in Kharzonov.

**Shadewalker** [Shadewalker]: (1) Common tongue for an agent of the Dark Lord (2) Mages who have been corrupted by the Dark Lords might.

**Shí Lû Dürr** [SHEE LOO DORR]: (1) The Grand Capitol of the Kingdom of Âldâmûr. (2) Where the seat of the High King of Âldâmûr lives.

**Sigrún** [SIG-roon]: (1) One of the five chosen that fought alongside Áslaug.

**Skëphthaüm** [SKEH-fth-owm]: (1) A race from across the great sea to the north from the ice lands.

**Sûl** [SOOL]: (1) High Mage of Vâloríâ.

**Suïl** [SUE-ee-l]: (1) City in Eldôria.

**Suñío̤** [SWAHL-thehz]: (1) Former High Mage of Vâloríâ.

**Swálthëz** [SOO-nee-OH]: (1) An Áírrmá unit of measurement, generally comparable to pounds.

**Sŷlphrót essence** [SEEL-froh-t]: (1) Essence from the sŷlphrót fungi that grows on trees.

**Thâlôr** [thah-lore]: (1) Leader of the High Mage Army.

**Thalirîthion Anvandrë** [THAH-lee-ree-thee-on AHN-vahn-dray]: (1) Elven Embassy, grand building in Vâloríâ, home to the last Elven dispatch outside of Illithría.

**Tháldrüm** [THAHL-droom]: (1) Province in the realm of Men (Âldâmûr).

**Théxaumíllíer** [THAY-ks-ow-MEE-lee-AYR]: (1) A title bestowed during times of great certainty within the mage's realm, when the roles of Grand Mage and Seer of the Enigmas are held by a single individual.

**Thórnwyn** [THORN-win]: (1) High Mage of Vâloríâ.

**Thrälfáylaín nectar** [THRAHL-fay-lah-EEN]: (1) Nectar from the Thrälfáylaín flower

**Thrângûnvôr** [THRAHNG-goon-vor]: (1) Last king of the Môrthŷl people.

**Thuczojle** [THOO-tsoh-YEH-leh]: (1) An elite group of fighters beyond the realm of elves in the south.

**Thŷndréll** [thee-NDRAYL]: (1) What would be the equivalent as the month of May.

**Tynnëmynnwn** [TIN-neh-MIN-wuhn]: (1) A river in the Kingdom of Âldâmuȓ

**Tôrgráth** [TOR-grahth]: (1) Ancient capital of the Môrthŷl people.

**Tôrthävn** [TOHR-thah-vn]: (1) City in Eldôria.

**Ûrvákënák** [OOR-vah-keh-NAHK]: (1) The prince of the dwarven kingdom.

**Wéil** [VAYL]: (1) A plant grown for its medicinal properties.

**Wéilwrót, crystalized** [VAYL-vroh-t]: (1) The root of the Wéil plant.

**Whelzorná** [WHEL-zor-NAH]: (1) Queen of Brâldôr.

**Wýrmwéb** [WIRM-web]: (1) A type of shot used in a ballistae.

**Vaerônthíloch** [VYE-rohn-THEE-lokh]: (1) The Áírrmá word for the High Mage Council.

**Valgârd** [VAL-gard]: (1) A sub-deity of the peoples of Cáelunárra.

**Valoríâ** [vah-lore-ee-ah]: (1) Capital of Eldôria.

**Valoríân** [vah-lore-ee-ahn]: (1) Someone of Valoríâ.

**Vassilios** [vah-SEE-lee-os]: (1) Caretaker of Valoríâ's Coliseum.

**Veðrvangr** [VETHR-vahng-er]: (1) Homeland of Áslaug and her four chosen shieldmaidens, famed for producing fierce and battle-hardened warrior women.

**Vígorrést** [VEE-gor-rest]: (1) A healing tonic that the mages use to heal muscles.

**Vôrmghôr** [VORM-gore]: (1) Warrior of Valoríâ.

**Vragmor** [VRAHG-mor]: (1) The capital of Kharzonov.

**Vränkëphlét** [VRAHN-keh-FLET]: (1) Known as the deceiver of the mages. (2) Led Mikhail and the other four chosen of that age to their certain death near Tynnëmynnwn at Ammón Cúrr.

**Vulët** [VOO-let]: (1) High Mage of Valoríâ.

**Vultzëmaegár** [VUEL-tseh-MY-gahr]: (1) A type of magic that is used for binding contracts or agreements.

**Xándriel** [ZAN-dree-el]: (1) High Mage of Valoríâ.

**Ythâríôn** [EE-thah-ree-ON]: (1) The original council of the mages.

**Zawxîne** [ZAHk-EE-neh]: (1) A race of dwarves that were banished from the dwarven homelands.

**Zolgulzier** [ZAWL-goohl-ZYE-er]: (1) The mountains west of Côrcaemán and the Eastern Pass.

**Zültzëmmë** [TSOOL-tseh-MEH]: (1) The Allfathers promise of ending the world in hellfire.

# AIRRMA SPELLS AND INCANTATIONS

**Achlàmen Ythráiál Ophtálínen** [AHKH-lah-men ee-THRYE-yahl OFF-tah-lee-nen]

**Achlàmen Ythráiál Ophtálínen Fínlïnántë** [AHKH-lah-men ee-THRYE-yahl OFF-TAH-lee-nen FEEN-lee-NAHN-teh]

**Anímaí Labyêsk** [Ah-nee-my-ee LAY-byesk]

**Fâräzŷënn Sâccûtrëâ Vûrrë Mŷëlûrn Ëltë** [FAH-rah-zyee-EHN SAH-kkoo-TREH-ah VOOR-reh MYE-eh-LOORN EHL-teh]

**Íncâttântä Vës Vrûth Elëmân** [EEN-kah-tah-tahn-tah VEHS VROOTH EH-leh-mahn]

**Sárrícírreân ôhr gô líscënâttén** [SAHR-ree-kee-REH-ahn OHR goh LEES-keh-NAHT-ten]

**Sŷërrë Sâccûtrëâ Azjŷërríc** [SYEH-reh SAH-kkoo-TREH-ah AZ-zyee-EHR-reek]

# KHA'ZO'GUL
# TRANSLATIONS

**Thruug grokran or atzlo!** [THROOG GROHK-rahn OR AHTZ-loh]: Translates to: "Come with us or die."

**Groz vrun enzok varzmag. Varz groznom drav grokran, or atzlo.** [GROHZ VROON EN-zohk VAHRZ-mahg. VAHRZ GROHZ-nom DRAHV GROHK-rahn, OHR AHTZ-loh.]: Translates to: "You have two choices, mage. Turn them over to us, or die."

# LUTHELLON TRANSLATIONS

**Týr ílar?, Hannah** [TEER EE-lar, HAN-uh]: Translates to: "How are you, Hannah."

**Ila sílvâthiël. Valëth ílar.** [EE-lah SEEL-vah-thee-el. VAH-leth EE-lar.]: Translates to: "I'm well, thank you."

**Illithría, Eldôria, Âldâmûr, Brâldôr, arë Blackmire Marsh. Ílarë var Valorië Cáelunárra. Ílar thalrîn var vathrion far ílar. Ílar ra-thalorin norath var Mûrríëthíêl arë Ancülí. Ílar ra-vathrion—** [EE-lee-THREE-ah, EHL-DOH-ree-ah, AHL-dah-MOOR, BRAHL-dor, AH-reh BLACK-meer marsh. EE-lah-reh VAHR vah-LOH-ree-eh KAI-loo-NAH-rah.EE-lar THAHL-reen VAHR VAH-three-on FAHR EE-lar. EE-lar RAH-thah-LOH-reen NOH-rath VAHR MUR-ree-eh-THEE-el AH-reh AHN-koo-LEE. EE-lar RAH-VAH-three-on—]: Translates to: "Illithria, Eldôria, Âldâmûr, Braldor, and last but not least the Blackmire Marsh, most importantly all the citizens of Caelunarra, we are here to fight for you! Against the tyranny of Mûrríëthíêl and Ancülí. We will bring the war—"

**Ón... Túr... Thír... Fâr... Vír...** [OHN, TOOR, THEER, FAHR, VEER]: Translates to: "One, Two, Three, Four, Five."

**Tír nôr, ílar?** [TEER nohr, EE-lar]: Translates to: "What is it, my friend?"

**Ílar var arith tharanë vathrion norathrîn. Ílar var thalrîn ithra sílvâthiël arë ílar var faral áylârdâr.** [EE-lar VAHR AH-reeth THAH-rah-neh VAH-three-on NOH-rah-threen.EE-lar VAHR THAHL-reen EE-thrah SEEL-vah-thee-el AH-reh EE-lar VAHR FAH-rahl AH-ee-lahr-DAHR.]: Translates to: "We must search the path forward for enemies. We must ensure their safety and that we can make it to the wood."

**Týr arith sílvâthiël?** [TEER AH-reeth SEEL-vah-thee-el]: Translates to: "Is the way clear?"

**Sílvâthiël,** [SEEL-vah-thee-el]: Translates to: "It is."

**Sílvâthiël, Mŷthrálôn** [SEEL-vah-thee-el, MEE-thrah-LOHN]: Translates to: "It is, Mŷthrálôn."

# ACKNOWLEDGEMENTS

First and foremost, to my incredible wife, Jessica — thank you for being my inspiration and for relentlessly pushing me to achieve the unimaginable. You unlocked a wellspring of creativity that had long been dormant, giving me a sense of purpose I thought I had lost. You've stood by my side through our greatest joys, from our wedding to the birth of our daughter, Lillian, and through the everyday challenges that life throws our way. Even in the darkest moments, when I know I can be unbearable, your kind heart and unwavering support have been my strength. Thank you for encouraging me to take on this project and for enduring the long nights as I obsessed over every detail. I am especially grateful for the forty-plus hours you spent helping me with final edits and proofreading, bringing this immense project to life and up to the high standard it needed to be. I adore you, and I'm so thankful you are the woman in my life.

To my daughter, Lillian — though you're too young to understand now, you've already given me more than I could ever repay. Your presence has made every challenge worth fighting and every step of this journey bearable.

To my parents, and especially my mother — thank you for always nurturing my creativity and for sticking by me during the darkest times, never once giving up on me. Your unwavering support has been a constant in my life, and I'm forever grateful for the love and encouragement you've shown me. Thank you for being there when I needed you, for listening, reading, and helping me bring this project to life.

To Mike and Scott, my two fathers — thank you for your steadfast support, for standing by me in every way you could, and for always believing in me.

A special thank you to my editor, Steven, and my cover artist, Daniel — without you, this book wouldn't have reached its full potential. Your dedication and expertise have brought my vision to life, and I'm grateful beyond measure for your invaluable contributions.

I would also like to express my heartfelt thanks to Jason and Katelynn Singer. Our paths crossed through shared professional ties, and I'm truly grateful for the connection that's grown from that. Your willingness to read and lend your time during the early stages of this book meant a great deal, and your presence along the way served as a quiet but meaningful encouragement throughout the process.

To Bob Perry. I know the process was long and arduous at the start, but your time, effort, and dedication have been crucial in getting this book to where it needed to be for release. And of course, I can't forget how much I appreciate you always listening to my rants at work—not just about the book, but about everything else too. You know exactly what I mean! Your support means more to me than I can put into words.

And finally, to all those who offered their support—whether through kind words, thoughtful encouragement, or simply believing in this journey—thank you. Each of you played a part in helping this story come to life, and I am deeply grateful.

# ABOUT THE AUTHOR

Scott A. Hatfield Jr. is a veteran who proudly served in the United States Navy as a Hospital Corpsman. He grew up in Ridgecrest, California, and now resides in the beautiful state of Utah with his wonderful wife and daughter. An avid outdoorsman, Scott has hiked the Pacific Crest Trail and the Appalachian Trail, finding solace and inspiration in nature.

Scott holds degrees in Humanities and Social Sciences, a Bachelor of Political Science, and a Master of Public Administration from Utah Valley University. He also had the opportunity to study abroad at Oxford University's Pembroke College. His professional career has been centered around various public administration roles, but his journey as a writer is a deeply personal one.

Scott's passion for writing began in childhood but was interrupted by a shift toward writing music and touring with the various bands he played in. After his military service, he faced the challenges with a Traumatic Brain Injury coupled with PTSD, and Ménière's Disease, which led to struggles with anxiety, depression, and thoughts of suicide. During these difficult times, he found comfort in revisiting a world he created as a child, using it as an escape. Following a hiking injury in the Bear River Mountains and while working on the project of establishing a thru-hiking trail in Utah, his wife encouraged him to pursue writing again, to fight the demons that came crawling back into his mind.

While *The Shadow of Cáelunárra : The Prophecy Unleashed* took only three months to write and nearly a year to edit, this project has been in the back of Scott's mind for nearly 15 years. It is the first book in the series he is writing.

When Scott isn't spending time with his family, in the great outdoors, or working, he enjoys watching his favorite football (soccer) team, Real Salt Lake, play at the football pitch.

You can connect with Scott through:

- Facebook: Scott Hatfield the Author

- Instagram: @scotthatfieldtheauthor

- Threads: @scotthatfieldtheauthor

- X: @Hatfieldauthor

- YouTube: Scott A Hatfield Jr. (Multi-purpose channel)

- Email: scotthatfieldtheauthor@gmail.com

# FUTURE WORKS

The Shadow of Cáelunárra : The Tides of Change – Fall 2026 / Winter 2027
The Shadow of Cáelunárra : Book III – TBD 2027/2028
The Shadow of Cáelunárra : Book IV – TBD 2028/2029

*\*\**

I anticipate releasing two to three additional volumes following Book Four. Books II and III are already written or in advanced stages of development, with preparations for post-production well underway.